SMUG DAD

JASON ROCHE

CRANTHORPE
—MILLNER—
PUBLISHERS

First published by Cranthorpe Millner Publishers (2021)

ISBN 978-1-912964-79-6 (Paperback)

www.cranthorpemillner.com

Cranthorpe Millner Publishers

For Mom & Dad

PROLOGUE

We are getting reports through, Clive: breaking news. I don't believe in all my years of television reporting I've come across a developing situation such as this. Simply unbelievable and quite shocking really. But we're not in the business of sensationalising news or reporting unsubstantiated stories so we'll be cutting to Doreen for the weather where you are, and it looks like another chilly one!

"We didn't take on this crusade to kill children."

"What in God's name will change unless the world takes note of every single infidel – woman and child – living in sin and disobeying God's will with every breath; every post on Instagram; every oppressed brother of mine. This family must die. All of them."

"The intention was to remove the adults and we have the wife, so let's show the world we aren't animals and let the children remain."

"Animals oppressed our people long before these infidels went to Waitrose with smug discontent handing products to our rightfully covered up sisters who scanned their decadence with a smile."

"I've spent the last three hours with these people; the kids are polite."

"Bombs. Plans. Beheadings. Guns on the street. Trucks on crowded streets. Kids in vests. None of it means anything anymore: the infidels desensitised by their lofty ignorance. So we make the one place they believe they escape all the pain the most unsafe. We take their homes and they die in their homes. Bring me the knife."

The house is completely surrounded – law enforcement on the scene immediately after the call was made from the house. There appears to be no ransom or demand situation, but the authorities are preparing for a negotiation. Another way to strike terror into our hearts, they claimed. Chosen completely at random, this house, and the terrorists not even from this part of Kent. So it appears the intention to strike fear and panic has shifted from the public domain into the private domain. An upper–middle commuter community rocked by this despicable home invasion. We'll have more on this story and other developments right after these advertisements; keep an eye out for the cute puppy in our sponsor's commercial!

Apologies to all viewers – we've had to interrupt those messages from our sponsors to return to our top story. A new development: Douglas Perfors, the husband and father of the hostaged family, has arrived on the scene and physically forced his way through the police barrier, in doing so striking one of the special force attachés. One of the cameras on our helicopter is clearly showing how the scene has escalated – Douglas Perfors approaching the house, hands raised above his head while the police cordon beckon him back behind the barriers. The front door is opening and we can see what looks like his youngest daughter; oh my god there's a knife held to her throat. Viewers should be advised this is live television and anyone with a sensitive disposition should likely turn off, mute or look away now.

"You're taking me instead. I have nothing on me – no guns,

weapons or wires. Don't hurt anyone inside that house. I'm coming in."

"If you take another step, I will kill your family! Get back!"

"I'm not going to give you a big speech but know this – I have nothing without my family, so either you do what I'm sure you don't really want to do and I come in to join them, or you let me in and we discuss the best way for you to achieve maximum impact from this venture."

"You stay back! I warn you!"

We can see a heated verbal exchange but we can't make out exactly what is being said. Oh wait, it seems that Douglas Perfors is removing his shirt – likely he is proving to the terrorists he's not carrying anything and– oh my word, he's taking off his trousers too! We talk about sensitive disposition here ladies and gentlemen but let me speak on behalf of all the ladies out there: DO NOT LOOK AWAY NOW. Rather apparent Mister Douglas Perfors looks after himself in the masculine physique department – we are witnessing something truly unequivocal and spectacular. He is wearing a pair of ManSize briefs for those viewers unable to read that on the underwear label. And it seems those too are coming off.

PART 1

CHAPTER 10

← →

Sarah Dice Patterned

How does one ever begin to explain? It was a cold and misty night and the shutters rattled in the storm … no, erm, it was a spiteful day when the sun refused to appear and the hurtful wind whipped leaves into a frenzy, circling exclusive pavement dog mess in spastic pockets around the neighbourhood. No. That's enough about the weather although it was an important factor that first day; the day that Smug started really going Dad. It was important because the weather was gorgeous and that meant Doug was able to wash his car with his shirt off …

Just as the car was about to be lathered beyond recognition Doug heard a faint, stifled scream towards the back of the house. Only Giorgia, he thinks, knowing how good she is at settling herself. The model child, he ponders, orchestrating the optimal amount of foam and tucking his discarded shirt into the back of his shorts. Ah the weather; the national obsession – the joy of soaping the car (a nice car and the fruits of a decent amount of corporate jailtime) … another scream, this time Magnus: the boy; the champ.

A noise not far away, towards Atrium Road, an edition of housewives and househusbands scuttlebutting home after a park day while the husbands stayed home to watch rugby and the children grimied their faces with a concoctory smudge of suncream, ice cream and kiddie sweat. He notices the kid with the moon face – James or John or one of the disciples – and remembers some incident in the park involving a tantrum, a puddle and his mother completely unable to control the frantic kid. What was her name? Nothing special, nothing memorable, nothing discernible – like most of them. Bit harsh for the COO of the fan club.

They approach. He knows they're looking and it should probably be a moment to shoot inside, cover up and wait until the train has moved through the station, but ah the weather and being flat bang in the middle ... The ladies step up the pace then slow down just short of Doug, each surreptitiously leaning in diagonal arches to sneak a tedium–halting torso peak. He nods to the group and they politely return the hellos.

"I can never get enough of that on the eyeballs," says Helen, without adjusting her expression as if reviewing a recorded TV list.

"The other day there was some problem with a few teenagers graffitiing a truck, and Doug steps in, tells them all to stop."

"Fearless," another commends, Yolanda perhaps.

"And?" the group questions, now slowing down to a pace where they'll have to find something to make them stop to avoid the obvious gawping. A neighbour popping out of another house up the road or a dropped bag perhaps. A bag drops. Doug looks up momentarily.

"All in good working order, ladies?"

"One of them – the gang – spouts some horrendous profanity right in his face. One goes scrabbling in a pocket, surely for a knife," the whispers continue. "So Doug," getting almost audible, "warns each of them then responds when the biggest swipes at him ..."

"It really was nothing," says Doug. "I think they're just desperate for attention."

They all stop and suddenly slide nearer.

"I heard you taught them all a lesson, Douglas."

"No, well not all of them. Just self–defence in essence."

"And there haven't been any more graffiti lessons on the truck since."

God, it was literally an impulse reaction: the kid swung, Doug caught his hand, bent back his wrist until he fell to the floor and the rest ran away. Quite simple.

Perfect. A cloud. The car's not washed and the ladies are still loitering but even in the face of it all Doug has a genial smile and time to chat to the local mothers. Perfect: because appearing around the corner drifts one of the heftier family 4x4s with the tinted windows unable to hide the flicker of built–in DVD panels on the back of the seats. The vehicle and the Sold sign unify with a slight bounce of the tyres as the car comes to rest in the driveway. The ladies stop chattering and even Doug's attention shifts towards the newcomers. The biggest house in the area if you count the driveway.

The kids are awake and quiet which is odd. That level of behaviour is normally reserved for the Perfors family. Out steps a man and a woman both coolly waving to the informal gathering of Doug plus posse, then the mother (presumably the mother, although of the extremely well-maintained, immaculate, yummy variety) proceeds to let the kids out whilst el–daddyo stands feet apart, arms on waist admiring the surroundings, Oakleys pinned to the top of his nose. Admiring his new kingdom. Doug's kingdom.

He points over to Doug with a pistol hand and clicks the side of his mouth, mouthing, "Hey there punter," and giving away a wink despite being concealed by the purple shades. Doug nods, slightly bemused then responds with a half–salute: does he know this guy? Is he someone from the firm? Maybe one of the other 42nd floor cohorts who knows him, or knows of him perhaps? And then suddenly, as though the whole episode was imagined, he's gone, yet the car remains glistening brighter than Doug's; bigger and with a driveway of its own nestled between a hedge and a stone walkway like the hottest of dogs.

And the ladies slowly disappear too, heads all cocked towards the new arrivals with Doug left standing alone, bucket in hand, Blackberry buzzing in the pocket and wondering if he's relieved to be able to get on with it or short–changed at not having given an accurate description of the teenager wrist bending affair. The phone buzzes again: there's some drama at the office to which Doug hastily responds by drying his hands down his bare flanks and bashing out an email response solution worthy of mediator of the century.

These office palavers: always solvable and never quite as dramatic as those in the thick of it might imagine. Doug's name rings out from within the house, it's Margot offering him a beetroot, coriander and strawberry smoothie. The car looks shit and that's just not acceptable so Doug gives it the quickest of once–overs and retires indoors to sap up the remainder of a splendid weekend. It's off to Paris in the morning then New York mid–week so rest, which, seemingly of paramount importance, is never required by the person cocooned in ease and success and …

Doug takes a shower and just after the spray from the wetroom has filtered through his hair he makes out the faint sound of a knock at the door. Why not just use the bell? It's brand new. Then Margot's voice and laughing; lots of laughing. Then nothing. Doug finishes his shower and wanders downstairs in his towel enduring a quickfire wrestle with Magnus and a kiss from MacKenzie in her cot.

"Who was at the door?" Doug asks while Margot fishes around one of the kitchen cabinets bending so far over that her shorts ride up her buttocks to the extent that an uncharacteristic patch of pubic hair reveals itself. "You answered the door in your short shorts."

"If I can't slop around wearing nothing on the weekend, when can I?"

"Who was it? At the door?"

"Our new neighbour. Oh God I've already forgotten his name."

"Must've been memorable. Where was his wife?"

"How do you know he's married?"

"I saw them arrive while I was outside. Another SITCOM I assumed with the T for Two I think not Three."

"But that could be his partner."

"Whatever; the mother of his children or whoever he chooses to live with or travel with or cohabitate with or procreate with …"

"No it was just him. What was his name? Shit! He wanted this." She reveals a half–empty packet of brown sugar.

"They've just moved in, come strutting down the premier tree–lined avenue with a brand–new Prado and need brown sugar? From our house? Let's avoid them. Too needy."

"We've been invited to a playdate. Sometime tomorrow."

The gun nozzle was pressed so firmly against the side of his temple he thought it might pierce through into his brain. The sweat mingled with various coagulated levels of dry blood then exposed to hot metal made an unnatural excretory–argentiferous roux, yet he never shook. He didn't see the point of shaking; two options: sit still and wait for the loud bang, (presumably) bright light and epiphany to the next level of existence or sit still and see exactly what the temple press was a request for. It had to be the latter. His instinct told him that if one of these thugs intended to kill someone or if anyone were to take a life for that matter then there would be no pre–event gesture: no push before a fight, no thunder before the lightning.

"I think we have a fucking hero among us," said the man pressing the gun, picking up a bottle of Uncle Punjab's Fire in the Belly Stir–in Sauce and hurling it at a crying woman wrapped around the side of the fish counter like a Band–Aid on an awkwardly placed wound.

Doug gave an ever so slight push back on the gun as though it hadn't happened or as though the man might believe he'd imagined it. The man pulled the gun away for a moment, spitting in Doug's face. Liquid warmth to counterbalance the solid cold sweat.

"I'm going to fucking shoot him in the face! I'm going to blow his skull up! I will."

Just then another man appeared, green balaclava pushed up above his brow, also holding a gun, his vest soaked in blood.

"What's he done?" muttered the other, squeezing at his lactating stomach wound.

"I think it's time for you both to lie down on the floor, put your hands behind your heads and wait for the authorities to arrive. That's the only way you'll avoid bleeding to death." He pointed at the man who now refused to hide his discomfort. "And the only way you'll avoid an unsympathetic judge who'll be so willing to get trigger happy with your sentence in an effort to quell the public's fear that scum like you walk free on appeal, that you'll wish you hadn't."

The lad at the fish, Aisle 11 – latest range of mackerel – stopped whimpering, daring to look as though viewing a self-inflicted staple wound for the first time. A calm stooped over Aisles 10 through 13 at Sainsbury's; the blanket suffocating the hostages and two armed men until Doug slowly got to his feet.

"As I said, gentlemen," Doug continued. "It's time."

I've got to get that gun; get the healthy one down or at least get him to fire a shot at me. Is there a third perhaps? There was noise down towards the cheese, yoghurt and butter section.

An almighty sound: not a gunshot but louder. The police barging in through the front? A bomb? A kid's toy from Aisle 16? A good thing: the man distracted just long enough for Doug to do something. And it's that something done that happened in less time than it takes to react but crystallised in slow motion for Doug, his elbow straightening into his utmost reach until his retentioned fist bunny hopped onto the man's throat. Let's take a second not to call him the man: the repeat offending criminal convicted of rape, assault and GBH in one year, back on the streets quicker than … Then something he'd never done before, his back arching to cast his head down onto nose, splattering the cartilage and dislodging the weapon.

This is bullshit. All of it. What exactly is there to fear? I'm sitting here pissing in my pants waiting for something to happen and it is happening; so fast that I'm rendering myself powerless because it's the most logical, most thought through, least instinctive thing to do. I'm sitting watching this filth violate a woman with a 2L Sprite bottle and my hands are bound by my own invisible bonds of wussyness. Wait, I can't look. The bottle goes further into her and then out again: jammed then wrenched back while the tip of the gun remains outside the back of her skull, pressing so hard that the menace of the intrusive bottle is somehow replaced by the imposing metal. This sort of shit doesn't happen to me. There are 24-pack Weetabix boxes above me for Christ's sake, the same kind I lovingly endow with 0.1% fat milk every morning, so I can jog to work, make money and return home in triumph.

"Get that fucking thing out of her," the man yelled "We have work to do."

His perfect life: is it all about to end now through one

moment of madness or does this define who he has to become to … to be … worshipped? But it isn't enough being an in–shape dad with cereal box–looking kids who behave well, wipe the formative years' classroom floor academically and kick oval balls left-footed. Having the unwavering coolness 365 ¼ days a year in the depths of a congested, overvalued suburbia – isn't that enough? How much does it take to wake up a hero every fucking day until you're so sick of the sound of your name, or the sight of your smug boat race smiling – looking dopey on the evening news or the half congratulatory, half I–think–you're–fit–and–want–to–fuck–your–brains–out looks you get when you're washing your car and a bunch of middle aged hens saunter past like some sort of overfed Dalek, spitting rays of suggestive glances, red line lasers knocking you over.

God, I must be near the end: using kiddie programme similes, but how long can I keep up this pretence that I am perfect and I don't have a clue that I am? Certainly not long enough to permit this indecency.

Another gunshot, this one far off in another aisle. The smack of the bullet entering something is distinct; hopefully an aubergine in Aisle 5 or some quintuple ply, small furry animal–associated toilet paper (pack of 15 – but only pay for 12). How did it get to this: standing over Magnus, his lifeless body crumpled together while Margot's legs twitch and her breathing slows down, inebriated from orgasm? He must be responsible. It was perfect before he arrived. Before it became this game, this contest; before all the heroism was not so obvious and his antics nicked more sewing circle tabloid spaces, found the prize in the circle and made him question how it had all been too easy up to that point. An easiness only called, bluffed then raised by his smugness. A smugness raised and raised and raised and raised until nothing really mattered except the raise. Ah but I digress (or he digresses, whichever you choose to follow first) … where were we? Something about an arrival, a perfect wife, sublime children, a playdate, then some other nonsense about a supermarket robbery, life–affirming bravery and most fascinatingly … a perfect neighbour.

CHAPTER 20

Dorm All Nay

Wake up before the alarm goes off. Every day without fail. Kick that duvet off; I mean kick it metaphorically so as not to disturb his sleeping angel. Jogging kit on including running shoes moulded around his specific stride, step and speed ('as near to professional' as they'd seen since the 3D modelling store opened). Out in the cold, the rain, the snow, the darkness, the rising sun, the whatever – to feel that push of the pavements up the quad like an old–fashioned injection pounding right up and out of the groin. No other joggers out.

No one as dedicated. Some babies already up, lights on in houses engulfed by the otherwise silent thick air. A few curtains quickly ajar to catch a quick view in case his shirt was off: the mother feeding, calming, soothing then that sneak of a glance like a mid–afternoon Cadbury's treat to take the reality of life away just for that momentary second. Still the quiet street. The odd dog, stretching, licking himself, stretching, half–heartedly barking as he speeds past. The pace getting quicker, the stride lengthening – into stealth mode, a track pumping from earlobe to earlobe inducing a slight flick of the toe for speed and a deeper breath to tighten the stomach.

Greeted at the door upon his return every time: his model children; how he could never understand those whinging parents complaining of lack of sleep and unruly behaviour. He knew the secret: kids embodied their parent's tainted traits, warts, fears and insecurities so the only option is not to have any. Not to have any kids if you have the traits; traits if you have the kids.

A luxurious shower in his wet room, the floor a jigsaw of organic shampoo, Dove soap foam and the smell of exercised man afterwards. A bit of blah and more perfect blah until we awake at Doug's office, his personal assistant under his desk forcing him inside her throat so that it tingles almost like his legs after the run. No really this isn't happening, rather his PA brings him a double espresso and follows up with a quick chat on his day, followed by her thoughts on the latest budget – not only is she smarter than any of the PAs in the firm but is also not north–estuary easterly orange and just basically beautiful, intelligent and part of Doug's world. And madly in love with him – so much so that she one time (only this one strange time when they were in New York and you know) did intimate she might have feelings. But Doug being Doug refused while not alienating their friendship, working relationship or diminishing her esteem. He only wanted good things for her, his Veronika.

Midday. Midday! The gargantuan daily meeting pulling friend and foe alike; admirer and admonisher towards a greater corporate sense of togetherness, a place where we should all write the same thing in snow with our yellow wands. The meeting where everyone has a duck and they jostle to get in a neat row so that their little tails and cute beaks are uniform; identical when all each duck really wants to do is fuck the other over so that in reality there is no row, just weak ducks face planted down in the soil, faces buried in career shame. The meeting where you get points for raising your palm to slap the duck next to you's back. "Good job, old buddy." Then the friend challenge: "Good point but I have to disagree," not because of real contradictory belief but because this is an actual value you get judged on come bonus season. Did he or she challenge enough? Did no one grow up in the eighties and watch the Challenger fail? Not Doug though.

Then the daily with the boss; the 'briefing note' meeting. Doug can't help noticing how his boss hangs on every brief part of the note and depends on each and every note in the briefing. As though the social hierarchy is flipped around: Graham (yes, Graham but not yes in a way that would be mocking because that's not Doug – his consideration of

Graham's role in his life is considered, respectful ...
sympathetic and not for his own selfish career progressing
aspirations either – that would be conscious, maniacal ...
calculating; to Doug it's easy does it, seamless as one of the
briefing note adverbs might issue) cannot believe his luck
when Doug shows interest in his personal life. And his work
dependence on Doug's people power, intellect and basic nice
guy demeanour helps Graham (yes, still Graham – the one
who has a barbecue with those Greek koftas, bought burgers
and over-spiced sausages versus Doug's where he's asked to
sing at one of his children's events or kite surfing in Norfolk)
earn more money and buy a more expensive desperate car
which fuels the office rumour grinder where the only
consensus is that Doug should be running the show. But he
doesn't and he doesn't push. Seamless.

Midday + 1 and the lads head to the gym and those young
bucks can have it because no matter how much sweat and
blood and lifting and hoping won't change basic genetics
where Doug has been blessed. OK the odd run but that's for
the buzz, to push himself versus himself to beyond the stench
of mediocrity.

"That Doug does sweet fuck all and he still looks great.
How the hell? He's never in the gym!"

*Really, it's not my thing – strutting around a congested
room gyrating on the spot just to look better. I need ball in
hand: try line or quivering batsmen on the horizon or just
rushing around the park with my kids. But they're right I do
need to up the ante a bit – the runs should be same distance
only quicker. And maybe something just to keep the spirit
alive – a spot of rock climbing or one of the boot camps in*

the park. Those middle–aged post childbirth women all look fit ... and unhappy.

The workday winds up – stuff has been done … well. People have been charmed and laughed; the right things have been said at the right time. Home time. The drive home: pleasant with a few knowledgeable route changes based on traffic nous; if Maddison Avenue is half–empty take Cromer Street; if full stay on Maddison. The parking spot – always there … except today. Who would? No wait, this is meant to be your typical day, one where Doug parks, locks, gets the attack greeting from the kids, kisses the wife, hangs his jacket up, has dinner, reads some poetry to the kids, maybe a bit of maths if it's Tuesday, checks in on his other business ventures and charity interests, shares a glass of wine on the sofa with the wife while she warms her feet under him, followed by a messy sex session of passionate thrashing about in the bedroom (but less so now the kids wake easily) then into slumber after another close to perfect day. But not today, for fuck's sake, there is a car parked in his spot and the kids don't rush to greet him and this is where it all begins for Doug. Begrudgingly Doug parks on the opposite side of the road, beelining for his front door when the rogue autoimposter's lights set the neighbourhood ablaze. The car pulls out and there is only a whisker of a hint that the driver veers towards Doug as the large SUV reverses meaning Doug should sway out of the way, even if just being cautious. But he doesn't; this is his kingdom and is that new prick of a neighbour actually aiming for him?

Stand your ground. I'm not moving. But that shit! That ...

Tank's rear bumper skims Doug's knee as he passes; the knee that rugby ruined; the knee that prevented the career. And if he hadn't moved it would be the pain and hospitals all over again. The car stops and Doug stands incredulous but trying insignificantly to hide the frustration. Keeping the neighbourhood sweet and all that contrived bullshit. The window lowers and the man who Doug spotted arriving the other morning leans nonchalantly out.

"Careful next time there, sport," he says chewing on a prehistoric cigar. "What are we doing tomorrow? I'm taking you out to play."

CHAPTER 30

←→

Corn Ping

"You collect it?

"I collect it. Some pieces are actually worth more than you might think. But I don't do it for the money," he says, ironically nodding and fingering what is either the beginnings of a hideous moustache or faster than the rest of the stubble. Doug winces hoping that top line of black regimented growth just happens to outperform the rest, but this guy probably could pull off a moustaka even though one was only last spotted in London two decades ago or on a foreign building site or in November.

Is that her heel? Looks round and artificially hard but perhaps the angle is obscuring the nipple. God, did I just think the word nipple? Tit. No, that's the whole thing. Or this whole guy.

"I've got some you wouldn't believe exist: Jenna's first boy-boy-girl; Devon's first anal; Briana's eagle before the work and even Jesse's home movie with everything on top, sprinkles and a red cherry pear tree."

"You watch this often?"

"Fuck no, just collect it. Porn is like women: you only want what's new. Once you've looked at it, experienced it, satisfied yourself – you're bored of it. Delete and move onto the next, keeping the classics for the memory bank and hoping you don't get bored of those when the time comes."

"Does your …"

"Of course. Doesn't yours know you, what's her name again? Good shorts. Margaret."

"Margot."

"I bet she does."

The screen shifts to another screen, distracting both men momentarily then holding their attention with a brief introduction, lazily re–enacting the signing of the treaty of Independence. The clarity of the screen can only be described using one of those words from the adverts.

Breathtaking. Astounding.

Better than Doug's, but that's okay not to put on show to the world that you're a couch potato whose life revolves around the set, as though you're unable to extricate your glare from its mind numbing power for one evening of …

Reading. Writing. Painting. Stuff you can't learn by listening to some reality hopeful making up for lost time. He'll be eaten alive in this town. No one gets out alive especially with the porn aficionado tag which'll be slapped on him ...

Like some corner store yellow price tag with the misaligned and smudged black writing, an exploitative margin and hiding the sell–by date.

But there is something about him. Something alluring. Something endearing. He believes he's collecting something or it's part of the 'dare to be different' tag. Or he just likes porno.

A completely shaven naked man is now having his balls licked by two women, but his legs keep knocking off their cowgirl hats.

"You like it round here?"

Does he?

"Yeah, pretty much. It has all the ingredients. Good for the children: open spaces, right sort of people, considerate neighbours. You know that mid–life crises appeal."

"Reg? You in the games room?" a voice emanates from somewhere above accompanied by high–heel clops down the spiral staircase. The porn doesn't miraculously leap away from the screen and Doug looks around nervously willing the remote to fly into his hand or the power to cut.

"You haven't met my wife, have you?"

"Um no, not yet." One girl spits into another's arsehole then darts her head back to the saluting phallus like a hurried cartoon character.

"What are you two gentlemen up to down here?" she says, almost facing the mesh of over-tanned skin bulging across the screen, the conquest of the West. "You being subjected to the 'collection'?" she says to Doug, putting out her hand. "I'm Deloris."

"Pleasure to meet you," says Doug, squirming in front of the set putting himself between her and yet another feigned orgasmic yelp. "Settling in?"

"Feels like we've been here forever; everyone's been so welcoming. I've met Margot. What a lovely woman. And your children – oh my God, they are the most beautiful creatures I've ever seen."

At last. Back to normal.

"Children certainly are creatures," Reg pipes in.

"We must get our troop of merrymakers to play with yours," she says without blinking as the man still wearing the blue regimental buttoned coat explodes all over his newly proclaimed patriotic countrypornostars.

"We absolutely must," says Doug. "It'll be good to help you acclimatise. Assume they're starting at the local?"

"Yes, Granger House."

"I meant Sundringham."

"We didn't know much about the area really, so thought we'd err on the side of caution and go private," says Deloris.

"Plus, not having my rats running with the local sewer rats," says Reg grinning.

"Sundringham's fine. It's meant to be the flagship school in the area. But who knows, you could be right. I considered Granger but had the North London sense of community shoved down my throat so many times I gave in. I'd have probably also gone for Granger had I my way."

"That thumb print," Reg laughs dragging the end of the word out, then again: "On your foreheeeeaaaaaddddd. I took that Margot to be someone who doesn't back down."

"It was a joint decision. And an easy one. Sundringham's results are better than Grange."

"But, my good man, as we all know it's the balance isn't it? So these kiddie drones get it hammered into them that they must write and spell and divide but the world is so much bigger picture. It's the network; it's the facilities. It's not helping others bring up the average."

Suddenly the porn score belts up to loud as the feature goes to credits, the black screen darkening the room. Doug, having momentarily relaxed as he forgot about the visual distraction, now feels a knot boring beneath his neck, a manhandled corkscrew eroding his muscle fibres. It's probably time for a run.

CHAPTER 40

Kit Some

The furniture is arranged exactly as it always has been. A lamp, covering a bulb which never lights, flanks the lived–in sunken single sofa which in turn orthogonalises the square glass table, sprinkled with dated magazines and a non–functional remote control. A Sony. And the TV is a Panasonic so the two don't connect, but the remote has to be there because it's always there and because that's the way she likes it.

Remind me why I'm here again? Tell me it's for all the right reasons. I'm close to her, I mean, in proximity terms: I'm edging nearer to the armrest slash door slash exit and she's over me, looming and swirling her glass of red wine in spasms of feigned emotion so that I don't know if I'm more nervous she spills wine on me (and I have to explain) or she spills herself all over me (and I don't explain).

The scene's the same yet the special guest star is different. She's the proverbial 'single girl in the city', 'always unlucky in love', 'quirky soulmate' material – at least to her friends, always supportive if 'flawed and funny'. Funny. This is the pre–watershed funny bit where we all know what's going on except the cast; this is not the post–10pm arched back, thimble of glossy sweatiness in that highly underrated Superman–shaped pocket just below a woman's Eve's apple, every taught contracted tendon, joint and muscle rhythmically pulsing in pick–up–sticks directions.

She is pretty and I know I've got to be funny now on cue or it'll ruin everything. We don't really hook up at this stage – that only happens at the end I believe. That's what I'm watching. Isn't someone meant to walk in now and catch us then we squirm next to each other on the sofa or I jump up and look at another interesting prop like the fake fruit or the wall clock in the shape of a mangled heart?

"You comfortable?" she stops.

"Yes V, thanks. You? All OK?"

"It's like I'm going through some sort of mid–life crisis, even though I'm not middle aged. Like it's all falling apart or perhaps it was never built to begin with so there was never anything to fall apart."

"I feel like I've been going through a mid–life crisis since I was fifteen."

[CUE LAUGHTER]

That's a great line.

She gets closer. Does the audience notice or is the camera edit such that one minute she's stretched across the dull fabric sofa like an oil painting then the next we're zoomed into her leg touching his?

The drive home is laced with a bitter taste. The radio is playing some forlorn love song, not where she kissed a girl but where he kissed a girl and liked it. And the sombre home street: all quiet and wet but not wet like a street is normally grimy wet, but fresh like a wet field with the scent of wood smoke in the air and the soothing reflection of porch lights onto hard wet night tar.

Serene but when a balaclavad shape casts up into Doug's eyeline to the side of the car, the Bejesus is scared out of him such that he swerves and dismembers a stray plastic bin, having run away and run onto the road. The figure now hunches over, hands on knees as though the wind has been knocked out of him only to emerge upright and shaking, convulsing in hilarity.

Who else? It had to be.

"Whatcha been doing up until these wee hours of the morning, my young marauder?" he whispers but in a shout, mocking the silence of the evening.

"What are you doing – you could have actually killed me or better yet, made me kill you."

"Ever hopeful I am," he says putting the balaclava back on and running up the street. For the second time that evening Doug isn't quite sure why, but he follows, this time on foot quickly parking the Volvo XC90 at a noticeably skew angle, something that he knows will bother him to the extent that he's sure he'll move it when he done finding out what Reg is doing a 2am running around in pink floral beach shorts and a balaclava …

I'm compelled to follow.

Reg is faster than expected as Doug shifts effortlessly into a symphonic stride in pursuit.

I should go running with this guy. He's nifty even though his stride is jolted.

The gap remains between the two, Reg stamping ahead on an unwavering quest, Doug now feeling the nibble of his pulse ascending and the effects of two–and–three–quarters of a bottle of Veronika's trying to impress him wine, as he sways momentarily, put off his line by the slightest undulation in the black wet tar. Doug regains his composure having lost precious yards, before giving into to a "What the hell are you up to?" shouty whisper which he knows Reg wouldn't, or really doesn't hear.

Suddenly Reg comes to a halt outside a neglected semi with peeling paint and crouches behind a dustbin that is overflowing with shards of rubbish peering out of a clear bin liner. He looks back at Doug, raising a finger to his mouth, then slowly pushing that finger forward as if placing a thermometer into someone's mouth and leaves it aiming at Doug, now hunched over some way back, the drips from an overhanging unkempt hedge clattering down his collar.

The Reg is in …

I mean actually in the house!

… through an open window.

How could someone leave their window open even in this, the safest of neighbourhoods?

It happens so fast that Doug doesn't notice Reg's approach to the house, jumping and backswiping at the security light with a large crowbar, shattering the light before hitting the path hard and deftly flicking the crowbar under the rotted worn sash panel and up as casually as calling tails. As he's in. And the road's silence hurts Doug's ears.

This guy's a friggin felon. He's going to pop out with something bundled into his jumper or a flat screen under his arm …

Nothing for minutes: double digit minutes. No lights going on. No screams. No bish bash footsteps down stairs and baseball bats flying. No Reg A–Team forward rolling out of the open window and screaming "Run!" in delight: a frat boy all Christmas wrapped in a responsible man's body, shorts and balaclava.

There's no way I should hang around. This is home time; this is past the fucking lesson bell. I need to get out of here, ban the wife and kids from ever venturing to 139 Crescent for tea, playdates, brown sugar or tips on how to fucking steal shit from some unsuspecting legal clerk or middle manager or pensioner. But the house doesn't look like it contains much in the way of nice stuff so why pick this one …

An arm appears from the window; Reg's arm flagging him inwards. Against all reason, better judgement and all that stuff he's been believing for over thirty years, Doug capitulates, crouch running to the window and spring loading down below the sill.

Doug grabs at Reg's arm. "What the fuck are you–" before the forearm twists and hurtles shut on top of Doug's, lifting him clean through and into the darkened room. The air in the room is close; heavy such that it feels as though each one of Doug's gasps for breath is being filled with stale balloon air, then shut off as Reg presses both palms firmly over Doug's face and holds his mouth shut.

"Don't fucking talk," says Reg. "Don't do anything except watch."

Then the glare of a multi–angled spotlight searing through the darkness in a haze of a million golden lights, Doug's head spinning, rolling over and into the two legs of a chair and the two legs of a man, bound and sweating. The sweat sprinkled onto the air, a condiment which Doug now consumes in rhapsodic blasts of hyperventilation.

"Oh my God, your face is such a picture. If I had my iPhone you'd be on YouTube and most people would be pissing themselves right now."

The man soldered to the chair looks down at Doug and screams through the tea towel tied around his mouth, the green–and–white seam jagging into the sides of where the top lip conjoins the bottom lip, a knife forcing open two mangled together slices of frozen bread. He's an old man, not an elderly man; a completely unextraordinary person except for the terror in his eyes.

"I need a piss." With that, Reg vanishes from the room, leaving a trail of active air in amongst the addled coagulated stench. Doug's alone with the man who looks up nervously and pleads with his eyes, tilting his head to one side and murmuring through the tea towel what sounds like a multi–syllabled "Don't."

Don't what? Help you?

In perfect unison with the distant sound of Reg's tinkle, the urgency returns to the situation and Doug tugs at the tea towel: once, twice, thrice then free, exposing the man's now almost blistered mouth so he can speak.

"Please don't; whatever you're planning. Take what you want; there's not much but take it all if you want. I have money. Take my ATM card and I'll give you the pin and you can come back if it doesn't work. You know where I live." The man pauses for a moment, with a sharp inhale of breath. "Wait. I know you. You've got young children. From down the road. Boy and twin girls. What the fuck are you doing in my house?"

A good question. Am I saving this man or wanking off my own curiosity?

"I think I'm helping you. I just followed R–"

"No great need for names at this stage," says Reg, wiping his hands on his trousers and lowering the balaclava back over his mouth with two clenched fists. "Let's ask our neighbourly neighbour just how much he knows about your kids."

A faraway dog howls – a stifled howl, the owner admonishing from an upstairs window – decimating the nighttime neighbourhood peace.

"I've got a buddy who's a DC – he has access to the offenders list and this guy is a first class, repeat offender, pedo–fucking–phile," shoots Reg.

"That's not true," says the man.

Smug Dad

"If this is all a big mistake, let's see if he wakes up tomorrow and calls the police on us. Actually let's see if he wakes up at all."

Reg now moves closer and …

Doug is motionless, frozen by the thoughts of this doddering bloke always popping up at parks, offering to help, commenting on the children.

Maybe he does deserve some sort of warning. But I'm not sure this Reg will know when to stop. And plus he knows my face and my home – he'll dob me in. Unless he's guilty …

Reg grabs a reel of fishing wire from his pocket and begins looping it around the man's hands, one loop after another in convulsive jerks until the green tightening mass begins turning the man's hands a blacker shade of crimson.

"You see," preaches Reg, "if he has no hands he can't touch no children. And if we leave him like this, they'll slowly lose blood, shrivel and fall off which hopefully won't kill him but leave him struggling to signal a cab or cup his hands over some poor child's mouth. What fucking goes around …"

"Reg, we really can't do this," begins Doug.

"Are you fucking for real, choir boy? This pederast, this … this … I overheard my kid and his mate talking about how this faggot touched one of the younger boys on his 'privates'. I'm going to stick a fucking needle through his balls."

CHAPTER 50

Astro Ginger Vitus

A relay: each in sequence following the same as the first, some sick recurring gag. Literally that is: sick times about eight then gag times four then perhaps a heave–ho for two to call and a flush beats the lot. Margot up first – fast initially almost double–heeling the duvet into a parachute, then combat rolling to the floor into crouching and hidden tiger–dragon followed by the sergeant strut as the screams bellow between the shock of the ribcage trapezing paroxysmally. First it's MacKenzie, the youngest; the start of the relay – the starter's pistol initiating the first generous splatter of lumpy orange mangled milk–teeth masticated 'could pass for trendy pudding' mess. Margot meets her in the shock throes, picking her up and whisking her towards the bathroom, half a decade of getting up practice making it almost mechanical. But remember, these kids are not like normal kids: they do NOT misbehave and have problems and issues and sticky–outey ears and big noses. As if by magic (to the rest of the world anyway) they've emerged through the baby and toddler realms unscathed with parental sanity maintained and not much in the way of nonsense, drama or imperfection. Which is why this little episode made Doug start to question everything up until now.

This must be a one off. I'll hop up and change the sheets and check what other help Margot needs. Big early meeting start, so I'll cancel the run if this continues ...

This continues. The 'stuff' is less thick, more sinewy and the heaves dryer. And the first few break his heart: the little munchkin all confused and distasteful at this rebellion of the digestive tract. And he wants to help her – let Margot alternate even though she doesn't work. He helps out. That is what he does. Pulls his weight. Plus he's never tired. Even when the little wonders were all young and up in patches during the night he could handle it no problem; a few more espressos than normal en route to work but no dip in performance whatsoever. Performance of any sort. During the next sweaty cool lull (between the end of the 8xsick and the beginning of the 4xgag) something happened to Doug that hadn't happened before.

Maybe I'll let Margot take it from here. I can feel I slight

ache in my lids and I'm not sure I've slept even during her
alternate shifts ...

"Baby, get the next few," she says, rolling into a squinched
thirty degree angle, the assumptions signed in blood that he'll
do it. "I'm broken. I can't face the smell anymore."

"Must be near the end," says Doug with the ever slightest,
hint of–, crumb of–, phytoplankton of–, minuscule taste (just
the tip of the tongue brushing – literally brushing – so that
one–sixteenth of a taste bud nicks a drop of savoury, sweet,
sour or bitter) of what can only be Fucking–RUSTATION.
"How much more can that tiny stomach hold?"

Then the baton change. Twenty-four hours, almost to the
minute, later: twin sister Giorgia, eyes car boot opening,
clutching stomach, the antithesis of peristalsis and the shout
for "Muuuuuummmmmmmmyyyyyyyy." This is something to
joke about at an upcoming dinner party. I mean we all know
that these bugs hop–scotch between kids like filed wire but
for heaven's sake, could it not be midday start to close of play
say, 8pm, allowing enough time for a glass of Cabernet
Sauvignon and catching up on current affairs? Twins, bang
on two nights on the trot is a funny story but one being right
in the middle of doesn't make the journey ahead any easier.
Giorgia reaches the bend, leaning into it ...

I'm not imagining that there was some lethargy during my
display in front of the Board today. Even Graham's
endorsing, nodding, inwardly clapping, 'you show 'em for all
of us' demeanour was dissipated, like he was a tickle
distracted or something. He couldn't have been. Or was I just
off my game? It can happen. Kids! Jeez, did I just blame a
four-year-old for something in my work life? That's what the

sap dad brigade monopolise, not me ...

"Daaaaaaddddddddyyyyyyyy."

Did she put her up to that? God, now I'm blaming her for my family's biology. Is there some weak genetics here? Weak biology? I must be tired.

"I'm going to sleep in the other room," says Doug, gathering his pillows like a tramp asked to clear off his doorway nook. "Big meeting and I've got Hamish out tomorrow evening for dinner. He wants to talk about Graham."

Margot doesn't respond.

... which is unlike her. We'll look back and laugh.

And into the final straight – or is it? The worst of all to come – the triple whammy.

And there should be no mention of heading down to A&E, because we all know what happens there apart from the oppressive waiting times and the condescending 'you're not ill' or 'missing limbs' looks – when the music changes things get critical ... any any medical drama.

CHAPTER 60

←→

Vicarious Precarious

A suitcase on the side of road. Something unnatural unless you're located on some type of landfill or those ever so downmarket areas where pretending–to–be–well–to–do folk leave their old goods outside their house so a neighbour (or wandering wilbury) will be accidenting past, notice an old set of golf clubs or kid's bike (or suitcase) and say with the little voice (not really!) somewhere alongside the other stupid voice, that always pipes up when you're on Amazon and you find some useless crisp looking cheap thingamajiggy that you have to not not have, which says, "Hey, you know what, I've never actually wanted or needed that in my life before, but now that I see it

now that I see it

I think I'll find a use for it;" or on this one rare, almost fate–esque situation, it says,

Have a peep inside.

So you couldn't make it more obvious: a loose panel haphazardly see–sawing above half a dozen or so plastic packets full of powder.

Call the cops. Don't touch anything because you know how this shit works. You watch Dexter. You used to watch CSI.

But this is all too contrived. A suitcase. In the middle of nowhere filled with drugs. Doug's head darts from side to side, his pulse quickens – he rolls, grabbing a pistol from behind his dusty belt and fires, two white doves flapping to obscure who he is firing at. But all is still quiet and Doug's on the floor rolled up in an odd ball, no gun and no white dove shit.

Doug deftly hides the case because he has to shoot to a rugby game.

"You ready?" he yells to Magnus, grabbing a ball from the cupboard.

"Of course," bounces Magnus down the stairs. "Bye Mum!"

"Bye love."

And they're out the door, the clatter of studs on path not dissimilar to a trotting street police horse.

"You all ready? You got the moves all down pat?" says Doug as the car ambles away from the house.

"Haydn's not playing today. He's sick."

"Shame. Well you'll just have to be the sole playmaker then, buddy. You psyched?"

"Yes Dad," says Magnus almost bashfully.

"Only joking, champ, the main thing is that you enjoy yourself. If you're not enjoying it you might as well not play. And as long as you're giving your all and doing your best you can't really ask for anymore. And the two are different: giving your all and doing your best; the first would be that final burst of speed through the defensive line when all you feel like is resting and the second that one play you've saved for a special occasion – the triple scissor nutmeg dummy for instance."

Car parked, the two make their way towards the field. They're slightly late due to a minor traffic incident off the North Circular, so Doug steps up the pace forcing Magnus to follow as the teammates warm up in the distance. The grass is just not yet muddy underfoot; that period just between when summer gives and autumn establishes an unrelenting stranglehold. And today's mild. Mild as in long sleeve t–shirt mild, the dollop of an open field enhanced wind to braille the goose pimples on even the most resilient fan.

As Doug approaches, he notices Reg, standing next to the boys warming up, wearing a short sleeve t-shirt. Reg nods towards Doug and Doug, thrown for a second, forgets to nod back.

"Come on, Magnus, we're late!"

Magnus throws the ball to Doug, a prefect spinning egg, then glides towards the gaggle of hunched over players desperately reaching for their toes.

Reg lights a cigarette. "G'day."

"I didn't know you'd joined?"

"I'm sure there are many things you don't know about me."
He offers a smoke to Doug.

"No thanks. I'm not sure it sends the right message."

"Oh for God's sake, they won't be virgins for ever. My boy
probably quicker than most. You play?"

"Used to. A while ago now."

"Any good?"

"Not really, but I enjoyed the sport."

"I heard you subbed into a league game the other week and
nailed three tries, plus slotted four penalties. A man after my
own heart: runner and a boot. Like being a lover and a
fighter."

"Wasn't a very strong league game; the opposition were not
at their best."

"Doug," Reg whispers leaning forward, almost annoyed,
"you've really got to stop this righteous, humble,
sanctimonious bullshit. Be proud of your talents. Swing each
one of them from your big dick so the world can admire.
Rehhhhhffff!"

Doug had failed to notice that the game had begun, one of
the home players taken off the ball.

"Your lad looks a bit slow. Carrying an injury? My
Timmy's going to be a fullback … Ooohhhf." He winces as
Timmy goes over for the first try of the match. "That's it,
son," he yells while exhaling, blowing a jetstream of smoke
into Doug's eyes.

"Excuse me for a moment," says Doug walking closer to

follow the game.

"Yeah, whatever. Good luck."

In the interests of fairplay and adaptability (given the scoreline flattering the home team something horrible with Timmy and Magnus sharing most of spoils) the coaches decide to mix the teams at half–time, "allowing some of the weaker runners to learn from some of the stronger runners."

"Fucking Darwin would've whipped this socialist prick out of the evolutionary stack by now," were Reg's reactory sentiments. But it didn't escape Doug's notice that Timmy and Magnus were in opposing sides in a race to five tries.

That start was encouraging with Magnus setting up and scoring to go two tries up early on, allowing Doug the mini–luxury of pretending not to be overly concerned and into the game like the flapping, screaming, vicarious dads, wholly unable to pass left to right or hit any ruck with any sort of on the feet balance. His head was tuned yet one eye and all the other senses couldn't miss a coat hanger of a high tackle – Magnus less unfazed than normal and Timmy glaring, psyched, pumped, ready to win.

Cheating little shit.

"Aw fuck that's gonna hurt," yelps Reg. "Man's game."

"Cheap shot," Doug now admits to being interested."

"Your little princess need an ice lolly?"

"Just a fucking game OK; a kid's game."

"Like I said – Man's game."

Not worth it. Let the play on the pitch do the talking. Where's Magnus?

In less time than it takes to lace up a muddy boot, Timmy scores a brace and the scores are level. His team wrestling the ride back, Magnus clearly shaken and shirking his responsibilities as natural playmaker, leader and talent well for the key moments. Another try to the opposition, Timmy's hattrick.

"You okay? What the hell is going on?"

Magnus doesn't hear Doug trotting back to the halfway line. Kick off and Magnus gathers beating the badly coached zig zag defensive line and through to the last line of defence: Timmy. Now Doug is not completely sure but Timmy seemingly trips Magnus – a blatant penalty – but in the act rips the balls, pleads innocence and darts through to score. Again. 4–2.

Then a cold wind blows and boy does a cold wind actually blow. Doug spots Margot approaching who *never* comes to rugby and her usual attractive yet understated appearance is but the tiniest morsel – the small bit of muddy grass that will not extricate itself from the underside of the rugby boot (the stubborn dingleberry up yow backside) no matter how many times you head bash the studs together – annoying. It's the top – the V without the harsh angles like a test tube shape arching down to reveal the fluttering tops of her breasts. And Doug can't quite make out his annoyance: Magnus shirking, Reg smirking, Margot lurking or Doug's fragile disposition twerking?

"What are you doing here?" says Doug, peering over to see if the score has changed. Magnus could've dragged one back putting it at 4–3, getting up with ball in hand but Doug can't be sure.

"Hello to you too. Charming. I was in the neighbourhood,"

Margot responds without layering her welcoming smile and joining Doug to peer for her son. "How is he doing?"

"What I mean is ... you normally call or something. They're down 4–2 or 4–3 I think."

"Haven't you been watching?"

"I have but–"

"That's your best kept secret, old man; your old lady or you're on one serious clock."

–I keep getting sidetracked by this manboy!

"I thought you'd met," says Doug.

"I would have remembered, that I guarafuckingtee," says Reg already crouching into hand and or cheek kiss mode.

"I'm Margot." She extends a hand.

Not Doug's wife?

Doug gets a whiff of her scent; so does Reg. Then a commotion – try disallowed – Timmy obstructing Magnus off the ball. Magnus, his rugby sense now seemingly back where it belongs, taps and goes to sidestep a retreating Timmy and Boyce, over the line. He spins the ball on his fingers.

"Wonder where he learnt that?" Reg and Margot in perfect unison.

"Freaky," says Reg. Margot blushes. Or does she?

Uncharacteristic.

The game is now appropriately tense. 4–4. Most of the other coaches and parents have gathered to watch. Doug's guard and cool are gone – squirted down the sink like old toothpaste. He is another anxious fan, so much of nothing riding on the game it hurts.

"This is well mashed up," says a voice not normally

synonymous with the rugby set. Reg lights a cigarette, his gaze fixed on Margot rather than the game. The ball is moved between multiple hands in Magnus's team, Doug frustratingly marvelling at the fact that neither of the Granter twins drops the ball and that the ball makes it to Magnus in space. Timmy is man marking Magnus rather than the channel marking structure Doug would have coached, as Doug hopes Magnus can spot this as a potential overlap and put someone else in space. But who? Who has the wheels to win this game? Only really Magnus thinks Doug and he's being watched like an East German suspected of wanting to defect in the eighties. Possession still held then Timmy rips the ball from the small, weaker James Granter and scores. That simple. Game over.

Magnus traipses off the field looking strangely undejected, hair ruffled with a holy cross of two cuts on his temple. He approaches Doug, the dejection now seeping into his face, crimson ink filling the bath.

"Maybe we should do some practice. Actually expend some effort on this game. Perhaps this is what everyone else is doing."

CHAPTER 7

⇤ ⇥

Okay Creaming Nonchalant

"It was never going to work out," says Veronica, bravely retracting the urge to sob.

He was never you.

"I tried to turn him into something he wasn't and he knew all the time. He wanted a dull life and I just wasn't willing to be part of the dullness. He wanted to hold my hand in the street,

kind of like I always fantasised with you;

he wanted slow walks and babies and to get on with the family and growing old and fat together. He wanted no TV, dinner parties with 'solid' friends, expensive meaningless stuff. Blinds. A bigger house. Companionship. Camaraderie. Hope. Dreams. Togetherness. To touch me softly."

Was there ever a time he'd do that? Hope not.

"He wanted everything I wanted

from you, Doug

and when that breeze turned the other way and blew back in my face, all I smelled was burnt rubber. And it made me sick. The sight of him. The touch of him. The smell of him. The him of him."

So I killed him.

"So you killed him?"

Veronica laughs; that laugh he knows: the genuine chortle not the practised, polite, socialite agreement chuckle. A breeze does blow; a hot breeze so that they both inadvertently taste the air for burnt rubber. Doug's coffee steams.

"Still the almond Americano even in this heat."

"Still the unnecessary cold sugary drink to wash it down."

"Some things don't change."

"That was likely some of the hardest fucking you've ever done to me. I can still feel you."

"You know if you hadn't dumped Dufuss Whatshisface and we hadn't rekindled ... this ... I would've left Margot."

Veronika stops sipping, taking Doug out of her mouth.

"You're not saying ... "

"Hear me out because this is just making sense to me." Now holding him at the base, round one complete with all fluids tidied up and round two on a knife edge between never again and right now. *"You filled this hole in my life; this*

incessant itch – this rash I could never explore with her. And when you weren't around, I couldn't manage the tedium with her anymore. I wouldn't have run to you either – likely it all ends up the same way when you share a toilet with someone and buy groceries from the same account. I might have found someone else but this is the balance which means no one ever gets hurt. Like you were saying: be careful what you wish for."

A squeeze and round two resumes.

CHAPTER 80

⟵ ⟶

flex Actor

This is one of those times you either stick to being a man of principle or give up on a lifetime of empty rhetoric. Plus how bad will it be? I might not even make the final edit. But I'm here; I've made it this far, sitting amongst these hopeless hopefuls. Sitting waiting. While someone belts out a tune somewhere down the corridor or in the gents singing into a comb or their fist.

Even if Doug was the sort to renege on a deal, they wouldn't have let him. Inky Pinky Ponky and Winkie; the four

Muskaqueers – driving him to the venue, giggling all the way like those overly enjoying themselves people in road movies, except without the convertible. The luck of the Irish, or in Doug's case perhaps the jinx of a third generation Irishman. He somehow recalls how the stupidity began and clearly recalls his reluctance to be a part of it. A silly after work loser–takes–all competition which spiralled into the cult echelon after no one could dispute it was a crazy–good idea. Winkie took the credit but in truth the idea, although throwaway, was directly from Pinky's goatee-enveloped lips.

So throughout the week everyone in the office picked their favourite song of all time. A rogue iPod became the vessel to inherit this unholy conglomerate of Kurdt–Kylie–Robbie–Madge–Marshall and the entire back catalogue from U2. Some keeno (Ponky) loaded all the songs on and the entire office gathered around to see who would take the cake. The mechanism was simple yet effective: put the iPod on shuffle and go to the one song put there intentionally to kick off the selection. They all listened as Leona belted out beyond her tonsils. Then the quiet before Doug's demise: the randomly Steve–Jobs induced selected song to be the winner.

The first few notes of Coldplay's *Yellow* followed by an uproarious commotion from iPod desk all the way to the coffee machine with most looking expectantly around and others (notably Inky, Pinky, Ponky and Winkie) pointing and laughing. Doug sheepish, not really believing the odds had gone against him; over a hundred must have been involved and his song plays. Of course, he graciously accepts, nodding and absorbing the back–slaps and general "You will go through with it won't you?" queries. Of course he'll go through with it; that's what he does. Gets things done. Even if it means belting out the second verse for Simon Cowell on the X–Factor.

I'm only human if I'm a bit nervous. But it feels different to be nervous in this situation. I'm convinced it won't get on the TV.

"So?" says Winkie as Doug stumbles from the exit like a prisoner being released. "What happened?"

"I'm not allowed to tell. For this round of episodes there's some has–been celebrity involved so we all had to sign conditions which stated we couldn't mention anything about the audition. Even whether we got through or how bad the rejection was."

"So you got pushed up against the glass while grassy forearms himself gave you a seeing to! I know it!"

CHAPTER 90

Anoint On Perturb

No matter how long or how transfixed he remained – his eyes like erect stalks pulling the ceiling nearer – it wouldn't go away. And the breath beside him: familiar yet in a strange context; an unacceptable one. What's the word that should be applied in these sorts of situations … philosophical.

Yes, let's remain philosophical about this.

As though this experience would somehow make him a better person. But this is the act he's been through a thousand times in his head and a further million in ways he would avoid this. So how had it happened?

God, a minuscule crack in the ceiling. One that you would probably only notice once out of every 5,386 times you looked up there. Please God let it widen and swallow me up ...

Like Veronika's wet cunt as he plunged into her, at first allowing the slow tensing of his arse muscles to tighten; inserting a needle into an arm, then the non–obligatory breathing out moan. The moment she'd been waiting for. Or perhaps he'd been waiting for. Then a gathering of frenetic thrusts so that his shaft gleamed in the bright kitchen lights, flicking her one leg onto a stool and pushing her head flat onto the cool counter granite.

I can't get out of here now. It was much easier back in the day when you hardly knew someone and you could make excuses and depart.

But Doug knew her well. He knew her likes (him) and her dislikes (his family, being alone, football); he knew she was always there waiting for some crack to appear. And aptly the crack looms above his head – now a proper in–yer–face, this–can't–end–well crack.

Philosophical. Manage the situation. How did this actually happen? How did this actually happen. Did this actually happen! Did this actually happen? This actually happen? Actually! Happen? Happened.

CHAPTER 01

Ray Gape

October never held surprises. Historically in perfect rhythm with the weather: a welcomed Indian summer complete with lawn just dry enough to mow in t–shirt and shades and a venture to the local garden centre in flip–flops. Then the crispness of a fresh morning, more clear than those new glasses relentlessly punted whilst in the latter stages of a required optometrist visit, the breath just beginning to melt the air in puffs of fresh steam, but with the obligatory oval mouth to heat the air on exit.

October was normally that final month of squeezing out a

set of runs just before the clocks went back: Monday fresh and calm, Tuesday crisp and tight, Wednesday rest and so on until November shifted all road panters indoors to compete on a whirring stationary NASA dashboard of a treadmill. Sardining into a gym where the whole place smells of chlorine, even the parking lot. Which is why Doug liked to take months off and top up with the odd insufferable trip to the gym; get as much running in as possible before he was forced to endure this mechanical 'trying to push or pull or grunt hard' festival in a tiny room where the weights always outweighed the IQs. Snobby? Not really – just a glorious appreciation for God's green earth and the patter–splatter of bespoke designed–around–your–stride Asics running shoes on manicured London tar.

So he'd struck a deal which meant his 'Winter Wheels' programme kicked in at Foddington's flagship gym: November start to February complete with additional price tag for being a Selective Months gym goer. And the thought of being seen there by some colleague or neighbourhood working dad – horrendous, as they might actually think he pumped iron to get that physique. Na ah. Fitness, gallingly good genetics and a shape born (or muthafucking Jason Bourne) from the pages of an immodestly altered men's fitness publication. What ridiculous section do they store them under in the shops, right next to the local porn, bondage, tattoo, piercings and interest so dull you're gobsmacked there's actually a monthly printed set of pages about it … what do they call it? *Men's Lifestyle*. Jezuz.

So this is Doug's current state at the apparently freaky turn of weather patterns in his cherished, ever reliable October. "And yes, you long glum faces," whistles the purposefully ugly BBC weatherperson, "we could even have a winterwonderlandoctober this year. Wouldn't that be fun? A snowman dressed as Capt. Jack Sparrow for Halloween. Wrap up warm whether it falls or not, me hearties!" His state is not pleasant, not nice, not unconsciously smug ... but not rude either; just inwardly annoyed. Running wiped out in October and the gym not budging on an early extension. So he supposed Reg's offer of a few free guest passes would have to do. Rather kind really and the offer was matter of fact enough (and accepted in a reciprocal manner) to not equate to the all expense, double fat, full calorie meal deal being bandied around Doug's head like his running shoes on a golden crisp October morning in 2009.

Nice of Reg through. Perhaps I have him all wrong anyway. So he says he'll meet me there as he has to sign me in the first time. I'll go, run on the treadmill, maybe a few pull–ups, crunches and some rowing and out of there to home for Magnus's chortles of laughter before bed.

No sign of Reg, but the employee womaning the front desk (beautiful and not in a gym sort of 'I was fat and now I'm toned to within an inch of my life and I still keep the parachute Levi's I used to own when I was sixteen draped over my bed acting as an additional duvet' or 'my body is styyyyyyacked baby, like I have abs OK – but my face looks like something that no small child, or human being for that matter, should have to suffer, so I'm orange and have enough make–up on to sink a bath') offers a welcoming entrance smile. Just beautiful. Plain beautiful. Doug notices. Jemima notices Doug noticing. All a bit (20p perhaps) awkward, masking the fact that Reg isn't around but Jemima kindly ushers Doug in on Reg's written request, offering him a tour of the facilities which he (regrettably but with some relief) refuses, substituting for some lame reference to only running. Fucking October: similar scenes used to be effortless, now everything is thrown off kilter; a time warp of annoyed energy.

Doug hits the treadmill (that could actually be an advert), arms pumping alongside his tight black vest, legs pounding a single spot which feels unnatural. He's run on treadmills before but it always felt just that bit contrived and sometimes there's the dizziness afterwards, a disorientated, almost drunk feeling. But he pounds it (another ad, or perhaps bolded extract from one of those <swallow before saying> *Men's Lifestyle* magazines) – too much – more than normal – harder and faster than any run that year. Steeeeeeep incline: belting up that imaginary hill so that his quads burn, his lungs squeeze and the black vest turns snooker–ball black from the sweat. When he stops, he is dizzy; so dizzy that he falls backwards sitting on the lap of another exhausted patron who almost welcomes the attention.

"Apologies. I, um–"

"No problem. Take it easy."

Traipsing back to the shower, Doug meanders, stopping at the ubiquitous water fountain to gulp and gasp and gulp gulp and gasp and gulp gulp gulp. The men's changing room is quiet – no usual banter of post work squash buddies pretending to be interested in the other's job, no clickety–

clack of OCDed blokes donning sandals to the pool/shower, no hairdryers. So Doug slows down, gets rid of the sweatfest that is his clothes and becomes showerbound, just like at boarding school.

The shower head opens like one of those sped up time lapsed flowers germinating on a nature programme onto Doug's face, and he welcomes the first cool then piping hot water down his body. He has to hold onto something, reaching up to lean against the front wall and putting half a shoulder against one of the two glass panels which flank him.

Ahhh. Nice. God that feels good. It's not that bad hanging with the overtryers for a couple of days a year. There's someone behind–

"Excuse me."

A man's frame fills the entire entrance to Doug's shower cubicle. He's completely barkstollock naked without a drop of hair anywhere (yes including there) except for the rough stubble outline of what can only be a moustache. Doug peers through the stream and steam in disbelief.

Does this guy actually own a moustaka? Is it Movember? No for fuck sake it's Fuckedtober! What's he–

The man reaches a golden arm out to Doug. "Would you mind if I soaped you?"

"Yes, I would," Doug responds, now regaining consciousness from his fatigued haze. "Look, I'm not that way."

"What way?"

"I'm not homosexual. I don't like men. So somehow you've got the wrong idea and now you're encroaching on my space and I'd appreciate it if you could leave and I could finish my shower."

"You're such a tease: you've been signalling the whole time. Plus you have to on your first visit."

A figure appears behind the man, then another behind him, fanning out in perfect held–bodyboard symmetry, the two gentlemen appearing neatly tucked under the triangle pinnacle's bowed arms. No clothes. No hair.

No fucking way!

The rest of the changing room remains silent but for the oddly intermittent spurt spurt of water from the pimpled nozzle, clattering onto Doug's back. He feels his shoulders tense and an unfamiliar antisocial feeling wash over him, like he actually has to do something here. Something that won't be agreeable; something where somebody is probably going to get hurt or at the very least restrained. But who?

This is not going to happen. Not here – not like this. Scrap that: what kind of a lame–ass–mother–fucker–action–hero– movie–rip–off line is that! Not ever – not in any way, shape or form. Lame–ass? What kind of an associative–

"We're going to take turns. Now you can choose – the full relay with baton change on completion of each leg or more of a free–for–all, 'let's just scatter the love' approach? Hm?" The three men now almost squashed together at the cubicle entrance. A big gay sausage factory and Doug's brain blocks out exactly what is happening below his eyeline as sausage squared on the right considerately reveals a tube of lubricant from behind his back and expels a clump or three in a zig– zag across his four (well–manicured) splayed fingers.

"What's it going to be, newboy? There ain't no one here to

hear you moan."

Something from way back – try to remember. Keep the attack down the centre: nuts, stomach, sternum, nose. Belt the nose. Belt the faggot rapist's nose!

Doug steps forward putting his face flush against the centre man's face; nose–to–nose then, pulling back momentarily, he screams before putting a firm shoulder into a lengthened arms down through fist into centre–man's face. Then the blood flowing everywhere diluting to a pink colour in the still–flowing shower and Doug's wrist stinging like he's cracked it or worse. Before he could either raise his much weaker southpaw or have another diagonal crack at one of the lieutenants, the other men were on him. Pinned between waxed golden bulging forearm and gorilla–paw palm cupping the back of his head, Doug was held as the other man standing took to wrestling with the lubricant. Forced onto the floor, the bloodied leader now back into the action, Doug could feel the men step onto his ankles pushing open his legs so that his hip bones scraped on the tiled floor. Doug kicked like a sadistic mule, his arms arching up in punches at the man holding him and his legs tightening like an old–fashioned Christmas nutcracker unable to separate the outer shell of an obdurate kernel.

The sound of faint laughter, almost dream distant laughter. Perhaps the happy disbelief unreality to shield the horror of what was happening.

But familiar laughter. I know that condescending cackle–

"Oh my Gawd, your face! When you thought. Oh – too precious."

Doug's face can smell the disinfectant lining the safe–coloured tiles as the now almost clear again water dribbles across his eyeline. His muscles relax – not because he thinks it will be easier and less painful but because … because …

The motherfucker. Is that meant to be funny? Perhaps that is funny.

… he knows the laugh. He's starting to know the man; sense of humour – timing. Reg slaps Doug square on his left arse cheek, his fingers akimbo so as to grip as much meat: a butcher lifting out a clump of lean beef mince from the display window.

"My boy. Gawd you thought your cherry was about to get pumped out right here in the gym. I should introduce Guy, Steve, Dennis."

CHAPTER 11

←→

Iraq's Seem Urging

Cold evenings were never a bother. Or perhaps they were yet Doug was just resourceful enough in the old prowess department to make it not matter; to make it more irrelevant than fresh air in winter. Or perhaps they always just did it with the windows shut. Or maybe the overdone gaudy graphic TV weather reports of the cold snap are true. Or what about middle age bones becoming old person brittle, so that the aches correlate more to dismissing cold techniques rather than muscle wear and tear.

Nah, something is wrong.

Margot is propped up on her elbows, repelling Doug's

attempt to put her calves on his shoulders. The act of defiance annoys Doug so he tries to flip her over as he might have done thirty five hundred times. Doesn't happen. Not going to happen. Then the cold reference, the inference so 'might not be worth it' Doug slumps back, wounded, dismayed, without further endeavour.

I mean missionary is a hunting ground I have never failed in but it is ... well ... missionary. Vanilla when the 101 starter should be at least wafer infused, nut flavour or perhaps pecan salted caramel.

So for the first time in like forever Doug actually considered masturbation. But only for a millisecond because his harmonious one–on–one time is shattered by Magnus bounding up the stairs whilst the credits role on a DVD distraction one Saturday. Doug mourns his situation: they've ignored each other for over two days now – a record in the Perfors household.

"Daddy, why do some people have grey skin?" asks Magnus, swinging on the study's increasingly loose door handle.

"Don't do that," says Doug, logging out and motioning towards the atypical monkey–like behaviour. "What do you mean grey?"

"I mean are bad people always grey skinned – like the Orcs and those people who carry the magazines and smell next to the shops?"

"The thing about bad people is that some actually look like good people – they're not always ominous looking with big scary eyes and sharp teeth like in your films."

"What does ominous mean?"

At that point the doorbell rings which triggers Magnus to swing again, momentarily annoying Doug just sufficiently not to have time to make it downstairs and answer the door. He misses it. To Doug, Monday now seems a long way off. The weekends used to be the respite but now for some familial self–pitying ostracised reason Doug has started to feel himself drawn into the Vortex that is Veronika. As though she's become the familiar; the constant able to worship from afar and aclose.

This is ridiculous.

"Shall we take the rugby ball down the park? Practise drop–kicking?"

Magnus is silent shaking his head.

"Aw, is it the game the other day buddy? Don't worry – you know losing is fine: it makes us stronger and it's okay to let the other saps enjoy their moment of glory," he says through wincing, clenched teeth, "because when you're running the country they'll be driving you some place with a car that lights up in the dark."

Magnus isn't quite sure how to take this so he leaves the room.

"Frozen yoghurt?"

CHAPTER 21

Affection Pain Gel

Everything had always gone according to plan for Margot. Her near–perfect start in life (complete with 'finest looks in the class' perpetually bestowed with seamless effort from all the boys and 'brains to go with the looks' from all the teachers) had been perfectly orthogonal with the next step (scholarship to top performing girls' school) and the next step (commendable degree at Oxford) and the next (marrying man–of–everyone's dreams Douglas Perfors) and the (oldest beautiful boy with red–cherry lips and eyes brighter blue that any touched up tropical island sea postcard) and (twin girls, both the spitting image of her and possessing her 'unwavering spirit' and 'calm demeanour') and and and …

Wherever Margot went there was a fuss – always skilfully disposed of with minimal bother. The aesthetic of a slender blonde woman with twin blonde girls normally drew the oooohhs and ahhhs from the old biddies, and the trendy yet way far away from anything revealing sartorial inclinations would traditionally quell the lechy whistles and sneers from the street's bright jacketed finest. Her poise normally saved her when she was without Doug: of a disposition so above attention that invariably when it came to rest upon her like a veil she would shoo it away and get on with the far more important task of being perfect and raising children and generally being a gift to the world.

Which is why the concept of playing away from home came none too digestibly to Margot, the thought more sinful than the act perhaps. She'd come across this often enough in her eclectic collection of friends from university days and newly acquired mummies–in–crime. But the crime would or should always end with breaking the sanctity. Or was it worse just thinking about this shattered illusion? Her friend Abigail had blown one of the fitter fathers in the toilet at a school quiz evening and given Margot the gruesome inch–by–inch rendition of the act. Margot had been torn between oblivious (I'm always the one to hear 'these things happen as long as not in my world') and feeling somewhat queasy at the mental image so painstakingly sketched by Abigail's multitude of facial expressions and discordant hand gestures. A potential replay of the latter had, in fact, actually squeezed the ever so slightest hint of Mediterranean couscous back up her gullet when exposed to Mr Toilet Head smirking and nodding at Magnus's nubile teacher while the two revelled in how his daughter was the second most progressive child in the class (to Magnus of course).

And the rather more enduring situation of one of Margot's closest friends suspecting her husband of making plans with his secretary, only for her to vengefully seek a revenge–fuck to acquire an inconveniently exotic STD, to then pass it back to her husband only to discover the secretary had gender designs of a more similar to her own sort. Only once the husband's condition worsened was she able to gather the courage to fess up, resulting in a drawn out separation and general life upheaval mess all due to the builder's assistant's wandering hormones.

All of which made Margot's discovery and her own disgust at the thought of considering it before the discovery even more paradoxical. The discovery, seemingly innocuous, had struck such a chord that, although the evidence was somewhat tenuous, there was very little Margot could do to persuade herself that it was all folly. Because her life was so scripted and perfect she almost made sure to not dismiss this, as though this was the one opportunity to test this ridiculously perfect notion. After all this perfection hadn't been generated from years of subservience but rather from the bold (yet disinterested) demeanour that had driven her popularity during the pre–glory days. Margot's glory days were now and ahead: mother of superstars and effortless calm, nice home, nice stuff with the hint of messy character to just take the Stepford edge off; yet Doug's (must be!) indiscretion didn't (when it should have) shatter the illusion of a perfect existence. It just meant she would have to taste of this forbidden fruit: something which had to be easier than actually thinking about doing it. But it would have to be fate. And it would have to be clean.

When the doorbell rang Margot was in the shower and didn't hear anything until the fifth ring, when the faint chime slipped under the barrier of the wet room door, it must have been fate. Margot rushed to the window to spy who the intruder might be, her hair matted like a woven basket dripping down her pronounced collar bone and converging in a Y–shaped stream between her breasts. It was definitely a man. She could tell from the stance more than anything – hips pouted forward, legs straddling the path. The doorbell went again.

Unable to whip something on in time Margot took the highly uncharacteristic play to answer the door in her towel; something not only way too out there for the North London yummy mummy rumour mill but generally not consistent with her decent upbringing. Maybe these types of things happen when you're under pressure, dripping wet running for a familiar stranger; your fidelity flashes before your eyes, but Margot couldn't help casting her mind back to her first time with Doug and how just plain sexy the hollows of the side of his backside had looked in the mirror, taking the full stride while his angular upper body remained perfectly still. She couldn't help but think of the lipstick smear she submerged into the white linen as she came with her backside apexed towards the heavens like a double scoop of praline ice–cream. The doorbell again and somehow she knew this was the final ding and dong.

Margot went clattering down the stairs yelling, "Coming!" leaving tiny foot marks of wet behind her and tightening her towel to conceal even a beggar's measly portion of cleavage.

"Do you choose to keep all your neighbours waiting?" said Reg lunging forward to plant a triple cheek medley on her wet face.

"So sorry; was in the …"

"Shower. Yes, I could hear. Was it a good one? Why do you need to shower in the middle of the day anyway? May I come in?"

A few minutes later Margot was dressed: a hastily concocted ensemble of 7 For All Mankind jeans with tight white long sleeve Karen Millen top and no shoes, while Reg nosed around the lower floor. At one stage she thought she might have heard him coming up the stairs and felt like she was being watched. Had she left the door ajar slightly intentionally or had she just not swung the door shut hard enough when dashing for her underwear drawer?

"What are you doing here?" asked Margot in a friendly manner as she handed Reg a Nespresso.

"Being neighbourly. Thought I'd tell you your man is a swell fellow."

CHAPTER 31

Pinner Darty

Was there any more insight that could be provided to further enhance the couple's reputation as knowing absolutely everything about just about everything, with that ever so profound sprinkling of a socio–political opinion. But not enough to offend. Certainly enough to impress.

"The banks can't be expected to understand how they invest when the organisations they invest on behalf of don't have a clue. They certainly know why though; we all know."

Splatterings of some pastry dish with cranberries and a savoury jelly–like substance until everyone's eyes are swilling around faster than the exponential increase in wine at the end of the evening.

The doorbell rings. They all ignore it the first second and third time until Doug, dragged from his captive audience status, finds a reason to extricate himself from Shelly's laser–beam stare and incessant yapping.

Why does she always look at my mouth when she speaks?

"I must get that," proclaims Doug slipping from the beam as though into shadow. At the door Doug was only able to make out the silhouetted figures of two individuals behind the mottled period stain glass window in the centre of the main door.

The movement. I know the movement. That ever so slight head twitch.

He fails to answer the door, standing motionless for a second or two, experiencing something ever so strange; something completely foreign to him: being anti–social. In that moment all he can think about are the boundaries no longer being flirted with with Veronika. The boundaries now sledgehammered out the way by an unashamed connection. Can a connection be solidified through depravity alone; was she his canvas or his plaything or his distraction or his fantasy?

She wanted me to take it from her arse and put it in her mouth. She requested it: not matter of fact but as some savoury sort of decree – as though there couldn't be any other purpose for it at that precise moment. And the dressing up and the feigned conversation and perfectly rhythmic ecstasy yelps.

He points. Doug does. And the channel jumps.

Is there an actual cruel dedicated channel for teen school dramas?

Sky Teen Angst. Sky Coming of Age.

How dissimilar to his first time in the dormitory of his private school – the door propped locked by his wooden study chair, back in the day when the only way to possibly quell teenage male hormones was to swap it for the principle of true love. Oh how her expression changed; the bright yellow condom attempt number three in trying to get a seemingly oversized object down a miniature rabbit hole, while the boys outside yelled posh profanity and dissent at losing a house game of touch rugby. At least one portion surprise at the smooth speed of entry – from oval peg into round hole to arm right through the sleeve in one fell swoop: a child down a slippy slide; another portion a hint of pain and the last portion the fire behind her pupils that this would be the most enjoyable course of action for the foreseeable future. And of course he was gentle.

Well that portion anyway.

Knockings at the door; kids shouting his name; the curtain blowing across his taught behind to momentarily flash the boarding house opposite; her muffled orgasm and his great finale deep into the bright yellow like some overpriced cocktail mix.

His initial excitement, as the prospect of actually fulfilling what seemed a lifetime of waiting, quickly gave way to that curious blend of guilt, shame, desired extrication from the situation and patronising concern. There she lay, dishevelled not beyond her rosy cheeks, but sufficiently embarrassed by her near–perfection nakedness for him to lower himself carefully next to her and hold on with a reassuring forearm – hiding behind her for those moments waiting for the guilt to pass, but with arm bridge linking them in virginity scorching symbolism forever. And they weren't even permitted the luxury of a post–coital cigarette – permanent expulsion for that but probably only a severe telling–off for what he had just completed.

So for reasons only beknown to the deepest, weirdest elements of his psyche, Doug no longer had Veronika anywhere near his thoughts: so far away he couldn't even taste her smell or remember her pre-, during or post-debauchery demeanour. As though it never happened – the enjoyable sordidness. But oh how the dorm room first time took place – the real and only threat to Doug opening his home to Reg and Deloris. Those couple of seconds now dragged as Doug shunned the noise emanating from the dining room with his body and stood still, asking himself why he didn't want to answer the door.

I know I don't want to open the door but why? Do I fear him or her? Is fantastical Veronika waiting to engulf me in the same void I might or might not have imaged last Thursday? Do I just think she's looking at me in 'that way' because it's become so commonplace in my world? Is Reg right – do I love it or have my years of pretending to hate it been just that – a pretence? Or do I want to give in to it for the first time ever and essentially cash–in on being almost as good as everyone else at everything? Am I scarred and scared of Reg being so much more risqué than me socially so as to render me one–dimensional and boring? But I have that edge! That twist! That controversial timing! Christ, I was just talking about the only two pure exploits to be porn and Poker – just to get a rise. Or do I just want to picture my cock scooping my juice out of her ass and slapping it into her mouth?

However many moments Doug stood completely still at the door – the same number of fidgets took place on the other side of that door. But no one departed. Like two blindfolded pistol bearers, aware of the general direction and which way to aim but uncertain of the outcome. Without warning one of the guests, the youngest of the wives, Pollyanna, stumbled from the kitchen door into Doug's path.

"Hello Doug. Oooh I'm sorry I was after the little girl's room?"

"A right not a left when you entered the kitchen."

"Is there someone at the door?"

"Well yes, but …"

"I see, you're hiding; you don't want the intrusion." Fiddling with her dress she whispers, "Your secret's safe with me."

"They're new in the area. Newish and we just don't …"

"Oh my gawd, you're not talking about Reg and Deloris – they're a hoot. We have to invite them in," she spouts, lunging at the door to reveal Deloris still standing patiently at the entrance and Reg already down the path en route home.

Oh so farking close. Within touching distance. But she might have stayed. Goal now – not feigned; not feigned; not feigned; natural.

"Hello, Deloris … have you erm been at the door long? So

sorry. What with the noise and everything. Do come in. Please."

Not feigned

"Thank you, Doug. Always wonderful to see you. Reg! Hurry up."

"And you. What's your poison?"

Not feigned

"Thought I might have passed out from excessive loneliness out there," yaps Reg. "What were you doing loitering at the door like that?"

"Who me? That's funny. If only I was that anti–social. My life mantra has always been the more the merrier, unless of course you're a football supporter."

So so feigned.

Doug was and wasn't sure what he was letting himself in for. Upon entering the Coleccion Alexandra dining room, Margot was the first off her seat, springing up from the mahogany Nicosia chair like a marble bouncing off a marble floor. Her treble air kiss was casual – Reg the second recipient – arching her angular shoehorn jawline roofwards, the dark contours of her spectacularly perfunctorily perfect complexion a complete tonal reflection of Deloris's. Doug reluctantly topped up everyone's wine glasses including dragging out a cork or two more from the red stash to breathe. Without knowing it he took a swig from the second open bottle, quickly concealing his misdemeanour from the group across, and continuing his hosting chores. In terms of sequence of events he was in that awkward space between main and pudding, when the exponential increase in flowing booze became cumbersome for both his legs (up down up down) and his arms (pouring over heads, shoulders, noses whilst avoiding the obligatory whiff of a fed up underarm). Margot began relaxing into her hostessing duties too, now having broken the back of the course procession with only a chocolate gateau, cheese and coffees to follow. Plus once the uncertainties of which vegan North London liberal was intolerant to which nut, lactose food and gluten carb, coupled with the portion dilemma (does loading a woman wrestling weight issues constitute generosity or cruel temptation, and conversely does a teeny portion remove temptation in a 'looking after my sistahs' manner or exhibit just plain nouveau stinginess?) were over, the rest would be soothingly mechanical.

Pudding bowls for each, the original Emma Bridgewater range, just mass market enough to be of the people yet worn and discovered early enough to be trendy. Small portions for the perpetual diet freaks but rich enough for the booze soaking–up gluttons. Then cheese: a gruyere, Vacherin soaked in white wine and baked, the essential soft goat's cheese for the laymen, Montgomery cheddar for the hard cheese aficionados and oat flaked/sesame sprinkled/chilli speckled distorted octagonal biscuits from that new trendy deli on the corner of The Avenue and Rosebush for the approvingly raised eyebrows. Coffee from the Nespresso machine, each guest gurglingly selecting the strength with the men dominating the 8–10 strength range and the women operating at below 6. The cups were ultimately the pièce de résistance and Margot's attempt at the 'final memory of evening' for each couple to take away and go off to try and find the limited edition, impossible to ever find, hand painted, collectors' items, East African 80z style cups in the shape of an espresso–size calabash. Mechanical, and luckily so, for Margot's mind was so far from the final few laps of the evening's impressive impasse that, all she could do to keep her thoughts from the other morning, was squeeze her legs together so tightly that the underside of her hamstrings ached.

On the other side of the table (and the metaphorical Universe for that matter) Doug was squirming whilst Reg sat beside him, legs crossed. Doug could tell he was ready to pounce. As though every time a small gap appeared in the conversation like sun biting through netted clouds, Reg was gearing up – sparks splattering beneath his chair, hopping and dicing.

Rocketman. Fucking up my world at the speed of li–i–ght.

Then as if Reg was actually plugged into Doug's thoughts, he stopped. Or seemed to stop, shutting out the rest of the table with his matador shoulder swing over towards Doug, casting a social barrier whilst simultaneously dismissing his chocolate gateau, his forefinger straightening as the white main dish clattered into the 'ready to go' cheese platter.

"You throw dull dos," he muttered to Doug, putting a reassuring hand on Doug's newly crossed leg. "Shall we try get out of here?"

"OK shall we. I'll just depart from my own dinner party. Shall we pick up a unicorn on the way and roast some brass on a magic carpet on the way to the chocolate factory."

"That's probably the most interesting thing I've ever heard you say. I knew I was right about you. Not a bad idea either.

The bit about the hookers that is."

No momentary lull in the conversation – the hum of paired chatting fluctuating across high girl and low boy timbres.

"Ladies and gentlemen," interjected Reg, "my dear host and I have had enough of your tedium and are going native to the local whore house for whatever six hundred squids will buy us. We bid you adieu."

Eruption, no! no! Torrent … cascade of the stuff coating every noun in the room OF LAUGHTER.

It had to happen. Love the daredevil. Hate the rest.

"So Reg, what is it that you do? For a living that is?"

"Reg, I do love your house – any chance we could pop around to take a peek at your loft conversion?"

"Reg, where did you snag that car – it has to be a collector's item."

"Reg, you absolutely have to bring that gorgeous wife of yours around. We're having a little soirée next Friday. Don't bring anything – just yourselves!"

Did I just notice his fly unzip like Dan Ackroyd's in Ghostbusters ... without the contorted constipated expression.

So Doug chose to do what any self–respecting person would do; making sure not to give away that anything was wrong. This juvenile level of jealousy had to be dispelled through gritted teeth at least: perhaps if you can't beat him join him. But this inaugural feeling of being disposed from the coolest man in the room was the real irksome thorn in his regal paw, not necessarily Reg as the embodiment of that prick. But it was as though Doug knew something was wrong: this lethal concoction of that teeny un–finger–putter–

onner in Reg's character, and the deep–seated tip–of–the–oesophagus feeling that his life was about to fundamentally alter its course the real concern.

At a skew diagonal tangent to Doug, just outside his eye line, Deloris made a real effort to listen to a doctor with more OCDs than specks of hair on a collar after a close haircut. The white wine glass had to be exactly in line with the red wine glass – almost to the degree; the bottom of the cutlery on either side had to line up with an adjustment – forth and back at least thrice a minute; the dapples of food or residual sauce had to be removed from the raised outer rim of the plate; the glass of water at one o'clock (although that probably more a product of children); the napkin end perfectly equidistant to the bone handled ring; and so on.

"I am so sure the entire medical profession aligns to Labour because they've created this compensatory bubble which ignores patient care but makes sure each random doctor is on the golf course every Thursday," she spouted, undoing her top button then redoing it immediately afterwards. "We have all become patient agnostic – including the specialists …"

"Would you excuse me for a moment," said Deloris motioning to stand up.

"… unless they're invoicing the overpriced private medical providers at an extortionate rate for half an hour of nodding at some corporate slave who ultimately want a definitive solution rather than a bunch of maybe scenarios."

Deloris got up to urinate. It might have been the constant pressure in her bladder that pressed her to stand up,

unnecessarily readjust her full length dress, bust Doug
watching her unnecessarily readjust her full length dress,
intentionally bump the doctor's soldier line of cutlery and
head upstairs to the loo; or it might not have. By this stage
some of guests had dispersed themselves throughout the
house like a Navy Seal team infiltrating a hot house. Men and
the token tom boy wife encircled the television set while a
seemingly electrifying sporting conclusion concluded;
couples popping their inquisitive noses into the drawing
room, scanning the shelves of old books with acknowledging
grunts and substantiations; an orderly queue of two inebriated
wives hung outside the master bathroom like backstage
groupies; the remainder marvelled at Margot's use of space
in cramming two bedrooms, a study and a wet room into the
loft conversion. This forced Deloris to seek out another place
to relieve herself as all the amenities were occupied upstairs.

Her travels led her to the little known basement after a
mumbled reference from one of the sports fans. With only a
lone door in the basement this had to be right and by this stage
she did actually need to go. On the left a beautifully hacked
together wine rack, the wonky compartments carbuncled
with a vigorous balance of old dusty prize collections and the
latest semi–respectable plonk to serve up to indiscernible
guests. But in reality even those were never really plonk:
Doug and Margot had the best kept secret for their wine, a
South African London–based importer able to tap into the
finest unattainable wines from the entire Franschhoek region.
So the adulation was genuine, the entire dinner experience
convincingly not let down by the one constant throughout the
evening (with the exception of vacuous chat) – wine.

The door was closed and latched, an old fishhook latch resting across the gap between door and frame like some flimsy taboo barrier …

Nice for a moment of quiet respite.

… but for an inexplicable reason Deloris ran her long fingers up the gap, effortlessly flicking the latch open, entering, latching again and pressing her bottom against the door in protest.

As though she knew.

She watched Doug, ever so slightly hunched over in concentration but not so much that it implied he was focussing on a small object, complete and shake. She imagined herself lassoed by it, the veins protuberant around her midsection, warm against her skin looping over her breasts, momentarily faltering at her unyielding nipples – first the left then the right – before tightening around her neck and drawing her in to the source. He was beating her with it like some large mythical tail, one swish and thump then another, leaving pockmarked red blotches of pain across her back, buttocks and face. The explosion of hot white molten lava …

"Are you lost?" asked Doug, casually zipping up and washing his hands without turning around.

"I thought we might catch up. We've not had the opportunity."

"It is nice and quiet down here. There shouldn't be too much traffic."

"Is that an invite?"

"The door was latched."

"That's how you roll: innocent enough to be the victim yet cool enough to walk away unscathed. As though no matter what happens it wouldn't be your fault. Absolving yourself before anything has even been done. God that is smug. I had hoped for more but expected this."

Is this me getting one over on the wonderful world according to Reg or me actually wanting this? Or the precursor to a master escape?

"I'm not exactly sure what's going in here," said Doug. "What do we get out of me pushing you over the sink for half an hour? Conversely what do we get out of starting this for the long haul? Lots of ducking around I'd imagine. Not really my style."

"You think too much; analyse too much. There might just be a moment in this somewhere; a moment you're intent on shattering."

For a second the hum of volleyed discussion infiltrates the space then dies down again. Someone had obviously stuck their head into to cellar entrance then retreated immediately.

"Shattering … strong term. Is this when I say, 'There's something between us isn't there?'"

"Then I respond, 'Hopefully nothing but a thin sheet of rubber?'"

Suddenly the pipes burst into song, Deloris jumping

forward with Doug there to catch her, almost expectantly.

Hardly a few feet from this, as the crow flies straight up, Reg had wasted no time in squatting next to Margot. His hand was on her leg, high up the thigh, his fingers walking towards her hipbone. Then her faultlessly manicured fingers, nails tailored in deep red polish, reciprocating up his lapel …

"You either have it …"

Tugging at the end so the unfold explosion should cascade in a quick then slow revelation of how well the batswing was tied.

"Or you don't …"

Same finger; same spot. Pulling the end to reveal a fastener.

CHAPTER 41

Shag Nifty Cent Mild

There was never a moment in his young life that Magnus wavered or was in any way uncertain. As a baby he'd cried only when absolutely necessary, almost as though his juvenile intuition had aligned to his parents' casual delivery of their seamless life like an intertwined koeksister. From his inaugural playdate he'd suctioned in admirers, friends and followers – both children and parents alike – moths gazing into his dark eyes and transfixed by the effortless ease with which he made them feel, for that very moment, they were near greatness (or at least near enough to have some of the great dust settle on them).

Throughout the toddler years he was one of the first children in history on his feet, and toddled with such ease his burden as the first additional member of family was hardly apparent. All the things parents dread and obsess about and read copious volumes of books about and subscribe to letterbox clogging volumes of publications to solve were neatly swept aside by Magnus's reign of impassive progress – solids were a slam dunk; no issue whatsoever with greens; long lazy sleeping mornings allowing the parents gratuitous respite; a changeover from cot to bed at 19 months; no teething; no colic; neat handfuls of solid poop with self–wiping at 18 months; a ruminative expression the substitute for tantrums; no drama at the prospect of an early bath or bed and of course a trusted parental relationship where independence was earned and not a blatant gold star on a chart like the other children.

It was like baby puberty and it all seemed to happen in a day.

Even the onslaught of siblings didn't seem to daunt Magnus. Where his first–born lesser–compeers resorted to violent anti–arrival tendencies to maintain the doting attention they'd had splashed all over them or the bipolar snail extraction into shell approach, Magnus had embraced the opportunities and, more importantly for his parents, the responsibility. One dry afternoon when his sister set the other alight, Magnus unceremoniously put the blaze out with a Wellington boot filled with water; it took three trips to the kitchen tap but no harm done except the stench of burnt wool which crammed the downstairs for days.

So was there some big denouement for Magnus, some big moment which would shatter his seamless entry, existence and future on this ordinarily overpopulated planet we call progress? Well no. Not really. Except to say that Magnus held his father in such high regard that any blip, even if the natural insecure progression that more of the uncreatives call 'middle age crisis', would be considered significant. But Magnus adapted. As though he knew, liked and loved his father to such a degree that he understood, and more importantly forgave. His soulmate was going through some shizzle. Not like most men shizzle where a Maserati of hot vacuous thirty-year-old would suffice, but a proper explainable 'life–adjustment' seemingly cataclysmic in the short term but ultimately digestible in the long term. He was the boy champ after all, priming to run the county. After All. And there was a lot of All. In Doug's defence though, thought Magnus, Doug could have done without much of the All.

Both Doug and Margot remembered the time Magnus was made, in fact the precise moment the champion sperm might have fusion headbutted the yolk to formalise this unadulterated cell union. Both casually aware that fertility for normal people was perhaps a longer struggle culminating in IVF and disappointment, there was no acknowledgement that falling (feet first) or not falling (standing tall) would be a problem. Doug had stored up for no reason other than busyness in business which meant that, although three had preceded, the was a large One simultaneously with Doug then a rare post act One, Margot certain that it was the actual conception. Doug less so, but it made for a good superhero baby story.

A lab. A dish. A sci–fi film. To create the perfect being; the perfect male from the imperfectly perfect male. Made. In. London. Made. In. Perfection. Made in perfect discourse.

When he smiled, a warning went out to old ladies all over the neighbourhood to avoid fainting, clutching at breastbones and other spasmodic adulatory gestures. Well the ones who were physically able to look at him directly anyway.

CHAPTER 51

←→

Wed Dive

"Have you ever thought about killing your wife?" asked Reg, scratching the top his eyes so matter–of–factly he could have been asking the newsagent why his prices were creeping ever–so–slightly upwards. "Before you give me that look," and he knew even though his head was cock–averted elsewhere, "think of it this way: it doesn't actually mean you'd ever do it or entertain the notion of the reality of it but at least tell me if it's ever popped into your head?"

Doug did need to think about this because there was that one time but it might just have been another too–close surreal dream; the ones that always happen during the Saturday lie–ins. And he didn't want to continue to be prudish in Reg's mind.

"Well of course, but …"

"I knew it. How'd you do it? Because mine was far less glamorous than Marg wrapped around the tyre of a monster truck with a machete sticking out of her brain. Mine was the perfect crime: clever, undetectable, alibi tight, poignant and best of all – thorough."

There was no discernible wind that day and for the first time in ages and Doug felt hot, like his collar was too tight or his jacket too small. He had thought about it. And in more detail than was perhaps normal. But perhaps this made it all normal.

"I'd never want her to suffer. Or be in any sort of pain. Or discomfort," said Doug looking aloft, a symmetrical Jesus pose failing to hold Reg's attention.

"I'd love to know how she'd answer that question. Your Margot."

CHAPTER 61

Pool Slayground

That year the school fete came around early. Annoyingly early for Margot who, in one of countless moments of proving that nothing was beyond her capability even when saddled with a self–started business, three children, a non–seasonally immaculate house, the patience of a foreign call centre operator and the demeanour of one gleefully stoned on a tropical island, had agreed to be class rep for another year and hence throw a grander, brighter, trendier and more profitable fete than the previous year (touted by many in most overlapping cliques as the best ever). So the late May early

June rains had not yet fully abated, leaving a sporadically drenched set of fete goers – in and out of shelter persistently scrabbling through their pockets for mushy ticket tokens.

One such couple: a now tired blend of Caribbean dark with not–quite–making–the–set South East pastiness had succeeded where countless others had spectacularly fallen short. Or probably a better term: fallen long. The school had long maintained its exceptional results (100% Maths, 100% English, 100% Science; 6th in the recent Key Stage 2 national league table) through only mopping up a very strict subsection of the catchment area; a grid of roads called "the Monets" and excluding the rabble. Simba was the rambunctious (the school's justification for future criminal) offspring of such rabble, having snuck in under the special–needs quota guise and wasted no time in *blinging* and *bruving* the class to within an inch of half the parents staging an exodus to the local (slightly less impressive) private school.

Simba was two classes older than Magnus and the two exchanged pleasantries every now and again. Most kids in the school of course knew of both of them for completely different reasons. Whereas Simba was one to steer clear of, Magnus attracted the masses. Simba was less aware of how to treat a star–performer like Magnus; he was more of the thinking if it's in front of me I'll push it and see what happens. So although Magnus was probably not used to the level of abrasion from one such as Simba, he was completely adept at reading people's intentions and influencing in a way where both were winners. The pre–pubescent embodiment of symbiosis. I'll make you feel special and you'll worship me for being the coolest, most unphased kid in all of the British Aisles.

Which is what made that day at the fete all the more confusing and destructive for Doug. Doug had not seen Magnus cry, well … ever. He'd welled up a few times when a physical injury had struck, the majority of whom would have reacted with an orchestra of grizzly yodelling basically until the cow actually jumped over the soothing moon. And he didn't actually cry this time. But something was wrong.

Doug could see the exchange between the bouncy castle and the slip–and–slide: Simba's head back in laughter and Magnus's downward cast eyes. Doug made his way over.

"Gentlemen," said Doug, approaching. "What gives?"

"Nothing," said Magnus.

"Simba, right?" asked Doug.

"Yap," answered Simba.

"Dad, I'm going to go get a drink. Please may I have some money?"

"You OK?" said Doug making sure that Simba was not in ear shot, having been distracted by three blonde girls in his year. "You can tell me if something is wrong you know."

"Yeah I know."

"What happened? I know something happened. Tell me."

The two stood silent for a while as the rest of the fete shouted and groaned and dispersed and regathered like some giant multi–coloured amoeban entity.

"It's just that …" hesitated Magnus. "Well Simba was saying he's going to root for whoever is playing Saracens in the final this weekend. Because I told him I play rugby for Saracens and that they're in the final this weekend. He hates rugby."

"What did you say back?"

"Nothing. I said they'd win."

"They will win. Listen, you go find your mother and grab one of those rice crispy cookies from the stall next to the fishpond."

Simba had lost interest with the girls and was now sitting on a wall digging into his left nostril, the right flaring in the shape of a 20p coin as the protrusion and the finger distorted the septum.

"You find anything?" said Doug, sitting next to him. "You play football, right?"

"Yeah."

"And you support the mighty Arsenal?"

"Yeah."

"Not a fan of rugby then. I believe you're supporting Leicester this weekend?"

"I didn't say that."

"Well good. Because next time you're watching your fag football buddies writhe around on the floor when some overpaid monkey friend of your dad's has coughed near them, you think about playing a real game. And if you feel the need to berate someone's team in a sport you know fuck all about, think again."

"That's not what happened."

"I don't care."

A distant whistle rang out from somewhere in the depths of the face painting corner, startling most due to a momentary lull in the muddled noise emanating from the DJ hub. Doug's nerves twitched ever so slightly: enough for no–one to notice; no–one except Simba. Perhaps it was the unnerving twitch in his eyes – a quarter blink, perhaps the half a degree unclenching of the fist or even firming up of a hamstring. Simba remained unmoved. Yet he did notice. Check.

"Be seeing you," said Doug, walking away.

"Yeah. Sure. Whatever."

CHAPTER 7

←→

Des E.T.

What would transpire (behind the scenes) over the next few months would leave an ugly taste in all mouths and in the end read like a whodunnit. Without anyone really knowing who did dunnit but undeniably that 'it' was in the system; in the circle of falsely–debauched infidelity.

There was no doubt in Doug's mind that Veronika was 'clean' – they'd been to the clinic together and, after waiting anxiously for clear results, had celebrated shortly afterwards with a full throttle precautionless session in the toilet at work.

The subsequent moments had been one geometric anatomically impossible trapeze feat after another, the seasonal boundary shattered each time with a new location, position, supporting apparatus or orgasmic height. This was underpinned by (and to a large degree the chief catalyst for) the mention of 'true love' and 'the one'. Well certainly in Veronika's world anyway. Disregarding a slightly chequered past where there were certain boyfriend 'overlaps' (without going as far to use crude term of double–dipping) she'd always at heart been a one man woman and there had been little doubt, both prior to, at the moment of first entry and post coital glow, that Doug ticked just about every category of being that one man. Even the most notable black mark 'attached' to Doug was in an obscure way the reason Veronika got the best of him each time they did it.

So Veronika spent most of the spare time when they were together convincing Doug of his 'one' status and unequivocal reassurance that there was nothing to be sought elsewhere. And Doug seemed convinced but for that almost inaudible cynical whispering at the back of his skull confirming that these types of emotionally charged 'never can happen' scenarios breed deceit and more tellingly the need for meaningless reassurance elsewhere. But she was convinced; and her conviction kept the canvas bare and the taboos down to a barrel–scraping minimum.

So hopping over the Joneses' fence firmly onto the lawn of the other adulterous twosome – the nasty had to be from one of them. Right? And the obvious candidate given Margot's once in a lifetime justification of the act – an itch which was unavoidable not to scratch and one that certainly didn't require regular scratching like the journey back over the fence. And it was only the one itch which Margot was scratching (which unfortunately in reality turned into a full–blown rash if we are able to seamlessly move from metaphoric to sun–don't–shine–down–there graphic literal body location). And with Reg's track record the obvious origin (of the neighbourly circle of fluids thus excluding more sinister origins of hookers, porn stars and under–age club regulars) was him. He took the blame too, and in his own inimical way he admitted the crime claiming it was 'all part and parcel of the back–arch inducing package you sign up for with a dollop of the Reggiemagic.'

But it wasn't him.

So how did the nasty jump back over the fence? Or how was it on the lawn in the first place? A sixty:thirty:ten blend of everything's–all right:seems like a good idea at the time:maybe this'll fix it, meant that the conjugal reunion happened every now and again: sedate by comparison but enjoyable regardless and most frequently in the lazy morning haze before breath is fresh, kids are awake or time has passed to consider the hassle of clean–up. The clue is it definitely went from intruder to intrudee but with the strength of Veronika's loyalty on unashamed show for Doug's eyes only, the originally infected party in the reality round–about of who contracted Molluscum Contagiosum was not Veronika.

It was Deloris … who gave it to Doug who gave it to Margot (and miraculously not Veronika even though the window between contraction and revelation was significant) who gave it to Reg (who never got it from Deloris despite his incessant advances).

Where Deloris picked this up from is next week's episode. We rejoin the action somewhere in the middle of all this without any fancyfree lover aware of the misery about to be inked across the already smudged couple copybook.

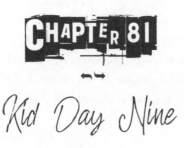

CHAPTER 81

←→

Kid Day Nine

Why is it that every good story has a dog in it? And by good I mean interesting, not wholesome, retributive and laced with platitudes. There are three kinds of dogs in London: those cute demure–faced perpetual puppies which children cheerily harass with a parent's sanction and those swollen–jawed primarily illegal social menace dogs which litter the papers every day with tales of savagery upon largely unsuspecting child victims. I did say three. Because the third category is a genre unto itself; so menacing it often leapfrogs

*the latter or worse yet becomes it; so mind–numbingly
repetitive you find yourself berating your own constant
nagging. But it is always the same. Nauseatingly so. The
beginning of the end of symbiotic terrace relations.*

Neighbour's dogs.

*By the strict definition this would only include animals
within the 'one property proximity' but when your fuck
pushover "yep no problem" if you slap a god–awful looking
dormer, smashing the period apex with some bright orange
imposing monstrosity next to my house neighbour allows said
category of dog (let's call him/her by his/her actual name:
Pruppin) free reign on the lawn, this in turn facilitates entry
into my garden under the beech hedge. Effortless. Despite all
efforts to establish natural barriers. Natural. Then unsightly
unnatural. Unnatural.*

*Slow drip torture: first Pruppin's evening song all night
long after being left outside for an extended holiday period;
then the odd two–day old fossilised turd between one of my
normally sensible brood's fingers, complete with quizzical
look head cocked to one side; then wanton destruction of a
flat rugby ball; then polite words to the neighbour; then not–
so–polite words to the neighbour; then Pruppin making his
way into the kitchen and snarling at me then that feeling of
helplessness until ...*

*Note to self: in amongst this domestic reality I must figure
out what to do with the suitcase. It must have been left there
by a dirty cop; a cop on the take. Or perhaps one of the gang
members who escaped from prison after the grocery store
hostage situation. They're sending me a message ...*

Smug Dad

When the phone rang Doug didn't recognise the number but uncharacteristically answered it regardless. It was a momentary lull at work between the mid–afternoon flurry of adulation and the high–fives to complete the day. Before Doug could even answer a voice interrupted him; a voice he knew quite well by now but not telephonically.

"I done you a favour," said Reg.

"How did you get my number?"

"Do me a favour – let's drop the big stand–off pretence. You need me. Especially now. Pop around to the house …

"The" house – way too grand for "my" house.

… say seven, no eight."

"I have plans tonight."

"You don't. See you later. It might mean we both don't go to jail for thrashing that paedo."

"We didn't, I …"

And just like that he was gone.

Doug's journey home that evening was more uncomfortable than normal: as though the normal average 360 degree space between commuters had been halved (or even divided by three) so that he could tell that the early forties blonde trying to look mid–thirties had just had intercourse and that the gentleman with an almost octagonal bald patch nestling below him at an insignificant 5ft nothing had just had a shit. And the windows were all shut, Doug's access to each tapered to remove any chance of a breath of fresh air.

Something about this country and how people love to breath in each other's old breath and flu and germs and Ebola …

I'm going to wash my hands until I bleed when I get home.

"I did just make that up to get you around," admitted Reg, pouring Doug a single malt. "I'm sorry, but I just had to." He grabbed Doug's hand and shook it avidly making Doug wonder if he'd indeed washed his hands after a similar nasty brush with the public.

"So what was so important that there was no other option but to drag me out on an early week school night?"

"I believe you have a little problem."

"What problem?"

"Margot told me."

"When did she tell you?"

"That's not important right now. That's another story. Suffice to say I've solved it. You won't be bothered again."

By this stage Reg had effectively ushered Doug through his conservatory doors into the garden. There was a strange stench in the air; Doug had smelled this before – it was the smell of death. Doug noticed an abundance of blood streaks across the dense bright green lawn. As though the lawn was a living organism having been slashed open in places by the gigantic claws of some prehistoric predator.

Perhaps you notice these sorts of things when you've felt the warmth of a gun against the side of your cranium. Perhaps you smell out the perp. Bit much? Which bit – predator or perp? Or both? Okay both fine.

"The little fuck was so excited at first, but they all hit that little revelation moment, don't they?" began Reg. "Where the wagging gradually slows and the white of the eyes darken. I do so love that change."

The stench then flicked at the outskirts of Doug's nostrils

more fervently, an invisible line of refractory discomfort from the tip of his nose through to searching among the canals of his brain. Was there ever the ever so slightest flicker of content in Doug's eyes? Did Reg notice this – or was it disgust?

"I'm here to help," said Reg. "I know you don't see it now or understand why but I am the part of you which has been hiding in amongst those false parents' party smiles; between the nods at your magic wand divine acts at work; mangled into your smug existence."

Reg revealed an old cardboard box with the words "Very Fuckin Fragile" scrawled down the one side in dark red writing from behind two chairs flanking the dining room table. Without hesitation Reg reached in and lifted the soggy remains of a small animal, an awkward knotted concoction of fur, entrails, teeth and mottled fluids. Half expecting Doug to reel back in shock Reg was contentedly surprised to see Doug's eyes casually scan up and down the clump of animal, as the fluid oozed out between Reg's taught fingers.

"We can cause some damage together, you and me," continued Reg. "If only you'd let me in." Unprovoked, Reg reached out his arms and held Doug within his embrace. There was nothing else Doug could do but cry, after all this was the man who'd tortured and killed Pruppin in Doug's honour. His life had to be easier now.

The drugs belonged to a local dealer known as Sonny Boy. He'd been loosely connected to the supermarket hostage episode which had left an indelible mark on all those who witnessed the horrendous ending; the extra man helping out a cousin by driving the getaway car. So when things got hot and shots were fired (and hostages killed) he'd fled the scene and was happy to go back to small time drug peddling without so much as a scratch of connection from the manhunt aftermath.

Sonny Boy's orders and distribution volumes were normally modest and leaning so close to the impure rat poison end of the scale that, had his clients embodied the actual biology of rats, they'd have been unable to throw it up and died back in the nest with their countless offspring. So when a big order came through from a Nigerian player higher up the hierarchy to one of his connections, Sonny Boy was only too happy to help 'break, brick and ship' his allotment. Sonny Boy was in fact pretty ambitious: in the narcotics world a middle–to–lower manager with aspirations of running his own niche product distribution line, achieving a healthy margin and maintaining a loyal customer base by upping the quality just when he'd get a sniff they were talking to his competitors. "Losing profit short term only to downgrade the shit back to junk bonds when my lifestyle is challenged."

So misplacing the lion's share of the shipment as one might misplace a letter due for posting was an elementary error which would consign Sonny Boy no higher than his current station in the drug pyramid and most erroneously, result in one single bullet to the side of his head and his body dumped in the New Forest. The plan was simple: place the non–descript bag in the rubbish bin of a known empty property. During the quiet time of the day when all daddies were keeping the global economy afloat and mummies keeping personal trainers in the black, go by the house and pick up the case. The proverbial unaccounted for issue: the fluid rubbish collection schedule. The bin men, in their infinite efforts to obey health and safety laws and avoid any bureaucratic–busting helpful actions, had deemed the case of an 'irregular size and material' for the bin and duly lifted it out, leaving it exposed on the side of the road. And if by fate, design, karma or whatever other nonsense was plaguing Doug during these harsh times – he'd found the case.

Instinctually there had to be a dirty cop involved and Doug knew this. This is why he didn't go to the police but rather stored the case in between the old wrapping paper and travel suitcases in the loft. This was the essential thinking time required for a decision of this magnitude. Someone would be looking for the case. In fact both sides were: a young dirty DC (so trendy – a logical way to supplement an overbloated pension and measly salary) and an old Turkish drug baron by the name of 'lick your lips Lemi'. For the first time Doug realised he couldn't do this alone. The only options available were Reg or Veronika. Sitting alone on the local park bench watching his kids indulge in frivolous climbing frame energy he realised he did not have a close friend whom he could trust with such matters; no confidant or trusted work ally able to step in and Teflon the bullet away from him. He'd lost his male soulmate to the 'weather exodus' from Britain to Australia and his female soulmate to the 'tax exodus' to Singapore. And this nagging feeling that he couldn't handle this on his own, instead of annoying his independence to the extent of making him step up and enjoy the satisfaction of solving the conundrum, had the opposite effect, making him feel at a new vulnerable low. He couldn't go to his wife either – not after what he'd done.

CHAPTER 91

←→

Dross Cress

Inky, Pinky and Ponky had a firm policy of never crossing swords or bruising a beautiful friendship and, more importantly, a viable business. Despite numerous spill–over occasions when one gay orgy had seeped into another room, balcony or unoccupied space, gorging and absorbing random limbs, mouths, cheeks and appendages like a cartoon snowball (as distinct from 'snowballing' as an integral part of the 'gathering'), this was an unblemished hard and fast rule. Inky's preference was always the youthful glow: not a hair in sight and protruding ribs a welcome bonus, whereas Ponky was the bipolar opposite – big, bulbous, sweat–encrusted carpet–hair from top to toe to get lost in for a moment or ten nirvana. It would have been too neat to position Pinky slap (the) clap bang (bang) in the middle or too convenient to sprout a niche fetish: anomalously long foreskin; bus–fitting gap in the front teeth; a penchant for pinching. The simple yet undeniable match was that Pinky didn't know exactly what he was into until Doug wafted through the door on his first day after the much touted appointment.

"I don't believe I've ever seen a male specimen more perfect not only in the aesthetic sense but one where you can just tell that every drop from his mouth will be interesting. And if ever one of our clients was in zero (nadda) need of styling it is this man. Although he could probably pull off a grey suit with brown shoes if he felt so inclined. I'm not sure I'll be able to handle his casual look. Beneath that suit and Prince of Wales knot I just know it's an uncompromising, all–natural granite body."

It was all really just in Doug's head that they had any interest in what he believed to be their day–job. Their real business collusion, deep seated passion and extended camp marketability was fashion: not theirs but others; finding the right space for some helpless soul riddled with 'you wear what!' clichés and stuck between middle–age catalogue tedium and anything accentuating a part of the body other than the belly. And they were good at it. So good that not only did the lucky contestants always come back for sequel 'you promise you stayed away from the tank tops' reassessments but managed to achieve some life affirmation along the way.

Cue emotive music …

"We actually get it on at least every two weeks now – my wife is back in my groove."

"My kids are no longer embarrassed when I drop them off at school – some of their mates have even wolf–whistled recently."

"I get so much more attention at the clubs now – it's as though they can see through the clothes and understand the new real me."

Each too had his place in the chain of fashion transformation. Inky the metatarsal man, treating no shoe as an accessory, giving respect and credence to the lesser known hand–made designers without letting the footwear dominate the ensemble, opting for classic understatement for gents and fabulous side dishes to sustain the arch, step and poise of a ladies foot. Ponky the exterior head to toe: beautifully constructed combinations of the latest fabrics, designers, colour contortions, textures and interlocking styles – often so simple in nature it would differentiate this show from the plethora of turgid gay efforts occupying the lesser slots. And Ponky – accessories (again minimalist) and the pièce de résistance; the one hidden fashion gem concealed in daylight but unleashed in the taboo comfort of each recipient's desirable inner circle – underwear.

Ponky had actually singlehandedly launched a successful male underwear range which had begun to not only make a noise, but occupy a rather large space in the men's intimate apparel market ...

ManSize - for the man With big thingz in front of him.

Doug's dress sense had remained both a mystery and a fascination for the trio – how could a blatant non–metrosexual seemingly ignorant to the allures of fad fashion and blind to the label trophies, pitch up every day at work (or even a simple trip to the local kiddies park for that matter) and look utterly magnificent? As though each stitch of cloth and fold of material and figure contouring line had been a bespoke fitting service from the full body attire equivalent of the little shoemaker's elves.

And Ponky had respected Doug's space in the beginning, probably more in teenager inhibited lusty awe than the etiquette of manners, but now that familiarity was an ever present part of their union, like a stain refusing to budge despite the efforts of a team of Vanish experts, Ponky had moved in for the tactile kill. A day could not go by without Ponky physically complimenting or faux mocking Doug, springing up with hands to flank like one of those kids' jack–in–the–box boxing toys. And Doug remained cool about it, duly noting the harmless attention until he spotted Ponky in Harvey Nics with what could only be described as an uncanny Dougalike; in almost every way conceivable except perhaps the dark beige tint in the skin.

Yet the manner was different; unnervingly different. Like he was getting his own back on the doting young man (Ponky was after all a C+ list celebrity) dominating his conversation, showing disdain at just the perfectly conscious moments, brutal shows of affection to get his own back. But for what?

Doug shuddered at the thought of what went on behind closed doors. And just when he thought he'd seen enough the two disappeared and Doug caught a glimpse through the three–inch ajar fitting room blue curtain of Ponky's creaseless forearms pushing with insurmountable strength on the back of the boy's head, his nose completely distorted below Ponky's navel. His face was a dark pink and there was saliva erupting from his lower jaw, his throat swollen with the intrusion.

They hadn't seen him that day and Doug felt fortunate for this modest mercy but equally unfortunate at knowing that this groupie was being punished for Ponky's infatuation with him. To make matters more sinister Ponky wasn't at work (for unexplained reasons) and then returned with an aggressive air towards Doug – as though his lived–out fantasy was spilling over into the reality of the workplace. Doug was normally quite good at nipping these false starts in the proverbial bud, but this had to be handled with a fair amount of delicacy. The opportunity presented itself like an eighties action movie stripper popping out of a cake: Doug alone in the secluded kitchen area on the 7th floor when Ponky wound up behind him to pinch his bottom.

"I'm not sure that's the best idea," said Doug, turning assertively.

"Some harmless fun. Plus you love it," said Ponky, leaning past Doug to grab a Kenyan Roast sachet.

I probably do, erm – have until this point. But someone has to end the charade, don't they? But the depths of Lucifer's sphincter has no fury as that of a gayman scorned.

"Listen Ponky," started Doug, "I don't want to make you feel uncomfortable but I know there's something going on here. And I'm not sure it's a good idea to be flogging it out for all and sundry to witness at work."

"I'm like this with everyone. It goes with the gay territory."

"I don't believe that – I saw your friend at Harvey Nics."

"We're not really friends per se – Donovan likes to receive and I like to give it to him as hard as I'm able."

Lovely image; almost as appealing as the forced gagging.

"How does that affect you anyway, Douglas? Donovan is my business."

"You're right – I shouldn't intrude in your personal life but I do consider you and your companions friends and I just felt that there was a destructive element creeping into this friendship. I'm sorry if I've got it wrong …"

… even if I know you're about to relent and tell me how much you love me.

"You have got it wrong. The whole world doesn't revolve around how fucking wonderful everyone thinks you are or how smug you need to be to talk to me about something so meaningless. God how the mighty fall."

CHAPTER 02

Jay B. Be No

The churn of foreign baristas at Doug's local coffee shop was high. Probably seeking a brief income injection in the capital before proceeding to backpack through Europe or the Lakes if the tips hadn't been as forthcoming as the new associative descriptors assigned to what is essentially a crushed bean … skinny, wet, wings, massimo, americano, flat, tallfatfreelattewithcaramelspunk, pumpkin spice, macchiato, grandeicedsoyvanillasugarfree, triple venti, creamy decaf, halfsweethalffat, extra shot – an industry with more jargon than PR. Doug liked this particular coffee establishment for three reasons – it was a breath away from the clone chains (*support the small businessperson*), the staff did seem to be genuinely friendly (*and not in that overly friendly grabbing at local slang to make you feel at home friendly*) and because it never smelled of coffee (*yes I want to drink a coffee but not sure I want to be gasping for breath hunched on all fours from the consuming stench*). And Doug was always polite – by nature of course and setting the example for his already polite kids, but also because it costs nothing to be pleasant to someone performing a task most of us would rather not perform. So that day when new girl Lucy served Doug it all seemed to change.

In stark contrast to new girl from a few months ago, Ruta. Up ahead in the (increasingly rare) queue Doug noticed how one of the dads he'd been stuck with for a long weekend during Magnus's summer tour could barely contain his excitement at looking Ruta up and down while she bent over the back counter to retrieve a five pound note which had gleefully slithered down the narrowest of escape cracks. At that's exactly what Alan? Andrew? Angus? got a jam–packed eyeball of. He could barely believe his luck, the whale tail rising up to meet the neatest of horizontal tattoos while the top of the two cheek mounds bobbled in retrieving effort like alternate winks, turned to Doug and nodded, sticking his lips out, lowering his nose and slanting his eyes in frat–boy appreciation. So Doug was forced to look. Not because he wanted to (or ever did) ogle girls just over half his age, but he needed to be certain in his distaste for the general male letch that characterised his generation. And Doug was an eyes man – not quite embracing the window to the soul bullshit but far more adroit at assessing a beauty from that angle than the little nodding man–horse in front of him. But it was impressive so Doug quickly diverted his attention to forcing one of his kids to be daring and have something with sugar in it.

"You come here all the time," said Lucy on this day, startling Doug to his core. She was English and quite simply splendid. Doug was at a loss. This was something he was relatively accustomed to surely – young, beautiful girl showing him attention.

"I suppose so. I don't think I've seen you here before."

"The other girls have mentioned you."

"None of it is true I can assure you."

Lame. Lame Lame.

Lucy didn't laugh. Instead she leaned back to one of the other barristers and whispered something Doug couldn't completely make out, something like, "You've oversold that one mate; he's not all that."

"Could I order?"

"Sure. What's your little one want?"

"A babyccino and a lemon cupcake. I'll go for …"

"Is that all for the little cupcake? God she is beautiful. I assume that's your wife's fault."

"Have you worked here long?"

"Long enough. I might have seen you before. Might not."

"I'd like to go for the usual – I come here all the time."

"Assume the 'might not' – what's your usual? Are you part of the denial crowd who have no shame in ordering the sweetest, sickliest, full of needless extras jargon–full drink or the macho it's only coffee 'I'll have a black Americano' set? Or the worst set, the middle of the road too bored to try something different medium skinny latte tedium?"

"Does that leave anything off the menu? I'll have a white Americano please. Minemo. Small."

"Ruta says you always have a medium skinny latte." Scuttling, no gliding gracefully off to quicken the order, Doug left pink foreheaded with a rare excursion into child control after a rambunctious exchange between Giorgia and a wonky chair.

"Here you go: your daily fix." Slapping the mass produced carton on the overly clean counter, a tiny ejaculation of muddy–coloured coffee, distorting the perfect swirls of cleaning fluid on the silver counter. "Why don't you find a more fitting fix – something that takes you out of the humdrum. You're not one of the masses who subscribes to mass induced habits."

"I thought your coffee was anything but humdrum. Doesn't the sign on the door say: 'Not your average cup of coffee'?"

"A fix like me."

Doug was at a loss for words and not because this flagrant gesture hadn't happened before but because he'd never been interested. In the split second between absorbing the 'fix like me' and the moment a non–response becomes socially awkward, Doug questioned whether he genuinely liked this girl (he knew he genuinely didn't like Veronika or Margot for that matter, or did he?) or whether he was now moving like an OAP backing his Ford into a disabled parking bay into being just another commonplace perv. Should he turn to the slightly younger man at the back of the queue and do the lips?

Smug Dad

He was literally speechless. She had him – the permutations of next steps were endless.

"I'm just fucking with you, Doug. Next."

CHAPTER 12

Stale Mippers

Deloris had always been one to play along and then tire of something excessively quickly. When that boredom set in she became the mercurial antagonist of whatever the flavour of the day was: liberal to the point of socialist when exchanging blows with a toffy Thatcherite; EDL–supporting right wing when yattering with a life Labour–loving liberal. And as a result she had a wide variety of friends (and censuring detractors) from old schoolfriends running PR firms to married housewives in the midlands with a thousand and one simple kids. And because of the cross–section of galpals across the Isles with this unnervingly broad spectrum on just about everything – including marriage (lesbians, sugar mummies, sugar daddies, cousins twice removed, mistresses, partridges, pear trees) – she'd been on the guest list for far more hen nights than she could either recount or care to recount.

So she'd become bored of watching all her friends' friends pretend to go through an emotional hiatus as they lost their soulmate to the dark side of couple–dominated utopia. Even the assortment of venues, themes, self–proclaimed character statements, outfits and cocktails made her feel nauseatingly normal. Granted, her slightly less well to do friends were mostly on their second or third marriages, so the encounters with paid for eye candy in the shape of orange, oily, photoshopped Firemen, Policemen, Superheroes, Geeks, Bears (yes) were somewhat diminished, which should have made her most recent encounter sufficiently rare to warrant some odd enjoyment.

The dim–lit club somewhere in the North where the bouncers seemed mass produced from a shop plumbing out condom–filled hazelnuts: a sickly tepid–brown smear of fake tan, metromoisturiser and roadmapped veins that actually lifted the impossibly tight shirt from the skin. And big nods – as much as the trunk of the neck would allow and a distinct demeanour change when the girls arrive, dropping the menace into a welcoming embrace. Deloris felt sick when one was near her. So much so that she had to tell him as much which almost resulted in the gaggle being removed before even entering. Without the deft flirting from the bride–to–be, the booked section might have been 're–allocated' ("Spell that three times quickly you gorilla") – *there is some strange ways up North*. So Deloris was already on the back foot when the girls poured into the area like sludge filling a container and, feeling slightly guilty at almost having ruined the evening, was perhaps more prone to being accommodating. But this took accommodating to a-whole-nother level. This was more showing off – a statement at the inane and easily corruptible nature of the situation. The rebel showing everyone what they were really giggling about.

"We have a special surprise for you," said the first lieutenant whose name was probably Kerry.

"Let me guess … he strips for a living but dreams of running the country and of being a movie star," Deloris said.

"Don't be such a killjoy – it's the theme that counts after all. And this one is so now."

As the lights dimmed Deloris became instantly more bored and downed two further drinks in quick succession. Two more followed in the eternity it took for the music to be cranked up and the two performers to appear clad in what looked like a three piece suit each. One had a rope around his neck and the other appeared to don handcuffs. Deloris wasn't interested, ordering more of whatever the fuck swill this shithole normally dishes out on a Fuckday night.

Above the noise, which sounded like a badly remastered grimy rap track, Kerry announced to the group – miraculously drowning out the deep base with her shrill chalky voice – that they were Lehmans' bankers. Get it? Deloris did and didn't and noticed how immediately the rope and handcuffs became the weapons of choice for the

Smug Dad

ravenous hens, pulling and clucking, squeezing and strutting. Unexpectedly Deloris, now facing away from the action, was lifted off her chair by hang–man while cuff–bloke grabbed her ankles dragging her into the circle of pseudo–iniquity. Obviously upon instruction either from the too–inebriated bride-to-be or the too–maniacal lieutenant. Either way Deloris kicked like a mule until the bigger and more golden of the failed bankers leaned down and slapped her perpendicularly on the forehead with his three–quarters swollen lumpy feeler. As though this was that Eureka, call–to–action moment, Deloris sprang into life seemingly playing along, gyrating to the beat, arms in the air (let's get the party started – ah yeaaaaahhhhh).

A gasp transcended across the predominantly yummies so much so that the DJ almost wiped the needle clean from the turntable. Deloris, on her knees took the now clad in nowt but a green–back thong pulled to the side into her mouth. The other swordsman arrived and there was a foreboding forbidden foreskinned crossing of the streams as Deloris plopped both into her mouth as casually as two regular morning multi–vitamins. They tasted different to the drinks she thought – a tasteless blend of sweat, moisturiser and heat. Entrant number one was certainly a bigger man occupying the lion's share of the parking bay until the latecomer rose for the occasion to claim more of his rightful berth.

For how long this continued no–one in the group was absolutely certain but it made the uselessness of the frivolous flirting, fussing and giggling seem even more fatuous than it was. Or at least Deloris thought so anyway. Those dumb ass bitches all pretending – it was time to step past the barrier of polite passivity and cut some sock. And then as sudden as the whole statement seemed the main attraction arrived – with both now ready to complete their mission all over her face, Deloris simultaneously bit down in the middle of the tip of both, the symmetry of the crunch resembling delving into a double fish finger sandwich with the golden crumbed contents being squeezed forth for consumption. The power behind the bite was significant enough to kill the music and for each expression to probably more closely resemble a Lehmans' banker than before. The act sent both men cowering to their piled clothing corners, two stray dogs wandering sideways with arched backs after that final owner betrayal. Deloris spat out onto the floor, smiling. And laughed. So hard that before she knew it, she was in the middle of the circle of irate hens having been summarily ejected from the club. Apparently there was a no violence rule or something. And this was not the point a nasty entered her system, although this was the night it happened.

It became a blur after that: Deloris numb from the intended ironic sideshow backlash and some sort of realisation that to act upon a toxic mix of fury and social resentment was neither wise nor profitable (if laughter, good times and good chat be the stuff of high margins). The group split into two with the 'I'm unable to speak I'm so ashamed and pissed off that the evening had to become about you' lieutenant–led brigade – unfortunately for Deloris – sweeping up the Qwhen (queen hen) and any chance of redemption. So Deloris ended up with three blatant losers which did at least provide her with some heart that the act hadn't been in vain, although one had what could only be described as interaction disabilities, the other beyond the point of no return and the third some modern version of a nymphomaniac intent on re–enacting the moment as a group with the first available legal posse.

When a serial–nice–guy happened on Deloris she was clearly susceptible to this sort of approach but unsuspecting that the worst of what he could've passed on he hadn't. Yet. In following with a sequel of the early indiscretion she failed to make him rubber up/raincoat on/bag the sausage, his dopey demure expression surely innocent enough to allow him this one bareback treat. The hotel he took her to was nice and most of the action was downward dog, so Deloris could have some emotionless think time with her enshrouded clumps of golden curls to drown out the slap–slap–slap thud–thud behind her. She might have actually come too had a police siren not unexpectedly cranked into life directly below their window, the only real outcome the splat of X warmth marking the spot across her lower back.

Then without provocation (or reason for that matter), whilst hunched in overblown TV drama rape victim knee clenched mode, trickle of worn out shower blabbering away atop her matted hair, Deloris broke into song. Not anything melodramatic (she had after all had the opportunity to finish herself off after sweet dimple man departed) but something uplifting, literally – Jim Lynne's *Lift Me Up* (sans the need for the broken heart reference). This was the first time she'd ever partaken in the dark world of playing away and, even though she knew Reg's indiscretions were more common than iPhones and less discerning than Blackberry, she felt the teeniest glass–shard–in–the–eye sting of guilt. And not because of Reg but because she'd done it all wrong ... the club, the Lehmans' bankers, the inadvertent nice guy – all too random. Spontaneity didn't breed joy. She needed to heedlessly erase this from the ticked and crossed memory bank and put it down to the thin air up north. She needed a plan and a goal and both culminated in striving for the perfect stray; she had to go for the title – seize the prize bull by the shopping–bag like gonads dangling between his prize–winning thighs and make every mistake from now on worthwhile.

This wasn't an itch. It was a lifechoice. If you want some action you have to take action.

CHAPTER 22

⟵ ⟶

Pack It All Cunning Cement

"There's nothing we can do; we've done all we can. Sometimes – and it is very rarely – but sometimes when the horse has been dragged kicking and screaming and its head forced into the water with the might of a thousand interested parties, we have to step back and let those interested parties realise that unless everyone does their job, the job won't get done," Doug said without any blink, twitch, hesitance, idiosyncrasy, word stutter or even a glance away from the depths of Graham's pupils.

"You're right of course. And I know you would have tried everything to get this to happen. Let me handle this with Steven."

Let me handle this with Steven! What kind of a response is that!

The reality that Doug's back was red numb raw from all the Steven slaps atop the highest branch of the tree made Graham's comment inaugural. Doug had always been happy to make Graham's worklife easy and under the covers Steven knew the engineroom, the doer, the impetus was always Doug. The reason he seemed to humour Graham by keeping him employed remained a mystery to Doug. As did this latest episode because in Doug's world nothing ever failed and Steven was inured to good news only; successful news where Ps outweighed Ls like the capitalist version of the tipping scales of cash flow, and news where nods, smiles and pride engulfing the eyes like a fish tank filling with water was the only news. So this recent failure, although in Doug's mind completely beyond his wide sphere of influence and the once in a lifetime circumstance where the group who deserved to be under the bus were actually being thrown there by Doug, was sure to displease Steven and the rest of the board. And the way this was genuinely being 'escalated' without Doug being the man standing on the escalator unnerved him. He didn't know how to be the person to take bad news to Steven as the good stuff had flowed thick and pure for so long, but the way Graham had taken this away from him to 'handle' could potentially pull the rug from Doug's feet and, more to the point, slap a glass ceiling above his head.

Doug tried to deal with this as he normally did though:

shelve it and get on with the day. But the nagging sensation in the pocket of his sternum made him accept a lunch invite from Reg. Predictably cryptic but nonetheless intriguing – dress code requirements 'suit and tie (with waistcoat if available)' to meet at an address in Tottenham. Doug left the building amidst a patchy yet drenching rain shower and arrived to find Reg and three others rustling through a suitcase outside a council estate, all suited and booted, the sun now livening each suit in brilliant contrast to the dull square brown brick of the worn building. Rusty satellite dishes adorned the sides of windows like wonky stalactites, above the sign 'This is a dish–free area' now spray painted to re–read 'This is splash–free diarrhoea.'

No one greeted Doug as he approached; instead, Reg threw him a grey hooded top instructing: "Take your jacket and shirt off and put this on underneath." He then threw Doug a bowler hat. The other men were already attired which made Doug hurry, each looking resplendently layered with the hood popping from beneath the neat designer shirt and tie, beneath the matching hats.

"These motherfuckers looting our great city; it's payback time. You chaps ready?" Reg said, pronouncing chaps as someone from the Queen's lineage might say it. Everyone nodded – then Doug nodded surprised at how flawlessly the black velvet bowler hat overwhelmed his dome. Doug wondered if he could keep it, his pulse now quickening as the men ran into the estate, knowing he would never get a straight answer of any type from Reg so dutifully followed second from the back. The last place was occupied by the smallest of the group carrying a camcorder inches from his sightline. It was rolling – Doug could hear the parp–click–wheez of the tape starting.

Upon bashing down the first door the group met an old black woman who started screaming so the men left. The second door had three black teenagers in a haze of dope smoke jumping up to confront the men only to then stop in amazement and laugh. With three brisk blows each was in a second frame hunched like a crumbled spider on the floor and Reg carried on to trash the living room and hand some select items of value to the cameraman. The next few flats were empty so the looting continued with the intensity of each raid diminishing; clearly Reg was looking for something more substantial. This eventually arrived when a gang of black youths armed with machetes and knives sprang from a room tucked off to the side of a grimy lounge. The first swung the blade ferociously and had Doug not had the adrenaline–fuelled foresight to duck he'd have clean lost his head – hoodie, bowler hat and all. Doug then slammed his shoulder into the attacker running him into the mantlepiece. He could feel he was strong and Doug was about to try and dislodge the machete when suddenly he went limp.

Doug looked up and there was a gun in his mouth. Doug looked around and the other gang members had also subsided into submissive pose, the dull clank of metal dropping onto the vinyl floor. Reg was holding the gun just above Doug's head and twisted the pistol upwards as though he was using a bottle–opener to angrily wade through the man's front teeth after one of the other marauding suits had exposed a stock of stolen electronics goods in the adjacent room.

"You fuckers are going to burn; burn for what you've done. This is a message from the capitalist tax–paying community … fahk you!" In spectacular form Reg lit a flare and brandished it across the curtains setting the room alight, the faces of the gang cartoonish in their terror. And for a second or slightly more Doug was terrified too as an explosion sounded nearby, propelling spears of pointed flame across the top of Doug's back and neck. He could feel the tiny hairs on his neckline quickly light, fizzle down to the base like a sped up candle melting and burn through towards the pain sensors deep inside his throat. In that moment he seemed very alone as his colleagues disappeared from view between the clouds of smoke and Reg's plundering noise ceased. He felt shoulders whizzing past him, undoubtedly the gang ratting to freedom, their bodies adopting impossible dimensions to angle through the rubble, furniture and Doug to escape. Another explosion … then more pain and complete darkness.

After a blackout, whatever constituted the failing of consciousness, be it oxygen to the brain or a sharp blow to the head, one doesn't wake up with an ice–bath jolt or open your eyes and the room slowly comes into focus. You're just awake. Like a blink. But there is a semblance that more time has passed than merely a blink which compounds the confusion and sometimes adds that lethal injection of panic – which is completely illogical because upon reflection if something really bad was going to happen to one it would surely occur when the said being is passed out. Surroundings play a big part too: once the brain acknowledges the change in state to lucid and the perception of elapsed time, the intake of the elements can be polar – familiar soothing and safe versus unfamiliar, which sends the brain asking too many questions in too short a space of time. Panic.

When Doug opened his eyes, he recognised the elaborate light hanging above his own bed and the ornate mirror at the base of his bed, which was soothing and safe. What he didn't recognise was the blonde to darker roots parting, like the brown and white quills of a flattened porcupine, bobbing quickly down and slowly up beneath his stomach. And then, unfortunately for the brain and Doug, darkness again.

CHAPTER 32

Wallow Heen

Bringing up children, in the eyes of the contemporary world filled with dual careers, fifty specialist kiddie extra–curricular personality–shaping clubs, activities and interests, competition with a bloated foreign–infused London population and the general unnatural modern phenomena of fidelity, was considered tiring. Even difficult. Which made the way Doug and Margot seamlessly flicked their kids between age group genres (baby non–rolls, toddlers, sensorimotor, terrible twos, the real terrible threes, preoperational, concrete operational) as natural as a straight line of wide steppingstones across a raging torrent. Now granted they were yet to splash their faces with the unpredictable formal operational teen waters but with some kids ya just know. Other parents are able to (in a second mind) look at a child and know they'll be a troublesome teen.

Next door: two young girls relatively sweet in nature at an early age followed by the slow unravelling of their characters into teen monsters. The neighbourhood would say it was because the parents never gave them anything to do, following their own indulgent paths to middle–class social glory. Or so Doug believed anyway.

Always the 'little girls' next door, Doug was confronted one chilly Halloween dusk by the oldest of the two girls, smoking at the front door and immediately pushing past Doug into the house. Margot and the kids were out trick–or–treating and Doug had uncharacteristically missed the exodus of delighted youths pushing off from his doorstep and down the road to be meshed with a series of other groups colliding like charging soldiers, parents pretending not to be frantic making sure all were accounted for. As Hazel pushed past Doug he couldn't help but notice she now had breasts as first the left then the right scraped across his ribcage like two marbles rolling in wayward directions on glass.

Doug had always been the sort of 'grown–up' who could relate to youngsters of any age which in itself carried a level of familiarity not usually afforded in the stranger danger era. He knew the parents and didn't particularly relate to either of them but always had an interesting slash amusing slash advisory note for the kids. He remembered explaining to

Hazel that it wasn't her sister's fault she was alive and that it could turn out to be quite fun to have a little sister, whilst the parents had popped out leaving Hazel to run amok in the garden, the cleaner-cum-babysitter watching daytime TV and too busy sniffing glue with her boyfriend.

But that familiarity, as Doug had recently noted, could easily be misconstrued now Hazel had slammed into puberty like an overly elaborate Hotwheels car crash – so Doug had carefully distanced himself from all things neighbourly and especially all things teen angst.

"You can't smoke in here. Plus do you know how small your lungs are right now? How each drag will be damaging every alveoli?"

"I've seen you smoking."

"That's different."

"How so?"

"Because my lungs are fully formed and I've been through the notion that cool doesn't necessarily equal cancer hanging from your lips."

"But I've seen you smoking. In your underpants."

She slumped down on the sofa and lit another cigarette, her legs wide open and vamped up to the point that the black fishnets and horny devil witch ensemble had been constructed from what could only be small adult wear. Would they let sixteen year olds shop at Ann Summers nowadays? Her legs maintained that hint of puppy fat peeping through the holes in the net like a series of organised cobbled stones. She lit another cigarette with a lighter which appeared from somewhere mysterious, quickly dragging on it, blowing direct smoke from her mouth then hunching over to purse a deeper toke, holding it for one–Mississippi, two–Mississippi, three–Mississippi before looking up through her hair at Doug, her elbows straining to etch out a sliver of cleavage, presented for Doug like some forbidden treasure down a dark murky hole. The one where you could stick your hand down but very well could have it bitten off by whatever lurks beneath.

"BTW I like your jocks. Briefs on a man of your age is daring. But I suppose your body is sort of designed that way, right?"

"Why are you here anyway? Do your parents know?"

"Trick or treat. What's it going to be?"

"Neither. This is not some secret smoke den. I'm going to have to inform your parents."

"About what? They know anyway. And if they don't I'm not sure I'd care … or I could say you're lying and make something else up. Have a bit of fun with the uptight PC middle–classes around here. I thought you were cooler than that."

"No huge aspiration at my stage in life to be 'cool'. I'm happy being warm."

"Cute. Great with opposites then. Bit like that guy who's always around. There's something about him. He's a bad egg which is quite different to your good egg routine. He's repulsive but he knows it and doesn't care which makes him sort of hot. I mean warm."

"What do you mean Reg has been around here? When?"

"Is that his name? Gawd. Is that short for Reginald? That makes sense. Maybe I'll trick or treat his ass."

"Was he here during the day?"

"Occasionally. I thought you were here. Aren't you two meant to be tight or something? Like not that tight or anything but into something secret … in the neighbourhood."

"I hardly know the man; he's a new neighbour and I'm in the habit of being neighbourly so we try to portray some semblance of community around here – looking out for each other's kids and all that."

"Now it's 'we' – I see. Your wife is stunning – that's like some sort of timebomb waiting to happen. Or happening. And your kids are just amazing. You're right I should be more neighbourly – do you need a babysitter? I'm cheap. And thorough."

"I have no doubt but I'm not sure I'd want a night out with Margot to return to a smoke den."

She lit up again this time shaking the pack in disgust at the residual sticks left.

"How many of those do you go through a day?"

"Depends how much money my dad doesn't notice is missing from his wallet."

"You're really selling it to me on the babysitter front … smoking, theft. Is there any teen angst box you haven't ticked? Daisy chain? Happy slapping? Shouldn't you be intelligent enough to know that this is just an assertion of your new–found independence? Keep it up – it is quite humorous, but make one slightly off decision and it could mean when you actually do grow up your choices will be severely limited."

"Severely! Woah – the tone's suddenly changed. Right

about now you're meant to be either filling me up with your chocolates or telling me to fuck off and waiting for me to light a dog turd on the patio. What's it going to be?"

"You probably should leave – I had hoped to have more of an adult exchange with you. It's disappointing all your responses are either threatening or some veiled innuendo."

"The thought of your disapproval hits me right here." She pressed her finger inside the lining of her shirt to squeeze the breast inward like the air–bulb of a table cloth pocket rolling from one side of the table to another. "But seriously you are still my favourite neighbour and I do feel for your plight."

Note to self: ban Halloween costumes in this household.

For the rest of the afternoon, and the week for that matter, Doug was unnerved. His runs became arrhythmic departures from cadence, almost as though each step was wading through sludge across a wobbly bridge. He wondered if the blackout might have slowed down his power, responsiveness and drive then abandoned the thought: it had already been weeks since the incident. The story had been all over the news and radio silence from Reg he assumed was a direct ploy to ensure nobody was caught. He'd found an edited version of the council estate raid on YouTube noting how when he ran then he looked more stable and compact. Like he was actually able to get from A to B. But B was becoming the issue for him. Where exactly was B at this juncture of his life? Was it slipstreaming Reg's boundary–popping exploits, which he couldn't deny lit probably the cliché of mid–life adrenaline sponsored entertainment which might (or might not) have been missing in his life until now? Was he that impressionable? Was B laying a deeper root base and isolating off from the rest of the intrusive neighbours and school friend parents, overdoing the marriage and father gig when up until this point just the right amount of sprinkle had been required to bake that cake to stodgy perfection? Would that mean he became his worst fear: a sappy flappy doting daddy? Was B beginning to believe the cracks were real when there was really no conceivable way they were: distrusting Margot when his repeated slip–ups were neither forgivable nor forgetful? Should B be an immersion in work, career and progression when all this time the ease of the skyward angled northward trending graph had been point one degree less seamless than breathing? Did B have a C or an A– with Veronika firmly established as that 'place' where he could fulfil his darkest desires and let go of the notion of every minute of every day being a procession of over–evolved perfection?

For the first time Doug was aware he was watching television.

CHAPTER 42

Shree Thumb

Veronika lay in bed smoking a cigarette. She was alone clad only in her most decadent set of Agent Provocateur undies, her legs folded over one another like two angular intertwined upside down Vs, as she toyed with her cigarette, almost dumbfounded by the simplicity of the design and how inversely proportionate this was to the resultant pleasure. She'd only recently started smoking yet felt like a seasoned thirty–a–dayer, contemplating upping her brand choice to something with more of a burn. She never felt sexy on her own; only the thought of her elongated legs straddling Doug on the edge of a sink or kitchen counter made her think all the perpetual male attention was warranted. But she didn't want any of that or them – her world was complete with Doug.

She always doubted whether he would actually come around or wake up one day realising this wasn't worth the hassle or the risk and bail in his nice–guy nicest possible way that she knew she'd completely understand yet still love him for it. Her titbits of him were worth it but she knew reciprocating in a way she had to believe his wife couldn't was a sure-fire way of keeping him baited and hooked. Although she could never really tell with him – his way with her was as she pictured his way with everyone in his life: a gentleman yet littered with enough humour, sincerity and charm to recycle any stray pants strutting across his path.

An hour earlier she'd shaved her anus. Not that it required any actual hardcore forestry but just to make sure the darkened pink indented fissures that greeted Doug would be so welcoming that he'd return the favour and put his strong tongue deep inside there. But her real enjoyment was taking that boundary from him, without so much as a hint of ever having explored at this level with anyone, substituted by his ability to take her into this void of depraved debauchery and taboo–smashing carelessness. She'd also spent over ninety minutes carving the front of her pussy into the neatest strip of beguiling pubic hair, and painted her toenails that dark green he'd once commented on in the office, and tried on over thirteen of her lingerie ensembles (settling on the light blue lace Rigby & Peller; the one which strained to cover the tops of the areola peeping out like some naughty schoolboy's puddingbowl haircut tiptoeing above a forbidden wall). She'd concocted an unbelievable four courses of nibbles which would keep him fed, nodding and impressed whilst still allowing time to come and come and come.

The doorbell rang, chiming twice then fading in Veronika's head. She couldn't move for that moment – what had she done? Was this that bridge too far or the single most exciting event in her fledgling sexual career? It wasn't for her. The shutters clattered together like a giant's chattering teeth, the house taking on the oral epicentre nearing in to swallow her whole, as the visitor reverted to banging on the front door. Still Veronika couldn't budge, her dressing gown in reach, her mind yanked left and then right with bubbles above her head showing how the scene might unfold. Then just as a thought reached the physical logistics of where Doug could poke his tongue if his other taught pleasure giver was occupied in quarters elsewhere, Veronika's sudden self–conscious fear took hold, further amplifying her stationary hiatus. There wasn't a cat's chance on this green earth her legs could be matched – 'Veronika Legs' they called her at school, but what of her trio of Achilles hang–ups? That speedbump below her navel; the dire need of one more cup's firmness; the fading glow of a once perfect porcelain reflection replaced by the annoying dusting of blotchiness. Silence now filled her bedroom for the first time, the only increasingly deafening sound her Titanic heartbeat growing closer to her iceberg sternum. Then her phone coming to life on the bedside table, an unknown number flashing sordidly.

"Hello," stammered Veronika.

"I'm at the address," muttered a foreign voice. "I ring the bell and knock. No–one is answering. They give me this number to call and ask for Jemima."

"Yes, Jemima speaking, I'm er … just out the shower. I'm inside. I'll be done in one moment. Can you do me a favour and wait?"

"Yes but time is starting now. The clock. Per hour."

"I understand. Did you wear the required ensemble? The attire – I mean outfit?"

Before anything of any reciprocated worth in Veronika's eyes was underway, Doug had confided to tell her about his first true crush, Joslyn Jackson, a crosscountry runner who Doug had become friendly with during his school years. Three years older than him, they'd corresponded during the joint crosscountry tournaments and through sincere handwritten letters. Joslyn had invited Doug to her final year ball, catapulting his kudos into the stratosphere being the only fourteen-year-old at the dance. Resulting in half resentment half romantic envy for Veronika, Doug had recounted how, after a solid hour of attempting the traditional butterfly for the first time ever in a rented tuxedo, standing amongst a communal bellow of post–pubescent timbre, JJ had walked in, resplendent in a low back, long black dress, her hair drifting down into the curve of her lower back as though there was only one proper destined place for it, the curls wrestling with each other in a clump like majestic eels jumping across each other in a velvet frenzy, and her ceaseless arms encased in long purple gloves. Doug had been unable to breathe yet took the initiative, putting his shoulders back and approaching her through the crowd as her entrance crafted a crescendoing hush across the hall. The rest he said he couldn't remember.

A light drizzle began to tempt the leaves to wiggle outside. With the drizzle the air suddenly became cooler and Veronika lassoed her thick gown around her shoulders and headed downstairs. The girl was beautiful, probably more striking than the web photo; her expression momentarily annoyed as the drizzle threatened to upset an immaculate pinned up do, then instantly into character to pull back the dark red pout, revealing a line of chewing–gum white teeth. She was quick to get out of the rain, hopping over the doorstep past Veronika, her respectable overcoat blocking the visual of what Veronika hoped was a vision of Doug's fantasy. She smelled strong but not in a sickening way – the waft sweeping through Veronika's hair and neck as though she were applying it herself. Her skin was immaculate and the youth in her jawline and tautness of her neck unashamedly apparent. She could almost fit under Veronika's chin which made her short by anyone's standards, but she didn't possess that square–set look of many big chested short girls; she rather looked small shouldered and petite with a frontal width that even Veronika had to admire.

"Can I get you anything?" asked Veronika smoothing out the sofa for the woman to sit on.

"We are starting now no?"

"Yes of course. Do I pay upfront?"

"Yes – for the first 3 hours then you pay at end for anything extra. Champagne drink please. I am Christina."

"Call me V. You are exceptionally beautiful. May I see

your outfit?"

Christina slowly took off her overcoat, handing it to Veronika who was busying herself lighting a cigarette. She motioned to Christina with the pack who shook her head with the fervour of someone allergic to anything smoke related. She divulged a perfectly turned out product – the caramel colour of her back and décolletage in discriminating contrast to the dangling voluptuary black dress. She wore the purple gloves as requested. Veronika took a breath and went into the kitchen to rouse the Champagne, which she'd pre–prepared regardless, feeling there was more than one way to treat Doug than hand delivering an exquisite fantasy.

Christina sat with her legs neatly crossed pecking at her drink a few times as if blinking to confirm she was awake then tilted the glass deftly skywards and put it away. Veronika refilled it then noticed Christina staring, almost disappointedly, at her tired dressing gown while she wrinkled the bulbous roll of cash into her purse.

"Are we staying together alone?" asked Christina. "Just us. Shall I come over to you? In here? No bedroom?"

"I specified on the phone that this was a couple request; did they mention that to you?"

"Yes but I just see you alone."

"He'll be here – later," she gulped. "And don't worry, he's not scary or anything; he's magical."

"I not worried."

"So is there anything you don't do … don't allow?"

"I do everything in price except one hundred extra for anal and on face. No hurting and your friend wear condom all time."

Veronika's phone buzzed as though on cue – Doug not being able to make it? Caught up at work? Running home to wifey? To kiddies? It's all over? He did say he had some big showdown with his boss that evening. What would she do if he wasn't around – always being a woman who believed in value for money would she 'get her money's worth' or demand some sort of refund before getting rid of her? Maybe she could just watch to see if there was any effect or perhaps ask Christina about some of her past exploits for new ideas.

She looked at her phone. "I'll just go change," she said, dashing upstairs. In below ten minutes there was a knock at the door – bedraggled Doug caught in the heavier drizzle, sans umbrella, his hair pasted flat down along his forehead in tooth comb tails. Veronika, with gown still intact, kissed him on his cheek, almost jumping to do so, and pulled him inwards mumbling, "Welcome lover," before dropping her gown to the floor. She was now wearing full suspenders, no pants and a black and gold push up brassiere which held her breasts like the charity coin grids at the McDonald's drive–through.

"I have a surprise for you," she said, trapping him by lowering his soaked jacket half–way down his back and easing down onto her knees.

"I do love that type of surprise but could I dry off first?"

Taking him almost immediately into her mouth – jack jumping out of box into the exhaled warmth – she managed to squeeze the words "It's even better," out.

With his arms pinned Doug discontinued the fallible protest, eventually freeing his arms and placing both hands on the back of her head while her multi–tasking hands orchestrated between his base and her mouth and undid his work shirt buttons. When he was naked but for his trousers around his ankles, she forced him down the small opening of her throat as if to congratulate his participation. With her free hand she found the ruttish warmth of herself, her crouched legs taut in an unrelenting squat position, Doug's back now uncomfortably arching past the dado rail in the hallway.

When Christina appeared a moment later Doug's shock was so apparent that he almost poked himself through the roof of Veronika's mouth. Veronika diligently held him in her hand, while lifting her head to spit a look of reassuring lust up at this face. She had this under control.

"This is Christina." Leading Doug upstairs towards the bedroom, Christina industriously following in her swaying black dress.

As the three stood motionless in the bedroom, the now persistent rain drowning out the deafening conflicting thoughts of each, Christina took the primary initiative to kiss Doug softly on the mouth running a long nail down his stubbled sideburn then along his jaw, neck and onto his chest, stopping at the rigid nipple to pinch. Doug politely pulled free then leant his pec back at her allowing this first time sensation. Veronika, fleetingly idle, kissed down Christina's back, the three at equidistant heights like a consistently good few months of sales figures on a barchart. Christina eased her shoulders allowing the dress to fall to the floor, circling her ankles, then slowly rolled down part of the left glove, almost the opposite of what Doug was about to have done to him,

Veronika thought. Without disrupting the scene Veronika put her hand on Christina's hand, ceasing her rolling, and bent down to shoo away the dress, easing her legs open by sliding two fingers down each inner thigh. Christina now lowered herself too, placing a hand on Doug still glistening from Veronika's exploits in the hall. Part warm up part clean up, Christina placed the tip into her mouth.

What came next was one third natural, one third Veronika's orchestration and one third Doug's embracing the licentiousness of the situation.

Doug stopped. There was a concept caressing through his inner canals that he couldn't shake, like a set of insistent groupies, their tentacles attached and gouging into his skin pulling the pores apart and embedding. Beauty. What was beauty? Was beauty these two aesthetically irreproachable creatures writhing around in contrived, B–movie nirvana or that split second of euphoria windscreenwiping across the eyes of his children with the mention of ice cream/movies/chocolate/midnight feast/toys/games? Was it something natural perhaps: the ever present giant orb representing a dozen different shades of yorange depending on landscape, country and photographer's lens or the ocean or the (puke) desserts or (puke) the (puke) (Puke)? No. It was something intangible … even more intangible than an emotion – something as soon as you tried to describe it or categorise it or put it as a polar black or white ("I'm hurt; you're wrong; it's beautiful") it became ugly.

As if by some sort of divine cork back in the bottle, the rain stopped making the flesh slap of flesh deafening. Veronika's old woman oil portrait, completely out of place in the bedroom, glared down first at Doug's back then into the top of his eyes then down the length of his vigour lined body.

"I need a change of venue," said Doug. "Shall we shower."

Being clean after a shower normally meant some rare television watching. While Doug waited in front of the TV everything got even more mixed up. Suddenly there was the prospect of another threesome in his life – the one that existed at home had been unnervingly effervescing along while the rest of the world kept shifting through the ad breaks.

"You sit slumped on your lazy arse the whole day," he recalled Margot bellowing one evening. This aimed at the most active man in the world he thought.

"Are you for real? Really?"

"Why must I do everything around here. Drop off. Pick up. Clothes. Lawn. DIY. School council."

"Income?"

"Fuck you with that card: you can't play that the rest of your life. It'll run out eventually."

"Something I'm sure you're looking forward to relishing. Don't you think it'll affects all of us? The kids."

"Ha, the kids! Are you planning to adopt."

"Ever since Janine came into your life you've become … become a wee bit judgemental."

Should I really have said wee bit?

"Janine! Janine!"

CHAPTER 52

Gall And Face

We need a Charlton Hestonesque voiceover for this segment…

Our wouldbe hero would need to fall before he rose again; slide before he climbed the ladder. He was good person – we know that – but his good nature and his good motives had begun to be questioned by those around him. Heroism came at a price. And a person's perceived heroism of one's self came at an even greater cost.

Walking (not running) home one evening he would be set upon by another pimply gang of no–good youths, but this time instead of controlling that situation to send every neighbourhood mummy into an adulating frenzy, he would stick one of the boy's heads into another boy's cheekbone, breaking the face in more places that one cares to imagine. He would not feel that same sense of guilt that he might have felt a few months earlier either; he would relish it – enjoy it, as though what people deserved they should get.

Through a more sinister set of faked witness appeals and fabricated police reports, he would ensure the local neighbourhood paedophile would take the wrap for his misdemeanours. The whole road stood and watched as they dragged the 'old bastard' out in chains, despite not having even considered any wrongdoing of any kind since the visit from Reginald and Doug. The teenagers would positively identify the man after a series of bribes and he would be sentenced to three years in prison, where his previously harboured desires were well known and disseminated down all the cell corridors and showers.

And in failing to take any responsibility for this spate of deteriorating retribution, Doug would confront Reg in a fish store. Now whether Reg had actually observed Doug's decline and tried to distance himself or, more likely, failed to fixate his attention on one person for longer than fifteen minutes, Reg had moved on to a new BFF. Simba's father, a reintegrated ex–con, complete with ankle tag and neck tattoo, piqued more frontier pushing curiosity boxes for Reg right now, so Doug would have to wait. Perhaps forever.

The fish ship incident would make the papers as an impressive array of mackerel, tuna, eels, octopi, gunard and coley were used as bludgeoning weapons by both men, an aquatic sword fight of sorts. With the victor uncertain and the NHS funded hospital bill extreme, including the surgical removal of scales from the facial region, the whole affair was blunt fish trauma.

Perhaps this is also the time to mention this other threesome gaily plucking from the so called marital bliss, a parallel universe of excitement, deceit, normality–crunching, tedium–rupturing climax. It started the day Doug first slept with Deloris. Doug wasn't sure whether Reg moved out, died or just disappeared – but one thing was for sure: he wasn't there. He wasn't at his home, no communication with Doug, no Prado Panzer. He was gone.

PROLOGUE II
JOCK WARS

Now Clive, this is a quite extraordinary business story. A continuation from the home invasion segment we covered a few months back; quite literally a rags to riches story, or should I say rags to underpants. Here's Gloria San Pellegrino with the business segment to tell us more.

"For the man with big things in front of him" – the tagline that would launch a billion men's underwear sales. Tapping into the growing world of male vanity and body dysmorphia, ManSize has successfully targeted an aspirational niche for

men with ... well ... big things in front of them. The cheeky innuendo combined with an innovative range of underwear levels would propel this small business into the big time, becoming the first exclusive male underwear brand and company to dual list on the London and New York Stock Exchanges.

Hi Gloria, sorry to interrupt, but would it be fair to conclude that the man who first brought ManSize to the wider world's attention was Douglas Perfors, whose heroics and gratuitous male nudity – we will never forget that will we ...

We won't.

... singlehandedly took the company from obscure independent clothing line to major global brand?

Yes Sienna, many in the business world would attest to that theory: a modern day hero without any marketing angle viewed by millions around the world, increasing sales in the brand's flagship product by over one hundred thousand percent worldwide in three short weeks, making an almost immediate impact into the sizeable global men's underwear *market, recently valued at $29.41 billion. Rumours are that Mr Perfors was offered a significant sum to model the apparel and, upon rejecting the opportunity, the brand would become even more sought after by international consumers, both male and female.*

I do hope my hubby will be donning a pair but doubtful he'll fill them quite so generously as Mr Perfors, Gloria!

Indeed. Let's now go behind the scenes at ManSize to discover a little ... or lotta ... more about men's undergarments ...

"Why in the front?"

"Because the Y–Front is the single most misunderstood garment in the history of men and women's apparel. Given a bad name by overweight seventies fathers everywhere."

From when he could remember, Nate was intrigued by men's underwear. But of course being from a generation of grey, white and black, with Calvin Klein seemingly shattering the mould more from the designer's use of suitable models than desirability of the actual garment, Nate felt impotent to speak up and dare to bare anything other than the boring majority of jock buyers.

ManSize!

"The name sucks" the focus groups shoved down his throat, each one entombed in a now increasingly tedious grey, white or black CK; likely a Father's Day present from their wives. The gay focus group hadn't been too complimentary either, wanting the underwear to reflect more on the inner workings or one's soul than the supposed outer workings of one's apparatus. Women loved it though – cheeky enough to pass abound at a hen do and serious enough to measure an aspirational suitor with (and perhaps measure they would). And this was when Nate had only five varieties, each hacked together in China really just to get ManSize out of his head and into the real world.

A business was normally something to share; spread around in an effort to establish the brand and increase sales, but Nate chose to keep ManSize his dirty little secret. And not because he felt any shame in revolutionising the male underwear market, but rather that, to truly do it justice, he needed the inspired taboo juices to flow into the creations like an author's dark characters and sinister motives.

And let's not feign compliments and bestow praise due to a noble niche idea to be flogged to a venture capitalist and eventually worn by David Gandy for M&S, but ManSize set everything apart; from the quality of the material to the design and form fit, to the colours, textures and adjustment for physical traits. But most of all it became aspirational – like you had to have it but either couldn't find it or weren't allowed to buy it like those new launch chocolate bars in the eighties.

ManSize CEO Nate Ponkington explains how he started the business …

"I realised a few years ago that the primary purveyors of cutting–edge, good–looking male underwear came from the gay community. So I decided to become gay for a short period as research.

"We experimented with many taglines and associative brand jingles to support ManSize …

'For the better endowed among us'

'Never boring'

'For big things'

'For the man with big things before him'

'For the man with big stuff ahead of him'

"Eventually settling on …

ManSize … for the man With big things in front of him

"ManSize is not a garment – it's a club; one where the genetic exclusivity and quality materials make it undeniable what the wearer stands for. 'Wearers' have multiple payment options including a monthly fee earning each 'big boy' free options throughout the year to reward the loyalty. There are bespoke options including rugby colours and personalised options including letters cut out of the backside. There are also garments that change colours when wet – all features patented and unique to ManSize."

"What about the aspirational tiers that have further defined the brand?" asked Gloria.

"Well as you know, Gloria, the 'tip' of the logo – the ridged overhang of the z – is very symbolic and again unique to ManSize. Each 'tip' signifies the level of customer loyalty and affiliation with ManSize employing the following parameters…

"Blue … 'New to ManSize' with a tenure of between zero and

three months.

"Black … 'Finding Your Niche' between three and twelve months.

"Platinum … 'Seasoned Wearer' one year plus.

"Purple … 'Exclusivity Tier 1 (members only)' where a membership fee is applied but with significant benefits like first look jocks, limited additions and exceptional discounts.

"Tanzanite … 'Exclusivity Tier 2 (invite only)' where we already have a few unnamed celebrities signed up – no Boybands though!"

"That's funny, Nate," laughed Gloria.

"And of course our first patron to achieve Tanzanite status was a local resident hero, male stripper to the masses … Doug Perfors."

"So Doug has a little – or large – Tanzanite 'tip' to all he owns in his underwear drawer?"

"We certainly hope so as we encourage 'wearers' to embrace the tier they are a part of and actively upgrade all pants as membership changes."

"Hand wash only?"

"Of course! Tanzanite items only use the finest hand backstitched Sea Island Cotton so should not be seen in the vicinity of any washing machines!"

"I wonder if Mrs Perfors likes doing that?!"

"Well we'd expect she wouldn't, Gloria. ManSize is likely for the modern man – who does all his own washing. Doug probably hand washes Mrs Perfors's underwear!"

"What we and the viewers are seeing now include examples of the different tiers; hope my man flies first class!"

"From a garment design perspective we really wanted to boast about the male physique; encase it in something mythical to be adulated, so all products (with the exception of ManSize W.I.P.) would be briefs. So the brand range is crafted into six categories – ManSize Excessive, ManSize Or, ManSize Statement, ManSize Daily Exposables, ManSize Directions and ManSize LifeSize – all with their own 'collections' to ensure each category has its very own uniqueness, identity and style – all the while being like nothing else on the market."

"Any chance we could get a sneak peek into the upcoming collections within those categories?"

"Afraid not, Gloria – although a few that have already launched include ManSize Load, ManSize Enuf, ManSize Below the Belt, ManSize Hore, ManSize Southpaw, ManSize Cherry and ManSize Early Riser.

Smug Dad

The remainder … that's an insight reserved for the next episode of Jock Wars."

Phew, Clive, might be time for a little lie down after that. Cup of tea perhaps.

PART II

[Ever Present]

CHAPTER 62

←→

Sea four Bug

Sometimes you have to. Simplify. No, reminisce. Well reminisce to simplify, or remember to declutter. Bang straight out of a just past watershed production: guessing a four–parter or even six (why are they always even numbers; when was the last five–part drama?). So the casting isn't stellar but enough home grown English has–beens and up–and–comers to keep the TV licence paying masses swooning for another Poldark–torso moment. To break the tedium of reality. Was it actually like this; before the Smug? Was a pre–kids couple being pissed off with each other and a job spunked with clichés and friends from the supporting cast manual and that young professional vibe HOW IT ACTUALLY WAS?

When you get this lost for this long in the drama, you can't turn off; or even dart to the loo for a whazz. Or blink. So simple it whined emitting static, a retro test pattern and a presenter still clinging onto the nineties. Or perhaps Smug was learned; practised; honed; perfected. Normal came wrapped in a domestic, on–edge yet tedious set of exchanges. Like the rest. Of them.

Present. Tense.

"She's staying and that's the end of it," says Margot, turning a page of her book and failing to acknowledge Doug's botheration. Doug's folded arms across his chest, half propped up by an entanglement of pillows against the looming headboard, don't deter her in the slightest. She folds back: four of a kind beats a full house. It's way past either of their bedtimes which doesn't impede Doug from one last attempt before Margot's patience completely drains away. Is there a magical straight flush he can pull from his sock? Royal flush? Now that would be magical.

"We've just moved in," he begins. "Everything is everywhere. Nothing is in order. The remainder of the furniture isn't even here and you want a visitor? For God's sake Marg, can't we just make some excuse? Something that's true for a change like we're in the process of moving? Or that your parents are coming to live with us indefinitely?" Immediately Doug wonders whether this would be worse. Most likely but at least he wouldn't have to stand on ceremony in a polite host meets husband routine.

"She's a friend and she's had a horrible time lately so drop it." Her tone wanes while her eyes continue to droop across the page of the gardening manual. Doug, too exhausted after a day he'd rather forget, now has to deal with the imminent arrival of a complete stranger, to invade his space and force him to behave properly.

"How long?"

"As long as it takes."

"As long as what takes?"

"Until she feels she is ready to leave."

"You must be joking! This is my house too you know and I don't feel like running a bloody hostel for all your down and out friends." Doug turns over, pulling the duvet with him. Nothing is said for a while until Margot turns off the lamp. The evening is well lit by splashes of moonlight that saunter into the room, unwelcome. Doug fetters up the tormented curve, a man without his crutches and receptor for anything beyond black serenity: the click of a light switch, hearing Margot's breathing change, her appearing breastbone now rising slowly and dropping quickly, the swaying naked bulb above his head, his feet over the edge of the bed.

Doug can't sleep, turning over in a futile effort to get comfortable. Margot, next to him bundled in the foreskin of the duvet like the cardboard bit of the loo roll, her pyjamas extending right to the top of her neck denying him any flesh but her face remains swollen with sleep. A tall cardboard box sits beside him holding his plastic mug of water from which he takes a sip. The warm liquid is unfiltered and he can taste it. He doesn't like this disarray; this disorganised mess. All he wishes to do is have everything sorted out and return to normal.

After a while he does fall asleep after removing his shirt to allow the breeze to cool the sweat bubbles forming across his chest. His rest is uneasy but he manages to achieve the prescribed six hours. Margot sleeps deeply and dreams of painted ceilings and Victorian fireplaces. She loves to redecorate and having a visitor will only serve to further establish her taste in the new home. Two against one is always going to ensure a cream room rather than a green one. But Doug had already given up arguing and now has to put up with a strange visitor staying for an indefinite period of time. For definite.

The following morning was customarily frantic, beginning with a loud peel emanating from Doug's behind; passive aggressive: his backside's way of being argumentative. Margot walks straight through the fog whilst applying her mascara and eating a raisin bagel at the same time. Her silence is enough of a scolding.

"I'm going to continue doing that while she's here you know," he says. "If I'm forced to live with a stranger in my own home then I'm not altering any normal bodily functions."

"If you feel the need to behave like a child then do so," yells Margot from the bathroom.

"When does she arrive anyway?"

"Two weeks."

"Two weeks! Jesus, I was thinking maybe a month or so. We won't even have the CD cabinet alphabetised by then.

What happened to her that's so bad?"

"Do we have to always have these discussions in the morning? I'm about five minutes away from getting intimate with a fat sweaty pervert on the train. You know what it's like if you shift your morning schedule by even five minutes – mayhem! People seem to be getting up earlier too. And you still want to talk about this?"

"We don't really talk, do we. I just get dictated to."

With that comment Doug instantly realises there will be a cloud of tension over the apartment for the next couple of days. It has been building though and Margot fails to kiss Doug goodbye as she departs amidst a flurry of papers and laptops, an action reserved for those special occasions lately when he has said something wrong. After she's gone Doug quickly wanks which means he knows he'll be later than he already is. He doesn't care because he needs the tension relief of an orgasm and justifies the rest of the day's happiness with these five minutes of intense tugging. He abandons a made–up fantasy instead opting for memory, the lucky participant a short Swedish girl he had sex with in the toilets at university. Immediately afterwards, although relieved to only have zero other people in the room to share the shame with, he adds masturbation to the abstinence list. Further list additions: start smoking … something heavy. Change career. Start running.

When it's all over he stumbles over the still wrapped coffee table on his way out. The day waves coyly to him rather than greeting him with a big smile. The heat is occasionally dispelled by sharp gusts of stale air that relocate clumps of dry leaves along the pavement. With his mind still on the trashed coffee table, Doug almost walks into a moving van crossing the road, the driver yelling obscenities which fade as he turns off. His mind isn't quite ready for another day of nodding contemplation and power cigarettes. But he knows he'll pull it off as he always does. Despite the nature of the work.

In the cab on the way to the client's plush building in central London Doug wonders if his management consulting days are nearly over. He is within spitting distance of being made partner but the effort and the cash outlay seems more effort without the associated reward. He's still young as well; young enough to dig down another career path. But he's good at what he does; what all consultants do: tell companies to cut costs by cutting staff. But it's the way he does it that makes him really good.

The day rushes past him as the flurry of life turns from suburban to urban, the green patches quickly replaced by vivid red buses hooting and unwashed buildings. The taxi is on the client but this doesn't enable Doug to relax. The driver is in more of a hurry than Doug, bumping over curb corners and flicking signals at other impatient drivers. By the time Doug arrives his nerves are shot to hell and his paper unread so he decides to calm down with a latte before turning his late unwanted presence into fashionably wanted. That's the art of it really. To lure the everyman into a delirium of trust until you make a recommendation of retrenchments only to blame it on the board. You must hide and duck and crawl in the trenches and then enjoy the view from the general's post.

His new abode still bothers him. It's now nibbling at his

conscious and the continual disarray, which won't be sorted anytime soon, doesn't fit with his persona. In the universe everything has a place; everything must be noted and organised accordingly so that its future use is accessible and seamless. This is not how he is existing at the moment with unopened boxes, slaps of tester paint in every room and stained kitchen surfaces. It is a beautiful property with plenty of investment potential which he would happily spend a fortune on to improve, but that would cause something just short of a holocaust. 'The more we do the more it's ours' rings out in his ears as he proficiently sucks the remainder of the foam from his coffee and gets up to depart. 'How can we let other people decorate our home?'

He's greeted in the lobby by a paradox of a large blonde woman with red teeth and a frail black man with a bayonet. The woman towers a good three feet above the security guard who stands, fiercely guarding the premises. The woman nods, gets up then sits down as Doug flashes his visitor's card across the scanner. 'Welcome Mr Visitor' reads the display screen, the voice announcement to accompany temporarily out of order.

In the lift Doug checks his effortlessly symmetrical tie as he does every time he ascends in a lift. He tries to remember the last time he was in a lift without a mirror or some form of reflection and reflects how this is the way business will always be: visual. A presentable picture is one your customer or your colleague will always respect. He nods to himself, not in vanity but in respect. Respect for what he believes and what he does. Every day.

Ted the mailroom chap is the first to greet him as he disembarks, getting his name wrong as he shuffles the trolley past. He's been with this client for almost two months now and finally the cracks are beginning to show. He knows today will not be a good day if already someone has his name wrong. The office is a mess yet a productive mess. Everywhere flow charts and diagrams decorate the walls and glass panels like billboards. The next four people, all on his team, get his name right which quickly snaps his negative attitude, rendering him positive, eloquent and creative. Not that it was going to be different anyway though.

A few boroughs away Margot is apologising to her secretary after reducing her to tears. The carefully constructed woman now sobs into one of Margot's tissues, the constant flow of mucus on the verge of not being ladylike. Margot was late which meant someone was going to have to bear the brunt. The usual recipient took it a little too hard for a change and, like a hydrant being knocked over, turned up the floodgates.

"Bonnie, I'm sorry. No excuses, just that nothing in this place ever goes according to schedule. It's as though there's a mass conspiracy to do the exact opposite of what I plan. It's not your fault."

"I know," says Bonnie, now raising her head to show bulbous clumps of mascara beneath her oval eyes. "I'm not having the easiest time here that's all."

"Me neither, but things have got to improve. The more idiots like Gardener that get sacked the better. He's gone now so don't worry. But that doesn't mean slack off, you hear? I know you are better than a sobbing teen princess. You've got to learn from this mistake you've made and emerge a stronger woman."

"I wish I could be more like you and have a man who loves me."

Bonnie's final words stick with Margot the rest of the day as she devotes her lunch hour to cleaning out her second drawer. While rummaging through it she finds a price tag for an Ann Summers outfit that Doug bought her. The date on it is almost two years ago and she vaguely remembers the purple panties and bra that she wore once and which now rest at the back of her cupboard along with the size six trousers and crop top. *Does he love me?* she wonders. *Is he that committed to us?* Her insistent demands for their imminent guest now fill her with considerable guilt. Before her next meeting, which ominously squats a mere minute away, she makes a note in her diary to call Janine and let her know that it is not a convenient time for her to visit. Despite everything Janine has been through; despite the support she needs. She's doing it for her relationship and she knows the real victory has already been won: he had agreed to the visit.

When the phone rings Doug is woven into a thick discussion on the implications of a paperless office. His face is wrought with concern and, in the space of ten minutes, he succeeds in convincing Gus, a senior manager, that Gus is the one who came up with the idea and is the only one with the business savvy to implement it. The red tartan Malt Whisky Fudge pencil container in front of him is the victim when he scrabbles forward to pick up the receiver.

"Sorry Gus, I'll just be a moment. Good morning Douglas Perfors."

"Hi it's only me," says the familiar voice. "Shall we meet up for lunch today? Our client just cancelled the storyboard presentation so I have a free hour. Leadenhall market?"

Doug is taken aback by the request because his visions of scoffing humble pie for the next few days are quickly dispelled. Under normal circumstances he would honour a lunch request from anyone but on this particular day he cannot. He has to be somewhere else.

"I'm sorry Marg, but I've got another appointment. Another time perhaps?"

"I'm sorry about this morning; about the whole Janine thing. It was unfair of me to impose this on you. I'm going to phone her and cancel."

"Don't be silly, it's me who should be apologising. She's more than welcome to stay, you know that."

"Well it's too late, I've already called her."

"How did she take it?"

"I left a message on her answer phone."

"That's personal."

"This is for you!"

"Well it shouldn't be."

"I have to go. I'll see you at home. Goodbye."

Doug, despite feeling slightly guilty at having deterred the visitor, is wholeheartedly relieved at the prospect of his home being his own again. His lunch with his old friend Michelle goes on for longer than it should and he staggers back into the office chewing strong peppermint flavoured gum and trying not to belch alcohol fumes in anyone's face. On his return there is an email from Margot saying she has to work late. The tone is formal and cold and the thought of a night on his own snuggled up with his cable and DVD player is not the worst a man can imagine. Pepe has invited him on a boy's night out but, for God's sake, it's Monday, an evening far better spent in the comfort of one's own home.

The key into his new home won't turn properly so he has to give it a bit of a jolt before it forces open. It's already dark and the street is sombre yet somehow tingling. All the streetlights work yet the darkness still dominates the long row of Victorian properties. Doug is at that stage of the day where he's stopped concentrating on the menial activities like walking and stepping over objects and the scattered coffee table again almost ensures his demise. The noise rouses something in the house and a figure appears from the lounge. At first Doug is startled until he makes out the shape of a small woman. She has her back to him now and is running down the corridor, the naked shine of her bottom cheeks lampooning his eyeballs, the landing quiver forcing an involuntary blink – first left then right then left again. The last Doug sees before she disappears around the corner is the flap of her faded purple t–shirt and the tiny clump of brown hair visible beneath her.

"Hello? Margot?" he yells, knowing that the woman is a good foot shorter and completely differently proportioned. Then she appears again in the latter stages of pulling up blue drawstring tracksuit bottoms. Her face is sweet and her smile quickly dispels the tension.

"I really must apologise," she says, sticking out her hand.

"You're Doug, aren't you? I let myself in. I'm Janine. I know I'm early but thought I'd surprise Margot."

"How did you get in?" says Doug, reluctantly shaking her hand, his world now crumbling around him.

"Old habits don't seem to die too hard: the front door key under the back door mat. Margot's been doing that ever since university."

I've told her not to do that a million times, thinks Doug putting on a brave yet bemused face.

"It is very rude of me, I do apologise."

"No it's no problem at all."

"I was up early this morning and dozed off on your sofa. I woke when I heard you arrive and realised I'd forgotten my trousers. I must have been out for six hours."

Doug tries not to notice but she is a beautiful woman in a young girl sort of way. Her blond waves seem to mimic her speech, jumping and darting with each exaggerated expression. Her eyes are steady and focused on his, yet all this doesn't dismiss the feeling of anxiety that he thought Margot had got rid of that afternoon. But he'll be polite. There is nothing else his nature will allow.

"Please excuse the state of the place. We've just moved and it seems that Margot has a special place for everything so it has to sit and rest until 'the place finds it'."

"Same old Margot. She told me you had moved. I was expecting a lot worse. It really is a wonderful place, this. Loads of potential. I would love to help out as a way of saying thank you for allowing me to stay. It really does mean a lot to me and I know it is a big sacrifice on your part."

"Not at all," lies Doug. "Please do make yourself at home

and feel free to do as you wish. Margot really is looking forward to seeing you."

Doug makes a weak attempt to tidy by emptying a few boxes which only serves to worsen the home scenario. What he really achieves is ignoring his guest until Margot arrives just after midnight. He hears the mass hysteria as the two reunite in the hallway showering each other with kisses and tight squeezing hugs. The usual platitudes are exchanged and Doug even mouths a few of them as he sulks in the bedroom: 'How've you been' 'You look great' 'It's been too long'. He ventures from the bedroom to join the party, still fully clothed and craving a bath.

"I see you've met our Doug," says Margot pointing at him. "I bet he was surprised."

Later when everyone is in bed Doug turns onto his side and whispers, "I thought you said she wasn't coming."

"She must have left the place where I left the message. I never managed to get hold of her."

"And what's all this coming early to surprise you bullshit?"

"It's just the way she is. Since I've known her she's always done these nutty impulsive things."

"How long is she here for?"

"Knowing her a day or a year."

The three finally sleep, the beginning of the week blues ordered into the subconscious. No cars move on the streets and the air takes a break from the gusts.

There is no slight breeze.

CHAPTER 7²

←→

Mother Ate

Michelle smokes a cigarette on her balcony after having had sex with a man with an ugly head. She's wrapped in a silver gown and watches as the ash trickles over the edge of her rail to disperse in the windless night that comforts her. Her fridge is full of food she knows she won't eat. She isn't hungry but forces a ripe desert peach into her mouth washing it down with leftover single malt whisky.

Her loft apartment is sparse but for the hints of west coast Californian furniture. When she returns upstairs the man is asleep on top of the covers, his nakedness turning her stomach. She shakes him gently and then rigorously until he carefully opens an eye, extricated from a peaceful dream.

"It's time you left," she whispers in his ear, standing up and handing him his trousers. His expression doesn't change and he dutifully gets up and dresses without asking questions. In a breath he is out of the apartment and calm is restored to her life. Into the early hours of the morning Michelle watches television: no show in particular just the soothing flicker of images on a screen. The scene changes distort the dimensions of the room as if each angle of the large space is mechanically shifting. Her low bright red sofa is hard yet comfortable and she snuggles forcefully into the square angle created by the harsh rise of the arm rest.

A few minutes later she is upstairs again and looking at her naked form in the mirror. This is the life she chooses to lead, she tells herself. There is no regret. Thinking of his clandestine yet obvious disdain for unnecessary body hair, her mind wanders onto Doug, her friend for too long, and how their lives regularly touch once a month. As though their encounters are structured but when they're together the spontaneity is the only thing that dominates. Lately though, she's worried about him.

When they met she was stripping at a classy club and he was out on a Stag Do. The sparkle in his eyes and the strength of his convictions at first excited her towards him and then cemented the friendship. It was a strange encounter: him, practically a married man, and her, a wealthy heiress, with nothing better to do than the unthinkable. The connection was apparent to both, nonsexual in nature and refreshing, Doug the only man in Michelle's life not to proposition her or demand anything of her.

She remembers how he called her aside and said he'd pay her to sit and just talk to him. With all of her on display, light blue frills barely covering her surgically enhanced breasts, it would have been difficult for any man to remain focused. Yet he did, his eyes fixed on hers, never wavering or following the excess of tanned glitter passing by. When one of his friends approached to whisk her away for a private dance she promptly made an excuse. That was the last time she stripped, the adrenaline appeal having worn off and the shallow clientele a turn–off. When he asked her why she did it she couldn't answer, a recurring theme in her life.

Michelle Opera doesn't do the relationship; she doesn't do the commitment thing. A cliché for a woman of these times but one that keeps her functioning. The guy from earlier she picked up at the video store. It's easier with uglier guys: it's as though you are rewarding them for years of patience and they will accept anything you throw their way. You don't need to know anything about them just that they will do exactly what you want. Her life is to go.

Her nonphysical affair with Doug is the one element of her life she fails to control. She understands why it must be kept secret and frankly has no desire to worm into the other elements of his life. She knows a woman of her appearance is difficult to explain yet something about him lately is drawing her nearer. She has never met Margot and envies her for her simple determination, exactly the way Doug describes her. And when he seldom talks of her it is always with the utmost affection and respect. Years ago this ideal would have made her sick, but for some reason on this still night she craves it.

When a television programme she wasn't watching ends she cuts a line of cocaine and snorts it from the glass table, instantly regretting her action. She can feel the substance remove her tiredness and once again restore the confidence and conviction of her lonely existence. She is a queen in her world again and smokes a badly rolled joint to calm her feeling of false euphoria. Doug is no longer in her thoughts and she knows he won't be until she dozes off and is pushed into a semi–conscious state of reality, only to wake up, perform her yoga and spend money on something she hasn't done before. Perhaps she'll learn to knit and knit some socks for Afghani children. That's exactly what she'll do, she tells herself, giggling. Or she could just buy a new car. The pot is still full.

❴ ↪ ↩ ↪ ↩ ↪ ↩ ❵

Across town an exorcism is taking place. An old woman is sprinkling powder in a bedroom and muttering words of faith. Leo is almost too scared to watch and Pepe watches with the intrigue of a child. The woman is dressed in black with a cacophony of wooden beads draped around her neck. Her skin is taught for a woman of her years, her eyes the wary give away.

"Did you feel that?" yells Leo at the exact second the clock chimes half past the hour of four. "You both did feel that?"

The woman takes no notice and continues chanting in a

deeper tone while Pepe twitches his head around the room trying to believe. "Feel what? Where?"

"The whole room went cold. He was here for that brief second and now he's gone."

"Do you want to stay at mine again?" says Pepe, fighting the convulsions.

"I'm sure this seems very funny, but this place is haunted. I'm not one to jump to any sort of supernatural conclusion but every night since I moved in, at exactly four thirty, he arrives and lets me know he's here."

"How do you know it's a he?"

"I checked into the past owners of the property and the most likely explanation is an ex–army officer who lived alone for twenty years."

"Are you sure it wasn't Colonel Mustard with a candlestick in the kitchen?"

"Very funny. The kitchen is actually my solace. I've spent a few nights in a sleeping bag next to the washing machine. There doesn't seem to be any activity there."

"Was this before you moved into my place?"

"I haven't been at yours every night, have I?"

"Leo, I really don't mind. I just think you're making this up in your mind; a product of a reporter's over-active imagination. You're looking for a story where there isn't one."

The sun is just beginning to light up the neighbourhood when the woman departs. Leo tries to compensate her for her efforts but she refuses claiming that it is God's work she does and there is no price for that. Leo is too scared to ask whether he will be back so doesn't, putting his desperate faith in her rigid posture and strong resolve. The two resign themselves to no more sleep and decide to pick Doug up for an early breakfast.

The ride over to Doug's is quick as the traffic is yet to coagulate. Doug answers the door and is the only one up in the apartment. He's shaved, dressed and ready to run from the mess when the doorbell sounds. He hears both girls stir as the bedrooms are beside one another and tiptoes to answer.

"We were just getting rid of ghosts and thought we'd pick you up for a filthy breakfast, seeing as you couldn't make the exorcism," says Pepe, pointing at Leo getting out of the car.

The two are huddled at the door as though trick or treating when they spot Janine staggering through to the toilet clad only in a long white t–shirt.

"Jesus," says Leo. "Looks as though you're the one with the ghost and she needs exorcising immediately. To my apartment perhaps?"

"Shhhh, you'll wake Margot. Let me grab my stuff and we'll head."

"Who's the fox?"

"I'll explain later."

The only breakfast available at that time of the morning turns out to be a greasy spoon with stale baked beans and cold coffee. The boys are jubilant, wired awake by their evening shenanigans and intrigued at their friend's new guest.

"It's funny because this morning he was a shivering mess, scared of a male ghost and then at the first sight of female flesh he's back to his usual form and raring to go," says Pepe, finishing off all his food, his glasses having slipped to the end of his nose.

"You really went through with the exorcism?" says Doug.

"Enough with that. I've explained what was going on but now I no longer have to worry: the black widow stung the ghost and he's gone for good. Fucked off back to the nether world or wherever," says Leo.

"So your days of sleeping with Pepe's teddy bear collection are over?"

"No offence or anything, buddy," says Leo, having not eaten much, "but we've got to get you a life. First and foremost we've got to get you laid and second, you've got to get some cool stuff. That's what it's all about: cool stuff. If a bird likes your stuff, half the battle is won and you're in."

"You could have always gone home," says Pepe, sulking into another fork licking episode. "To your wife."

"Janet thinks I'm away doing a story on Central Africa. I'll have to think of something when I fail to appear on the evening news. She always buys it though: I act a bit pissed at having my story canned and she's sympathetic."

"She doesn't suspect the pad?" says Doug.

"She wouldn't suspect it if I did a story about myself in it! I think I'll end up in Africa in a couple of weeks anyway. Who's the babe in your house anyway?"

"One of Margot's friends," says Doug. "An old university friend visiting for an indefinite period of time."

"Is she attached?" asks Pepe.

"A girl like that is always attached," says Leo. "More importantly is she available?"

"There's no way I'm letting you within ten feet of her. If Margot ever found out about your nocturnal activities I'd be joining you in your haunted house. You are a pillar of investigative reporting remember."

"Maybe you could get her out without Margot knowing," says Leo.

"The only place I want her out of is my house," says Doug. "She arrives virtually unannounced and makes herself comfortable like she's a relative. All because of some trauma she's suffered."

"Girl is on the rebound," says Leo, flicking his fingers. "It's like clubbing baby seals."

"Is she nice?" asks Pepe.

"Don't know yet and don't really care. To me she's a nuisance in a home that needs attention. With her there nothing will get done."

"I have a plan," says Leo. "Why don't you invite your stripper friend along with this, uh, what's her name again?"

"Janine."

"Janine girl over to my place and we can all live happily ever after. That Michelle won't be able to go on much longer denying her obvious attraction for me."

"She's thinking of getting a restraining order against you," says Doug.

"Are you serious?" says Leo, his floppy hair falling across his forehead.

Doug laughs and wipes his mouth beckoning that the breakfast must end.

"Sorry boys but I have to see a man about a man about a horse. It's been a pleasure."

"Introduce me to this new girl Janine," says Pepe after a

prolonged silence. Doug looks at Leo who looks at Pepe, waiting for a change of expression. Nothing comes and Pepe's serious face dispels any sarcastic retort from Leo.

"Once we're settled, you are welcome to come around," says Doug.

"I'm going to have to take you shopping first, little man," says Leo, paying the bill and winking at the overweight waitress wiping her hands on her apron.

CHAPTER 82

Bumble Huge Innings

All three of them are huddled around the makeshift dining room table eating with a mismatched array of plastic cutlery and cardboard plates. After a full day of unpacking and decorating, the take–away Chinese food never tasted so good, each scooping mouthfuls of egg fried rice soaked in sweet and sour sauce into their faces. Janine has a menagerie of crimson paint and wallpaper glue strewn across her face while Doug and Margot can barely feel the softness that once existed on the skin of their hands.

"It really is wonderful to see you again," says Margot after a purposeful swallow of chow mein. "And for you to help us get this place ready really is beyond the call of duty."

"It's the least I can do to thank you for having me to stay. I insist on paying board and lodging on top of the labour, you know," says Janine looking at Doug.

"That is not at all necessary and you know that," says Margot. "I just wish your stay could be more fun. I'm sure you hadn't planned to spend your free days decorating someone else's home."

"Well there's only one corner of the ceiling left," says Janine pointing to the grimy corner of the living room where damp has collected and turned the wallpaper light brown. The bubbled paper creates an almost perfect oval above their heads.

"We're getting a damp specialist in, so I think wait until they've had a look," says Doug.

"That's no problem, I'm sure there's plenty for me to do around here."

"Do you have a job?" asks Doug, instantly receiving a scolding glance from Margot who has no real table to kick him under.

"I did have a job but left. There was just too much attention after the media circus. I am actively looking though and intend to keep my word regarding the board and lodging."

"You really don't have to pay rent, especially if you're unemployed," says Doug.

"Would anyone like any more Chinese? I feel as though I could give birth over here," says Margot, pushing out her belly and trying to change the topic.

"I suppose you read about me in the papers so it's no mystery what happened." Janine's eyes are downcast, her fists delicately clenched.

"You don't have to talk about it." Margot smooths the back of Janine's unruly curls. "Only when you are ready."

"I might as well get it out in the open."

"Please, not on my account," says Doug struggling to look away from her eyes.

"I was living with a man who decided he'd had enough of everything. He ended up murdering half a band and torturing the rest before getting himself killed. I was carrying ..."

Suddenly a loud jolt from above echoes out sending all the living room inhabitants gazing towards the ceiling. The clatter of loud boot-laden footsteps then follows along with a regular banging.

"It's that bastard trying to make a point," says Doug. "I'll have to have a word with him." The next second there's an assertive knock at the door, the visitor opting out of using the doorbell. Before Doug has time to reach the door the knock again sounds out, this time louder and more forceful. On the other side of the door is a bald – but for a dozen hairs – squat man with a pink face holding a letter and waving it in the air.

"Good evening," says Doug.

"We had the same problem with the previous owners and again we have to put up with shit from another young couple. We will not stand for it anymore! That we won't!"

"My name is Doug Perfors," says Doug, extending a hand. "And you are?"

The man is caught by surprise but continues to rant. "There

is a noise problem in these flats and we are seeking legal advice to rectify this. In due course you will be putting in false ceilings to eradicate this problem. Do you understand?"

"Is this how you welcome people to the neighbourhood?"

The man's face changes colour for the fourth time in as many minutes. The lines on the whites of his bulbous eyes darken and he shoves the piece of paper at Doug, who is forced to accept it. "I will be seeing you in court. That or I will keep you awake for the rest of your life, young man! The noise you just heard was me dropping a bowling ball. That noise will continue as long as yours does and until you fit your ceilings."

"We weren't making a noise. We were just talking over dinner."

"Life is all about choices."

"That's right and if you chose to pursue this course of action, we will challenge you in court. I am used to dealing with bullying tactics, sir, so feel free to proceed as this is a familiar area for me: a safe place as it were. But be warned for you have a choice too. There was never going to be any animosity in this relationship and you have chosen to start it off on a bad foot rather than an amiable symbiotic one. So good evening and see you in court."

Doug shuts the door softly in the man's face leaving him breathing heavily and knocking again. Doug does not answer and motions for the girls to relax and enjoy the rest of the evening. He returns from the kitchen with a bottle of red wine and a cheese platter, the earlier events as distant from him as the water long ago departed from the duck's back. The noise momentarily resumes upstairs and then subsides as it seems a scolding ensues. Doug sips his wine, unaffected while Margot clears up and Janine stares straight up at the ceiling, her eyes circling the oval patch of brittle paper.

After dinner and a brief tidy consisting mainly of sweeping sawdust away and shoving boxes in the storage cupboard, everyone retires to bed, exhausted from a gruellingly physical day's effort. The teeth brushing procession is kicked off by Margot who ends up fast asleep without the customary bedtime read. Doug is in the ultimate stages of his brush when Janine knocks and enters the bathroom. Doug is standing with just his boxer shorts on and Janine walks up beside him, squeezing into the gap between his arm and the wall to moisten the blob of toothpaste that sits atop her brush like a perfectly broken turd. Doug feels the edge of her nipples rub against his flank, each breast swaying beneath her t–shirt.

"I think what you did was exactly right," she whispers, conscious not to wake Margot, whose distant snores now resonate down the corridor. "Bullies like that should be taught a lesson. They don't like people standing up to them; people like you."

"Well, we'll see how idle his threats are sooner or later," Doug whispers back, motioning to the silence around them. "Good night, Janine," he says, leaving the bathroom while Janine bends over the sink to spit a mouthful of the water–toothpaste–saliva concoction.

In bed, Janine is restless, staring above and counting the number of feet across and wide. Her light is off yet the room is light. For a moment her hand finds its way down between her legs and then the idea is abandoned when she starts thinking about Doug's job question. She would get a job the next day no matter what and keep true to her promise. And Doug seems to like women with jobs, successful women. The ceiling is segmented by three lines and Janine traces out a square in one of them with her index finger then turns onto her side to tackle the burden of rest.

you wanted attractive girls between eighteen and thirty for photographic work."

"That's correct. And you are a very attractive woman."

Still the Japanese man sits behind the security of oversized dark glasses, his dual pinkie rings sparkling in the spotlight's glare. He hasn't moved in the entire time Janine has been in the room, but for the inadvertent chewing on the left side of his face.

"Just relax, my dear, take your time."

"Okay, I like tulips, red wine, a good bowel movement and watching people die slowly," she says, waiting for reactions. The Japanese man stirs ever so slightly but enough to give something away. Janine giggles, which seems to put the men at ease who laugh nervously.

"How tall are you?" says Mike Reef.

"Five foot six. Five foot five."

"You're too short for ramp work. Hold up your hands for me."

The Japanese man now leans across and whispers something to the casting director while Janine wishes she's given her nails a treatment after all the renovating.

"We might have a special project for you, miss," begins Mike Reef, pushing his chin drawing an imaginary egg, "but it might involve some nudity. The money is good though, almost three times as much as you would receive for glamour work. Mr Mochizuki here runs an adult production company called Phayze Productions. He is currently working on something you might just be perfect for. May we see your body?"

Janine stares ahead and can hear the regular rhythm of the video camera. It's not the first time she's bared all and casually takes off her blue sweater, the drag above her head lifting her hair, creating a strobe effect with the light. She is naked and the Japanese man nods in approval after analysing the camera picture. He takes off his glasses revealing two almost non–existent slits cowering above buckets of dark rings.

"When you begin?" he asks.

Ten minutes later Janine is again fully clothed and Mike Reef has sent all the other applicants packing. Mr Mochizuki has left as well and the casting director now circles the new recruit like a coin circling the dark drop of a hyperbolic funnel charity donation box. His brow is mottled with sweat and he departs to make a phone call in the toilet before returning to the casting room, having instructed Janine to wait to sort out the paperwork. There is not a sheet of paper in sight and Reef closes the door, bowing in humble apology towards his guest.

"It doesn't usually happen like that, you know," he says running his extended fingernail along the back of her neck. "Mr Moch doesn't always like what he sees the first time. It must be your attitude because he usually demands a greater show of um, talent if you know what I mean."

"Isn't there something I have to sign? Your commission percentage or something?"

"You see he only deals with me as his agent," he whispers next to her ear. "Without me there are no girls and he knows it. Phayze Productions is nothing without the culinary British delights of Mike Reef Castings. This is why I need some reassurance that you will deliver the goods."

Janine can see the door behind him is a long way off and he'll surely resort to force should she make a dash. She sees his nervous twitching mouth inches from hers.

"What exactly do you want me to do, you naughty boy," she says running a hand up his inner thigh. "Do you want me to spank your little pale behind? Well you'd better go stand in the corner then and think about what you've done."

Mike Reef shakes his head slowly laughing to himself. "No, no, my little fawn. This is far more serious than a little domination game. If you come to me you work for me – Mr Moch might tell you something different but there must be a clear understanding between you and me as to where we stand. The two of us."

"I work for you, that's fine."

"Do you know what that entails? Do you know how many little girls like you work for me?"

With his last words two men enter the room and lock the door behind them. Janine tries to scream but is thwarted by Mike Reef's sweaty paw which covers her mouth, clutching it shut so tightly her teeth grind together, feeling as though they're about to crumble. One of the men moves in to assist while the other repositions the video camera. "There must be a constant reminder," yells Mike Reef, ripping at her clothes, "as to who owns who here, who is in charge."

Janine begins lashing out but her small frame is no match for any of the men. Conscious not to leave bruises one of the men gets her head into a chokehold and applies restrictive pressure until her delirium is reduced to droopy eyelids and frequent blackouts.

Janine washes herself in the shower, relieved no one is home. She is unable to clean herself, the yet–to–be–powershowered water pressure too painful on her skin, so she resorts to careful splashes of water from the basin. She watches how the remnants wash away with a swirl and the sucking noise of the pipes, remembering the director's words on her departure.

  She doesn't cry, the only sign that anything happened the occasional wince with every step. She continues redecorating, focusing her efforts on the damp-ridden corner of the room. She must finish the job today and becomes more determined as she cuts away the paper with a Stanley knife, revealing a brown muddy looking ceiling with cracks all along the plastering. A bit crumbles and drops into her open mouth leaving a stale bitter taste to accompany the excessive toothpaste. With the knife she slices an elongated hole in the ceiling and spends the next few minutes examining the sliver. The soft underlay of the carpet is now inches from her dry eyes, as she looks at her wrists and decides to abandon the lengthwise slit for the one above her head.

CHAPTER 03

Eye Tea Victory

Margot returns home from work early to find Janine crying in the spare room. She quickly pulls Janine to her and kisses her on the forehead.

"What's the matter?"

"I just miss him, that's all," Janine replies. "Despite everything, I did love him and things were good towards the end."

Janine nestles more firmly into Margot's underarm and moves her lips to touch Margot's neck. The sobbing resumes, this time deeper and more intervallic, as Janine delicately moves her lips in slow kisses around the dent of Margot's clavicle. The telephone rings and Margot pulls herself away, running clumsily to retrieve the receiver before it resorts to voicemail.

Doug is welcomed home to a discord of laughter and hot chocolate, Janine's visible sadness now almost dispelled. Doug's day has been a blur and he briefly enquires before retiring into the lounge after being giggled at. Instead of being annoyed he lets the two embrace their feminine bonding and sips a bottled beer whilst trying to find the beginning of a news bulletin. The two women join him and settle down once a fascinating story appears on the screen.

Before long, the two are fast asleep in the lounge, Margot visibly spent from another combative day in the office and Janine, an emotional wreck, the tiny lines of smudged mascara her betraying accessory. Doug watches as the two breathe in perfect unison, their breast bones pushing vigorously upwards before withdrawing down past the rapid eyelids fluttering. A lot has been accomplished in the last few days: the built–in cupboard two doors from completion and every hole and crack filled and sanded. The painting has started, brief scrapes and splashes of tester colours now the graffitied interior shootouts and Doug is daring to settle down into his new environment.

He thinks he dozes off and is not sure whether or not he dreams that Janine is standing in front of him without clothes on. But it doesn't matter for her stance is unassuming and instils a sense of calm and well–being upon him. By midnight the room is filled with the flicker of a black and white movie and Doug stretches on the sofa, removing his feet that have become nested beneath Margot's breast. She doesn't stir and he lifts her, sauntering carefully across the wooden floorboards to their room, semi–undressing her mid-air and laying her down. She mumbles something, kissing his neck and falling back asleep. When in bed she clutches the duvet towards her, rolling over to enter another night of stolen consciousness.

Janine is in the same position, curled in a dainty ball on the buttermilk single seater sofa. Doug instinctively lifts her up, her weight providing little resistance for a man of his size. Just as Margot did, she nestles into him, holding him close as a child would a parent. When he reaches her room, after narrowly missing knocking her head on the corner of the odd shaped passage, she is reluctant to let go, her subconscious attachment an impenetrable bond. Her fingers are curled around his neck, her nails on the verge of piecing the skin and Doug is forced to lift each finger one at a time and lower her softly onto the bed. She's not wearing shoes so he pulls the duvet up and over her, hopeful that she will rest peacefully. Just as he's leaving the room, he thinks he hears her say "Thanks Doug," the dart of a disjointed breeze muffling the noise. He shuts the door behind him.

In the middle of the night Margot and Doug end up holding one another in a tight embrace that quickly progresses into half–comatosed passion. Doug can feel that she wants him too and is fully awake when he enters her. The reality of the situation settles like dust upon the resistant lovers when

Margot moans "No," waking up and pushing Doug from her. The two have not yet made love in the new home and the sleep induced scene seemed like the perfect ice breaker in a relationship where the physical side is now glossed over and not often spoken about. "Why not?" whispers Doug, approaching the subject with desperation, remembering the days when they could hardly get enough of each other's bodies.

"She'll hear," says Margot, pulling up her knickers and getting out of bed to go to the toilet. Doug lies back, too dejected to finish himself off and pretends to fall asleep before Margot returns accompanied by the hiss of the flushed toilet.

{ ➡ ⬅ ➡ ⬅ ➡ ⬅ }

Pepe embarrassingly enjoys a public lunch with his Mexican father and Chinese mother. It is a weekly family ritual that his father insists on, and seems to never be without a verbal display aimed at an unsuspecting waitress or manager. Pepe instantaneously reverts to child mode on these occasions, his father's dominance and mother's consistent fussing the reasons for the reversion. Pepe smiles from behind his large glasses as his mother wipes a bit of pasta that has escaped his mouth and rests on his cheek. When she dabs her napkin in the mineral water to wipe it further she is told off by Pepe who tries unsuccessfully to change the topic from potential girlfriends.

Pepe's kind nature is splashed all over his face, his

unfortunate inherited traits probably the best he could have hoped for: unavoidably macrocephalic, his short stature overshadowed by his head, looming in unison with his glasses, ready to fall off. His cheeks are red and slightly scarred from a bout of pimples as a teenager, his eyes dark brown with hidden pupils. His shirt is always tucked in and trousers always too high.

But despite his physical shortcomings he has the patience of a saint and a smile to change anyone's perception. Doug and he have been friends ever since Doug rescued him from a bunch of zealous bullies at senior school and has always looked out for the poor fellow. Doug's matchmaking attempts have been tremendously unsuccessful, a host of Margot's friends the unlucky recipients. Pepe's efforts always come across as too severe and it is this approach that is the most difficult to verbalise to him. His theory is one of the second date being the clinching moment but the dates never seem to progress past the main course.

When he has finished the monotony of being told how he should be living his life, Pepe makes for a designer store where he is meeting Leo to pick out a shirt. He's mortified at the idea of buying clothes with a male friend and only agreed after a persistent hour of nagging. Leo is not there when Pepe arrives and he waits anxiously outside while the shop assistants swarm upon a well-dressed man who looks like a city banker. Pepe peers in and then strolls by as though perusing the abnormally shaped male mannequins that adorn the shop windows like plastic security guards.

Pepe waits for fifteen minutes before Leo rings to say he

cannot make it because the studio need to re–shoot an interview with a parliament member accused of statutory rape. His apologies are genuine and Pepe accepts, secretly relieved. The indecision in his mind makes him stop a few hundred metres from the shop, turn around and retrace his steps back to where he was waiting. His dinner invite from Doug was that evening and he would have no time to construct an outfit to impress the newcomer from his wardrobe which Leo called a cross between *Little House on the Prairie* and *Footloose*. The words now ring in his ears as he fights the urge not to enter the store.

The door jams and only gives way after a forceful shove which sees Pepe stumble forward, creating a much unneeded spectacle. His cheeks brightly flushed, Pepe readjusts his checked collar and nods at the attendants, trying to exude a disinterested demeanour and browse through the shelves of shirts. No one comes to help him until it is painfully clear that he is looking in the wrong gender section and his cover–up when the assistant tries to measure his neck, only serves to worsen matters.

He selects a green shirt with thick white vertical stripes and takes it to the assistant asking where the changing rooms are. The woman with an exceptionally long nose bridge stares down at him informing him that the size is too large and that a size 14 would probably be more suitable for a man of his frame than an 18. She retrieves the exact shirt and sends Pepe on his way to the changing rooms, noticing that his trousers have become lodged in the crack of his arse.

Once inside the brightly lit cream cubicle Pepe checks that he has signal on his mobile and rings Doug. The phone rings twice before Doug answers.

"Doug, it's me," he whispers, trying to peer over the door to see if anyone is waiting.

"Why are you whispering?" asks Doug, excusing himself from the executive lunch.

"I'm in a changing room trying on shirts and I need your help." He puts on the shirt before fully examining the disproportionate shape of his body in the angled mirrors.

"Is this for tonight? Wasn't Leo meant to be there?" asks Doug.

"He couldn't make it so I'm stuck here with a green shirt and too many choices."

"Pepe, don't treat tonight as a date. Just take it easy and treat it like a friendly get–together. Once it is labelled a date the nerves set in and the evening starts wrong. You are great company and it doesn't matter in the slightest what you wear. Just be yourself."

The words send a lump into Pepe's throat as he jumps, hearing someone ·else enter. "What colour do you recommend though? What colour do you think, um, will suit me?"

"Stick to the basics. Get something that fits and stay away from patterns or too much colour. Buy what makes you feel comfortable. Okay?"

"Thanks Doug."

"No problem, just don't be late. Janine's cooking a bolognese so make sure you're there ..."

"Are you alright in there, sir?" yells a voice from the exterior.

"Yes fine thank you," says Pepe, fumbling the phone shut and cutting Doug off. "Please could you bring me a plain white shirt in this size?"

"Certainly," says a woman strutting off in her high heels and visibly shocked by the confident tone of Pepe's request.

"And a light blue one."

The evening has a chilly edge and Pepe arrives armed with an expensive bottle of red wine. His hair is gelled into organised spikes that make him look older and this new look creates a little stir from Doug when he answers the door.

"Looking sharp," whispers Doug, relieving Pepe of the bottle and welcoming him into the hallway. "Nice shirt."

"The place is looking great," says Pepe before greeting Margot with an awkward kiss on the cheek and shaking Janine's hand. Pepe can feel his palms are sweating and he tries unsuccessfully to wipe the moisture away before the introduction.

"Pepe this is Margot's friend Janine and the proud originator of what she's called 'Janine's Double Death Spag Bol'," says Doug.

"Nice to meet you, Janine," says Pepe, visibly taken by her earthy beauty but relieved to be eye level with a woman for the first time in ages.

"And you," says Janine, rushing off to check on the garlic bread in the oven.

The evening begins with the usual doses of segregated male and female conversations but eventually the four are slurring their words across the stocked dining room table. All have red teeth that resemble bloodied fangs having indiscriminately tucked into three and a half bottles of wine.

"I think that meal might be the end of me," says Doug, leaning backwards and tapping his stomach that he has forced out.

"That really was a fantastic meal Janine, thank you," says Pepe.

"Really very easy I promise," says Janine, leaning over to tap Doug's stomach who flinches back to an upright position.

"Anyone like some coffee?" says Margot, rising from the table.

"Let me do that," says Janine. "I'm the visitor, remember."

Margot sits back down and laughs then has another gulp of wine. All their faces are merrily glazed over while the music softly intrudes in the background.

"Well if that's the case then I'll have to give you a hand," says Pepe, picking up the salad bowl and a few pieces of unused cutlery.

"Well dear, I suppose we should just relax in our own home," says Doug, sending Margot into further drunken hysteria.

In the kitchen Janine scrapes the remainder of food into the dustbin while Pepe fills the kettle.

"So are you enjoying staying here?" says Pepe.

"They really are fantastic people. I had never met Doug but heard loads about him. He's a wonderful husband."

"Are you working at the moment?"

"Yes I am. I'm doing some acting work."

"What kind of acting?"

"Do you always pry into other people's affairs?"

Pepe doesn't know what to say as Janine's glazed expression has been replaced by a wincing stare straight into his eyes.

"I wasn't, I mean, I was just asking questions."

"Did you think this was going to be a hot date? Did you think I'd fall head over heels for a little toad like you and that we'd end up fucking in the toilets? Did you really believe that someone like you would have any sort of chance with someone like me? Did you?"

Janine walks up to Pepe and places her hand around his neck squeezing until her nails are one Newton away from breaking the skin.

"You're a pathetic little man. You're nothing compared to Doug and I suggest you stay away from him. All he talks about is what a burden you are as a friend and how embarrassed he is to have you around."

"Doug wouldn't do that," says Pepe, his eyes filling with tears while the steam from the kettle rises above his head.

"Why do you think he invited you? It was so he could make fun of you and your new shirt."

Pepe pulls free from her grip, wipes his nose with his forearm and salvages his coat from the flimsy rack. He leaves and in their drunken joviality, Doug and Margot fail to notice until Janine informs them that he had to leave because of some commitment he had early the next morning. Another wine bottle follows until the three are scrunched together on the couch like puzzle pieces, allowing the music to dominate the mood and staring at the ceiling.

The noise of a person arriving home radiates from the upstairs flat, the thud of footsteps ascending wooden stairs arousing everyone. The clamour subsides momentarily until the footsteps are heard directly above their heads. Janine turns the music volume higher seconds before there is a creaking echo in the corner above the damp patch. In the next second the ceiling gives way and a human form falls through along with a flood of rubble. The form buckles when it hits the lounge floor, the crack of a broken bone sobering up the inhabitants with a whiplash.

She is a small elderly woman and screams hysterically as she clutches her ankle, her eyes visibly swelling inches above her face. Doug jumps to his feet to help her while Margot telephones an ambulance. She is bleeding in a number of places and her neck looks as though it is set at an abnormal angle.

"Just keep still," says Doug, stroking her forehead with his fingers and shifting bits of masonry from her body. He looks down at her ankle and winces at the sight, struggling to hide his expression from the purple headed victim. The bone of her ankle protrudes through her flesh, the skin torn and in tatters. There is surprisingly little blood and the exposed bone glistens in the artificial light.

The ambulance arrives quickly and gently stretcher the woman before shuttling her off to hospital. Doug rides along to make sure she's okay while Margot tries to contact her husband who is apparently on a night shift. Janine fishes through the rubble, cleaning up the debris that now decorates the newly decorated lounge. And the streetlight flickers while a passer–by kicks his toe on a raised piece of concrete, blissfully unaware of the happenings within.

CHAPTER 13

Be Bee See

"This is the first sign of dissent against the Mugabe regime as the Zimbabwean president spends his final days as the country's leader. There is renewed hope as the election draws to a close, the opposition supremely confident of a resounding victory. This is Leonard Sayer for Sky News," finishes the news bulletin ending with an intrusion of smiling faces all peeping past Leo at the camera as though it were a strange species.

"So that's your friend?" says Janine, eating from a tub of chocolate mint ice–cream.

"Are you eating ice–cream in the morning?" says Doug, still in his pyjamas and evidently relieved to be lazing about on a Saturday.

"He's quite good–looking," says Janine, hearing Margot getting out of bed in the other room.

"He's married," says Doug.

"He's still good–looking." She scrapes the bottom of the cardboard container. "But not a touch on you, Doug."

"Did you like Pepe?"

"I can't say he was really my type and, for the record, I'm not looking to be set up."

"It wasn't a setup, just a gathering of friends."

"He was like a dog on heat when we got to the kitchen. I had to actually restrain his advances. I even grabbed him by the throat."

"Pepe? Surely not? He's about as unassuming as you get."

"Well it must have been the wine or something because he certainly made his intentions clear. Have you spoken to him?"

"I've called a few times and only got his machine. He hasn't called back."

"Listen, Doug, I don't want to bad–mouth a friend of yours or anything but he said something that wasn't quite acceptable, if you know what I mean. Don't tell Margot–"

"Don't tell Margot what?" Margot emerges swollen-eyed in blue vertically stripped pyjamas.

"That I ate all the ice cream," says Janine looking sternly at Doug and jumping up to greet Margot. "Coffee on this fine weekend morning?"

"I can't," replies Margot. "We don't have time. Kim and

Steve are having a champagne breakfast today and we're already late."

"Oh my God," says Doug. "I completely forgot. How much time do we have? Never mind, I'll be ready in ten minutes. Come on, Margot, we said we'd be there."

Janine scratches the side of her head, her expression dropping. After Doug departs for the shower, Janine leaves and shuts her bedroom door behind her. She had planned to take the two of them for a picnic in the park; a surprise thanks to let them know how much she appreciates their hospitality. But now they were going to Kim and Steve's to make polite conversation and pretend to be the perfect couple. Janine's calm once again supervenes as she discontinues brushing out her curls and lights a cigarette in the house. She knows Doug and Margot don't smoke regularly and she does not try to hide the smell.

On their way out, Doug smells the stale cigarette smell and looks quizzically at Janine who looks away in disdain. Doug lets it go and departs, Margot following seconds later but not before kissing Janine on the cheek as a farewell gesture. There wasn't even an invite. She pulls on her knee–high leather boots and applies her make–up. While she's getting ready the telephone rings and she lets the machine answer it. The voice is Leo's calling to say he'll be back in three days' time and has a new number. She deletes the message and leaves, glancing momentarily at the hole in the wall and slamming the door shut. Seconds after she returns to smash a pane of new glass that Doug has recently purchased for the kitchen door. She then stomps on the glass until each piece is ground into a million miniscule pieces and vacuums the mess up pouring the plastic Dyson contents into a brown paper packet and putting it in her bag.

The day is annoyingly bright and she haphazardly puts on her sunglasses and hails a cab, the driver absurdly pleased to be picking up a woman in this attire. She barks the address to him, lighting another cigarette and blowing the smoke directly into the cab. She makes a call, her tone in complete contrast to her mood as the driver enjoys the generous cleavage in the rear–view mirror.

When she blows in at Mike Reef's studio apartment in south London he acts pleasantly surprised even though he knew of her imminent arrival. She exits the cab throwing a twenty into the slit of the window and walking towards Mike who still remains in his slippers and tracksuit pants. He hasn't got a shirt on and his hairy stomach hangs well below the line of his tracksuit pants which are already below where they should be. Janine leads him into his own home, the squeaking of her leather shorts exciting him to exhaustion.

Once inside she removes her skimpy top to reveal her breasts. "You were right, Mike," she says dropping to her knees and pulling his pants down. "I needed to be taught a lesson and now that you have taught me this lesson I want to make sure I never make the same mistake again."

"I knew you'd see the light," says Mike, breaking into an instant anticipatory quiver as she takes him into the warmth of her mouth. The event is over quickly which suits both of them. Janine goes to the toilet to spit out the load while Mike gets a few grams of cocaine from his cabinet.

The apartment is messy but brand new with an excess of

electronic equipment. Cameras decorate the walls and shelves along with palmtops and wires.

"I know why you came," says Mike, cutting a line of cocaine with his credit card. "You want the work. Well as I said before you've nothing to worry about. You were a good little girl and Mr M loved you so things will start as soon as he's back in London."

He snorts a line which immediately induces a dabble of sweat on his forehead, exactly like the kind that dripped on Janine's back in the studio. She emerges from the bathroom, still with half her clothes missing and dives straight into the feast of white powder that now adorns the glass table like a dirty tablecloth.

"I'm staying today," she says sucking a wallop into her brain and closing her eyes tightly. "And tonight."

When Doug and Margot return, the house is empty and disturbingly quiet. An unnerving breeze blows through the slits of plastic that flimsily patch the hole in the ceiling. Doug, at first opening the door for Margot, beckons for her to stay back as he creeps into the murky corridor. Each of his steps creak and he tries to dispel his concern by walking quickly into the lounge and turning on the light.

"It's okay," he says throwing his keys onto the bookshelf. "Something just didn't feel right."

Margot walks in and collapses on the sofa yelling for Janine. No reply comes bellowing from within. "Where do you think she is?" asks Margot.

"No clue. Maybe she's at a movie or visiting friends. She'll be back later. We mustn't treat her like a child."

"She doesn't have any friends in London and she hates movies."

"It's not our role to police her every move. She can do what she pleases. She is an adult you know."

"Shall we have a bath together?"

"I was going to visit old Mrs Denerich in the hospital this evening. Take her flowers. Didn't we discuss this?"

"No, but you go off and play saint. I'll wait for Janine."

"So you don't want to come with me? I shouldn't be too long."

On the way to the hospital, Doug calls Michelle who coincidentally answers the phone in the bath.

"This is a surprise," she says.

"Sorry to call this late," says Doug, realising his seatbelt isn't buckled. "How was the interview?"

"They offered me the job but I turned it down. Couldn't really picture myself slapping ludicrous make–up all over my face and strutting up a catwalk as though there's something stuck up my arse. What are you doing?"

"Driving to St Leonard's and trying to find some flowers."

"So you're in the neighbourhood. There's a flower shop just around the corner from the emergency ward. Easy to spot and I think it's still open although you might not get the freshest. Do you want to visit when you're done?"

A car's abrasive hooter interrupts the answer and Doug swears under his breath, having failed to signal whilst changing lanes. He puts his seatbelt on and turns off the radio.

"Sure. You won't be asleep?"

"Doug, I just got up. You know my hours. Are you hungry?"

"I couldn't eat a peanut. We were at a champagne breakfast this morning that turned into a feeding festival. At this rate I'll be joining the Sumo little league sooner than I had envisioned."

"You couldn't put on an ounce of fat if you tried. Did you go with Margot? Silly question. So you don't want me to whip up my favourite: takeaway?"

"No thanks, I'll only be a while. It'll be difficult explaining hanging around a hospital for the entire evening."

When Doug arrives at the hospital there is a commotion outside between the father of a pregnant teenager and the limp armed boyfriend. The girl looks no older than fourteen and the boyfriend nonchalantly smokes a cigarette, blowing the smoke in the direction of the father who is being held back by two stout female orderlies. Doug weaves through the rabble, spotting the flower shop and running towards the seller who looks to be closing up. There is one bunch remaining, bitten to pieces by bugs and broken from a hundred fingerprints. Doug persuades the shop owner to reopen the shop and pays him ten pounds for the bunch. After a brief rearrangement and a dose of manual pruning the flowers are in presentable shape and Doug proceeds to the ward.

The interior is as most hospitals: shiny and smelling of disinfectant with colourless walls and stern nurses. The clientele in the emergency ward look surprisingly sedate and consist mainly of homeless people seeking free drugs. An old man with a matted Rastafarian beard is banging on the glass threatening a small office official and falling down in the process. Doug proceeds to where he knows Mrs Denerich is and opens the door to the communal ward quietly, the soft hum of a television screen failing to entertain a fast asleep patient in a neck brace.

Mrs Denerich is sleeping peacefully, her hands folded across her chest and her broken ankle contained in a cast and propped up by a pulley. She is the only patient without a list of paraphernalia to decorate her side table and Doug places the flowers softly down beside her. The ruffle of the leaves startles her and she opens her eyes.

"I'm sorry to wake you," he whispers, crouching beside the bed. "I just came to see how you were doing. Has anyone managed to track down your husband yet?"

Her eyes are rolling but remain open, the Valium wearing off. She reaches out to Doug who takes her frail hand in both of his, moving closer and smiling.

"He won't be back for a little while yet, my dear boy," she says. "He goes when he feels the need and returns when he is ready. There is no way of contacting him."

Her benevolent face is peaceful and the regular nature of the departure makes Doug decide not to pry any further and just sit with her for a moment while she dozes. The pipes from her arms look too brutal for so feeble an arm and Doug smooths away the coarse hair from her brow.

"You are a good boy," she says, crying. "I wish I had a good boy like you."

At that instant, a male nurse noisily walks into the ward to discover Doug whose appearance evokes a special stare.

Once the obvious attraction is over the nurse reverts to duty mode and scolds Doug for visiting out of hours. "You will have to leave now, sir," instructs the nurse propping Mrs Denerich aggressively up for her next shot. "Before the doctor arrives."

Michelle's nomadic nature does not lend to visits and Doug's presence is somewhat of a surreal occurrence. On hearing the bell, Michelle answers and instructs him to go the top floor in the lift and to the penthouse suit, giggling at the precocious nature of the instruction.

She answers the door in jeans and a cut off t–shirt, kissing him on the cheek, painfully aware of the time she spent picking her casual outfit. This is the first time she has ever deliberated over any man let alone Doug and this strange hysteria unnerves her. She welcomes him in and quickly pours herself a straight gin in the kitchen then offers him a drink.

"How is the old lady?" she says, returning and handing him a glass of white wine.

"I don't think old people deal with pain in the same way as young people. It's as though she's already given up and that accidents like this are par for the course with every waking second after the event a bonus. I don't think I'm too good in situations like that, where you know you're the reason for the accident."

"That's exactly what it was: an accident. It wasn't your fault in the slightest and she knows that."

"The thing is that it is my fault. There was a damp problem

where she fell through and I had initially telephoned a damp specialist to look at the problem. The damp was the reminder and I forgot as soon as it was papered over."

"Did you paper over it or was it, uh–"

"Margot, no. It was Janine: a friend of Margot's who's been staying with us for a while."

Michelle is horrified that she cannot say Doug wife's name. The words are not physically able to escape from her mouth and she wonders whether this recent jealously will affect their platonic relationship. As she watches him from across the lounge, she notices how striking and unique his features are. His jaw line is strong and his skin jagged with stubble that accentuates his handsome smile and dominant eyebrows. His body is also well proportioned with a wide spread of shoulder width above a lean and muscular figure. But the things she loves most about his appearance are his hands: strong yet with long deliberate fingers and trimmed fingernails. For the first time in forever she wishes to be held by those hands; touched and forced into erotic submission.

"You've got someone staying with you and you've just moved in? Isn't that a little difficult?"

"That's what I thought at first but it's turning out to be alright. She really is a sweet girl and she's been more than helpful around the house. Margot is very comfortable with her around too: the two seem to have an invisible feminine bond."

"Why is she staying with you?" asks Michelle, taken by the news of the visitor.

"There was some drama in her life; some tragedy that was in the papers. As far as I know her boyfriend went off the boil and killed a few people. I don't know whether she was in any danger but the whole situation has definitely shaken her up."

"Do you know anything else about her?"

"I'm not one to pry and the situation is a lot better than I thought it would be so, for the meantime, while she rebuilds her life, she can stay. But it won't be permanent. I tried to set her up with Pepe but don't think they hit it off. But enough about my crap. How've you been?"

As Michelle delves into her insubstantial activities, she hates herself for the feelings flooding through her mind. Perhaps her loneliness is convincing her that she needs to love the nearest to her. Or that her yearning for him is purely physical. Either way she struggles to extract the image from her conscious, desperately embarrassed that it is all too apparent in her expressions. But Doug seems not to notice, content to share a drink and a chat with a friend. A friend who his wife doesn't know about. A friend who is an attractive female.

When Doug departs, he kisses her goodbye on her cheek and places a warm hand on the flesh of her side. She wills it to stay there a second later when he lets go and makes for the lift. When he is gone, she forces herself to cry to make her feel better but it only serves to make matters worse. She calls an ex–lover who is not home and then tries another who promises to be over before she's put the phone down. When he arrives she turns him away, much to his dismay which eventually spirals into begging and abuse. When she does eventually let him in the passion is brief and insipid and he lets himself out.

When Doug arrives home Margot is already asleep and Janine is not home. After a quick wash Doug climbs into bed and puts an arm around Margot. He is asleep quickly and dreaming of broken ceilings and stale cigarette smoke. This strange craving for a smoke wakes him and he finds himself rummaging through Janine's drawers for a cigarette.

When Margot notices his absence, she finds him sitting on the porch wrapped in a yellow blanket blowing weak attempts at smoke rings. She says nothing, just squints through the darkness and returns to bed.

CHAPTER 23

I Arm full Hint Tent

When Mike Reef wakes, he is alone, ensconced in his satin sheets having fallen into a drug–induced sleep with his partner for the evening. He has sweated most of the toxic substances from his body and lies drenched among a pile of Janine's clothes. He feels beside him. The sheets are cold yet her clothes are still there which means she hasn't left. He can't remember much of the previous day and now just wishes to extract his guest and get rid of the headache that thumps against his skull like the beating of a tin prison mug. As he is slowly rising Janine enters wearing one of his gowns.

"I made you breakfast, you love machine," she says not going any nearer to him.

"I feel like shit," he replies collapsing back down. "How much of that shit did we do last night?"

"It was the whole day and if I remember correctly we used your entire stash."

"Everything! The entire fucking caboodle. We should be dead!"

"You were fantastic."

"I was?"

"You couldn't stop. You were like a horny bull elephant. I didn't think a woman could come that much."

Mike is impressed with himself and jumps from the bed to smother Janine in his bulbous arms. The hair on his shoulders smells of urine and Janine reels playfully back.

"Steady there, Romeo, you've got breakfast to digest."

In the kitchen Mike notices that all his papers have been rearranged. The general discord is not out of sync with the rest of the place but his golden dollar paperweight is indisputably facing the wrong way. He knows that Janine has been rummaging through his stuff and turns to face her. She has a glass of orange juice in her hand which he slaps to the ground, cutting her hand and garlanding the white tiles. He then bashes her with the side of his hand and gets her in a stranglehold forcing her face against the kitchen counter and spitting with rage. For a second he recoils clutching his stomach and then continues to choke her.

"You thought you could go behind my back you little bitch!" he yells, squeezing her throat as she paws at his grasp, the blood from her hand smearing rainbow shaped patters on his outer paws. "You thought you'd contact Mr M and cut me out. Well that doesn't happen to Mike Reef because he always collects!"

Janine cannot speak as Mike wrestles her across the kitchen, dragging her with one hand on her throat and one ripping at her hair. He walks across the spilt orange juice to shove her into the fridge when he steps on pieces of broken glass that he'd taken such care to avoid. He again grasps his stomach and collapses to the floor letting her free.

"What the fuck is this?" he says, picking up bits of white glass that do not match the big portions of bright blue glass from the cup. He again winches, this time the agony more apparent and the discomfort more long–term. Janine re–gathers herself, relishing the opportunity to suck in air, albeit filthy used smoky air in an apartment with no open windows.

"It's glass, you pig!" she yells, keeping a safe distance. "Glass that you were meant drink. But no matter. I've already called Mr M and he, like me, has had just about enough of Mike Reef and his fucked up commission structure. Do you think we fucked the whole night long? Do you think your stomach cramps are a coincidence? Once you fell asleep it was as easy as smashing a baby's skull. Your mouth is not the only place where glass can hide."

Mike now makes an advance towards her and slips to the floor, his face slapping the moist surface and further lacerating his cheeks. From where he has been crouched on the floor the orange juice has become a light red and the lower back portion of his gown is soaked in blood.

"All those drugs inducing a small bowel movement?" says

Janine, casually wiping away her fingerprints. "I'll tell you what I did just in case you make it to the hospital and have to explain your symptoms. All I did was shove a few blocks of ice up your arse and down your throat. That's it! But these ice cubes were a little bit special because frozen inside were a million tiny pieces of glass that are now ripping up your colon. Not a special feeling?"

Janine leaves Mike and returns to the bedroom. She does a thorough check for video cameras and retraces what she might have touched. She puts her original clothes back on and takes the gown she has been wearing. She doesn't take the bed linen as she purposefully avoided spending time in the bed. On her way out she says, "Oh by the way Mr M says you needn't bother calling him again," and kicks him in his face. He tries to grab her leg but she effortlessly shakes him off. His bleeding has intensified and it looks as though there is blood oozing from his hairy stomach. He gets up, clutching his bottom and sobbing hysterically before crumpling into a ball, still breathing but in a state of unconscious shock. Janine leaves through the front door.

When she returns to what she now considers her home she believes no one is home. She carefully checks around the house before running a bath, pouring a healthy dollop of 'peace' scented foam bath into the tub. Margot's special foam bath. There is a note from Margot on her dresser instructing her to call as soon as she returns, the tone caring yet concerned. Janine picks up the phone but doesn't call Margot, rather dialling the number she memorised the previous day. A woman answers identifying herself as Mrs

Sayer and Janine immediately hangs up.

In the bath she masturbates to climax, the exertion of the morning's activities heightening the pleasure. When she is out of the bath, she continues her self–stimulation on Doug and Margot's bed, breathing in their collective smells and burying her head into the bulging pillows. With flushed cheeks she re–straightens the room and calls Margot, apologising profusely but offering no explanation. Margot is in the middle of a meeting and offers to talk later. Janine then calls Doug who is not available to take the call so she says she'll call later, not leaving her name.

Moments later the telephone rings, the noise startling Janine to the point that she spills ash onto the floor. Before she is able to make sure that there is no lit ember she answers.

"Welcome home," says Doug.

"How did you know I just called?"

"How many strange female voices are there in my life apart from Margot?"

"You tell me," says Janine, contemplating how *in* Doug's life she is.

"I was worried. Are you okay?"

"Yes, I was just–"

"No need to explain. Your business is your business. I was just worried about your safety, that's all. There are parts of London that are, shall we say, less than salubrious."

"Did you stay up thinking about me?"

"I'm just glad you're back, that's all."

"What time are you back tonight? I have a surprise for you."

{ ➥ ➥ ➥ ➥ ➥ ➥ }

Leo boards a plane on a rundown airstrip in the African city of Johannesburg after covering the lead up to the Zimbabwean election. He is spent after days of circumventing Robert Mugabe's security force, finding solace in the northern suburbs of Gauteng. He is pleased with himself and feels as though the story was one of his better ones. The plane is three quarters full and the air hostess makes him comfortable as he reflects on how the satisfaction of a well–covered story surpasses anything. And for a change he's missed his wife, now anxious to relax with her and purposefully steer clear of his infidelity pad that has kept him sane for much of his young married life. It's not that he actively seeks to be with these hordes of women behind his wife's back but rather that he acknowledges variety as an integral part of his make–up and the silent glue that bonds him to his wife.

Leo is asleep before a shaky take–off and woken by the air–hostess briefly afterwards with a hot towel and a champagne flute of orange juice. She clearly recognises him instantly, paying careful attention to his needs for the rest of the flight. The flight is overnight and Leo spends the time drifting restlessly between the on–flight movie and deep sleep. The seat next to his is vacant and his outstretched legs are disturbed when the air hostess steps over them to nestle beside him while the rest of the aeroplane sleeps. There is no noise par the drone of the engine and a few muffled baby cries from economy class. The two are alone in the row.

She leans across and whispers something about fucking him in the toilets, putting her hands beneath his blanket. Leo is so taken by the audacity of the situation that he lets it run for a while until she is blinking her excessive make–up just inches from his face and rubbing the outside of the bulge in his trousers.

"This'll sound really pathetic," he whispers to her, "but I'm just too tired to be in the mood." He fights the urge but eventually ends up saying, "Why don't you give me a call when you're next in London," handing her a card specially designed with his secret apartment's number printed on.

"I'm not in London much," she says, persisting. "And I'm a big fan."

Leo's efforts are futile and he leans back in the seat as her head disappears below the blanket. He feels her placing his hand on her breasts, forcing his fingers down the front of her stewardess top and squeezing his fingers around each. He notes their firmness and the rigidity of her nipple on his touch. She's at a slightly awkward angle and he moves her so that he is able to fondle her chest while she presses her mouth down on him. His mood is reflected by his penis that remains unresponsive for the first five minutes of petting. When eventually he is aroused he can feel her press her face right down so that his tip is well into her throat. She holds the position for seconds at a time and rubs the muscle between his testicles and his anus with her index finger. This seems to speed up the process and before long she is back to her duties having swallowed a modest amount of his semen. This puts him into a permanent sleep and suitably doesn't see her until he is disembarking on a chilly London morning. She winks, waving the card at him and he steps onto the platform instantly wishing he'd held onto it.

After the heat of Southern Africa, London greets him with the verve of a paralytic snail. A fine rain fails to dampen his dirty hair and short bursts of wind firmly reaffirm autumn's presence. His luggage is first off and he wastes no time in hailing a cab and heading home to the heart of Chelsea. In the cab the driver is chatty and immediately shunned by Leo who slumps in silence, disappointed in himself after the euphoria of the story.

This is the end; the end of justifying the need for other women. Doug and Pepe's words now ring clear in his mind and for the first time the love of one woman is enough. But maybe it's just the usual post affair guilt that's stirring up these emotions, albeit stronger than usual. Perhaps his friends will no longer respect him in the way they do if he changes his ways, despite their pleas. Perhaps that is the only reason they like him at all. The flood of thoughts entering his head induces a headache and he quickly calls his estate agent telling him to put his secret pad on the market. Instantly he feels better knowing that he has done the right thing and the sticky sensation beneath his boxer shorts is one he has experienced for the final occasion.

∫ ↪ ↩ ↪ ↩ ↪ ↩ ∫

Margot sits at her desk and is convinced that something is in the air. For the first time in God knows how long she is aching for sex. So much so that her back aches and a slight bout of nausea ensues. She tries to trace the source and merely puts it down to ovulation after struggling to nail down the longing between her legs. She's putting a storyboard together for a high street bank launching exchange traded funds and finds her hands resting innocently in between her legs. Slowly and deliberately she runs two fingers up her inner thigh and then summarily dismisses the notion once her eyes come to rest on the final frame and she tears it off, substituting the ending for a tag line in order to strengthen emphasis and save on media buying expenses.

Margot has lunch in the office cafeteria with a male colleague who she is fairly certain has a crush on her. Amidst the shine of metal trays and salad dressing bowls he offers to pay for her meal, the price drastically reduced from the company subsidisation. She politely declines and pays for her modest salad, settling into the seat he has saved for her. The cafeteria is full and she nods at select colleagues as she passes them in the urgency of eating. For a change she has time to kill but this doesn't stop her from wolfing down her meal while Donovan regales her with a story about jalapeno peppers that once came out of his nose.

After she has made her retreat, she spends half an hour browsing through expensive boutiques in a mall that previously housed the stock exchange. The shop assistant's polite as the clientele is minimal and feeding through the doorway like spasmodic showers of rain. In Paul Smith she catches a glance of a man through the half–open curtain of a changing room. He has his back to her and presents half his bottom which peeps around the bright blue curtain. She watches him try on designer underwear even though she knows it is not shop policy to do so and stares transfixed at his hairless behind. Her mind drifts to Doug's behind: harder and with cuter round bits at the bottom when a woman catches her, smiling while passing the scene.

She walks back to the office, once again in a state of fevered sexuality and almost completely disinterested at the thought of an afternoon's work. She decides to do something completely outrageous. Her hormones have her in a nasty stranglehold and she cannot resist the urge to call Doug, have a quickie somewhere in his office, the toilets perhaps, and then resume her duties. The thought scares her: what if Doug refuses outright. They haven't made love since buying the house and their initial exploits of christening every room in their old place seems to have completely vanished. She hangs up, the thought of rejection too difficult to stomach and the practicality of the situation too ridiculous.

The urge creeps upon her again as she begins to dial whilst passing a hairdresser. Before the phone rings she notices Leo wrapped in a protective gown, the cloth tucked right up to his neck, making him look like an ant heap with a head sticking out the top. She notices something else too; something which makes her hang up the phone. The salon is busy and stylists slide from patron to patron amidst the plethora of floppy wrists and colourful hair. At first she thinks it might be her imagination but then becomes convinced that Leo is playing with himself beneath the cover. No one is fussing over him apart from a skeletal woman who every now and then massages his scalp. When she sees his expression change and his hand stop moving, she hurries on, scarcely believing what she has just witnessed. She blinks, shakes her head and giggles a bit, glad to be relieved of her spontaneous urge. There's plenty of time for that.

When Doug returns home, he is again greeted by a silent home but this state only remains for a short while when Janine enters instants later. She greets him with a savage smile and before any words are exchanged hands him a brown envelope sealed with two flimsy elastic bands.

"This for the drug bust, Sergeant?" says Doug, offering her some wine.

"It's rent money," says Janine, brimming even more. "I hope it's enough. I looked at a few properties in this area in an estate agent's window and came to a guestimate. If it's not enough I can pay you more without any hassle at all."

Without opening the envelope Doug hands it back to her saying, "Janine, you know this is not necessary. We cannot accept this."

"You don't have a choice," she says, her face narrowing and moving closer to him. "Now tell me about your day."

Doug beckons again to hand her back the envelope and she places her hand on his folding it over the package. "I insist," she says.

"You can sort this out with Margot," says Doug, leaving the money in her hand.

When Margot returns Doug has just finished showering and Janine is prancing around the apartment noticeably pleased with herself. Margot dumps her bag in the room to find Doug facing the cupboard revealing the exact pose of the man in the dressing room. She saddles up behind him and places her hands under his arms cupping his pectorals and resting her head against the striations of his back. For a moment Doug lets her hug him and drops his arms to the floor. She moves her hands lower and is just about to reach his dark patch when Janine bursts through the door.

"Oh I'm terribly sorry," she says, backing out of the room. "I really should have knocked first."

"That's okay," yells Margot, retrieving the situation by rushing out of the room to join Janine while Doug finishes drying off.

"I have a job," announces Janine as Doug emerges to join the two in the dining area below the now adequately patched hole in the ceiling.

"That's fantastic," says Margot. "What are you doing?" She receives a scolding glance from Doug, whose wet hair is crumpled like paper above his head.

"I'm doing some acting for a small Japanese production company. Small bit parts really but well–paying and with the opportunity for further work."

"What kind of acting?" says Doug, breaking his own rule.

"It's sort of an art house collage with plenty of still shots and mood setters. The work is fun but, most importantly, I can justify my stay here by paying rent."

Janine goes to bed uncharacteristically early after an exhausting day leaving Margot slumped on top of Doug's thigh while the two watch television. Bleary eyed she sits up and tries to draw his attention away from the screen.

"I saw Leo today," she says sipping from a mug of water. "At the hairdressers."

"He must be back already. How is he? He hasn't called since he got back."

"Well I didn't speak to him I just spotted him from a distance while he was having his haircut."

Doug's silence and a knowing look reveal that he knows there is more to come. Margot waits patiently while Doug changes channels in order to metaphorically alter the subject.

"You know about this don't you?" she says, Doug looking purposefully confused. "You know about his little habit in the safe confines of the barber shop. What is it all about?"

"It's just his thing really. God if he knew I was actually telling you. He likes to knock off while he gets a haircut. He's done it since he was thirteen and has kept count ever since." Margot's inquisitive expression warrants an immediate answer. "About three hundred or so and he's only been caught a dozen times."

"Why didn't you tell me this before? Does his wife know?"

"This is a male-orientated topic; boys' chat. This is not something you discuss with your wife. Men brag about these sorts of things: I know it's pathetic and silly but it's part of our primeval instinct; it's just the way we are made," concludes Doug, blatantly aware of the juvenile wound he is attempting to leave bleeding.

"What else don't I know about?" says Margot, altering the timbre of the conversation.

"Nothing." He doesn't look at her.

"Is there nothing you're keeping from me because we've always sworn to be honest with one another?"

"You're paranoid. When would I have time for an affair?"

"Who said anything about an affair?"

"I don't want to have this discussion now. I'm tired."

Atypically Margot backs down from the topic and snuggles closer towards him, anxiously trying to dispel the trivial tension. Doug is responsive to her emotional and comfort needs but shuns her sexual advance by pushing her hand slowly away. "I have to be up early. I'm off to New York for business for a couple of weeks. It only came up today, I'm sorry."

Doug eases out from underneath her and makes his way to the bathroom. Margot hugs a cushion and turns the television off, sitting in silence and darkness while the tears wobble in her eye sockets.

When she hears Doug go to bed, she joins him and the two precariously hold one another while Margot remains secretly annoyed at not being told about the trip sooner.

In the other room Janine is asleep with her hand cupping the five slice wounds on her hamstring decorating her flesh like a cat's whiskers. In the morning neither woman hears Doug packing for his trip and he's out of house by the time Janine reluctantly slips from beneath the duvet. She's wearing a t–shirt and underwear and softly knocks on the couple's door. Margot stirs and invites her in, rubbing her eyes with the back of her forearm and sitting crookedly up.

"Doug gone already? That's early, even for him. Want a tea?"

"He's gone to New York," says Margot lifting the duvet up to cover her naked body. "For a couple of weeks."

"And no one told me," says Janine biting on her teeth and sitting on the edge of the bed. "I mean what if I'd planned something for the two of you?"

Margot bursts into tears saying, "He only found out he was meant to go yesterday. One of those short notice emergency consulting trips. But I feel the same way."

Janine then climbs into the bed and takes Margot to her, pressing her smooth hair encased face to her free swaying breast. Margot sobs hysterically for a while and the spray of emotion surprises her, the usual resolution nowhere to be seen. Janine can feel Margot's warmth from her naked taller body radiating against her own. The two are friends but now something more that there is a mutual need. Janine notes how slim and firm Margot's board–like body is and how her dimensions are so much more elongated than her own.

For a second Janine backs away once Margot has seemingly finished crying and then presses her face forcefully against Margot's mouth. Margot is at first uncertain what to do, keeping her mouth still yet open. Then Janine pulls away again and continues to softly kiss Margot's mouth, biting at her lower lip and tracing circles around her teeth with her tongue. Margot says nothing, allowing Janine to explore her face, even reciprocating slightly as the physical contact begins to stir a pang in her belly.

Janine sinks to Margot's neck while her hands rest precariously on Margot's angular hips. She kisses her clavicle and then descends to meet her flat eye–shaped navel, purposefully having omitted Margot's willing breasts. By the time Janine is placing her face cogently between Margot's legs the anticipation has grown and Margot arches her back in orgasm clutching the covers and opening herself more completely. Janine maintains the momentum this time tonguing Margot more vehemently and placing moistened fingers inside her anus. Janine now stops and removes her shirt to reveal her rotund breasts in stark contrast to her tiny frame. She grabs the back of Margot's head and pushes her into her, rubbing her face and moaning in anticipation. Margot sucks on her toughened nipples like a baby, hesitantly participating in the aggressive sexual encounter. Janine then straddles Margot's shoulders, sitting down on top of her face and twisting to face Margot's feet so that she may continue to give Margot pleasure with her hands. The two climax and flop down holding one another while their breathing steadies.

Janine dispels any ominous awkwardness by nuzzling up to Margot as a young lover might. She kisses her faintly, tucking her hair behind her ears and assuming the dominant role. They make love again before Margot is forced out of bed to get ready for work. She leaves Janine in bed, slightly confused, clearly relieved to have released the physical build up. At work she is unable to think about anything else and, as the day bobbles on, begins to dread going home. Her betrayal of Doug sits at the forefront of her conscious and for the first time in her controlled existence she doesn't know what to do.

Doug's flight to New York is in stark contrast: uneventful without even a spatter of turbulence to liven the trip up. His early morning departure facilitates an early morning start, thrust straight into a client meeting before he is able to settle at the hotel room. The situation in New York also contrasts London, both management and employees tense and expectant as though the imminent failure of the company is the only alternative. Doug has a rushed lunch with a female colleague who is also part of the London consultancy and has been based in New York for almost six months. As she eats, he watches with interest how she only chews twice before swallowing each mouthful. It's as though to chew thrice would waste too much time. The concluding discussion at the overpriced Italian diner reveals a mutual acquaintance and, to Doug's surprise, this colleague and Michelle are friends.

When Doug retires to his hotel room later in the smoky evening of a New York autumn there is a note under his door. It's from Margot and he decides not to call back as it's probably too late: Margot's probably already in bed. After a long soak, Doug smokes a cigarette on the balcony and watches a rabble of twenty somethings stagger into a bar on the corner below. There is much activity on the streets tonight: children yelling at their parents, couples holding hands and even a runaway dog with lead following. Doug's time clock has succumbed to the jet lag as he flicks through the channels before slipping into a foreign sleep.

When he wakes, he notices another note under the gold-framed hotel door. This one is from Michelle who claims she will be in New York that evening so would he like to meet up. There is no number just a venue and a time so Doug, even if he wanted to, is unable to cancel or reschedule. He feels slightly better this morning having slept right through, the noise from outside conveniently dying down as the night wound to a close. He shaves quickly and deftly without nicking himself, the magnified circular mirror extending from the wall like an antenna providing a better than accurate reflection. It's going to be busy day he thinks to himself straightening his tie and thinking of Margot briefly before closing the door behind him and making his way towards the elevator along the rich yellow carpeted hallway.

Margot awakes with a start again realising she's late. She got home late the previous evening obviously avoiding the confrontation with Janine. To her relief Janine wasn't home but she wakes to find Janine lying beside her, eyes open.

"I'm going to be late," says Margot kicking the duvet free and trying to get up. Janine grabs her wrist and pulls her back down to the bed.

"Margot, don't avoid me." She digs her nails into Margot's arm. "I know you came home late because you didn't want to see me and I cannot accept that bullshit. So you know what I went and did? I went to a club and got a guy to take me home and fuck me."

"I do feel bad about what happened between us, Janine. I don't want it to affect our friendship. I think you caught me at a vulnerable time. I don't regret what happened but it has to be a one off."

Janine lets go of Margot's arm who has now stopped resisting. "It doesn't have to be that way," she says. "That's exactly why I fucked a guy last night. To show that we can have separate sexual lives and still be there for each other. I know Doug doesn't meet your needs and that's why I'm here.

To be with you when you need me."

"What goes on between Doug and me is our business."

"But it's not anymore is it? I'm involved now and unless you let your inhibitions go there might be situations beyond our control."

Margot is silent, not sure whether Janine has just threatened her. Janine tries to initiate sex, stinking of stale smoke and male sweat and Margot pulls solidly free, heading for the shower. The skirmish both excites and angers Janine who follows Margot to the shower climbing in with her and pinning her to the wall, placing a cupped hand in between her legs with a slap and forcing fingers into her dry cavity. Margot soon subsides and the two shower in aggressive harmony, walking the tightrope between pleasure and attack. The emptied shower gel bottle and water rushing over their mangled bodies provide the much needed lubrication and Margot exits just short of her orgasm. Janine finishes herself off in the shower yelling loudly while Margot dresses. Before Margot's departure Janine tiptoes to kiss her on the forehead and wish her a lovely day at work. Janine's soaked body, dripping in the corridor, is the last thing Margot sees before closing the door behind her and swallowing the tears on the way to work.

CHAPTER 33

Angst Acts On!

In the dim study of a square council flat a makeshift kettle in the form of a copper pot on top of a hot plate plugged into the chipped wall boils over, the water spilling in all directions. A man with a straight middle parting rushes in to discover the mess, salvaging the remaining water for his wash. The room is speckled with clothes and pictures, the carpet beneath peeping through at select points. In one corner of the room is a collage of pictures, some colour but mostly black and white amateur shots.

The man takes the water to the bathroom where colonies of moss dominate the porcelain panorama. He takes off his shirt and pulls his vest aside to wipe the warm water under his arms and down his neck. He has a small moustache which is assembled precariously below his miniature nostril holes. It covers a scar left by a dog when he was attacked in his crib as a child. Once he has cleaned himself, he brushes his hair neatly flat with a brown comb making sure to taper off each stroke so the finish is even.

A voice yells from the bedroom and he rushes to meet the request. His sister has defecated all over herself in bed again and he is forced to clean up the mess despite having just cleaned. He gathers the potty beside her bed and scoops the mess from around her before wiping her clean with the same warm cloth he washed himself with. She falls asleep while he wipes her, the television in the room her noisy comfort.

When he has finished, he combs his hair again and retires to the study where he hopes to be alone for a while. In a shoe box he flips through a disorganised leaf pile of notes, being careful not to make too much noise. He hides the shoe box behind the desk even though he knows his sister literally does not have the legs to find it. With his hands still dirty from fingering the money he scribbles a verse on a bit of paper then relieves himself sexually all over the floor, all the time transfixed on his collage on the wall. The first one was taken inside the club and is still his favourite. You're not allowed to take cameras into the club and he was thrown out for doing it but managed to salvage the film to sticky tape his masterpiece to the wall. It captures her almost completely naked, the club nights slightly obscuring the form, but, to him, it represents everything about his imminent future.

{ ↦ ↤ ↦ ↤ ↦ ↤ }

The set is made up to be a ship and even sways using hydraulic gears to create to genuine effect of being at sea. Some of the crew even feel seasick, the constant yet sometimes spontaneous rocking back and forth upsetting members who spend the afternoon clutching their guts. Janine is one of the few to be unaffected and leans from the bow clad only in a fish net. Mr M watches on, blank faced yet blatantly proud of his discovery. The morning involves a series of still shots of Janine in various poses on the ship, her natural curls accentuated to create the effect of a woman of the sea. It's easy work and she laps up the lens having trained formally as a model.

The afternoon is slightly more tricky as Mr M dismisses most of the crew who are ill and decides to shoot the scenes where the sailors attack Janine. He decides to roll the camera although the focus remains on still shots. Three hefty actors are meant to wrap Janine in the net, tightening it around her neck, her breasts and her upper thighs. They're then meant to ejaculate all over her as she tries to wriggle free. Everything goes according to plan and Mr M is jumping up and down at the artistic value of the shots when one of the men is having trouble getting it up. He barks something at Janine who takes him in her mouth, biting down hard enough to draw blood. He bashes the side of her head to release the clamp and Mr M sends two of his bodyguards to remove the man from the set with a medley of cuts and bruises.

Once the shots are captured and Janine has cleaned off, Mr M invites her into his car for a drink. Janine is anxious to get home to Margot but accepts. He politely opens the door for her and she climbs in, the interior fitted out with a complete bar and two opposite seats.

"You do good job," he says scratching his eyebrow and pouring her a drink. "I pleased. Market love work. Selling well." He reaches into his pocket and retrieves another envelope, Janine hiding her surprise at being paid more than the agreed amount. She glances at his crotch knowing that nothing comes from nothing, dropping to her knees and undoing his belt. The little Japanese man is too surprised to allow the thank you gesture, settling anxiously back in the seat for an impatient variety of failed attempts.

Janine sips her martini, her mouth dry, as Mr M buckles up and continues in his broken English. "What doing now soft. Lower end of porn market. Real money higher end. Phayze making new strides into harder market. Your choice. More money. Plenty. But hard work and long hours. Take time to think. Come Monday with decision." He begins ushering her out and she responds knowing that to talk amounts or details with him is futile. She knows all too well that everything he says is magnified: more money means bucket loads; Mike Reef disappearing means permanently; hard work means just that. But the thought excites her, now that she is comfortably settled in her new home.

Janine makes her way to the hospital which is a long way out of her way. She had called to meet Margot for lunch but she was unable to take the call so instead Janine decides to pay the neighbour a visit. The hospital is quiet for this time of the day and the hollowness of the wards echo as Janine clatters down the corridor clasped in a swollen overcoat. Compartments of sunlight greet her at each door as she peers in, examining the sullen patients. Towards the end of the corridor she comes upon the woman who fell through the ceiling.

The strange stillness in the room alters once Janine enters, her footsteps failing to rouse any of the patients. The old woman is asleep, the lower corner of her mouth drooping down and cupping a pool of saliva. Janine checks her watch and makes her way through the ward to the bathroom on the other end. The door is closed yet the bathroom is vacant and Janine locks the door behind her holding her breath to avoid the sick smell. From inside her overcoat she pulls out a nurse's outfit that she had worn in one of her scenes and deftly squeezes into it, pushing her breasts flat, a contrasting portrayal to the film. The bottom strains to cover her upper thighs and she tears her fishnet stockings free to expose her satin legs. She stuffs the torn stockings into her overcoat and hangs it behind the bathroom door before wetting the side of the bath.

When she emerges the ward is still silent and no one seems awake although she continues as a nurse would: checking charts, looking at intravenous bags and mulling over the patient lumps wrapped in the rigid hospital sheets. When she arrives at Mrs Denerich, she wakes her quickly by ripping free the cords inserted into her arm and ushering her out of bed under the pretence of a wash. The elderly woman is so disorientated that she makes a severe effort to comply, sitting upright and flinching from the pain. When she cannot physically get off the bed Janine lifts her free from the sheets. Despite Janine's small frame she manages with relative ease to carry the old woman to the bathroom.

Once inside she locks the door while still carrying the terrified woman who has now begun to tentatively question the situation.

"I usually get washed in my bed," says Mrs Denerich, her hands shaking as Janine climbs into the bath still holding her.

"You must learn to wash yourself now," says Janine. "The hospital is sick and tired of wasting valuable time on your kind, now stick your legs out."

Janine now clasps the woman under her arms as she uncertainly lets her crooked legs hang from beneath her hospital gown. Standing in the bath and facing the back of the woman's head, Janine lowers her like a child into a crib until her feet are level with the side of the bath, then suddenly forces her legs apart so that she is forced to take the weight of her body by standing on the sides of the bath. Janine, still holding her shoulder with one hand climbs out the bath, the woman grabbing onto Janine's wrist and beginning to cry in short choking bursts.

"Don't make a noise," says Janine. "Not now. Not ever."

When Janine shakes her hand free the woman has nowhere left to hold and her legs buckle, slipping along the cool smooth ceramic surface. Janine watches as she slips backwards her head meeting the bath with a sickening blow and immediately turning the porcelain crimson. The woman is motionless, her matted grey hair soaking up the chunks of blood that decorate the bath and her eyes closed. Janine is conscious that the noise might have alerted other hospital residents and quickly pops her coat back on and dashes through the remainder of the dazed patients. Once outside she cannot contain the laughter that has welled up inside her and giggles hysterically as she makes her way home.

❴ ↳ ↰ ↳ ↰ ↳ ↰ ❵

The restaurant is more like a bar and sits back from the hive of activity that surrounds the area. The smoke from within creates the misty effect as the patrons slump over dingy tables and sip drinks with no ice. When Michelle enters she struggles to see if Doug is already there and peers around as the people shift comfortably on their seats. He is nowhere to be seen and she is early so she orders a spritzer at the bar pointing to a table in the corner. She cannot resist asking the barman whether the place has changed ownership, her past experience in complete contrast and being completely aware that of all the places to invite Doug in New York, this is the best she can do. The barman is unsure and she abandons her quest settling for the drink. As she's leaving, he makes a comment about her breasts which she ignores.

To her relief Doug arrives moments later and she rises to greet him. He has a bemused expression when he kisses her and she meets his approaching question.

"I know what you're thinking," says Michelle, "but in my defence it was very different the last time I was here."

"How long ago was that?" asks Doug, sitting down once he sees a waitress heading in his direction.

"About two years ago. Used to be the hidden gem in New York: live Jazz, trendy crowd, a lot of character. Now it seems like the only character left is in the alcohol. Do you want to go somewhere else?"

"No this is fine. And plus it's near to my hotel so I'm not complaining. It's been one of those days."

"Not enjoying the trip?"

"It's not that. There just seems to be no harmony between New York and London and it's creating tension. Americans work in a different way. The Atlantic umbilical cord is more like a broken telephone wire. But enough of that, how've you been and what are you doing in New York?"

The question is sufficiently innocent but Michelle is eager to dispel any hint of an idea that she might have followed him here.

"I had this old ticket," she begins, "that I had to use before next month. I spoke to Gail – isn't that bizarre that we both know Gail? – who said you were in town, so I thought I'd pop over for a short break." The words reflect the innocence and Doug's expression seems to suggest that he thinks nothing of the sort. "And there is another reason."

"What is that?" says Doug, casually ordering another round of drinks after gulping down the first.

"It's nothing really. I don't want you to get all worried or anything but I'm having a slight problem in London. It's probably paranoia but I think someone is watching me; stalking me or just following me around occasionally."

For the first time Doug's expression does change and he puts his glass down, looking concerned and quizzical.

"I've received a couple of strange letters. At first I thought it might be you playing a joke but as I read further I realised it wasn't. They seem harmless enough but they're written as though the person writing them knows me. It's bizarre because the letters are almost love letters and written beautifully if I might say so. It's as though the person writing them is a distant lover from the Middle Ages and I'm their lost princess. So I thought nothing of it when the first one arrived, thinking it might just be an old boyfriend but then when the second one arrived I became nervous. And it's those nerves that made me believe someone followed me home the other night. That's the reason for my hasty visit to New York."

"Have you spoken to the police?"

"There's nothing to report really: the letters aren't threatening, in fact they're quite appealingly written. The cops would have a good laugh searching from a serial poet!"

"You're sure it's no one you know?"

"I have racked my brains and as you know there's not a whole lot to rack but it could be. I know I'm getting myself in a state about nothing but something about the situation unnerves me. I'm boring you with this."

"Not at all, I'm just thinking what you should do. I suggest the police. Do you have the letters with you?"

"No, they're in London. I did keep them in case. Let's drink some more."

When Doug wakes up his jaw is aching from sucking on cigarettes and the front portion of his brain feels as though it's going to burst from his skull. Lying next to him in his hotel bed is Michelle and the sight of light breathing beside him instantly sobers him up. It's early in the morning so he doesn't have to rush to work which means he tries unsuccessfully to fall asleep again. After a sip of water from the glass beside him he eventually drifts off only to wake, this time late and beneath Michelle's limp outstretched arm. For a second he watches her and traces the line of her arm to her body. He can see that she is wearing a bra and watches how the outer bulge of her rounded breast protrudes from the side of the light green lace. He manages to slide from under her arm without disturbing her and makes for the shower. He is so late that he fails to shave and is out the hotel door before Michelle has woken. For a brief second he contemplates writing a note and then disregards the idea closing the door mellifluously behind him and deciding to let his head clear before they speak again. For the first time he misses his disorganised home.

{ ⇥ ⇤ ⇥ ⇤ ⇥ ⇤ }

Leo feels as though he's fallen in love for the first time. His conscious fidelity has ignited an eccentric passion for his wife and the two share an ice cream in the bath after a romantic dinner followed by soothing sex. Leo notices how perfect she is: clothed only in bubble bath with the top of her breasts peering above the foam like gorgeous frogs. They sit facing each other and he soaps her foot, handing her the soap to return the favour. They share a glass of wine from his expensive collection and laugh at one of his faltering impersonations of a fellow reporter he works with.

Although it's late Leo decides to give Pepe a call, not having spoken to either Doug or Pepe for a long while. Despite his wife's coy pleas to come to bed he puts on a gown and calls from the lounge. The phone rings for a long time before there is an answer.

"Hello."

"Pepperino Pepperoni! How goes in the land of saddled horses and prison women? Where've you been, my little friend?"

"Leo," Pepe's voice creaks, lacking its usual gregarious naivety. "You're back."

"Of course I'm fucking back and I've got news for you and the Dougster. Where is he anyway?"

"He left a message saying he'd be away for a couple of weeks in New York."

"Well the three amigos will have to ride again when he gets back. I've got news for you sailors. Are you okay?"

"Yeah, fine. Just tired I suppose. I'm going to stay with my parents for a few weeks. I'll give you a call when I get back."

The conversation is over as suddenly as it began and Leo is left staring at the receiver dumbfounded. He knows something is wrong and decides to wait for Doug to return before figuring out what is up with Pepe. It unnerves him slightly, Pepe's lacklustre tone, and he places the receiver down before frolicking through to the bedroom and into his wife's loving arms amidst the floral hangover of a bedspread. They don't make love again but rather hold each other until the gift of sleep is bestowed upon her and Leo is left staring at her shiny forehead in the relative darkness. Although he is in some way proud of his new direction he regrets his actions and somehow wishes he could tell his wife but justifies it as another selfish act of self–gratification: not only would he ruin the reuniting of two lost souls but the motive would be wholly to relieve his guilt. It's time to move on: a Leopard can change his spots!

{ ⇥ ⇤ ⇥ ⇤ ⇥ ⇤ }

Margot knows she can't avoid Janine forever despite her recent spate of good fortune and resolves to treat the experience as a new millennium expression of femininity, opting for frivolity over the culpability of disloyalty. Janine is painting a section of skirting board when Margot returns home from work and Margot greets her, approaching her boldly and kissing her on the cheek. Janine makes for her mouth but Margot stops her face with a forefinger, her expression mischievous and potentially suggesting later. The act serves to dispel the tension and it's just like old times again: the two laughing over a glass of wine complete only with take–away Thai. The room is filled with tactility yet remains of an unsexual nature and with harmless intent, lingering fingers and moist palms washed away with the Tom Yum Goong.

The early hours of the morning arrive and Margot traipses

through to bed, half drunk, once she believes Janine has passed out on the sofa. She passes out fully clothed but not before wringing her shoes free from her feet and rolling into the cover. Dreams come quickly to Margot and are quickly dispelled when she awakes to Janine climbing in beside her. At first she takes Janine into her and then stops.

"Not tonight, Janine," she whispers in the darkness. "Let's take this slow; let's adjust."

Janine says nothing and continues to wriggle in before Margot pulls up her feet and extends her legs against Janine's stomach, forcing her from the bed. Janine stands up and leaves, slamming the door behind her.

It is still dark and Margot dreams that she is being tied up. Her arms are above her head and she feels she cannot move them down: a cold metallic object preventing the movement. Fantasy becomes reality becomes fantasy when she realises Janine has handcuffed her to the bed post and is standing above her, clad once again as a nurse, the outfit fresh with the old neighbour's terror scent. Margot tries to cry out but is promptly gagged with a used pair of Janine's knickers. Margot still has her legs free and begins thrashing the lower half of her body around, forcing Janine to leave the room and return with an extension cord, harnessed with great difficulty to tie each one of Margot's legs to a corner foot of the bed.

Margot stops wriggling when the effort becomes too much and reflects on the hilarity of the situation when Janine retrieves a whip. Janine can see Margot is laughing and proceeds to whip her stomach so that dark thick pink lines appear on the flush exterior. Janine then straps on a large yellow dildo and squirts a load of lubricant all over it, the puff of the tube signifying its exhaustion. She briefly licks Margot between her legs, biting on one of her labia and spitting at her groin. She then lifts Margot's torso and places a pillow below her so that it is raised at an angle that presents her anus. With one decisive thrust Janine plunges the object deep inside Margot's arse and immediately begins thrusting at her. Somewhere during the act Margot stops crying and comes so violently that the explosion is enough to force Janine from inside her. Janine stops and unties Margot's mouthpiece, snuggling in next to her yet leaving her bound for the remainder of the morning.

{ ⇥ ⇤ ⇥ ⇤ ⇥ ⇤ }

Michelle is still in the hotel room when Doug returns, the sun already set and the weekend's activities fittingly underway. He loosens his tie as he disintegrates onto the bed beside her. He places his arm over his face so that the front of his elbow cups it like a boomerang. Michelle awkwardly touches his arm.

"Rough day? About yesterday," she begins immediately, "would you like a drink? Do you want to talk about this now?" Her nervous muddle of questions touches a soft spot in Doug's being and he relents.

"Can you order me something with too much ice and no alcohol," he says peering around his arm and smiling for the first time that day.

The two are settled: Michelle cross legged onto top of the made bed and Doug sitting upright in a gold sleeved chair.

Each sips tentatively waiting for the other to start.

"What's happened, happened," begins Doug, "there's no going back now. The only thing we can do is discuss where we go from here. This is the lamest most adolescent excuse but I can't even remember what went on last night."

"Doug, I sat here the whole day contemplating what to do. It was a strange night for me: I'm not used to feeling alone and scared; I don't usually need anyone on an emotional level. As the day wore on the events from last night began to come slowly into focus. We were both drunk and somehow we moved our festivities from the bar to another to another to your hotel room. One thing led to another and we're still here, you having endured a day at the office and me having searched my soul for a reason not to lie to you."

"I think I'm more confused than when I woke up next to you this morning."

"I wanted something to happen. I mean I didn't set out with that intention but when I was up here with you in a foreign country, I wanted us to be together. And the whole day I wanted to lie to you and tell you something happened but I couldn't; I couldn't be dishonest to a man I've fallen in love with."

Doug gets up and holds Michelle as she convulses into tears. She knows she risks losing him completely but could not continue living with that knowledge inside her, eating away her cells like corrosive caustic soda. She had been strong for so long but it was all too much.

Doug leans away from her and kisses her on the forehead. "You are one of the most important people in the world to me," he says. "And I do love you. But nothing can ever be.

I've sworn to another person and my heart will always be with Margot. The number of times I've been tempted and wished something would happen between us, God only knows. But I'm glad it hasn't. Not only because I haven't betrayed my soulmate but because you and I have preserved our more than special friendship. I would never want to lose you to a silly affair."

Michelle again spends the evening in Doug's hotel room and, despite his restless sleeping patterns, he holds onto her for the entire evening, keeping her warm and safe while a heavy thunder shower erupts outside and the swollen leaves fall to the floor, leaving a moist yellow and red carpet.

CHAPTER 43

Railed freed Damp Shin

London's winter drizzle unceremoniously crusts the row of Victorian properties covering them with a fine film of water and darkening the ageing orange brickwork. The wind picks up, strengthening the drizzle's resolve, the liquid slits becoming angered swollen scattergun globules. The bay windows receive the brunt of the lashing, jutting out: in vain defiance against the inanimate invasion, peeled paintwork delaying the inevitable rot. One or two lights in the street flicker and then shine brightly as day becomes dusk and premature darkness silently fills the spaces not inhabited by the rain.

Doug is on his way out and kisses Margot on the cheek proceeding to don his suede jacket and fish through the pile of keys haphazardly embroidering the kitchen counter. He takes his car keys off his house key ring and sloppily throws the loose black plastic headed key back into the metallic mess. He leaves and then returns for a scarf and leaves again not repeating his goodbyes.

He catches the tube into the city knowing he'll be consuming a fair amount of alcohol: nights out with Leo are seldom any different. Yet that fills him is a sense of keenness. He hasn't seen his old friend in a while and a night out seems like the perfect return to normality after his shenanigans across the Atlantic.

When he exits the tube station an arrow of cold air blows straight through his bones and he wishes he'd worn another layer, always stubborn and refusing to accept the advent of cold weather. Leo is predictably late and Doug makes himself comfortable in an upmarket coffee street across the road, where he can look out for Leo's panicked arrival.

He's been back for a few weeks already and still the events of his business trip haunt him. He feels as though his moral fibre had begun to degenerate. Maybe this is what happens to a person his age; perhaps this is why so many older men ending up running off with their secretaries. But despite the rocky patch he still does love Margot and justifies this love by his refusal to be with Michelle.

When he returned the house was empty even though it was a weekend. Once he had finished unpacking Margot returned home laden with groceries, looking bedraggled after being trapped by the first of the winter storms. On first eye contact there was clearly something wrong and the polite hug illustrated each's lack of desire to talk about their situations. Janine was away on a shoot in the south of France which gave the couple time to themselves most of which they spent apart.

Doug spots Leo flipping open his latest mobile phone and rushes out to greet him before his phone rings, leaving a note on the bent table as he departs. A warm handshake is exchanged and the two make their way for a drink in the upstairs bar at Sugar Reef before proceeding downstairs to the club. At the entrance a woman is accompanied by two bouncers possessing all the correct traits: monosyllabic responses, sloping foreheads and tattooed forearms the size of Bigeye Tuna. The woman is probably attractive beneath her layers of affected makeup and cocks her head as she notes the two good looking gentlemen in front of her. Leo pretends to know her which thankfully doesn't damage the visual rapport they have already generated as she calls them from the back of the queue to enter.

Inside, the DJ downstairs is styling his mixing, drowning out the almost elevator eighties classics that adorn the ears of the sparsely spread out patrons at the bar. Doug and Leo discard their coats in the coat room and make for one of the many available tables signalling to a waitress even before they have settled. Doug unwraps a fresh pack of imported Peter Stuyvesant Extra Mild and lights one with the complementary light blue matchbox sitting in the ashtray like a hors d'oeuvre.

"When did this all begin?" says Leo trying hard not to

notice a dark haired woman noticing him at the other table.

"You know I always have a couple when we're out."

"Yeah but a couple usually takes place after the tubes have stopped running and the shot invasion is well underway. That habit will spank you before you know it. Is Pepe coming tonight?"

"I must have left over a dozen messages and he hasn't returned one."

"He's gone to his parents for a while. Something's up with him."

"I don't think I've not spoken to him for this long since we met. The last time I saw him was when he came around for dinner. He was deliberating what shirt to buy beforehand."

"Ah yes, I was meant to help him and couldn't. For once it was a genuine excuse: I had to fly out to Johannesburg on short notice. Do you think he's pissed with that?"

"No, I spoke to him during the ordeal and he seemed fine at the meal. It's not like him to be pissed at anything or anyone so I can't understand it. He seemed to be hitting it off well with Janine."

"That's right, your sex machine of a house guest. Maybe the two have eloped and are raising funny looking children in a village near Puerto Rico."

"Do you know when he's back?"

"Not a clue. We'll have to form a task team and launch an assault on his premises once he's back. Get to the bottom of this mystery and then slap him silly for changing."

The two start drinking shooters earlier than planned and launch with apple schnapps which makes Doug gag and Leo wince like a schoolchild who has just eaten a rotten mulberry. The club opens and the two totter down the stairs and into the dimly lit area filled with leopard print and cigarettes held aloft. Doug has already smoked half the pack and has barely extinguished one before lighting up again. On the way to the toilet Leo is cornered by three females who recognise him from the television. Doug is accosted by a small chihuahua–like female with sparkle all over her face and a waist so narrow she could probably wear her watch around it. During his getaway he leans across to see Leo tapping his wedding band and disappearing into the gents.

"Am I hallucinating?" says Doug once Leo returns, drying his hands on his trousers. "Did you just tap your wedding ring and tell those fighting females you were a married man? I didn't even know you owned one."

"Well I took a long time to find it again but it was somewhere between my VHS collection of Little House on the Prairie and my leg warmers."

"What about the pad?"

"It's on the market. I'm a new man now; a one woman man. I was getting too old for this sort of nonsense anyway. And things are good between us; really good. We're even going to retake our vows."

"Good for you, man; I'm pleased."

"What about you and Margot?"

"We're going through a bit of a weird patch lately. I think it's adjusting to the new apartment and not seeing much of each other what with the respective piles of work."

"Make the time, my friend, make the time. Falling in love for the second time is better than the first."

Janine has returned early. Most of her physical injuries from the shoot have healed or are healing. She sits in the corner of the club wearing purple rimmed sunglasses and a dark, straight-haired wig. She sips on a Sea Breeze and dismisses a city banker with a pink tie trying to pick her up. As the evening wears on she watches what Doug and Leo are drinking, occasionally talking to a stranger so she doesn't stand out.

At half past midnight the club is heaving at full capacity: both sexes gyrating on the dance floor and blowing bucket loads of money on copious amounts of alcohol in the form of imported beers and exotic cocktails. Doug and Leo surround a small table in the chill out area and are harmlessly talking to two women. Janine leans over the bar and lets a generous portion of cleavage flop in front of an underweight barman like the rolling out of an electoral poster. He ignores her and struts off with a gay swagger to serve a spiky haired androgynous female at the other end of the cluttered bar counter. Janine again exposes herself to another barman who quickly approaches, his eyes struggling to break away from the matching mounds.

"Do you do deliveries?" she says, leaning further forward so that her face is inches from his and rolling out her tongue to lick his lips. Like an adolescent he lunges forward trying to shove his tongue in her mouth until she is forced to stop him. "I need a favour," she continues. "I need you to make a delivery for me."

"We can't leave the bar, baby face. That is until closing

time and when that time comes, I'll be more than happy to make an express delivery." The noise adds to Janine's disinterest as she blocks out the particulars of his speech.

"Here's a hundred pounds, you dumb fuck! Now listen carefully or I'll call your manager and tell him you were trying to swallow my tonsils on the job. Bring me a Millers and a Budvar and then get ready for your excursion."

When the barman arrives at the table, Doug and Leo are engrossed in conversations about the recession and the lack of quality noughties porn. The barman yells above the thump of the bass, "Those ladies over there would like to express their gratitude at having 'such a fucking sexy face to stare at on the telly' all the time. They sent these drinks over." He hands them a tray with the two beers and points towards the bemused faces of the women who accosted Leo at the toilets.

"That's very kind of them," says Leo, taking the Millers. "Tell them the gesture is much appreciated and tell them to keep watching and keep the ratings up."

"Okay whatever," says the barman, departing without an expected tip.

When he returns to where Janine is sitting to hopefully collect a further reward, he is met by a fist clutching his neck. "Why the fuck did you give the blonde one the Millers! I fucking told you to give it to the dark one!"

"He just took it," says the barman, trying to wrestle free and genuinely scared. "I took them over like you said and he just took one; I don't think he even looked at the bottle!"

Janine lets go and sits back in her seat, leaving the barman to recover his breath and his composure. In the fray Janine's wig has slipped slightly to the side and she quickly relinquishes her bar stool and makes for ladies. Inside, having just engulfed herself in a mountain load of cocaine, is the woman she approached earlier.

"Hey," says the woman, dragging the end of the word in unison with putting her arms around Janine's neck. "How'd you like the pills?"

"Do you have any more?" says Janine, ushering the dazed woman into one of the cubicles.

"I gave you twenty. And those are strong MDMAs, girlfriend, no rat poison, so you be careful: little bit of speed; little dab of heroin and a healthy dose of good old charlie to spank it all together. How 'bout you and me get a little better acquainted?"

"No thanks, I have business to attend to."

Doug doesn't notice Leo's vitiation because the descent is gradual. His verbal diarrhoea becomes incessant and on the verge of obnoxious. Doug is far too gone as well, the alcohol inches away from removing his balance. On his way to the toilet for the umpteenth time Doug almost stumbles over the placid Nigerian handing out towels and gum and decides that it is time to beg a cab driver to take him home. On his return Leo has a woman on each knee and is harping on about a story he did last year.

"Come on, mate," says Doug grabbing Leo's arm. "It's time we cut our losses and made a move."

"So you boys are together then? I always suspected it," says an accommodating blonde haired woman with a fake tattoo on her cheek and too much fake tan smeared below her hairline.

"I can't go now, man," says Leo. "I feel as wide awake as a pussy in a pussy slapping contest!" The girls laugh on cue. Doug is too wasted to realise that Leo might be resorting back to his old ways and says his goodbyes. He clambers to the top of the steps and miraculously remembers to pick up his jacket then takes a full twenty minutes to hail a cab. His efforts to remain awake fail when he wakes up outside his home with the taximeter more swollen than the journey warranted. He pays the driver and makes for his much sought after bed.

In the club Leo is being talked to by a dark haired woman with sunglasses and has his head in between his legs and his hands on his ears. Everyone and everything is screaming at him as if each inorganic object in the venue is now alive to accompany the sentient life forms and actively seeking to imbed themselves beneath his skin. The woman easily persuades Leo to leave with her after numerous appeals for home and the two jump in a cab. Janine directs the driver to a nearby hotel and then changes her mind after going through Leo's wallet to discover a card.

"Where's this number?" she says, kissing his ear.

Leo glances up and then slumps down again. "It's my pad. My own pad. My place I'm getting rid of; throwing away; letting go. For my wife. To be with her. No more pad. Sell. Sell. Sell."

"Where is this place?"

Janine has Leo's arm over her neck and precariously climbs the steps to his apartment past the sparkling new 'For Sale' sign that stands guard at the front of the property. Leo is grinding his teeth together and bites the inside of his cheek, swallowing the blood and instantly vomiting, the warm liquid bouncing off his stomach like a ping pong ball. Janine forces his head the other way so as not to get the mess near her, the resultant victim an ageing pot plant beside the cement banister.

She manages to get him upstairs and as soon as she's closed the door behind him his mood does a complete one eighty and he's once again the life and soul of the party: chatting vicariously to her despite not knowing who she is. In another second he's clutching his stomach and hurls through to the bathroom, frantically tugging at his belt buckle. With an ear to the door Janine hears his bowels explode, the noise double jointed. She casually goes to the kitchen to fix them both a drink.

"What did you say your name was again?" says Leo in rapid speech, emerging from the bathroom followed by the most awful reek. Before she answers she hands him a lit cigarette which he drags from although he never smokes. The sensation is in complete contrast to a first time smoker: no clenched lungs and violent coughing but rather sheer pleasure. In the kitchen Janine drops her tight fitting black trousers and turns around presenting two perfectly rounded golden cheeks dissected by a white g–string. While still smoking a cigarette Leo's visual appetite goes into overdrive, the sensual curves of her form drawing him nearer.

"I want you to spank me as hard as you can," says Janine, further extending her pose. "And then I want you to put that smoke out on my arse." Leo is too absorbed with the ecstasy and having gleefully escaped the digestive agony, failing to hear her as he drops to his knees to kiss her. He kisses the outside of each cheek with gentle, deliberate pecks and then suddenly launches himself at the gap, ripping her underwear off and lifting her light body so that she is draped over his arm. He then tongues her from behind, pushing his face right into her depths and pressing back with his arm. He wants to taste her and spreads her anus open with his fingers while he drinks her juices.

Janine reaches back to feel between his legs and confirms her suspicions to find no sign of rigidity. Leo looks down and giggles at his aberrant inability to get blood down to his weapon and then furiously continues to smother his face into her. She doesn't climax and succeeds in pulling herself free to stand in front of him. She pushes him to his knees and makes him continue from the front. Then she drops to the kitchen floor to join him and undoes his trousers while he lies back on the cold tiled floor.

His unresponsiveness lasts for a while but eventually due to Janine's persistence he manages to achieve an erection and she instantly forces him inside her. The sex begins as gradual and loving, Leo's eyes acquiring a soft reminiscent look, so much so that Janine is unnerved by staring into his pseudo drug induced loving expression and instantly bends over on all fours for him to insert from behind. The two fuck for an hour solid until Leo comes on Janine's breasts and collapses on the kitchen floor.

Without cleaning herself Janine rushes to her bag from the kitchen counter. She walks delicately with her back arched so as not to spill any of Leo's semen that decorate her breasts like barnacles on a velvet rock. Leo conveniently vomits beside himself and then sprays a pool of shit between his legs and Janine captures the scene with a deft finger. Then, avoiding the mess, she checks that her wig is in place and refastens her sunglasses, placing the camera on the antique pine breakfast counter ready for a series of three self–timer shots. Once the red light is flashing, she hurries to recline next to him making sure to avoid the mess at either end. The first shot flashes with her hugging him, her face to the side and obscured. The second she takes him again into her mouth holding her breath and the third perches on top of his face.

She then lights a cigarette and extinguishes it on her arse, the sizzle of melted flesh clouding the kitchen like steam. The remainder of the spool is used to capture her chest and arse and she uses the final shots for close–ups of Leo face. His pulse is faint but still present and she pours herself one more drink while she gets dressed. Before leaving she playfully spits on him then kisses his cheek, making for the door and twirling the spool between her fingers. The morning has arrived and the sky is light with no sign of the sun. She takes a deep breath of cold air and blows stream from her nose, descending the stairs towards the wet street below.

〔 ↪ ↩ ↪ ↩ ↪ ↩ 〕

The air inside the room is still, almost anticipatory in nature. The smell is clean yet with a hint of sordid activity. All the curtains are drawn which further accentuates the obscurity. The bed is haphazardly made as is the bed in the spare room.

Glass shelves lined with an assortment of exotic seashells adorn two walls of the bathroom. The soap has only just dried, caked froth coating its outer edges. A light suddenly turns on, instructed to do so by the timer, startling the visitor to such an extent that he lets out a meow–like yelp. The light struggles to gain momentum then shines bright, pasting his slight shadow against the glass panelling in the lounge.

He feels lucky to have got inside and vaguely relieved that she wasn't in, giving him real time to get to know her. At first he checks her fridge only to find half–drunk wine bottles and unopened preserves. He shakes his head. She should really be eating at least five portions of fruit and veg a day. He will tell her this when they are together. He sits on the rigid red sofa and tries to create an elusive comfort then scolds himself for dictating how she should lead her life. He loves her for her and that's enough.

In the bedroom he picks up a few of her clothes strewn around the room placing them neatly into a pile beside the overflowing laundry basket. He picks up a pair of her knickers and a large-cupped bra and shoves them into his blue wind breaker. He fluffs up her pillows and breathes her in, intoxicated by the tiny remnants of her scent and doughy eyed at the allure of her eyes in a picture on the set of drawers. He looks under her bed and carefully goes through her cupboard.

There is a television set and video recorder in her room and he pushes play, seating himself smoothly down on the light blue cover. He crosses his legs over, flattening his already flat hair. The picture leaps onto the screen and immediately the man feels sick. He sees her pleasuring another man on her knees and then allowing the filthy swine to impurify her with his manhood. He watches how the man dirties her person and how she enjoys it. Barely able to look, he is pleased when she extricates the man with aggressive words. She then faces the camera crying saying the words "It'll never be Doug," and then leans across the camera to turn it off. The static changes the comportment of the room completely.

{ ↪ ↩ ↪ ↩ ↪ ↩ }

"I'm home," yells Janine laden with bags, her sunglasses resting atop her bleached curls. "Anybody home?"

Doug emerges from the study to meet her, kissing her on the cheek and welcoming her back. He'd almost forgotten she was staying after her prolonged absence and in a strange way enjoys the thought of her return. The house decorating is almost finished and the place has transformed.

"What a difference," Janine says, handing Doug the heaviest suitcase. "I can't believe how much you've done. A new picture rail, the gloss and the new carpets have arrived!"

"A lot of the credit should go to you and Margot. You two did a lot while I was in New York. I just merely continued from where you left off."

"Hopefully," says Janine under her breath, making her way down the buttermilk and barley white corridor.

CHAPTER 53

Cope Son Collusion

The monotonous clatter of the dated clock fills the station with an impending imminence. The sun is not yet up and destined to be hidden beneath a modest layer of cloud. Pigeons rummage along the lines of the track occasionally launching into flight only to settle back amongst old toothbrushes, crisp packets and cans. The air is chilly but not cold, the biting sting a welcome absence for the three travellers who remain alone on the silent platform.

Doug is hidden beneath a Gore–Tex blue jacket and blows feebly into the air, adding to the fumes that rise from the track. He gets up from the bench disturbing Margot's now heavy head and goes for a meaningless wander along the track. Margot, still in the clutches of sleep's oblivion, flops onto the shoulder on her opposite flank, this one remarkably bonier and less comfortable. Janine doesn't stir as she turns the page of a glossy women's lifestyle magazine and continues chewing her gum in unison with the clock.

Doug looks over the billboards that titivate the station like obligatory jewellery. His efforts to stay awake have been successful and he scrapes the remaining crust from his eyes, lighting a cigarette and shielding the view from his companions. The taste is foul this early in the morning but he persists, anxious to take the edge off the day and step into break mode with a token amount of effort. The smoke from the front of the cigarette suddenly blows up his nostrils burning the inside and strangely making the remainder of the inhalation more bearable.

There is a poster advertising an herbal remedy for constipation and Doug can't help noticing the pained expression on the young model's face. Is it the stuck turd or the anguish at having to do the advert? Further up the station an organised whirl of graffiti is intertwined with more advertisements. Doug notices a billboard for the company he works for: the smiling male model with teeth more perfect than any consultant Doug knows. He's promoting the company's technology capability and wears an expensive suit surrounded by smiling gadgets. The accompanying cartoon multimedia all seem to worship him, bowing down to his superior knowledge of their genre. He has been unable to escape the graffiti acquiring a host of earrings, a curly moustache, breasts and an abnormally long penis which ends in a laptop's mouth beneath him.

Doug is so tired that the picture fails to even evoke a chuckle. He probably would have cared about such a blatant dismemberment of corporate identity a few years ago but now nothing, as though his decreasing ineptness is equal to his waning loyalty. He flicks his cigarette onto the train line which almost seems to ignite the line with a metallic creak signalling the approaching train.

But for a handful of weary travellers the train is empty. Most are slumped against jackets and handbags as they drift between dozing and yawning. A small Chinese man drools on himself; his mouth open as the stop fails to deter his mystical dream. The three easily find a comfortable seat and Doug ends up facing the two girls from across the grey table. Janine is awake and smiles at Doug who shrugs a brief smile back at her while fishing around his bag for a newspaper. Margot is fast asleep having resumed her pose on Janine's shoulder. The train shakes from side to side before a muffled announcement commences the journey.

An hour in, the ticket collector rouses everyone followed closely by the refreshments trolley. Doug has joined the sleep procession by dozing off and his book precariously rests atop his chest, falling to the floor as he scrambles to find the tickets. The girls are awake and both order a coffee which Doug pays for adding a black tea to the order. The day outside the rocking carriage is grey, the green manicured fields in stark contrast to the demure sky.

"No one for any food?" says Doug stretching.

"Coffee's fine for me," says Janine. "What time are we due to arrive?"

"Another hour or so. You sure this is all okay?"

"Of course! He'll be there to pick us up."

"If it's any imposition, we can easily revert to our old plan. It's not too far away."

A look of disappointment comes across Janine's face.

"We've been through this already, Doug," says Margot now more firmly in touch with the world around her. "I think it's very kind of Janine's friend to put us up."

Doug is not yet comfortable with the situation. The whole idea had been to get away with Margot for the weekend: a welcomed break and perhaps an opportunity to talk about the degradation of the relationship. He had booked the holiday to Devon last minute and the mention of the excursion sparked Janine to suggest staying with a friend of hers who ran a quaint bed and breakfast near where they were due to stay. The suggestion had initially been shunned out of politeness and a general desire to be alone, but after a lengthy discussion there was always only going to be one persuasive outcome. After all, the trip would be fun and a much needed break from the city.

On arrival, the three disembark onto another deserted platform. Behind the waiting area is a car park with a lone man standing with his hands crossed across his groin. Janine strides ahead and kisses the man on his cheek enveloping him in a polite hug.

"This is Jack," says Janine. "Jack used to look after me when I was a kid growing up in the area."

"Near here?" asks Doug.

"Ottery St Mary. Jack's been running the B&B ever since. Business been good has it, Jack?"

Jack grunts what sounds like confirmation before hurriedly loading the bags into his van.

During the drive Jack says very little, playing his country sounding music too loud and turning the heating in the van too high.

"We would like to pay for the accommodation," says Doug, leaning forward between Jack and Janine who reside in the front.

"That won't be necessary," says Janine quickly, turning around and facing Doug. "My family and Jack's have been doing each other favours for decades. This is no problem."

Jack seems not to hear the offer, remaining focused on his excessive speed and jerky breaking.

The lodge is compact and a little run down. The front is clad with fake gold decoration which separates black wooden panels. The name in bright white lettering greets the recipients along with an elongated plastic moose head. The moose is smiling or perhaps wincing. There are tiny green mould marks which are splattered over the black wood creating an almost camouflaged effect. The front door is the one redeeming feature: large and Victorian with an authentic round doorknob. A few daffodils and primroses remain on the outskirts of the building's perimeter.

Inside, Jack makes arrangements for two rooms next to one another. The establishment doesn't seem fully booked although dabbles of local patrons sit slumped at the four corners of the bar sipping half–empty pints and scoffing peanuts. Jack doesn't show them to their room, rather pointing and grunting in the general direction, instructing an Albanian porter with not an iota of English to escort the threesome. He does so gladly and humbly, bowing and gesturing onwards.

Inside, he accepts an excessive tip from Doug and backs out of the door still clutching the note. The room is modest with worn curtain linings and an awkwardly positioned bathroom which has recently been replaced and is in stark contrast to the bedroom where the wallpaper is flaking. Margot bursts into the bathroom in desperate need to urinate, dropping her trousers aggressively and letting off a little exertion wind as the noise of her spray fills the room. Doug shuts the bathroom door and flops onto the bed bouncing up a couple of inches, impressed at the bed's spring. The television doesn't work and Doug gives up trying to execute a miracle. He hears Janine settling into her room next door: the walls must be thin.

When Margot emerges from the bathroom her trousers are still unfastened and the look on her face is one of sheer relief. Doug notices a neatly shaven tuft between the harsh edges of each side of the zipper and realises she isn't wearing pants. It's a strange sensation because he feels as though it is the first time he's ever seen it and again strangely he wants it. Not a desire want but rather a fulfilling want. Margot settles on the bed next to him and he tries to hide the fact that his eyes are fastened upon her slim frame. It has been so long; too long he thinks. How does a man approach such a situation from the wilderness: kissing is certainly out of the question and if he were to feel her up the situation would either end in rejection or embarrassment.

Margot closes her eyes and turns away from him onto her side. Her loose trousers now show the top portion of her intergluteal cleft and Doug reaches out to touch her when she reaches back to pull them up, denying his view and his intentions. He goes back to relaxing alongside her, his mind wandering back to a work project that has been troubling him for some time. Almost as suddenly as his shift in mindset he thinks back to the ludicrous cartoon enhanced advertisement complete with teenager graffiti. Is that what he has become? A well–dressed big smiling idiot with his cock in a laptop?

Margot flips herself to face Doug but keeps her eyes shut. Doug turns to face her too, also using the guise of exhaustion. He slips down so that their faces are mere inches away from another. With all available courage he raises a hand and places it against her face. As if expectantly relieved she raises her hand and presses it onto his, her eyes now open and filled with care. He then moves his hand down her flank skimming her breast as he moves towards the top of her loose trousers. Still looking at her he places his palm inside the material and quickly around to the front so that he is cupping her warmth. Margot again closes her eyes this time slowly, welcoming the oncoming sensation.

A loud knock at the door interrupts the contact and pulls the two back to reality. A knock again while Margot fastens her trousers followed by: "What are you doing? Are you ready for a walk in the countryside?"

"Be just a sec," yells Margot but not before Janine has opened the door and entered. Doug has rolled onto his stomach to hide his erection and Margot is in the bathroom pretending to unpack toiletries.

"No lazing about on holiday," says Janine, jumping on top of Doug's back so that not only is the wind squashed out of him like a whoopee cushion but also that his unwavering erection digs into his belly.

"Where are we going?" says Margot, emerging unflustered from the bathroom.

"A place I used to frequent when boys where something you scowled at rather than howled at. I hope it's still around. I have the picnic paraphernalia all ready!"

Glimmers of sunshine are disobediently peeping through gaps in the grey although the air temperature remains cold. The high grassy banks line the road and enclose the damp tar, each side reaching towards the other as though attempting to form a tunnel. Janine walks between Margot and Doug who each carry elements of the picnic. They follow the road for what seems like a long while until Janine darts off through an opening between two hedges. Surprised, the two follow, Doug having to crouch low to fit himself and the backpack beneath the low overhang of crumpled bush. A twig sticks into his head and scratches him as he bustles through the mess to emerge in a wide clearing.

For a second the scene literally takes his breath away: not a building in sight and an expanse of fluffy green that rolls in hemispherical mounds all the way to the horizon. The bluebells dance in the slight breeze beckoning the explorers to join in. Doug is so mesmerised by the scene that he doesn't realise that the other two have entered into another gap just to his left. Only when a gold bracelet encircled arm reaches from the depths is Doug symbolically ripped from his stupor. Trekking for the next half an hour is tough and Doug struggles being a foot taller than most. Janine is convinced she remembers where to go and forages forward through the growth that has evolved into a damp forest. Doug, the designated bag carrier, spends most of the time digging nature's paraphernalia from his hair and mouth.

Moments before the journey becomes unbearable, they stumble onto a hidden paradise. Janine is pleased and silently congratulates herself as Margot and Doug take stock of their intimate surroundings. A small stream weaves through a succession of smooth brown rocks which are dabbled alongside a flat clearing. The smell is jasmine yet none is to be seen and the trees that surround the enclosure shield the scene, an impenetrable, untamed fortress. A squirrel startled by the intrusion waits a while longer to challenge the onlookers but is soon deterred, scuttling up a strong tree to view from above.

Janine lays a blanket in the clear, opting out of reminiscent stories of her childhood. She allows the surroundings to seep into everyone and stretches across the textured rug so that her stomach is revealed as her arms reach above her head. Her exuberant stretch reveals the bottom of her lace brassiere and she quickly crouches her arms down, offering a subtle apology. Doug dumps the bag of food beside her and Margot takes off her jumper: the wet heat from the stream amplified by the energy expended to find the place. Janine opens a bottle of wine and the three relax in the depths of the forest, completely oblivious to the outside world. No unnatural noises filter through the forest, only the soothing hum of nature at work and play.

With the only disturbance a stray pinecone cartwheeling across the blanket after dropping from the high boughs above, the three doze after an excess of prepared snacks and red wine. The morning becomes afternoon and the constant temperature of the forest contributes to the eyelid strain. Doug is last to drift off whilst watching Margot's consistent heavy breathing. The blanket is just big enough for the three of them and Janine lies curled in a petite ball at Doug's flank. He awakes suddenly after being asleep for only a couple of moments. In her sleep Janine has placed her arm along his thigh so that her hand rests between his legs. Margot is also closer to him huddling her body up against his and following the line of his angle.

Doug again drops off and is woken from a sexual dream to discover that Janine's hand is rubbing up and down his erect penis. His initial reaction is to jump away but then notices Janine's rapid eye movement. He is unable to move away slowly as the pressure will surely disturb Margot who has almost moved into a position on top of him. Janine suddenly opens an eye and stares at Doug who remains frozen. She smiles and closes her eye again, not discontinuing the gentle strokes. She now begins rubbing his balls and moves closer into a better position. Margot begins blinking beneath her eyelids as though she is about to wake up and turn over. She begins smacking her lips together, the dried remnants of red wine keeping the bottom and top lip reluctantly stuck together. Her one eye opens and then the other and, just before Doug is able to turn over with his back to Janine and wrestle his groin free, Janine lets go and pushes her head towards Margot.

For Doug what happens next is somewhere precariously between shock and excitement. Janine kisses Margot on the mouth and Margot kisses back, the two female heads intertwined on Doug's chest. Margot is not yet properly awake and the whole episode seems like a dream when Janine pushes Margot's head down to Doug's bulge and begins licking Doug's lips. Before Doug can object or quantify or make sense of the situation, Margot has him inside her mouth and Janine has her tongue deep inside his throat. The instant warmth on his groin renders him useless to resist and he leans back, Janine following and Margot taking him deeper into her mouth.

Janine now straddles his chest and sits upright removing her top from above her shoulders. Doug is unable to look away from her magnificent chest: her two fleshy mounds propped up by a see–through brassiere. His face is engulfed by her chest and he begins frantically tonguing and biting at the nipples he has just exposed. Both her breasts are propped above the wire at uneven heights and he squeezes one with a tight fist while Janine laps up the pleasure. She resumes kissing him forcefully on the mouth before lifting her pelvis momentarily to pull down her pants. She turns around and sits on his face, pulling Margot up to her and tasting Doug's saliva. Margot reluctantly leaves Doug's groin and sits across his rigidity still fully clothed. While Janine orgasms she rips free Margot's breasts, motioning for her to turn and face the other way.

Margot resumes on Doug, this time plunging her arse high in the air to meet Janine who places fingers inside her and nibbles at her moist innards until she too climaxes. The tempo uncharacteristically stifles before Janine bashes Margot's head from Doug so that she stumbles down a small bank into a clump of harmless thorns. Doug is unaware and Janine seizes the opportunity by straddling him and pressing firmly down so that there is no daylight between their pelvises. She lifts off the shaft and then pulls her legs from under her, landing on Doug. Janine hardly notices Margot who returns and crouches behind her in order to tongue her anus. Janine leans forward and whispers in Doug's ear while her forward thrusts continue to bobble at Margot's head.

"Are you close?" are her words as though scolding him for being near climax. She feels him swell inside her and moments before he is past the point of no return she leaps off and hurtles through an opening behind his head. Unsure what to do Margot chases after her which sees Doug following while trying to force himself back into his trousers. He comes into a clearing filled with the brilliant yellow of rapeseed and spots the two semi naked females darting towards a train line. He pursues, his erection now painfully pressing against the cool metal of his zipper.

He is surprised at how fast the two are and arrives to find Janine holding Margot down to the track while she kisses her chest. She is lying on top of Margot and has one of her wrists in each hand as Margot reluctantly struggles against her. The sounding of an approaching train echoes out like a screech and Margot rolls out from Janine down a bank of light yellow jagged stones. Doug's heart pauses for a second when he sees that Janine is not moving. She turns over to catch his eye then presses herself onto all fours and places her fingers in both rear orifices. Doug knows she will not move and the juvenile dare stands as he approaches and drops his trousers behind her. She lets out a full throttled gasp as he slams himself straight inside her. The train's sound draws nearer and Doug tries to lift her off the track only to discover her hands firmly clasping each raised dark brown metal rail.

"You finish first," she says, clipping her ankles around his calves. Margot is speechless and has no strength to yell, unaware of her bloody forearms, feeling the heat of the approaching train. Doug's fear-fuelled fervour is translated into vigorous thrusts that quickly bring Janine to orgasm. He continues, the train a hundred yards away and bellowing forth as the driver sounds the alarm. He can feel he is close and concentrates, trying to block out the amplified noise of the train. Janine's moisture means he lacks the pressure for orgasm and he pulls himself free before plunging himself into her moist anus. The pressure forces a violent ejaculation from both and, seconds before the smeared coagulation of cowcatcher, metal train wheel and glistening flesh, he jumps free pulling Janine with him. The two land as the track wilts, the driver shows a hand signal and Janine breaks free from the sexual lock. Margot's tears are already dry and dusty.

PROLOGUE III
WOK JAWS

Clive, there is no getting away from this story; I think you know that. Now of course we are not saying on behalf of the channel that this rivals a presidential result, mass scale terrorist atrocity or huge celebrity dating scandal; but we are ensuring you, the viewer, is kept appraised on all emerging stories. And I will confess ... guilty! As charged! That I have a slight penchant (not as strong a word as fascination but an interest perhaps) for the well underwear-attired modern male. Clive, you have to get with the times!

PART III

[Episodic]

CHAPTER 63

Cow Two Hint And Ate It Out

EPISODE 1

Pig(n) – A member of the genus Homo, family Hominidae, order Primates, class Mammalia, characterised by erect posture and an opposable thumb, especially a member of the only extant species, Homo sapiens, distinguished by a highly developed brain, the capacity for abstract reasoning, and the ability to communicate by means of organised speech and record information in a variety of symbolic systems.

My knees are barely able to hold the weight as I hover precariously above a brand new plastic cup, squatting over the steaming liquid. Leaning forward to make sure the toilet door is bolted I overbalance backwards and dunk the testicle that hangs lower than the other into the frothed coffee which sends relays of tiny spasms down my hamstrings and into my feet, collecting in balls at the tips of my toes before trumpeting back up to my balls. The constant pressure from tucking the team between my legs for days on end does nothing to numb the pain and I am forced to cup the spherical wounded soldier as the cup cowers below me like a pebble in the shade.

There is just enough room in the cup for me to spray a few drops of urine into it. One–and–three–quarter inches. Enough of a sample not to alter the taste but to make sure that a man in the office somewhere somehow ingests the pee from a woman. Just as we are taught to do. The proper procedure, of course, is to bring your urine to work in the homemade equivalent of a catheter bag. When I joined, containers were anything from that new Tupperware (that isn't actually Tupperware but will always be known as Tupperware despite exhaustive efforts to extricate the association) to freezer bags, the former not only more durable and watertight but particularly more inconspicuous with shaded green walls to hide and cool the nitrogenous waste.

Just as I'm about to create a stream not too powerful but enough to fill the cup; just when my nut has cooled down to above room temperature, opening my sphincter and allowing the urge to urinate to fill me with warmth and imminent relief, the main entrance clatters open in a flurry of intermittent high–heeled steps. I clench, motionless and still, balancing as the urge leaves me with the insipid blue board prison of a toilet cubicle encircling me like the exaggerated closing of a giant's hand around a helpless princess. Then there's a cough.

A signal? If so, an extremely casual one. Too casual to risk so I wait, extending my legs straight and opening my mouth in a pathetic wince as my leg muscles readjust to being idle. Another cough, this one as casual as the first and delivered with such imperceptible dexterity that sheer curiosity sees me cough a light feminine cough into the collar of my suit jacket which runs dangerously close to being completely inaudible. I search my mental cavities for remnants of whose being encapsulates the casual cough as the silence once again greets from the wash basin, which is gracefully leveraged open to release water which sounds like forceful air expelled from a tractor tyre. Oh how I wish the whole ability thing extended to sounds!

I cough again, unaware of my disregard for the high pitched squeak as I lie buried in the bowels of the female toilets. Two coughs are returned to me as the running water subsides and I respond with three more. When I'm about halfway through my third cough, four ring out from directly outside the cubicle, bouncing off the insulated ceramics within the room. I unlatch the door and try to zip up before the intruder joins me for a little imposed urine therapy. It's Beth from Sales and she immediately latches the door behind her, licking her teeth and taking off her panties from beneath her knee high light grey skirt. I'm hopeful it will be that functional, as simple as the coughing regime when she sees the coffee cup below me.

"Who's that for?" she giggles slyly, her eyes deepening into their sockets. I have to think quickly and accidentally blurt out a guy made redundant six months ago which she either disregards in her haste to abuse me or confuses with someone else. My fly is up but my belt buckle dangles impotently down one side of my flank which means Beth is easily able to rip down my trousers and turn me around, dropping to her knees. On the way down I feel her tightly held breasts bang against the top of my buttocks, the clash not supported by the silkiness of her blouse and more like a steel hammer coming down on a motionless railway sleeper. Her mouth nestles in the chasm of warmth between the pert bulbous humps and it brings back scary memories of the initiation night. The first time I proved my loyalty to the A.M.S. Subsequent encounters of this sort have been relatively few and far between, the gratuitous ability to test my loyalty a far greater weapon in many respects. But Beth is from Sales and probably too stupid to know any better so she embarks on her quest like a child with a new toy.

"What about the cup?" I mutter, not completely loathing the sensation. "Daniel's going to wonder. Why don't you? Go on."

She emerges, lipstick daubed across her beige cheeks and teeth shining. It takes her a nanosecond to go, her aim and volume control near perfection, dispelling two urban legends and preconceived beliefs in unison. Girls do not get stage fright worse than boys and certainly can control their wee–wee, maybe not to the extent of drawing monsters in the sand but to an extent worthy of some praise. Or perhaps not, for this is no ordinary woman for no ordinary cult. Before she departs and while retracting her underwear, she puts both her lips into my mouth, ferreting out my tongue with a vacuum slurp. When she leaves, I go to the toilet in the toilet.

As I make my way back to my desk, I greet Gus, Nick and Zander, all of whom have sampled the nectar from my temperamental bladder. Not that I fetch drinks as a matter of habit but rather that I like to exude a polite reciprocatory demeanour; I'd hate to drop the title of 'nice guy of the office': my life is happy when others are happy with me. And they are usually happy with me because I remember stuff. I possess this ability to remember stuff. This is my curse.

Access code equals the daily closing FTSE 100 index. A pig is an animal. A pig eats, sleeps and recycles its own shit. Pigs were put on the planet to procreate without procreating. Pigs are the reason we exist. Pigs are the reason we punish.

Section 4(a) subsection 3 (iii) paragraph 6: no pig shall exist in the A.M.S. unless initiated according to section 7(b) & (c).

A man stood on a street corner, shadowed by the overhang of a rusted bar sign.

Slumped at my desk, I almost take a sip of coffee, raising the cup precariously close to my dry lips. I can see my reflection in the now smooth fluid as perfect circles of clasped bubbles move from the centre in regular intervals and burst, dissolving. Beth's bubbles. A pile of mail is slapped down next to the coffee cup by a new mail guy with a purple bandana falling off the side of his skull. He's new because I don't know his name; I would remember his name if I only heard it once. This is my gift.

The coffee is still piping hot as I make my way past Beth towards Daniel's office. Today the office is uncharacteristically busy, shoes skating across carpet, skirts flapping beneath waists, keyboards cracking under fingers and voices bellowing above hoarse mouths. Daniel is not in his office. His office is cold and seat vacant yet the indentation from his oversized butt cheeks impresses the neutral grey seat that faces me. The wall is spruced with white board, amok with formulae, figures and charts. One look is all I require. There is no ordinary.

On exiting I notice the new receptionist talking to Beth. They both look in my direction at the same time and I pass back an awkward smile. Beth notices me still holding the coffee and struts purposefully over, her lips bunched and arse pursed. As she passes me, she whispers, "Get fucking rid of it," then stretches her mouth to an open smile almost as though tent pegs are keeping her teeth showing. The new girl looks confused; she's looking at her computer and then up at me, almost in desperation.

"Need any help?" I say, the coffee cup now annoyingly stuck to my palm.

"I've given up trying to find department cost codes. Do you know where to find–"

"Which code do you want?"

"Development," she says tapping hopelessly on the keyboard.

"DVL003TMN9456Z1."

"You're kidding," she says, smiling.

"No. Which others do you want?"

"Sales."

"SLS009FNX3256X3."

"Oh my God, so if I need anything, you're my guy?"

"Sure."

"Can I return the favour? Perhaps pass that coffee on? Doesn't look like you're going to drink it."

"Thanks, that'll be helpful. It's for Beth. The woman you were just talking to. I forgot to give it to her. She'll be pissed if she remembers I forgot so would you mind putting it in a new cup and giving it to her without telling her it's from me? It's still warm."

{⟶⟵⟶⟵⟶⟵}

I'm one of the last to leave the office as I had to photocopy a list of DVD titles for the meeting tonight. The cold air greets me turning my exhalations into smoky clouds that singe the air in front of me. Bob the square security guard tips his hat as I leave. The venue is within walking distance so I bundle up beneath the secure confines of my duffel coat before breaststroking through the smog.

We gather in a rented apartment bringing completed assignments and new material, but only for group submission if the content fits any of the database criteria. I remember Callum Hollith's empty promise last week about a grade five discovery. Everyone remembers as Callum's time with the Porn Aficionado cult is limited.

I notice another man from the cult on the street outside the apartment. He smokes a cigarette and glances towards me without showing a trace of recognition. Cult members never fraternise outside the confines of the meeting place. Rain trickles spit across my glasses and I'm forced to wipe them with a corner of my under t–shirt before entering the building. The journey up in the modern elevator is lonely and the creak of the cogs makes me think that not many people hibernate in these flats. They're so modern the board walls seem ready to fall over with the introduction of a loud sneeze or fart. The chairman of Porn Aficionado owns the apartment, apparently. He never attends any of the meetings but rather relays messages through the secretary, Hans.

"We have catalogued the Tera anal and the Devon DP. Thanks to Mike and Reg respectively. Callum?" Hans finishes speaking, motioning towards the floor circled by single cream sofas squatting on crisscrossed slabs of sparkling wood. There is no drinking until the official viewing. The drinks are provided and tonight it is my turn to provide the viewing material. I've gone for nothing flashy just stuck to my mandate. Summer Cummings.

The strictest rule of this cult is no admission to any ugly men. The axiom of bald, salivating, desperate men being the only purveyors of quality pornography is firmly dispelled here. This is for the true connoisseur of porn; not someone with sexual deficiencies or relationship issues, but young men with a healthy fascination for the study and analysis of the pornography industry. There are discussion forums pitting the late seventies early eighties films against the mid nineties; there are film analysis questionnaires and there is assigned star tracking. There is no sitting around wanking. But where this moves from a silly male society to a cult is the action.

A cult is more than a society. A cult is action based. A cult's beliefs are such that the action taken must have a definite visual outcome that will change the lives of others and demonstrate to the world that something must be changed. Sometimes cults are obscure, sometimes misleading, but always passionate. The minute a member of a cult is perceived by the others to be not all there is the second their membership ends and sometimes with scary consequences. All cults have rules; all cults have extraction policies.

Tomorrow is Wednesday. Now that combat training is done and dusted we have moved onto bomb making. Thursday means an illegal radio press release showing the comparison between Jack & Jill and Bill & Monica. Friday is A.M.S. and Saturday is assignment night with Born Free.

Outside the window a cleaner stares in, unable to believe what he sees on the wide television screen. Summer's locked one of her piercings onto her partner Skye and is stretching back so that her labia is extended like a fresh slice of ham from the butchery. I know most will be disappointed with this. Hans pulls the blinds and suggests moving to a new venue.

CHAPTER 73

Cow Two Hint And Ate It Out

EPISODE 11

Memory(n) – a state of serious mental deterioration; significant loss of cognitive functioning and intellectual abilities – thinking, reasoning, empathy, independence – and behavioural abilities to such an extent that it interferes with a person's daily life and activities.

I'm too young to have grey bits in my stubble. This I know because there is too much of a discernible difference between blonde and grey. It seems to stand out in a dark beard more than blonde, haphazardly muscling in amongst the champion dark brown specimens like an unwanted relative.

The reason I spotted the unsightly half dozen growths was because I slit my wrists while staring at my eyes in the mirror. This was an exercise. Dissimilar from an assignment. An exercise is for you to learn; an assignment for others to learn. There was no easy way to do it and what really made me follow through with it was because I was told to. Arriving at a meeting having failed to show any attempt to complete the exercise and not armed with enough theatrical brilliance to expel the notion that it wasn't for me but that I was still worthy to be in the group is my greatest fear. So in three quick manoeuvres I grabbed my safety razor, pushed the insipid veins in my wrist skywards and sliced along. My face never changed, I swear. The basin did though, acquiring desultory drops of freshly brewed blood like a commuter without an umbrella on a rainy day. Now I'm scared for the exercise involves sharing the expression we see in the mirror and I have none to report on.

No one heard the screams from the cargo holds of the slave ships; no one noticed when the Bosniaks screamed in their beds; no one felt pain when humans replaced all peace-loving species on the Earth. We must know this pain, be this pain, hope for this pain until all our sins – past and present – are washed away.

Bethany called this morning fresh from her safari in Kenya where she said she tried to suffocate a lonely traveller with his sleeping bag. Bethany is the reason I am climbing the cult ladder within A.M.S. – she was the one who first took me to a meeting. The first man at an A.M.S. gathering.

I met her in a video store. Without blinking she asked me if I thought women who watched videos on their own were sad, hopeless, closet soap opera stars. I replied that I didn't think so. She then asked me if I believed that a woman's pussy would seal over if she didn't have sex for a long time. Again I replied in the negative. Finally she asked me if I thought she was attractive and I replied in the affirmative.

At her apartment at about three in the morning after a marathon of fluid exchange, whipping, strapping on and tying up I watched as she sobbed in her sleep muttering something about Stewart. She clutched the duvet under her chin and her lower jaw twitched up and down like a feeble jackhammer.

We saw each other frequently after that, not romantically but more functionally. One night she arrived at my house with scratch marks across her mouth and a broken cheek bone. When the hospital formalities were over, I made her tell me about the group of men she had induced to beat and rape her. It was her first assignment.

At work I am forced to regurgitate every piece of legislation relating to derivative based products for the legal team. The new girl, Jasmine, sits taking notes in the meeting, and watches me spew forth every clause and cause after reading the regulatory papers. Her stare puts me off and I am forced to readjust my stance, straighten my tie and clear my throat, the cough not sufficiently loud to dislodge anything in my lungs. She likes me I think, but not in that way. She smiles at me a lot which is innocent enough I suppose. She must be ten years my junior.

Ginger-haired and continually scratching the inside of his nostrils is South African lawyer, Piet. He stares directly at her, twirling his pencil around his chin leaving tiny lead dimples all over his pink face. The grapevine strangled me into believing that he asked her out and she politely refused, maybe basing her decision on his marital status (or perhaps that his sightline seldom rises above nipple height). Anyway, so why I have some sort of a weird soft spot for this girl is her innocence: Piet has taken to crude innuendoes around her and she modestly doesn't get any of them; not in a stupid way but rather that her dignity is held too high aloft to either throw them back in his face or acknowledge their existence. Beth has also taken to her which concerns me more.

At lunch it's party time for me: I'm the clown with the photographic memory. Members of the team take turns picking novels and I vomit whole paragraphs, sometimes pages back, at them. They giggle and clap. But it would be unfair of me to scold my affliction and wish it away. It has served me numerous times. My involvement with the cults for instance. Initiation into a cult involves a dedicated level of knowledge and understanding about the ethos and formal doctrine. There is no way I could juggle my involvement in so many cults without the afflicted mental library that innocently rests inside my head. It's not random either. All of it is ordered and I suppose I just figure out the order quicker than most. Or perhaps it's there for a reason. Whatever the case if I read something it is stuck with me like grey beard hair for the rest of my natural life.

Porn Aficionados does not exist for self–gratification. It does not exist as a forum for men wishing to bring themselves to climax and then turn the tape off or close the page. It exists for lovers of quality porn and those willing to share this subtle underbelly with the masses who choose to degrade the industry by ostracising those within it or quick fix junkies.

Porn Aficionados has begun producing films. The relationship between a shoestring budget and champagne tastes has meant the initiation of an actual production has been stagnant. But now we have a silent fund provider, eager to spread the word through production. The production house is called Phayze Productions and my specific role is the casting director.

No one notices the tightly wound bandage around my wrists even though it shows through my long–sleeve white shirt. It hurts a little more and I can feel the blood has not ceased pumping out of the wound. I am forced to change the bandage several times during the workday. In the evening we meet, all wrists bound, many with dabs of sparkling blood beginning to seep into the outer material.

Self Affliction for the Pain of Others understand that the world suffers. We understand that the world bleeds, that every second of her existence, mother earth and her children are scared and raped and beaten every second. This we believe to be our purpose to pay for those sins: to take our bodies down the righteous path of salvation through the true understanding of pain. No one will harm us in the afterlife; no one will disturb our sanctity throughout the fiery years when our skin will scorch and be saved for mother earth and her children. Death to all hypocrites.

The sermon element is the one that kills me. Often all they do is repeat what is contained in the doctrine, yelling the words, breaking down the syllables and spouting forth like an out of control fireman's hose. The other evening at Self Affliction a guest speaker from Canada made a member of the audience swallow his own tongue on stage and then waited while the helpless sod writhed all over the manicured wooden stage like a disorientated salmon. It was a waiting game: Professor De Ju Pain Lover versus the gawps of the audience. I of course was too far back to rush forward (and too scared). So we sat and watched as the man stopped moving, his hands crumpled in clenched claws and his face turning the colour of a swamp. When it was way past face explosion point the great professor retrieved from his person a plastic ruler and snapped the man's tongue back to civilisation allowing a burst of air to escape down his throat. And then everyone cheered and began hugging one another and beating their heads for pain and biting their tongues and bending their fingers. And the moral: let others relieve your pain.

The frequency of the cults can play havoc with your schedule. Some are weekly, the same day every week. Some are monthly in the same vein. Some are ad hoc at the discretion of the governing body or super supreme master or council or champion nigger hater.

Death to all niggers! Fucking die! Death to all Paki scum! Fucking die! Death to all Asian trash! Fucking gooks! Fucking die! Preserve the purity of the white race! Death and pain to those who stand in our way!

And being a member of many cults means that sometimes they overlap and this is never a good idea. The decision comes down to the importance of the gathering not the cult. If A.M.S. are running an assignment such as the 'drunk banker campaign' on the same night that the Puritans are gathering to chant at a picture of Hitler, the former is preferable. But there always has to be a great excuse and miss two in a row and you're out. The organisation must take preference over everything: family holidays, life threatening illness, croquet, court appearances, death. The beliefs you hold or pretend to hold must not only form the cornerstone of your existence but define who and what you are through your waking years. On your deathbed your biggest regret in life must be not having done more for the cult and your biggest ambition must be continuing the good work into the afterlife.

So the idea of just leaving a cult as you might a gym membership is completely unheard of. A woman named Sybil Carter at A.M.S. became pregnant and tried to put everything behind her for a new life with her child. As rumour has it when she awoke her legs were bloody and her baby was gone. Some said accidental miscarriage. Some said the society had drugged her and removed the baby in the dead of the night.

Another misconception about cults is the standing of the participants. True cult members are not hacks so bored with their own lives that they find cults to express their latent desires. Cult members are professional, qualified, intelligent, well–off people who have held the beliefs they express for their entire lives and now have a collective more powerful platform from which to enact their convictions. Many pour extensive resources, not only financial, into these organisations including premises, legal assistance, medical care and the like.

This is why my situation is increasingly dangerous. I now belong to over a dozen cults, none of which I am easily able to slip away from. Some are easier than others but as a general rule it's difficult. And would you believe that most of my admissions have been purely by accident! I didn't go seeking places where I could thrash corner shop owners, steal greyhounds, believe in the three blind politicians and make bombs. My mind remains hungry though, like a godless foul being from the sewer, only coming out at night to feed on any new material that might cross its path.

Bill & Hilary went up a hill
To fetch an American presidency
Bill fell down and Monica blew his crown
And Hilary went searching for the spoils

CHAPTER 83

Cow Two Hint And Ate It Out

EPISODE III

Dawn has an annoying habit of being over much quicker than dusk. Granted during the brief interval when the groaning dark is replaced by the water pistol curls of sunshine, fewer wary souls are admiring the splendour than when the effervescent ball sulks behind a screen of purple–grey smog. But dusk seems to linger longer, almost as though the day refuses to relinquish, gripping, fingernails stretched and ready to split free, onto the final visible remnants of luminosity, until a black sheet is cautiously thrust over the land and those who are unseen are able to do what is unseen.

Many of the meetings take place before dawn; before work, elasticising the brief beginning of the morning through the sunrise and even when the clouds hold back the fair–haired jolly flaming ball, there is no denying at what point the earth twists just far enough to allow the day to commence. Wherever I am, inside or out, I give the sunrise preference. All the prescriptive barking becomes a dampened blur of expressionist torture as the sun blocks out – just for that brief second – the world around me.

This morning was the longstanding and increasingly underattended Lovers 4 Lucifer cult. This was one of the earliest I joined when satanic worship and cult were frequently used in the same sentence. Now, of course, it's not particularly trendy to be in a satanic cult: everyone has an Ouija board buried in the confines of their attic or understairs cupboard; everyone played glassy–glassy and supposedly felt it move and spell out a significant platitude; everyone had been there and done that.

And the gatherings have grown boring; stilted now that the leadership has changed over a dozen times and everyone has slept with everyone while rolling in lamb's blood. The humble beginnings of pagan worship holding hands dancing around in a circle – not dissimilar to a hippy festival – followed by sensual lovemaking beneath a rock later in the fetid depths of the forest was when this cult meant something. Sometimes we were witches practising magick; sometimes pagans. Unlike the cults of today and some of the more extreme satanic cults there was never any coercion to join, no one was hurt or damaged and there was no slave teenage labour. I suppose it fell under the satanic umbrella simply because in those days it seemed tacky to join a cult without some form of lower purpose and the occult was the ideal scapegoat. There were strange periods though. During the reign of a satanic priest called Lurid the Spent.

Lucifer, o hail, is the brother of Jesus Christ. He was cast out of the gates of the holy kingdom for the sins of the wicked dwelling within the kingdom. We believe in the Christian way and chose not to obey it. O hail Lucifer, lord of evil. We will avenge the deaths of our brothers in the middle ages, hunted down and slaughtered like pigs. We will avenge the deaths of our sisters: the witches and pagans of the middle ages. O hail.

Lurid decided we should accumulate points for deeds with rich reward for those reaching higher levels. So instead of a free tin of baked beans we were rewarded with virgin's blood, prime position in the afterlife and promotion within the cult. Everything from digging up graves to burning crosses to graffiti to sacrificing animals within the magik circle could earn you points. Then there were the virgins.

Ah there it is: the sun, as I make another lunge forward, bowing towards the old priest who looks as though he's dozed off. The sun's presence sends a flurry of quicker bows and chants all at the same time, the creak of the cheap mats we kneel on sprinkled between the low toned manic gurgles like the call of a lark during a foxhunt. If everything goes according to plan this will be my last meeting. The only thing keeping me there is Tim.

Before my knees have recovered from the strain the sunrise is over. Tim is beside me and smiles, the left side of his one lip unreasonably higher than the right. The burns on his face have almost completely healed after months of rehabilitation and his hair is beginning to grow back, each feathery patch extending its tentacles towards the other making the top of his scalp look like an ancient map of the eastern hemisphere. Right about the time I'm trying to picture how Chiang Kai–shek made it from mainland China to Taiwan a commotion ensues at the chipboard altar. Everyone is crowding around the priest, pressing two fingers against his throat and fruitlessly lifting his head up, not to make him drink but trying to rouse him and, in the process, creaking the top of his spine. Watching his old beard flop to the side of his exposed grey hair encrusted nipple, my scepticism surrounding his credentials once again fill me. To me he was always a candidate for escaped mental patient of the year with his chants suddenly switching to an in depth discussion about the state of the Crusades then instantly onto American Idol. Unlike the other leaders he never tried to entice the women of the group, probably mainly because the remainder of the depleted consignment now only consisted of Dora, the Ukrainian power lifter and Dorris, the great grandmother of Lucifer himself.

"He's dead," a creaky male voice spurts from the crowd. "O hail Lucifer, take him into your bosom and protect him from the evil of God's wisdom! Take him now!"

The chant sends everyone scuttling back to their mats, bare feet slapping twigs bust on the slightly damp concealed wood, while Tim and I stare at one another bemused. The old priest is left at the altar, his chin stapled close to his breastbone until the frenzy that has become the death ritual transfers its verve towards him. A short man with a miniature replica beard picks up one of the flaming sticks yelling, "O Lucifer, we know you choose not the age of your servants but take this old disciple as though he were a young vibrant virgin! Take his impure soul! Take his magik!"

With this he points the stick towards the priest and sets fire to his limp beard. The result is instantaneous, the old features swallowed in a halo of yellow flame, some of the surrounding dry grass catching. The beard releases hula hoops of grey smoke rings as all the members of Lovers 4 Lucifer watch in awe. When the old priest suddenly stands up and begins tugging at his burning face is when star struck bewilderment becomes real human panic. The man who set him alight goes charging off into the bushes yelling Lucifer's name and skipping on every sixth's step. Others begin running away until a path clears for me to charge, wet bouquets of mud in each of my hands, and slap a face pack on the frail priest as he tries to escape the inescapable flames. Tim brings up the rear with mud pack number two and by about five the priest is extinguished, smouldering, cross–legged and bowed towards the altar.

{ ↦ ↤ ↦ ↤ ↦ ↤ }

At work my memory lets me down for the first time I can remember. Perhaps the flames planted the bug or maybe Tim. Whatever the case my error sees me take a half day holiday and drive to Highgate Woods for an assignment. Wasn't overly keen on this one as had never bashed anyone let alone a gay person but I joined during a lull and there was really no …

Jesus fuck is this where this is going? So encouraging initially – even quite liked the chap but gay bashing? Hopefully he doesn't go through with it …

X2 … X6

Looks like he's getting his arse kicked!

X12 … X30

Let's zap through the other episodes …

OK … priest is dead … new woman arrives … older lady … big tits … our man trying to make a difference … ends up burning Tim's face … must be a flashback. Man standing on dark street corner … lots of pornography … bomb making … an explosion … he's OK though. Beth doing something quite perverse to him … then discovering something … his memory talent seemingly fading by the expressions. Tim walking away … his lame duckling perhaps … young Asian girl … greyhounds and horses running around the streets … freed

Smug Dad

... some comic book superheroes and kids fairytale books ... transposed over news clips ... Bill and Monica.

CHAPTER 93

Adorn Pie Doll

"It needs to, like, have a good ending. Yeah."

"Yeah, a good ending"

"And, like, a good beginning. Yeah."

"Yeah, a good beginning."

"Because that'll, like, make you actually want to watch it. From the beginning."

"And a good middle bit."

"Yeah, a good middle bit so, like, when the beginning bit is sort of closing up and you're, like forgetting about the beginning bit, then WHAM! The middle bit hits you and it's, like, awesome."

"WHAM! Awesome! Yeah!"

"But not as awesome as the end bit. Or maybe as awesome but not more awesome, but maybe more awesome than the beginning."

"Yeah. Awesome. Yeah."

"And that is what makes a good show. That's what makes me want to buy a telly."

"A telly. Awesome."

"When do we get paid?"

"Yeah, and where's the free food, dude?"

No noise comes from behind the glass, but it wouldn't matter because supposedly these things are designed to be soundproof. The teenagers mutter to one another, agreeing, nodding, being surprised as the moderator leaves the room. One of the participants, driven by a combination of hunger pains and the smell of warm cocktail sausages wafting into the space, approaches the two–way mirror looking like a zoo animal: confused yet knowingly suspicious of the watchers' presence.

"Do you think they, like, actually watch us all the time?" he says, tilting his head and lifting his top lip to investigate for the manifestation of any remaining lunch bits.

"They video tape the whole fucking thing, man," explains the young girl, joining the onlooked onlooker, jumping at the mirror in a mock frightening. The two stare emotionless, waiting.

"I suppose at a basic minimum could we at least have

included in the profile teenagers without their own children and preferably those still living at home with easy access to a television?"

The remaining two people behind the glass remain silent: one, an old man in a black shirt has dozed off; the other caught in limbo between an excuse and an admission of guilt.

"I'm sorry, Eb. These things never seems to hit the desired result. The company probably did the deal based on them ticking the 'I own a telly' box. I'll pay them and get rid of them."

"Dave, I don't want to be involved in any more focus groups, or any more of these. This is a waste of your time and most importantly my time. When Bolger wakes tell him he can keep the fee and find someone else to come up with the show," Eb finishes, standing up to leave.

"But there isn't anyone else, not like you anyway."

"I'm tired, Dave."

"Just give me something. Some tiny little idea that I can throw into Bolger's melting pot and get the wheels rolling for the end of the year. Please, Eb. Jesus. What do we do? Run a reality show with an awesome beginning, middle and end!"

Ebenezer Vim takes a moment to enjoy the comment. Dave's gormless face mixed inextricably with his gentle yet well–meaning nature doesn't change when he chooses to throw his final plea in. It's funny and Ebenezer can't help chuckling to himself. The room now feels damp as the heating splutters and chokes into another cycle. The teenagers mill, sloped shoulders, scowled expressions, around the chairs. One lights a cigarette and is promptly told off by the moderator which doesn't seem to make a difference, the smoke filling the room and clouding the mirror like a horror scene.

"You need to shock and never explain why. That's your beginning. Your middle is the development: the explanation but always with a twist – and not a corny twist. Reality has a habit of creating its own twists – it's how you manage those without forcing too many imposed surprises or derivations. Keep the middle original. The ending can only be poignant. Audiences do not want to end a television series relationship with a grin and a chuckle. They want to be moved; to feel somehow inspired by the basic human emotion of the conclusion. The only other option for the ending is extreme sadness. This should only be embarked upon under extreme circumstances."

It really is now time to go. Ebenezer has a phone date with his ex–wife and his kids and doesn't want to miss a brief chat about all things American after their recent departure to New York. It's not right the whole being away from your kids malarkey. It's just too cold and too permanent. David B. Burlingham tries unsuccessfully to absorb all that has been bestowed upon him. He recites the formula in his head and eventually scrabbles in his boss's sleeping pocket for a pen to scribble on his pale hand. The pen's ink does not transfer onto his palm and Ebenezer notices his franticness.

"Please stay on this project with me," pleads David, hopelessly lost without his mentor and more concerned about the trudge of bringing a project to the small screen without the chance to work with the great Ebenezer Vim than the prospect of another flop for the production house. Eb breathes in, genuinely sympathetic but unable to go any further in this venture.

"OK, Dave, here's an idea. Take the perfect male specimen: an Adonis meets Brad Pitt. Trawl the modelling agencies for some good–looking prick. Make sure he's also got a few bits upstairs. We need this guy to have won the genetic lottery. An all–rounder but his aesthetic appeal is the key. You can make the audience love him as the show progresses. Pay him a stack load of cash for what he agrees to do. Take twelve rather unfortunate single older females: these women must be pitied; they must be between thirty-three and thirty-eight and single and lonely. And most importantly broody. One of these girls – the ultimate winner – will win the right to father this man's child. A twelve week reality contest for the perfect sperm. To win they can do all sorts of shit like go on dates, go to dancing lessons: the usual crap. Make him fall for one of them. That way your follow up docusoaps will make you a fortune."

"You are my hero. That is more brilliant than me or any stinky teenager could have come up with in one whole million years. No, one ba–zillion!"

"Dave, that's a crap idea. More of the same crap. But it will make it to channel. And you will get the credit."

The flicker of a lone streetlight provides Ebenezer with momentary clarity as his shoes slap the damp concrete running along the pavement in knitted cracks and grungy tones. The street's characteristically quiet, an unusual rarity for central London at any time of the year. The ubiquitous unlicensed taxicab, a relic from the mid-eighties restored with pride and smelling of a pine freshener, nowhere to be seen or found. So the walk progresses, the strobe effect only slightly apparent as Ebenezer shortens the distance between himself and his apartment.

❨ ➜ ⬅ ➜ ⬅ ➜ ⬅ ❩

Gaynor lay awake staring at the ceiling while her dad bashed everything in her mum's room and left before her mum could aggravate him enough to bash her. She heard the frenetic rattle of the door chain following her father's lunge away from the flat, ripping the door shut behind him and the doorframe bouncing back into shape. More yelling. Gaynor humming to herself, not so pathetic as to be wounded by what had become the norm but naïve in her youth and impressionable enough to know and yearn for the boundaries beyond this. All this. The chain snaps: he's back. Her dad enters the council flat, spitting something at his estranged wife in the corridor and pushing past her, his footsteps interrupting the humming and getting louder so that the sudden swoosh of her door opening actually gave her a fright. She cowered, peering above the covers, eyes flickering as her father stood still staring at her without really registering she was in the room. She started humming again this time louder and with a less discernible tune.

"Where is that fucking thing?" he belched, clenching his fingers on both hands into claws, unable to place either in the desired destination.

"Hmmm hmm hmmmm hmm hmm hmmmmmmmmm …"

He scrabbled through the applausive array of make–up and

beauty products adorning her dressing table, becoming more and more frantic until all the pieces were scattered on the floor and he was on top of her pushing the duvet hard down against her mouth so that the material pulled at the sides, muffling and distorting the humming.

"Don't make me ask again." His heavy hands bulbous and dirty like swollen seals on the ends of hairy stumps. Her mother entered, screaming, threatening to call the police and lumping on top of him, her frame contorting like a lava lamp, only serving to split the side of Gaynor's lip from the pressure and meaning that he accidentally kneed his daughter in the groin in an attempt to steady himself from the flying mum.

"Hmmmmmmmm hmm hmm hmmmmmmmmm mmm mmm; *cough; choke; splutter*; hmmmmmm," the pain shooting up through her stomach throat bound and then all the way back down again to her crotch and down her thighs, the nausea far worse than the time she showed Jermaine Charvis and his kid brother Leon how to fit both of them in her at once. Or at least when they showed her how to fit both of them in her at once as she lay on her stomach full of glue and booze and dope, being held down on the floor so that her soft cheek acquired an impressive array of bits of old glass, stones and even a sweet wrapper.

But the memory gone and thankfully so (lip and fanny now hurting like a mofosonofabitch!) and the humming still soothing of course (at it usually did) but with her ragged father playing WWF with poor old council loving, fake fur worshipping, leg warmer clad, five kids with three different dads mum. The price you pay she thought for not strapping on a jonny even when you didn't want to which was most of the time. Of course. Except for the kid known as Lieutenant whose name she couldn't really remember (think! Think!) but whose face, peering above the clump of matted pubes and gathered tartan skirt while his tongue performed some sort of miracle, remained. Probably the first real, you know, the big O. Don't tell but now mum going to the dresser and digging through aiming at – no, please! – the third drawer and fishing in the back. How the fuck would she know? The compartment coming away like a chocolate wrapper and the chipped nails clutching at the Adidas circular pouch.

"Here it is, you fucking scum," she screams, holding it aloft.

No don't! How many hours of scooping ice cream and adding extra sprinkles and M&Ms and nuts and those irregular caramel pieces that the black boys really favour? How many extra handouts for blowjobs around the side of the store, her knees raw and now permanently chipped and scraped like an old wooden toy? All the notes in the pouch in her mum's hand. No please don't throw it over. Now she does. "Take it, you son of a fucking animal's whore, just get the fuck out before I ring the gavers."

At lease twelve, maybe thirteen. Enough at least to get on a plane. Somewhere. Like the land of opportunity or something.

{ ↳ ↰ ↳ ↰ ↳ ↰ }

The night sky stung his lungs as he inhaled. The way he figured it wasn't the night air because the stinging was only when he looked up, gazing aloft at the nondescript sky: too hazy for any recognisable flickering objects be they man made or man observed. Everything always felt better when looking up, as though the searching stare would somehow pull down salvation from the heavens, or at least a rare UFO sighting to break the monotony.

Nothing was the same anymore really (a premature lament, sure, but something almost unavoidable after an evening such as his). Plus he was walking home and that was always the place to reflect, the place to dream; the place to move past what was always in the way. This time not an imposed restriction by some studio boss determined to follow a formula or deliver on a successful focus group, but rather a child's old bike, tangled in upon itself so that each dangerous metal protrusion became almost impossible to avoid as he stumbled through the obstacle miraculously unscathed.

At home: the television calling to him to peruse the prescribed junk that he had come to shape in every form. The black rectangle in front of his vision like the opposite of a bright afterlife tunnel. It never used to be like this. He poured himself a whisky, crouching down beside the freezer door to retrieve ice cubes then abandoning the idea. Sheer superficial effort. The whisky should taste the same without the spiked chill of an oddly shaped ice cube. But it doesn't.

Unable to find a suitable CD, Ebenezer relents, turning the television on and crumpling horizontally into the sofa, the victim of a Venus flytrap. The light of the phone message box flickers yet he ignores the intrusion, cavorting through the channels knowing that the only programmes being aired are half-baked versions of his own masterpieces, now pitifully soiled by the mere mention of the term reality. Reality then was something novel, something like an introduction of fresh air before the term even existed. Even before fly on the wall existed. When it wasn't about degrading the human soul through parading nobodies into celebrities as they argued with one another and their pasts were all splattered over the tabloids but when each programme was a triumph of the human spirit; a study in the everyman's psyche; a celebration of the something new; something shocking. A good night for a lament.

When Ebenezer wakes up, hugging one of the pillows for brief warmth, the light on the phone machine still flickers. Beckoning him to listen, to accept another same–old project. Leave the wretched thing. In fact, get rid of it altogether. Take a holiday. Drown the mobile phone. Teach the little black book to fly out the window. Destroy every television in sight. Pour another whisky.

The bottle's empty so Ebenezer makes his way gingerly back to the kitchen, a portion of his hair protruding from the side of his head: axed on Halloween. The slosh of the liquid sobers him up again because he's forced to concentrate on opening the bottle and pouring without spilling. The clock within the microwave display panel shines 2am, penetrating the murky darkness. His head hurt, not all over just the front bit in an arc with the pain radiating west-east at the two sides. To amplify, the sides of his mouth hurt too – his temple's throbbing wingman – crusty and foul tasting, the butt of his hand unable to wipe away the muck.

At this present position, standing almost on one leg in the

kitchen, reluctantly slurping down another warm whisky, bed's a million billion freakin twillion miles away. Of course, the couch is close, rumpled and made into a mould of his human form, ready for a second doze. At this time of the morning he shudders to think what's on: perhaps a camera inserted into one of the royal family's horse's arses to capture a day in the life of a prince's polo match. Or maybe a camera peering from every council estate television in the country, enabling viewers to select the family they wished to watch fight and pull hair and swear and make up and feel better as a result and thank the programme and mankind in general. His stupid idea (desperate sperm hunting women for god's sake!) and giving it to poor David; knowing it would be a minor success but knowing that each step with the flow was actually a step backwards. It was perhaps time to quit the business. Reality TV had run its course and Ebenezer Vim, the great granddaddy of reality TV, creator of Between the Walls, My BFF's Dilemma, Lives Less Ordinary, should now (more so than ever) hang up his idea factory and preserve what morsel of sanity was left as a viewer of the kind of mulch he had conspired to produce. All those years back.

That was all a really great idea and probably enforceable had the phone not rung at that exact second of hiatus in Ebenezer Vim's life. But it wasn't the call that would put together a series of events that would change his whisky induced flee from his path, but rather his fumbling with the controls to delete all the messages only to play one from his younger brother.

The heating crackles the radiators: pellet gun shots in a

Smug Dad

silent home as the silent outside air held back from pushing the curtains aside to bless the solid air with reprieve. A neighbour's dog coughs and chokes then coughs again, seemingly far away only to snort and then go back to silent sleep. Everything in Ebenezer's life was as it is in this precise moment: numb and empty; silent and congested but above all boring. No day to hold promise for the adventure of a new series; no anticipation from millions of viewers as to what was to happen next. What would happen next? Diarising and missing classes, drinking sessions and long–time family commitments to watch his shows, see what happens, back the favourite. So boring that when the post was shoved through the letter box the next morning …

CHAPTER 04

Adorn Pie Doll

EPISODE ii

The next day the sun rose. Not that the dawn was particularly bright or anything, the ghostly patches of London morning smog creating a maze for the emerging sun to wangle through, but there was a distinct feeling that the actual act of visualising the flaming ball surge past the horizon meant hope. Hope mixed with a generous sprinkle of despair, but how else would the hope be realised without despair.

When the phone rang, Eb was halfway between giving up trying to force down a dry piece of toast and picking up the pieces of the broken mirror, whose bits of sabre–toothed obstacles had almost created a bloody foot bath after a clumsy fumble in the early hours of the morning before any appearance from the sun. Eb had deftly negotiated through the fragments, at one point resting his entire weight on his big toe in a pirouette style twirl to retrieve the safety of his slippers. The ones he never wore.

If the phone was anywhere but on the opposite side of the apartment, the glass bits might have proved less of a Berlin Wall, the resultant charge might not have scattered further joy for the bad luck club and also not torn through the never worn slipper to more than tickle that arch part of the foot that no–one ever wants touched, which equated on a pain threshold scale to only the grooves behind the ears and the testicles.

"Son of a … hello!" Eb shook the slipper free and then retrieved it again so as not to bleed on the buff carpet.

"You were always on my mind," a familiar voice rang out on the other end of the line, the words spoken casually rather than lyrically.

"*Little Tommy never contact* or should I say *estranged family remember never again seen after disappearing from first London then the earth!*"

"I owe you nothing, ooh–ah, nothing at all."

"How've you been? No, where've you been? No! What is the ransom amount?"

"Living in America."

"Where?"

"California. Knows how to party. In the city."

"So what brings you back to the land of warm beer and black trousers?"

"Knees weak; arms heavy. Vomit on his sweater already."

Eb accepted everything and anything that had come to define his younger sibling. In the past, the speaking in music lyrics had annoyed Eb to such an extent that he had often … but now it was just good to hear his voice and he accepted his quirky eccentricities. It was now such a part of his brother's persona he hardly expected anything less; a failed song writing career that had spiralled into a drifting on expenses à la some forgotten grunge publication the most logical explanation. They were due to meet that evening so Eb knew his journey from hangover hell to recovered socialite had to not only be a quick one but an effective one.

Not only did his head hurt – the door knocking inside beginning to push his eyebrows off his temple – but now his foot too. And his dear Georgina, now entering his conscious and reminding him that he had forgotten to call the night before. Just as he said he would. A midnight call to catch her before her first big school excursion in the land of the Merlion: Singapura. Another let down. Well, at least he was proving consistent in one area of estranged parenthood. Jill would make a meal of this no doubt.

When he had cleaned the wound and the apartment to the best of his ability and slipped an extra twenty in the cleaner's hand whilst apologising and slipping out the front door before her protestations, Eb decided this was the day to flog his property for a ridiculously cheap price, take the cash and either put it all on black in Vegas or buy something away from London. Perhaps so far away from London that the closest thing to an irate black cab driver would be the local kids beating a donkey up a hill with a pail of water. In some warped fairytale perhaps, he told himself. There was no more debating it really: the end of his creation and dream for reality television and the subsequent commoditisation of the genre spelled the end of his production days; the end of being anywhere near a camera or even a television set for that matter.

The estate agent, despite being handed a gift of a sale, wasn't overly animated at the thought of a quick sale without squeezing out every possible pound's worth of commission. Eb even offered to pay an additional flat fee if the spotted twenty-something, his teeth way too white, could flog it, exchange and complete within the week. As Eb left the estate agent he wandered down the broadway, the sun now completely obscured by the despotic cloud cover. Needing a fresh pack of something (maybe cigarettes maybe gum maybe halal nuts) he swung into a corner shop, the bell on the door turning the shop assistant on like a child's toy. Each greeted one another with polite grinning nods.

Aimless days meant aimless activities (freedom, Eb would now say, freedom from some mighty prescriptive force; freedom to pretend to have new ideas) so Eb picked up a few mags and flicked though. The mag shelf held extensive variety: from cars to books to DVDs to laptops to fitness to politics to gay to photography to, of course, the porn mags titivating the top shelf, most of which wrapped up away from prying young eyes, like an ancient council of jurors looming above his eyeline. So Eb stretched his head and perused the mags calmly and casually; the shop was empty and what was really wrong with a middle aged man looking at girlie magazines? Surely it was more healthy than an obsession with the FT!

The variety within the porno section quite astounded Eb: the obvious differentiators like age and chest size then with more obscure stand–outs including specialist porn star publications for the industry's so–called elite and …

Just as his fascination was peaking, Eb noticed a familiar cover. Without hesitating he grabbed the magazine from the top shelf, rustling the neat display which almost seemed to put a frown on the other front covers. On this cover, now on top of his flat palms, a bright blonde stared back at him giggling. He knew this face. She knew he liked her; she had that look which knew that everyone who picked up Luscious Ladies Lambasted would want her. That confidence; not that you would want to rush off to finish yourself off but that you wanted to be part of her world somehow: know her dreams; know her desires. And he did. He tried to focus on her face, her round eyes and mouth of perfect triangular symmetry; tried to ignore the two burly forearms lassoed around her chest and easing her breasts up so that the taut moieties were touching her chin.

Watch Kimmy take on The Sperminator and Captain Arsealot the caption read. And her breasts, so big and in your face (or her face in this instance), the catalyst for sparking the remembering neurons. She was a short girl, he recalled, with extremely bad teeth. She had been a contestant in one of the earlier airing reality segments and shot to fame as everybody's favourite girl next door. She was actually pretty big until celebrities began to be created like thrown confetti and PR men and women clambered to punt each joe and jill average on a reality TV show to stardom. But she was different, he remembered. Shy but determined to make it in the world of television and stardom where her looks had initially opened doors and then closed them just as fast. She had confided in him once after the show on how her only dream was to be famous and happy and that the two were hand–in–hand as far as she was concerned. Now she had Captain Sperm and Lancelot or something to contend with. Yet strangely she looked happy; fulfilled; content; like she'd arrived.

"Do you plan to buy the magazine?" rang a voice from just below Eb's shoulder. He turned to look down upon the small store manager whose turban was slightly wonky. Eb wanted to tell him so but decided not to.

"I'd like to buy this," he said, fumbling for a few more to cover up. "And these, because I'm a real car nut you know."

My head in a bucket. Scrap that. My head in a toilet. Why can't I finish? I'm in this! I'm part of this! I'm in this? Nobody's perfect, all of the time. Nobody's perfect, we are what we are. I'm the younger brother, aren't I? That's my relationship with – what's his name – Ebenezer Vim. I'm the wall not the fly.

… so desensitised he knew it would work. Taking what would traditionally be the most exploitative industry against women and turning it into something empowering; affirming even, the masses cheering in support even if some of the categories were – well – base. Not like they were intending to be – and nothing funky – just that these are what the general populous would be familiar with. And we have to root for the aspirant; the heroine – likely escaping heroin. And, of course, done in a tasteful manner, dealing with the most tasteless topic. Of all. Giving into to our most basic …

… does not exist as a forum for men wishing to bring themselves to climax and then turn the tape off or close the page. It exists for lovers of quality …

Jesus, this is how I justify now? And I'm almost aware that I'm crossing wires here: when you're at the shop, dicking around a lonely Waitrose aisle, and you remember being at that exact spot a day or so earlier, except you're staring at washing power rather than nuts and snacks. And there's no gun in your face? No 'Heroes please apply at the Self Checkout' sign? Wait – that is something completely different!

… and those willing to share this subtle underbelly with the masses who choose to degrade the industry by ostracising those within it or quick fix junkies.

Denial for being a …

These 'contestants' would actually do anything, thought Ebenezer. So he thought he had to find someone the viewer would feel was reluctant morally but willing to do anything to change their station in life. Represent 'it' as a business but not necessarily male led; enough male though to be scorned and enough female to feel it was okay before the channel changed – behind the camera. And the judges – he would get the most famous crossover of them all – Faith Fellation. And add a cooking episode! I mean, who doesn't delight in food as another of life's true pleasures? Cooking would give the everyperson appeal and spark the bingo hall "her mushroom and parmesan risotto was a revelation" chat. There would be critics – by gawd he knew the controversial Samson Saskatchewan would be shocked and repulsed in equal measure – but that press would be vital, as long as the channel wasn't synonymous with filth. Goodlooking cooking. Getting rid of the sex shame. Opening up so the audience got to know the contestants and the act of perceived depravity was more to unbolt the viewership door than be laboured on as the weekly tumbled in, changing perceptions, increasing advertising flow and keeping television sets firmly switched on. The heroine should be switched on too: not planted, but a credible underdog, to be fallen in love with. Until that final episode. That final choice. The classic British voting twist.

... *master baker.*

A triumph of the warped human spirit, the headline would read. Shockingly real and uplifting – a show for the times. Never before has one television programme exposed our most basic desire for fame and fortune set against the blurred boundaries between mainstream and underbelly. It was only

a matter of time before a celebrity signed up.
  Porn Idol.

CHAPTER 14

Clack Jump Silliness

A potbellied television on its side in a pool of adequately spilled beer separates coupled clumps of human bodies. The crusted lips bobble hopelessly at moisture in the air and most are too afraid to raise an eyelid and allow destroying light beneath a lid. The television splutters static, unable to move to a channel, the tangled cords immersed with the remote control in the golden froth that collects in pockets of sunken carpet.

The first stir emerges from the host, clothed in flattering

underwear, alone and hotdogged in a cream duvet bunched into three of the corners leaving a foreskin inserted between the heels of her feet. She doesn't know what century she's in, surrounded by her guests in her own apartment, the ceiling weak from repeated bashing from the upstairs neighbour. Her tongue, plastered to the roof of her mouth, wrestles free to touch the tips of her teeth and pulls back from the sensitive sensational shock. At first her head is numb until her eyes find a spread apart packet of cigarettes containing broken soldier sticks, half–eaten and unused. Then her head is alive, pushing ephemeral signals to all corners of her cranial globe, forcing her to wince in pain and make sure she hands her purse over to the hangover in gentle and uncompromising union.

There is a man three feet from her asleep on his back with an inverted empty punch bowl covering his groin. Both his hands are clasped over the decorated bowl as if he were a dead body pushed into a mid–price range casket being wheeled down the tunnel of doom for a quick singe, scatter, tear and forget. Jenna's head is not ready for a soldier with a big glass hat on nor the memory of a brother's ashes scooping back from the urn and into her mouth and down her shoes and under her fingernails. And a washing logistical nightmare using uncle Casius's broken shower where the door doesn't lock and cold and hot are mutually exclusive.

Her safety net. A party to celebrate a parting. He would have wanted it that way. And to smoke again. Ah the beauty of once again not making excuses for three years of excruciating abstinence and pulling on that golden social habit that gives your hands an enduring activity and lungs the relief they so badly deserve. The glass bowl falls away from the man's groin.

Inside her bathroom are two women locked in an embrace kept prisoner by the high Victorian ceramics. They are bone dry. In the kitchen most of the cupboards have been ripped free to form a makeshift fort on the floor, housing a naked couple asleep with their curved spines arching fiercely at one another. A crusty condom has somehow become wrapped around the man's toe and in his slumbered state is unable to shake it free. The kicking, first toe then heel, almost unsettles the angular fort but does nothing to deter the sleeping pair.

Swallowing water fast. The cold filtered liquid escaping down her gullet to ease the suffering on her liver and recreate the cells that scorn her in every corner of her body. She wraps a gown around herself, not visibly cold but nevertheless naked around all of Ben's friends. His musician friends. The ones she met at the funeral. The ones who knew him. The ones who could explain who he was. The ones who have become scattered around her awkward apartment like her brother's ashes.

"Ben would've rocked at this pad. It's good of you," they'd said as the flat metamorphosis bulged and choked to acquire more guests; more of Ben's friends until it didn't really matter anymore. "Take a few days off," her boss had barked under his breath. "But come back ready. Something's brewing at the Jones's". And now a pot of marijuana and black coffee and sugar, bubbling and brewing on the stove top, the tiny filaments of green herb sliding up and then down the brown bubbles of caffeine, but still lying motionless.

Soaked and unsmoked.

A clothesline of underwear, male and female, has been joined from the bookcase to the desk. Jenna doesn't recognise any of her own in there and is even more surprised to find no one inhabiting the worn out room, now reluctantly receiving slats of sunlight through the window. In the main bedroom a human pyramid spills over all sides of her double bed, faces buried in armpits, hands slipping between legs and round bottoms peeking from among the human remains like spotlights. Amongst the mayhem, immaculately preserved, almost enshrined by an inanimate glory, rests Ben's guitar.

Inside Jenna's cupboard is a choir of empty beer tins. Forty-four bottles of beer on the wall! She pulls on a pair of old jeans underneath her dressing gown failing to upset the tins. She abandons her stained Sunday top for a new tighter fitting one; one that she recently purchased, didn't fancy too much yet wears for the sake of wasted income. In the hallway she is forced to hopscotch another chapter of partly clothed bodies. Who are these people in her life, here for a death and an evening to return to their garage jam sessions and small club gigs and busking to support the habit? Consciously departing from a stilted existence to hear the right sound; a well-timed mix of instruments and syllables packaged and titled for the pleasure of cyclical age bands.

Outside is warm. Jenna's hands are warm and shaky and it takes her a few attempts to submerge her keys in her jeans pocket. The key ring cumbersomely juts into the solid part of her thigh muscle. The blur of the day is annoying. Everyone is already at work. Where she should be. Toiling away to make a difference.

Smug Dad

A truck driver passes and whistles, sticking his tongue at her and allowing his head to follow her form until the taillights have disappeared below the ridge of tar. She tucks her hair behind her ears and slumps onto a bench circled by an effect of tall trees and bus stops. An old woman waves and boards a bus. Jenna tries to smoke a three quarter cigarette. She coughs hard, the mucus from the previous evening's activities collecting below her chin, and persists as if completion will lead to some sort of unnatural redemption.

Her face feels smeared everywhere. Her fury teeth drip sweat and her jaw hurts from maybe laughing or smoking or talking. She's forgotten what it's like to be outdoors on a weekday, the reality of her only excuse to enjoy it being the death of her brother providing no respite. This is not her; this inactivity; this waiting for some kind of healing. What would be next but another strange encounter, which would only further serve to show her that her life will not be any different now that her brother is gone.

Back at her apartment the guests are still all comatose. The man with the glass bowl has rolled into a pocket of beer and the wall mirror has now fallen from the wall without shattering. Jenna changes clothes and washes her face. The application of a quick, respectable amount of makeup and a haphazard teeth clean is all that will suffice before she returns to work. She calls her parents to check on them before departing.

{ ↪ ↩ ↪ ↩ ↪ ↩ }

An arm slides through Jenna's arm arc before she has time to breathe in the static office air; before the spats of forehead sweat have formed; before the wrought brows have greeted. A hairy arm, capped with a clump of rolled up white office shirt and heavy, but not like a paperweight heavy, rather a dense piece of salami heavy. The arm drags her past her desk, past Frieda, a helpless, surprised expression passing her photos on the constricted desk. Frieda shrugs. The arm owner, channel executive director, Larry 'the Game' Platonofsky breathes heavily, straining along the worn green flooring of the office suite situated in the same building as some of the contracted studios.

He shuts the door behind him; his office with stolen calendar, music beat piles of dog–eared paper and Kerry, the golden retriever like researcher with glasses roosting on her scraped back hair (who does that anymore?), figure hugging designer suit and pen poised to work hard, beat others and spank into a senior management position. Jenna's hardly ready for this, still reeling from a cocktail of cocktails, her palms sweaty and stomach distended with pukey waves continually spitting upwards towards her mouth. Kerry smiles, her perfectly adjusted teeth catching the fluorescent lights in triumph and her pen tapping on her pad reminding Jenna and The Game that time is a wasting; her schedule is full.

An extended merry band of drummer people pound inside Jenna's brain. The beat is so loud she's convinced they can hear. Perhaps they'll confuse this for mourning. Her eyes must look beetroot red, roadmapped and watering, her ducts exhausted from agitation. Kerry clears her throat. The Game smooths his arm hair, one arm then the next so the numerous curly hairs buckle forwards, sticking for a millisecond then shaking free. A ceiling fan would be good. A quiet cosy day reading email would be better. Anti–Inflammatories would be the best if they stayed down.

"Kerry, good work on the drama series," the Game starts shuffling through a desk drawer and then, abandoning the idea, kicks the drawer shut and pops an old-looking mint in between his stained teeth. "Jenna, condolences. But seeing you're back, let's jump straight in. This fucking thing cannot wait. All our good work this year can be undone in one half season if rumours are true."

Kerry's textbook posture sends spasms through Jenna's hunched pose, jolting up as if waking from a dream. Without moving her perfect head, Kerry glances over and purses her face in some sort of condescending disapproval or knowing. Kerry wants to talk. To speak. To be heard. She keeps breathing in to bestow words upon the audience and is continually met by The Game's raised finger; no words just pacing.

"A house; a big fuck off house is being rented to none other than Peter Granger for the next seven weeks. Trucks outside. All the time. I'm thinking camera equipment. I'm thinking cables. I'm thinking live feeds. I'm hoping nothing of the sort. Prove me wrong."

"Larry, far be it for me to tell you how to run your team but could we put in place the structure necessary to make sure we all optimise our efforts," spells Kerry. The 'our' is pronounced like a slow motion movie. Kerry turns to face

Jenna who taps the tips of her shoes together in time with the fax machine splurging forth a brown smudged contract. "I feel strong about this, Larry. I refuse to run around alongside someone else aimlessly gathering information. I want a formal reporting structure."

The Game's mind now distant, jutting towards the ongoing roll of fax paper and then back to his notepad. "Get it done. Whatever it takes."

Afterward Jenna makes her way to the ladies, dipping her fists into the cool basin controlled water and dabbing her forehead. Kerry interrupts the fourth dab, lowering Jenna's hands to gather her complete attention, scrunching her nose towards the evenly layered base coat of makeup skilfully applied across all crevices and excessive smile lines.

"So we have everything clear then, Jen–Jen. Once you have your information report it in to me and then I will feed it all to Larry, making sure to provide credit where it is due of course. I have a little mini–itinerary for you. I've emailed it to you. Most of the initial work is library work which as you know is what makes any reporter the real deal. Don't go near the house. I'll be handling that."

The hand dryer spontaneously starts, the supernatural bathroom gods throwing Jenna a dissolving bone. Jenna glances sideways and Kerry waits expectantly, pushing Jenna for any sign of acknowledgement: a nod, a yes, a salute. "Oh and sorry about the whole brother thing. These things always have a nasty habit of happening at the worst possible times." Jenna pushes past Kerry and shuts herself into a prisoned cubicle, now unable to stop the flow of gastric juices trampetting from the depths of her stomach through the lower oesophageal sphincter, up the oesophagus, through the throat and into the bowl. Mixed fruit.

❴ ➡ ⬅ ➡ ⬅ ➡ ⬅ ❵

Dust swirling in the city so that eyes remain clenched and people spit, tongue flicking deliberate lines of dust from the end of lips. Jenna waits, head facing down on a convenient bench: a bus hints to stop then continues forward punishing her for not standing to attention. Frieda relieved so that she cups the limp flame of her old lighter towards Jenna's mouth, the polite refusal against Jenna's desire. A cyclone of blue chip packets, old bus tickets and dust swirl around the two momentarily and then off to harass an old lady hobbling without a cane.

"Where you going?" mouths Frieda, sharing the struggling for an end to whatever this is.

"The Game. New Assignment."

"Any help? I mean anything? I can kill Kerry if you need me to or at least spike her coffee so she's in the loo for more than practising her smile."

Jenna stands, another bus wobbling towards the stop, the driver expressionless then furiously swerving into the stop blinded by Jenna's waving. The mustard bouquet in the bus makes the side of Jenna's mouth curdle and she sits down in the section normally reserved for old people or cripples. She sits facing a child with a mum and dog attached, the mum annoyed with the child's incessant reading, the dog panting towards the exit.

"Why was Jack so clumsy, Mummy? I'm sure I wouldn't have fallen down. I would never break my crown if I had one, Mummy."

The kid is too pretty for a boy, thinks Jenna, scrabbling out a pair of fake spectacles from her purse: black rimmed and obvious. She applies her lipstick and, even without the normal seesawing bus, she gets it all wrong leaving an arch on the left side so that she might be covering a cleft palate. She ties her hair up tight so that her skin on the sides of her temples pulls backwards. Her collar is fastened. And her shirt tucked in.

The house squatting between an isolated plot and a fenced wooded enclosure is deserted but for two guards circling the perimeter by yelling across to one another every time something exciting happens on the radio: goals flanked by gratuitous celebrity headlines and beheadings. If only. Jenna emerges from the taxi walking purposefully towards the guards, shaking her head vehemently and strutting so that the clatter of her solid heels alert the guards. One stands up and Jenna alters direction, heading into his sternum like a deep breath.

"Christ. Jesus Christ. Stephen is going to have my balls with a side salad for his God Damn breakfast tomorrow," she says, flashing identification towards the guard. "Today is what? Thursday? That leaves us two fucking weeks! And what do I go and do to fuck it all up?

She's hot but nope. It's not working, cocked wrist in that Indiana Jones whip motion which ALWAYS works, not working.

CHAPTER 24

Laughter Wife

Oliver Wallace stares back at his body. It's like he's looking into a mirror but at a funny angle. Everything is not as it's supposed to be yet there's no remorse, just phlegm. He can see the hospital staff continue their plight, angrily barking orders at one other and inserting apparatus into his skin and orifices. The noise from the flat green line on the monitor rings inside his head and he is forced to place both hands in cup shapes over his ears. The noise fails to subside and still the pretend saviours continue until the time of death is recorded and a bloodied sheet placed over the corpse to rest in peace.

The peace and the silence are now deafening and Oliver is alone in a surgery ward with himself. All he can see is an out of shape lump of human concealed as if the sight were too sore for dead eyes. He wished one last look at the body he formerly inhabited but is not afforded the opportunity, or at least that is what he believes, frozen solid in the evergreen hospital with shiny walls and unpronounceable machines. For a second he believes he sees himself twitch and instinctually darts to call for help before realising the ludicrousness of his action.

He is dead. He is a dead man. Oliver Wallace. Fifty exactly. But a few weeks before his death. From his state of inertia he hears the voice of his wailing wife in the corridor. He wishes to go to her and console her and explain what happened but cannot or will not, whichever seems more suitable. His arms hang at his sides, motionless and tender like a baby's, unable to flick open his penknife and trim a fingernail; unable to throw a tennis ball for his dog to fetch; unable to take his grandson in his arms again.

His wife's screams become more muffled by the consoling rabble of concerned mutterers around her. He can make out the false sympathy from Dawn Madden, an old family friend, as she systematically pats on her head and clutches her wet face. He hears Dawn's daughter, Julianne, the one who was his daughter–in–law. Married to the one light and salvation that could have prevented the end of his existence. And then his voice with a quiver, struggling to believe the emergence of tragedy that has befallen the family, but still trying hard to be the brave soldier. He still has a heart because he can feel it race when hears his son's voice and, before he can figure out whether dead people are able to cry, he is somewhere else. Somewhere he has never been before (not surprisingly, having never been dead before).

He's not flying as he might have imagined but there is no doubt in his mind that he is not stationary. His movement feels as it might if one were submerged in jelly: every turn a squeeze, every lick a mouthful. This is the first time he contemplates the whole idea of the afterlife and the thought at first annoys him because he has been an atheist his entire life. Perhaps he is still alive and has merely dreamt of his premature departure from the world. Perhaps those doctors and nurses are all only moments away staring down on him on the emergency table like a dissected insect. This feeling of utter solitude is probably what many have described having been so close to death. Yet there is no door, no tunnel of light and certainly no stairway to heaven (or escalator to hell). The jelly numbness now fills his eye sockets and he feels all his cells being massaged into oblivion before he disappears somewhere and is gone from somewhere else.

He is fast asleep and on his way towards an event.

CHAPTER 34

Laughter Wife

He is suddenly awake and immersed in a sea of people. He feels like a pinball being shunted around effortlessly despite being a man of considerable build and height. There is no clear direction the people are moving in, each one a manic version of the next. For a second he sees the irony in wishing he were dead but the thought is quickly dispelled when he is knocked clean off his feet onto a smooth cold floor and then trampled by a billion pairs of warm toes. Everyone around him is barefoot and now begin scrambling in one direction when what sounds like a hooter wails. His confusion is meaningless as he is filled with a complete lack of desire to stand up.

A kind old woman lifts him to his feet and he does not thank her. The momentum of the crowd moves him forward, his limp body a loaf of bread atop a baker's basket. Every face around him displays clear and uncompromising determination; a determination which he does not share or wish to share. He tries to take note of his surroundings and notices that there are none. The human mass seems contained by a stretch of barrier that has no form or colour. Everyone knows it is there yet cannot see it or feel it.

This same phenomenon now presents itself up ahead. The crowd split into two as an invisible wedge creates a huge fork in the path. Where Oliver now stands, he is heading directly towards the split and does not care that he is in danger of slicing in half as he approaches with fierce velocity. He doesn't care because nothing means anything anymore and after everything he has done in life it is time he paid the price in death. He's dead and he wishes nothing upon himself, only that he be at the mercy of those who determine fates. Those so–called higher beings, dare he say God. Whoever, just do it quickly.

He thinks he hears his name amidst the low hum of people exerting and dismisses the notion. Again the words "Mister Oliver Ford Wallace" ring out, this time accompanied by an exacerbated "Stop!" He manages to turn around and sees a small bald man in a light brown suit waving papers and a torn briefcase in his direction. The man is clearly trying to get his attention and he ignores it before the man is lifted from the crowd and carried to safety, before Oliver is forced to the right of the barrier and through what feels like an electric curtain. In a second everyone around him is stripped of their manic state and an austere calm ensues, the procession now single file and in orderly rows. He does not wish to follow this way yet cannot explain why he is prevented from following his own course of action. It is as though he were free to choose before the barrier split but now has no choice. This makes him exceedingly happy as he slumps into a worthless trance, hoping now more forcefully that his end will be painful but still quick.

CHAPTER 44

Laughter Wife

EPISODE III

The sleep awake thing is starting to annoy him when again he wakes after what he believes to have been sleep. He is somewhere in the afterlife. Nothing has changed. Still he is unable to make out his surroundings and control of his movements is not precise. The only constant between life and death is his mind and complete inability to hope for anything beyond what he deserves. He deserved death. That was his punishment for life. That was his sentence. Now he is here, ready to serve out his sentence far from content wishing rather to cease existing in a box in the earth or scattered on some abandoned farmyard.

Where is the booming voice from above? Where is the bearded Christ? Where is the horny little devil with flames? Where are the clouds? Where is the judgement? That is what he needs: judgement. Clear and honest judgement to rid him of the part he played in life. Instead there is this nothing void that could not be painted or described or wished upon anyone. Not even him after all he's done. He's not the worst here, of that he's convinced. He's sure there are worse dead people out there, but none that had the choice. The choice that he created. The choice that he failed to shy away from.

He senses he is inside a room and knows he is alone. No one around. Again the solitude but this time different as though the air is expectant in nature, the force of a clear picture imminent. He feels others near him yet not, each one, unlike him, wishing to know where to next; what left to do. A man enters his room and faces him, his brow sweaty and a bunch of papers crumpled in his right hand. He is the short bald man from the crowd, his expression one of exhaustion as he cowers like a dog. He speaks to Oliver the prisoner and the words erupt from his mouth in a normal fashion. He is small and fat and Jewish and has the beginnings of a combover. His imperfections warm the room and give Oliver his first taste of real life in the afterlife.

"Mr Oliver Ford Wallace, my name is Garth Solomon and I am your 'Assigned'. Let me extend my sincerest apologies at my complete lack of punctuality earlier and welcome you." The little man does not extend his hand but does smile, showing an adequate set of teeth. "Thankfully, you took the right path, an action which I can only think of as the most fortunate of the rest of your afterlife. And no thanks to me either. Perhaps we can start again and treat this as the beginning of a most optimistic and prosperous partnership? Now I'm sure you have many questions. New 'Gimmlers' always do. That's what we call the new recruits: Gimmlers. It's a derivation of 'Glimmer' because that is what most are holding onto as they attempt to enter. A glimmer of hope!"

"I don't have any questions except one. Is there no way I can just cease to exist? Be dead and be quiet and forget everything that has gone before?"

Solomon now looks more confused than he should and loosens his collar before proceeding. "Mr Wallace, you might not understand at this present time how exceptionally fortunate you are. For most choosing the correct path was not a matter of luck but one of instruction. Granted had I found you earlier you would still be here but that is not to be taken lightly. You could have been one of many to not be preparing for your journey but rather one already at his destination."

There is no silence in the room yet everything is still. Garth Solomon has a chubby, kind face which reaches out to Oliver whose constricted demeanour shuts him out like blinds preventing the sun entering a room. "I know things are disorientating and confusing, but everything will become clearer. As your journey progresses all your senses will begin to react differently: you'll see things differently and be more of an integral part of your surroundings. At the moment what surrounds you is merely a product of your own psyche, a creation in your own mind. I don't know what you see but it is completely different for others in your position," he finishes, looking nervously at his wristwatch.

"Just send me to fucking hell!" yells Oliver, suddenly scaring the lawyer–like creature in front of him so much that he shudders away.

"Oh please don't speak that way, Mr Wallace. That is not something to be taken lightly, I assure you. Now unfortunately I'm late for another Gimmler, again! I will be back shortly to discuss the first level of your journey. Please take care, Mr Wallace, and try to get some rest. It will set you in marvellous stead."

With that, the little man scuttles out as fast as he entered leaving Oliver alone to be dead. This is juvenile, he thinks to himself. My little journey like a schoolchild. The big test. Pass or fail. Heaven or hell. Dead or dead. He now thinks of his son and tears that are not there well in his eyes. With that spout of emotion a small bed appears in the room and he lies on his stomach with his arms limply straddling either side. His beautiful son, full of the goo of life every unfulfilled person in the world is looking for. What he was looking for all those years ago: the beginning of the end. And his son such a stark contrast to himself, completely in control of his selfish desires. Yet still best of friends until the end. Until he could no longer live with what he'd done. He must be punished for his action, this he truly believes.

CHAPTER 54

←→

Laughter Wife

EPISODE IV

He's hungry so food appears which he shoves down his mouth with his hands, failing to spark a need for a fork or a spoon. He doesn't even care what he eats as long as he does, as though the hunger creates the food rather than him: a genuine feeling. Still he's hungry and still he continues to eat until he's so full that he has to lie down again. He tries to make himself sick by sticking his finger into the depths of his throat but nothing emerges except spit and the saturated feeling remains.

There is no going back, he keeps telling himself and this is a good thing, he tells himself again. How could he return after the multitude of lies and deceit? The 'Assigned' Mr Garth Solomon has not been lying as with every reminiscent thought, the world Oliver knew when he was alive begins to return. The room is no longer a square but a high ceilinged Victorian room with a matching picture rail and cornice. There is a large old fireplace that burns brightly without giving off any heat. Oliver watches as the flames manoeuvre themselves from side to side as they lick at the upper lip. He puts his hand in, feels nothing and then his face but still nothing. There is a large cast iron candle holder in the centre of the room which Oliver tries to drive through his heart but to no avail: the stick crumbles and disappears.

The commotion is silent and Garth Solomon nonchalantly pops his head around the corner of the polished wooden door and says, "Come with me now, Mr Wallace, it's already time for your first stage. There's been a cancellation and you've been moved forward. We've got to be there very shortly and I haven't yet explained what will transpire so walk with me and listen carefully."

The corridor is long and windy and colourless with a faint odour of activity almost seeping from the walls. The two men walk forcefully with Oliver, despite having almost double the length stride, lagging behind Garth as he frantically jabbers away. "Just do what comes naturally to you, Mr Wallace. This is not a game so don't treat it as such. Let the situation bring out the truth. There are ways of influencing this, even contorting it, but I wouldn't recommend it as eventually you will be discovered. You see up here it is impossible to monitor all eight billion people that are alive, so the next while will paint a picture of what you were like alive and whether you are worthy for progression onto the next phase. Do you understand, Mr Wallace?"

"No, but I don't care so we should both be happy."

"Here we are," says Garth, stopping at a doorway. He runs his fingers over something directly above his head and nods. Then he inserts a card or something into a hole that looks as though it doesn't exist and the door opens.

There is no mist or smoke just another empty room. Oliver enters, his face clearly not in awe of anything in the afterlife. "Good luck," says Garth before the door shuts and Oliver is once again alone. Before he has time to settle in, he notices an old man with sagging flesh hobbling towards him. The man's appearance is somewhat unnerving and Oliver takes a few steps backwards to view more clearly the man approaching. He holds a smooth dark wooden walking stick which he now raises and points directly between Oliver's eyes, the rubber bottom's fluff and dirt clearly visible in every detail.

"Do you know who I am?" says the man.

"No. Should I?" replies Oliver.

"I'm an old man. An old person. I am the majority in this place. That is what happens: old people die. Frequently. What do you want to do to me?"

"Nothing I don't think."

"What do you think of me? Do I repulse you?"

"Yes you do repulse me. This whole place repulses me."

"Let's get back to me for a second," says the old man. "I need to fill you with a feeling. You must let me and everything I represent fill you with a feeling, a range of emotions. This will shape your experience."

"I don't really care about my experience," says Oliver, feeling suddenly drowsy. "I just want out. I don't want to play these silly games."

"You are reaching your threshold now. In a few seconds the room will change colour which signifies that I have filled you with enough feeling for you to select the correct scene from your past. Do not worry about your anger. Your true self will be revealed."

Moments after Oliver passes out and collapses to the floor, the room goes a deep red, almost crimson, and Oliver's eyelids start twitching. The old man places a metal helmet on top of Oliver's skull and proceeds to project whatever is going on in Oliver's mind onto a screen connected to a recording device.

Oliver, his tiny arm in a cast, sits swinging his legs on a rickety old white bench that is too big for him. He looks lost on the immense expanse of wood and struggles, with only one arm working, to dismount. The lawn in front of him is not well kept yet beautiful in its disarray. Small purple flowers burst from the rich soil shrouded by a haze of miniature insects all hastily assembling plant matter for their nests. A yellow billed hornbill sits atop the washing line that dissects the lawn like a hair parting and lets out a characteristic disjointed call that echoes through the farmland.

Oliver casually strides across the lawn and towards the chicken pen where he runs his free hand across the mesh creating upheaval among the chickens in the roost. He is eight years old and visiting his grandparents on their farm. He loves the outdoors but not enough to spend every waking second there. His indoor activities are just as important to him and this particular excursion is one that possesses neither logic nor intention, just a child with a broken arm on a farm.

A plum tree rests aside the large enclosure and Oliver picks a few ripe specimens and eats them appreciatively after washing them under an old tap, just as his grandmother taught him. There are a few unripe plums which are higher up than the rest and Oliver skilfully climbs the tree to retrieve them, again just how his grandmother taught him but warned him against doing with one arm. The unripe plums are perfect missiles as they're hard unlike their ripe counterparts. He opens the cage and begins firing them into the chickens, the panic creating a spray of feathers and bird shit.

As he's about to fire his third a burly hand catches his and twists it around until he's wailing on the floor. "I'll break your other arm, you little shit." The stench of stale Brandy bellows forth like a hot breeze. His grandmother's husband lets go of his arm and staggers backwards before sitting flat in a patch of cabbages, passed out with vomit on his light blue, short sleeve shirt. Oliver gets up and wipes the tears from his face before firing one last plum at the lonesome cock in the pen and then rushes to fetch the hose from a nearby wall.

What flashes through his mind as an eight-year-old is not what he's about to do but what has happened before. He struggles to eradicate the memory of this man using the back of his hand on his grandmother. He still sees her cheek split open and one of her teeth protruding through her bottom lip as the man who would never replace his grandfather continues in a drunken rage. He also remembers how he ran in to hug his grandmother as she cried in a heap on the floor, aside the foreboding clink of a belt buckle being unfastened. He'd never seen her like that, so broken, so humiliated and it filled him with such anger and fear and hurt. The man would then rush at him, lifting him by one arm, swinging him off the crying elderly woman until the bone snapped and the numbing sensation set in. And how he'd flung him towards the ceiling and continued at his grandmother. Then how in hospital the next day he'd cried next to Oliver's bed saying how sorry he was and bought him a plastic truck to buy his silence.

These were the scenes that filled young Oliver's mind as he pushed the faded green hosepipe down into the unconscious man's throat and turned it to full. There were no regrets as he watched the water fill up the man's lungs and he drowned. He was saving his grandmother, the beautiful woman who had raised his mum and shown him more love than he deserved. He hadn't intended to kill this man, just stop him inflicting pain and hurt and tears and grief. Stop it for good. And that was what happened.

The lifeless corpse now lay in front of the boy, the smell of Brandy diluted by the water. Still the hose continued to pump, leaving a pool of mud and wet, green cabbage around the large form, the hair on his hands glistening dark black in the fading sunlight. Tears spill out of Oliver's eyes as he pulls the hose free from the man's throat and places it back where he found it. There is no going back now. He wipes his tears with the back of his hand, vowing to never hurt another living thing again. He locks the chicken pen and dutifully heads back to the farmhouse to explain what has happened.

When Oliver wakes, the old man is gone and the room is back to its original colour. He has a severe headache which rattles as he gets to his feet. For a moment he thinks he is going to fall over but manages to refocus his vision and remain upright. There's a glass of clear liquid in front of him which he pours down his throat. It reminds him of the scene of his step–grandfather's death which is strangely vivid in his mind. He cannot stop the memory, hidden for so many years, bombarding his conscious. He has no regrets even now that he is dead. His grandmother only lived for another three years but remarried to a postman who, despite his shortcomings as a gregarious soul, treated her well and looked after her in her dying years.

It makes Oliver wonder whether she's around here and whether the man he killed is too. The whole bullshit idea of being reunited scares him. What would he say? Presumably there were no secrets up here. Up here? Why does he presume it's up? He could be in the fiery belly of the earth's core; this could be hell. Maybe that's why he's so unhappy and can only think about being somewhere else. He doesn't want to run into his grandmother or his grandfather or the stand–in grandfather he killed or the postman. He just wants nothing. He's already given up and now just craves peace. Everything he lived, and now died for, is gone. His scratched records. His matchbox collection. His sport. His medals. His son. His dear son given to him by his subservient wife. His loving wife who, like the postman, spent her days trying to make him happy. But she never could. Not him. Not Oliver Wallace.

Solomon personally fetches him from the room and asks him whether he is feeling alright. He doesn't want to converse with this silly man any longer and shrugs him off as he makes his way down the corridor. "You're going the wrong way, Mr Wallace," says Solomon.

"I don't care," replies Oliver, stumbling and turning to return in the opposite direction.

"Let me help you. Please?" He forces Oliver onto his stocky shoulder and carries him a few feet until he is able to walk properly himself. Back inside Oliver's room, Solomon puts him to bed, putting more water by his bedside and turning off the light. "You take care, Mr Wallace," he says. "If you are a good person, it will be apparent." He leaves uncharacteristically quietly, closing the door behind him.

The room is even clearer for Oliver now even though he is semi–conscious and not fully able to absorb the additions. There's now a bathroom which he feels like using for the first time since dying. The water from the tap tastes like water from a tap and his needed nourishment is the only thing that keeps him awake. Now his bones ache and he feels like a fifty year old again, unable to take control of all his bodily functions. He's bored even though he's tired and for the first time wishes he was alive for the sole purpose of finding something to do. There had to be more to do when he was alive than now. The silence has become his enemy and he yells towards the ceiling before nodding back to sleep and dreaming about times that will never again be and times he hopes never to have to rekindle again.

Smug Dad

This must be it. The only plausible outcome. If you take the D out you are left with Eath which makes no sense. Or are you left with Evil?

CHAPTER 64

I Kill Till Salty Facts

Standing ankle deep in wet mud and gagging from the percolating stench in the middle of the night hopefully atop the undiscovered grave of that cartoon character is where we find our reluctant heroes. That is until Jake, the shorter of the two, makes too much progress with his spade thrust and falls through the cold air and into the sludge, catching the corner of the sharp edge of the spade on his descent. An open neck artery and a fetid stewing faecal stew is never a convincing combination and now Hugo is scrabbling at his partner's neck, trying to stop the bleeding and scoop the contaminated liquid away from the wound that belches blood as though a gasket has been blown. Jake's eyes are soft as he stares up at Hugo, unable to look away yet unmistakably aware of the consequences, Hugo breathing more rapidly, dispelling the attempted calming of the situation and holding Jake on his lap pressing the side of his neck.

With the heel of his shoe Hugo feels that Jake's fateful dig has found the brittle top of the coffin which proves Harry's scribbled map is no fake and the job is no dud. Jake now clambers onto Hugo's rusted shirt as attempts to lift Jake from the pit are foiled by the flashlight of a security guard, exposing the whites of their eyes, two pairs of brights suddenly off automobile lights in the darkness. Hugo is forced to drop down into the pit and clasps his hand over Jake's mouth after whispering to him to hold his breath. The two quickly submerge, Hugo still clamping the gash and keeping his own mouth tightly shut while the smell induces little splats of vomit to bounce into his mouth.

When the two surface, the flashlight is darting along the horizon further away and Jake has stopped moving. Hugo listens at his mouth to find no breath when the flashlight, its range annoyingly vast, skimming the top of his matted hair. Jake is dead and Hugo is alone in a smelly pit. The night chill momentarily releases its grip as Jake bursts awake, the neurons coughing up their last collective ball of phlegm, then slumps back down Hugo's forearms and into the rose coloured liquid to float and stare up at the characterless sky which stares back without remorse.

Hugo is about to go numb: he has been working with Jake

for a couple of years now; met his adolescent daughter with a stud through her cheek; persuaded a client not to stick a knife between his thighs; watched Jake feed his fish. And now he doesn't even hold his hand as the corpse drifts slightly away from him before colliding with the worn mud bank and drifting back. The protection means nothing; a vain endeavour to feel parental perhaps. The clumsiest of errors now dealing the two of clubs and a grave full of bones existing beneath.

An hour in the mud is enough to see the back of the flashlight but with the imminent return an obvious consideration, the only option: step up efforts. Clearing a path to hack through the casket required the removal of the body, further digging and scooping. The noise from the axe imbedding itself into the solid wood would attract attention and would need to be random like a shot in the dark or a gate slamming shut. Three strikes and still no daylight. Four and the remainder of the blood and sewage drain through the slit eye gash and into the warm cream coloured interior, immediately darkening the pristine environment and moving the feeble skeleton to one side.

The hum of the electric jigsaw now dulls the night silence as Hugo efficiently cuts a generous hole into the coffin. The skeleton is not scary even though the jawbone has been dislocated from the mouth to reveal the ex–being yelling at the invader, willing him through centuries of patient horizontal contemplation to turn around, take his friend to the morgue and wash himself with warm lavender soap that comes in those scented boxes. But he doesn't. He's not programmed for that. He's not looking for that. What he is looking for is not around.

Scrabbling through hungry bones like an eco–friendly scavenger without a gloved hand sees a shard of bone lodge itself in the centre of his palm. The immediate pain jolts him back so that his hand clatters at an abnormal angle against the top of the coffin and he drops the torch from between his teeth. Another clatter sounds inside the coffin as though something has dropped from the ceiling. Hugo retrieves the torch and curls his hand into the darkness beneath, coming to rest on the abdomen and then the side of the femur. Everything still feels like human bone which is exactly not what he is looking for.

When his hands comes to rest along a cool wooden shaft Hugo realises his accident has dislodged exactly what he came for.

Finding something worthwhile is nigh on impossible. Especially when you've seen all that is worthwhile. Like you know before you've watched. The reviews tell you so. And the hype; the marketing eons before launch date: the non–muted return of the series.

Open that dusty trench coat, I want to see your member ...

Something motivational called 'Today' and the follow up 'This Day' – not even a nah; more like a no way. Even at this stage, in this state, this trance, this void, there will be standards. Still flashing. Born when she wakes up – lives a whole day – dead when she goes to sleep. But not Groundhog because it is different each day. A different life. Sometimes a black woman. Sometimes a painful death. Little variation or twist that it sometimes prolongs for two days then stagnant for years, reverting to 'One Life in One Day' the Ones equal opposites and winking back at one another. That's a nah because Doug is tempted. A little like the graverobber heading towards some sinister construction and organised sick–ass crime ring: intriguing but not enough to stifle these violent awakenings; this increasing awareness of self.

A twisted thriller set in an asylum? Seen it.

A woman kidnaps a refugee thief then falls in love? Too now.

'Good is trendy' – good things to teach? Too Robin Williams.

Serial killer takes victims according to The Lord of the Rings? Too traumatic envisioning Frodo strung up by his ring.

'Pink Tools' – a story about a gay tool shop in backwater colonial Africa. Maybe.

'Tackling Lomu' – a father son saga with the metaphoric bringing down of the steroid freak by the father his one final act of self–affirming defiance. Maybe maybe.

Serial killer by phobias. Back to nah.

'Heading Towards the Dark' – the tunnel enshrouded by light as a vision towards hell not heaven. Rings a bell.

Smug Dad

Animal Rights retribution by someone so aggrieved it then moves onto Muslims? Odd but nah.

Let's fuck nah up here, thinks Doug. What's all the rage, what can't people get enough of. Dystopian YA of course. Cast looks half decent and the screenwriter and director are the same person.

Worth a nose.

CHAPTER 74

Energetic Anger Earing

 EPISODE I

Hoping in vain (and needlessly in fact because what else does it bring other than a mini vitamin D-induced tickle of warm optimism?) for the pesky clouds to open in a childbirth gesture to allow the remodelled Life Orb (version IX) to spit a ray, Grenoble procrastinated. So much so that The Unity might deem it so unacceptable as to leverage a Late which added to a similar offence a year ago and, of course, The Exchange, would most likely result in a significant loss of privilege for the season: full water retractions for a month, office working or worst of all – assignment to the Fields.

Nothing remerged, a single obdurate cloud tending towards redemption then reneging as if specifically instructed to conserve the limited energy as a direct command from The Unity, buttoning onto a larger reinforcement sweeping in from the west. Grenoble reached his neck forward, staring at a Dyson angle towards the ground, uncomfortably squeezed his collar fastener and walked to his Zone.

Creating order was something Grenoble understood and endorsed through his Basic behaviours and Development Goals. Although officially everyone was directly or indirectly employed and Embraced by The Unity, Grenoble's Zone was part of a genetic data processing unit within the structure's Core – the single most important part of The Unity's administrative management of growth and furthering of the human species before The End.

What keeps us from the End is the Future

Three blocks out from his Zone, Grenoble happened on The Future: a group of six Futures out of uniform; a neat symmetry of three Xs and three Ys. He quickly averted his eyes as was not only custom but now law, the imagined memory of the Life Orb still leaving an indelible tunnel every time he blinked. Grenoble could feel he was slightly taller than one of the Xs as she breezed past dragging a clean curve of scent up his jawbone. His face went flush but none noticed.

Since the Futures had been allowed to integrate with the Zone workers there had been no troubles – but rather the opposite. A campaign of tolerance and assimilation had been introduced into the Programme some time back, even at Fledgling stage which had initially drawn some criticism from the Right. But through a series of test cases the Unity had eventually unanimously (because every directorate, mandate, decision or Life Improver was always unanimous) agreed to screen for the Inclusive Marker, something most in the Sector believed would increase their chances. But there was no real change in the Filter numbers into the Programme which meant the Unity Left were left with the complete assurance that those in the Sector were not inclusive, at least not the type of inclusive the Programme (and ultimately the Future) was after.

The minute Grenoble was a horse's length past the group, one of the Ys turned to greet him then stopped as if the idea had passed quicker than Grenoble. As if sensing the expectation, Grenoble stopped without turning his head back and waited. The group was gone before Grenoble could enjoy a benevolent compliment on the Forward Doing (not Thinking) work he was getting done as part of his Zone whilst staring at his shoes. He wondered if they'd seen his collar – tropical sea blue showing excellence greater than his station and a commitment beyond the realms of exceptional. His pride at the blue collar wasn't evident – although there was always pride at grassing out law breakers and Concealers, stories had begun surfacing about what became of the offenders. Assigned to the Sector indefinitely, rumour had it that the Unity was initiating a way of destroying the Concealment by using offenders as test subjects. Grenoble had done his duty.

The Zone was characteristically quiet. Interaction wasn't

strictly necessary – everyone knew this. Grenoble's tasks were specific, targeted but not menial – nothing could ever be construed as menial when it was selfless for the greater good. This behaviour had been eradicated in our human nature, almost like the past frowned upon drink driving habits; no one cared for selfish agendas and no one thought about exercising the instinct to better on one's own behalf. Grenoble reached his allocated output target exactly on schedule when, without warning, his station shut down. This was a rare occurrence indeed, so rare that the last time Grenoble could remember it happening was pre–Danish. What followed back then was a sustained campaign to quell concerns and invest more Future resources in technological betterment. Not that Future resources ever became visible to the Zone but the perception was that things would get better. Zone reallocations flourished.

The power returned with little discernible delay; Grenoble wondered if he'd imagined it. Ever since his magnificent blue collar award after reporting Danish for Concealment he'd had a few similar episodes: lost time, mini–hallucinations, aching eyes, memory problems. He always wondered how she'd found the time to make regular illegal trips to the Sector and, more importantly, what she was planning to do when she reached the due date. He'd been part of the Construction ballot too but not even made it past the first round, most likely due to his brown eyes, looping nose, curly hair and splintered pockmarks on his cheeks. The improvements to the Ballot system had mostly taken place since his initial screening and were now performed at birth rather than puberty. His brother had been the same: first round failure but not on the aesthetic front, rather purely academic and behavioural or so Grenoble assumed. So as not to create stereotypes and feed insecurities the rejection letters were standard leaving people to muse, ponder and wonder. What might have been. Grenoble's sister had reached level III – a celebration and mystery in equal measure for the brothers.

The modern father of Gengineering had received pinnacle success based on years of false dawns by his predecessors. The Unity had been forthcoming in their later stocktaking: an all–media assault which ran for over a year.

Defeating the past to craft the future

All inadequacies had been voluntary and almost exclusively physical – he must be tall; she must not wear glasses; cobalt eyes; calf muscles; perfect teeth; no excess body fat. Which made the Breakthrough something of greater actualisation relevance. Within six years of Y1's life he'd discovered the cure for Entipididees, the single biggest organism destruction mechanism of recent times, effortlessly passing between humans, animals and even holding a detrimental effect over some plant types, particularly those important to the sustainability of life on a more industrial scale. With most sufferers already in cordoned off sectors, world powers were able to gift them all a longer life whilst avoiding angering whatever higher power had instructed the Entipididees plague.

Dr Sheln had then gone on to create a group of Xs and Ys – the first leadership group who would begin the improvement and form the basis of The First Counsel of World Unity, later to become The Unity. The group had been raised together, all twenty, with three dying within the first year, another a year later and the fifth killed in a freak accident a year before taking a seat on the Counsel. With a worldwide genetic screening campaign of suitable Parents across the globe, the selection of the group had been carefully split into making sure a balance was established – incredible cerebral problem solving to cure diseases; creativity to design our future; leadership to take us there; empathy to understand our plight; physical and mental fortitude to withstand the challenges ahead.

Certainty was now with us, Grenoble mused. It hadn't been like that back then: balancing on the exacting smooch of where the slope of a knife's edges collided, slipping North into oblivion and South into this … this … Certainty. Grenoble had never known anything dissimilar, hatched into the Light Years and assigned to the Pre Zone from his earliest recollection – knotting a brown–and–yellow tie every morning to complement a full khaki ensemble with dark blue boots and a matching belt. Even at Pre there had been Temporary Reassignment of under performers, notably the bottom five in each class spending a term in a Sector school followed by Complete Reassignment for a consecutive bottom five report. And once in the Sector that became almost definite, the only real opportunity to progress presented by The Defining. Grenoble's Pre Zone had been easy going as the region was large and the danger of falling towards the bottom limited, but when he'd graduated to

Primary Zone and the class sizes had been streamlined he'd had to push himself to the point of breakdown to stay up. Testing criteria had radically changed since then but when the parental support allowance was raised one year, Grenoble had found himself third bottom and sent to Fleepen Boys House in the Sector. The experience had changed him and, upon returning to Primary Zone the following term, his results had excelled, despite the continued apathy from his parents. This design of lessons learned would have been noted as a key contributor in Grenoble's successful Zone career.

Progression never halts for the determined soul

The days had started to get shorter. Normal for this time of year with the Life Orb powering down across the North but Grenoble couldn't help feeling that a few minutes here and there were being drained away, as if the seconds of the clocks were that iota quicker and morning arrived more suddenly and without warning. On his way home Grenoble took a slightly different route, passing the Central Unity College. A commotion was taking place directly behind the wall when Grenoble suddenly no longer had control of his senses. A boy's face loomed over his then blackness. The most perfect face he'd ever seen.

CHAPTER 84

Energetic Anger Earing

EPISODE 1

Even when it was hot it was cold in The Fields. The sun bore down on those outdoors like an innocuous pat on the head and was denied for those indoors, the cold in the Recs sometimes fatal. Most in The Fields knew that through an ingenious reflection technique pioneered by The Unity, the Life Orb could focus heat, life and sustainability directly on countries, regions and even households. Initial efforts to power the Life Orb up and down had resulted in inconsistent output which meant, once the reflection was conceptualised, all efforts quickly swerved from power to allocation. So where one gained, one lost and the relative order of allocation was debated between The Fields and The Sector. Many attributed the relative warmth of The Sector to the human congestion, further fuelled when a whole Field of outdoor workers froze to death some time back.

Kleyopatra was often mistaken for Royalty, despite being a regular in The Fields. Her height, chewing–gum stretched legs and honey complexion were betrayed by what Engineers diagnosed as personality instability resulting in frequent bursts of selfish, inconsiderate behaviour and an Asperger's–like disassociation to human emotion. And she was volatile, to the point of disregarding her own safety and long–term wellbeing to honour the expulsion of perceived injustice induced frustration. During one of her frequent stints in The Fields she spurned the advances of one of the Netherworld's most consistent offenders, gripping her powerful hands around the man's throat until the blood lines in his eyes swelled and the red tinge scraped across his face illuminated into deep purple. She's received further Field allocation for this during the coldest season of the cycle.

Kleyopatra's family lived in The Sector. Although family was most likely not a word anyone would seamlessly associate with this genetic misnomer. If the entire genetic profile was a disused latrine with matter consisting of months of misuse, Kleyopatra was the result of a diamond thief's peristaltic efforts to conceal the treasure only to have failed in their retrieval. Her brothers were all short, squat, a sickly–milky colour, repeat offenders (both in the eyes of The Necessary and even the most hardened lifer whose family line had remained barnacled in the Sector), of a unique bitter odour, fat fingered, monobrowed, low hanging butted buttheads. They'd never found time to respect or even consider their goddess–featured sister and much of her maligned behaviour, although identified early as a specific genetic trait that even the stricter behavioural efforts couldn't alter, clearly spiralled as a result of the years of verbal and physical maltreatment.

Kleyopatra's field work had worn away her striking aesthetic like the deliberate erosion of a classic automobile. Without the care afforded to normal citizens, she'd damaged her lower back to the extent that she now walked permanently stooped as though always ducking through a low doorway. The lack of Life Orb had not diminished her brolly handle coloured complexion but the rich flavour of her sand sprinkled brown hair, the parting previously erupting from her scalp as though trying the escape more dull and flat, now lay mouse brown dead across her brow, no cow available to lick for miles.

The only access to The Fields was a dilapidated train joining the mainland to a series of near–shore islands, most of which were used exclusively as FPLs (Field Production Locations). Security was strict on either side of the journey, The Necessary patrolling the departure and arrival stations with a heavy hand to make sure those reluctant to serve their penance did so with enthusiasm, yet the train remained unregulated. For a woman of Kleyopatra's appearance this was neither safe nor welcomed. Mostly men and mostly of an uneducated or anarchical disposition, regular Field workers cussed, spat through their sparse teeth, drank unsavoury liquids and hurled abuse at anyone within swinging distance. Although due to the sometimes flawed logic of allocation to The Fields, someone from, for example, The Zone could easily end up on a first–time train journey resulting in a severe beating and sometimes death. The bodies were left on the train sometimes only discovered months later when the stench of a decaying corpse would be too much even for the regulars.

On one such journey Kleyopatra found herself standing atop a deceased man, mid–thirties, brown hair – his glasses mangled into his face like the remnants of a car accidentally merged into hot tar. She noticed how his one eye was still open, staring intently ahead as though waiting for rescue. The cold months meant there was no real decay, only a solid platform for Kleyopatra to crouch down on to avoid the ubiquitous attention. When a man no taller than her chin approached, stood aside the body and began to grope at her she had no choice but to mash the butt of her hand into his nose. A call to arms scream rounded the unsavoury posse with a few interested do–gooders mumbling reluctant discontent only to retreat to the back of the baying queue when it mattered. The other women in the carriage distanced themselves even further.

"Now now, gentlemen," said a voice, scything through the madness and emerging eye–level with Kleyopatra, meaning his height equally her elongated altitude plus the body. "All good things come to those who wait … and learn," he explained swinging a square wooden pole at Kleyopatra's head, not directly connecting but not missing either, catching a chunk and relocating this rogue set of cells onto the window. Then the man collapsed with a needle in his neck and suddenly the crowd dispersed. Kleyopatra felt the warmth of blood toothpasting down her cheek and collecting in a pool at the corner of her mouth. It tasted sweet she thought as the man took out a bottle, daubed it onto a cotton swab and slowly raised it towards her as though calming a rabid dog. Against all better (and lifelong lessons learnt) judgement she lowered her fists.

"This will sting and you might feel dizzy, even pass out," he said, "but I'll be here in case." Once the swab arrived at her cheek it was like two opposing forces colliding: magnetic north touching magnetic north; she flung herself back arching to escape the searing million–needles–into–skin pain.

"The beginning is always the worst, but you have to persist. When I'm done there will be no pain and the only remnants of this vile episode with be an almost imaginary shadow of a scar. If you leave it in these conditions it will become infected, you will suffer and—"

"Why are you doing this? The world's a bit short of good Samaritans at the moment so what am I beholden to once you've 'healed' me?" The wound spouted more blood, the arterial river interconnecting hole and mouth.

"I hadn't really thought that far ahead, but for now you're bleeding and you need me to attend to this. I'm a physician."

"On a train to The Fields? Christ, The Unity must really be expanding the care they provide to us – all the way up from nothing. That or I'm an undercover spy getting beaten up as part of my cover."

"You shouldn't say that … about the Unity; not where people are within earshot." He stealthily moved closer to her. "You'll be on this train for the rest of your life—"

With the final spouting of the word 'life' he lunged at her, pinning his forearm across her neck and shoving the swab down onto the wound. Her knees flew up furiously at his groin region without finding their mark. He could feel she was a powerful woman; probably more powerful than him which meant he knew he had to catch her just right – it was his only opportunity. After a good five seconds of struggling the serum hooked into the tissue and Kleyopatra let out a gasping fading bellow to escape the pain. Her nails had dug steppingstone arcs of blood into his arms and he placed his face directly in front of hers, not smiling but with a reassuring gaze until she went to sleep.

When Kleyopatra woke, she was in a bed; not a flea–pit, dusty blanketed, wooden slatted, back crunching, glorified cot but a bed with a mattress that felt like it could single–handedly solve her back problems forever. The room was warm too. Life Orb rays trickled through the gaps in the curtains, the lines soldier still as there was no wind to disrupt the tranquillity. A wind chime made from what looked like Tanzanite hung motionless at the entrance to an expansive garden: double–doors of considerable size sealing the warmth inside the room but no barrier to the equally inviting warmth outside.

Kleyopatra noticed she was clad in a thick yellow woollen gown, her original underwear still intact. She instinctively raised her three middle fingers to her cheek as the most recent memory suddenly injected the peril back into her eyes, heart and mouth. She zigzagged her head, arcing her sight around the room for any sign of a threat. Her cheek no longer had a hole in it, the only vestige of the train incident a fleeting ghostly ridge of scar neatly melded down her sloping cheekbone, a petal laying delicately squashed into a soft grass bank. When she tried to rise her head hurt, so much that she lay back down and closed her eyes. This onslaught of cerebral pain would not normally have deterred a person of Kleyopatra's resolve, but something about this place, this room, this warmth, made her not want to run from it and seek enemies within.

"I'm sorry," said a voice some distance behind her, entering through a narrow corridor she'd failed to notice. "Sorry that I forced you here and sorry that I left you here so long but perhaps an explanation will vindicate my actions."

Kleyopatra purposefully ignored the intrusion without even the obligatory glance spat in his direction. She felt the wind of his movement rustle past her face, dislodging a strand of hair nestled insecurely behind her ear into a new location sheathing the scar. The host, or perhaps more like the kidnapper, retrieved a glass of something from behind a metal cylinder in the corner of the room.

"You should take these," he said, handing her two star-shaped powdery capsules. "If not for a current headache then to further aid the healing process."

Kleyopatra didn't move any part of her body bar the eyes peering up at the man with a lethal combination of disdain and circumspection. That was her power: those eyes saying a thousand words in one flung stab.

"I'm a qualified physician as you know although I must confess to having recently had to brush up on my basic medical training for my train excursions. I'm in Research rather than a practicing physician. And my name is Gherod Dastongular."

The name put the ever so slightest tinge of recognition into Kleyopatra's eyes, giving away her stand–off position – she knew of him.

"Are you up to taking a walk with me?" he said with an outstretched hand.

Clad still in yellow gown with the addition of fluffy slippers, Kleyopatra had the door opened for her, an expanse of undulating velvet lawn winding in multiple directions before her. The rich colour of the greenness stung her eyes as she closed them for a moment. With eyes still softly closed, she spoke "Do your own gardening then?"

"I have been known to sprinkle seeds and activate the mowers – but I wouldn't say it's my forte," he responded still loitering behind her as her eyes acclimatised.

"You're more the superhero wannabe, making sure Field workers arrive unscathed then return to your home after a good day's saving," the word home emphatically pronounced as a question.

"I'm not the biggest proponent of the transport system accessing The Fields. I'd written countless letters despite my father's protestations and nothing was done about it so I decided to do something about it."

"So you singlehandedly solve the hurt and the pain and the beatings one dumb bitch at a time. When do you want me to thank you in the way you're probably accustomed to?"

Gherod paused, for the first time uncertain of himself, and Kleyopatra almost witnessed his significant frame wilt, but not out of his own shame but out of disappointment in her comment. He knew she wasn't offering but rather taking her natural circumspection of his motives to a new place – somewhere out of this fairytale setting back into the real world.

"It's not like that at all. I do have influence – they know who I am which is why they leave me alone. The same doesn't apply to the victims – men and women; the trains are too frequent to control all but perhaps in some way it might deter the next incident."

They reached a bench enshrouded in white and yellow orchids, entangled with a passion fruit plant bearing fruit and complementing more sweet notes to the atmospheric aroma. Kleyopatra didn't want to leave the glow of the Life Orb so remained standing as Gherod knowingly shifted the bench away from the shelter of the decorative vegetation. Kleyopatra sank into the chair and looked at Gherod intently for the first time. His features were sharp but with a complexion that could only have been mollycoddled through this life of comfort, this life of opportunity, this life void of his own suffering.

This would turn out to be their only encounter. That still day when Gherod wanted to say so much yet could only muster brief glimpses of why he was the way he was and, more potently, why he had shunned The Unity and his Royal roots. Instead they just were: Kleyopatra unable to maintain her swinging arm distance long past lunch when both, in a morbid realisation that this encounter was fleeting, dropped forced facade in favour of letting the day be theirs.

They would end the day together; with each other. The next morning Kleyopatra was gone without a whisper of evidence of ever having been there (having taken the gown) bar the bench upsetting the neat angles of the enclave.

CHAPTER 94

Energetic Anger Earing

EPISODE III

The game was simple; simple for those Preferred for CUC. Accuracy, speed, vision and most important of all – bravery held the key to success in Even Standard. And because winning was a dated, almost heathen concept, the team and individuals deploying the most acute plan to display these traits would often usurp the team with the higher numeric score, so that, even when they waved hands (no longer shaking what with hand–bacteria still rife even amongst the elite CUC) at the end of the derby, deep behind sky blue and sea green eyes, victory was apparent. With six balls in play and twelve on each team, the object remained to gather and protect all 'in–play' balls by the end. There was no real physical limitation to how the ball was procured with the only rule that if you were caught without a ball and pushed beyond the barriers of the field of play you were marked 'sidelined'. If a ball was lost over the sideline it became 'out of play' thus reducing the number of 'in–play' balls. Any ball willingly or purposefully played over the sidelines was deemed 'could play' and punishable.

Ersone was as natural an athlete you could expect in that he wasn't engineered. Blessed with balance skills and a lionheart engine capable of getting up and pressing on when all around him were short of breath, huff–puffing in acute spasms towards the end of each match. His handling skills had been acquired, although a basic genetic predisposition to ball–games helped. His ability to pass off both hands, propelled by the opposite thrust of the hip bones meant his Even Standard 'reach' was near the best of the lot. The one real difference between Ersone and his teammates when it came to Even Standard (or any of the approved Formats) was his knee: deprived of cartilage and a lower patella positioning that might have won a Superman–badge shaped Mr knee–cap competition, the location meant he was prone to dislocations. Something he'd spent his early teens strengthening against and, more importantly, covering up. At the bottom of a pile of bodies during a seasonal match he'd felt something snap, followed by searing pain needles syphoning up his thighs all the way to his brain and down to his toes. Almost instinctively he'd rolled once (failed) then twice to jam the knee–cap back into joint and hide the hobble in the excruciating post–pile–up plays. This condition should have meant circumspection in receiving and dishing out hits, but for Ersone there could never be that restraint. It was not what he was; it was not how he was made.

Ersone's season's statistics for sidelining opponents was high; not the highest but combined with his total possession durations figures he was considered the most accomplished all–rounder in his age group. Most opponents were intimidated by CUC due to their far–reaching reputation but, with the coach gearing more towards the Quadrennial Unity Gate than hammering home the advantage week after week, they seldom needed to break a sweat playing regional competitors. Plus the unwritten engagement rules were always well respected so the brutal physicality of the more skilful teams (haphazard rash challenges resulting in injury more a product of carelessness than intent) meant the process of continuing to water the future leader seedlings through healthy competitive endeavour remained intact. The only real competition out there came from The Fields with Ersone, rousingly aware of this, arranging an underground league to test the boundaries of the team.

Ersone's group of teammates and his extended CUC group were all part of the now well established SelectGen. Even if someone had come into the CUC through the other less frequent feeder mechanisms, the CUC Board went to great pains to create all as a starting equal point so as to assess development within the environment and ultimately the best options for the betterment of progress. SelectGen had been introduced when the incessant research into genetic isolation had proved stable enough to offer initially to Royalty. The next phase had been touted as genetic enhancement but gone quiet for some time as the SelectGen initiative took grip and bore fruit. With no boundaries on procreation for Royalty each couple had the right to select from a list (initially narrow – a menu balancing expected success rates and demand) – gender, eye colour, height, exclusion of certain genetically–predisposed diseases, prone to holding body fat, longevity, proboscis size, testosterone levels (boys), child–bearing ability (girls), hair colour, hair density, body hair density and eyesight. This was prior to selection outside of the existing gene pool so parents selected based on their own view of their individual genetic prowess; a maternal or paternal bias, dubbed 'Daddy's Girls v Mummy's Boys'. Without any guarantees, Royal parents were given hierarchies of selection as well–

Total darkness. Lightning storm of all things. Power cut. Reestablishing the box will take some time. Red light terminator extinguished. For now.

PROLOGUE IV
THE END OF THE BEGINNING

Rather a sombre development on this unfolding story, Clive. My favourite 'Jock Man' Douglas Perfors, largely credited for foiling a terrorist home invasion and singlehandedly launching a male underwear brand in the process; then widely discredited for his supposed fabrication of a grocery store heist, was found to be telling the truth all along.

Footage of his destruction of the grocery aisles was proven to be fake as police investigate the bizarre motives behind this. Witnesses involved are being interviewed with many changing their original stories, citing coercion, bribery and confusion as reasons. "I just couldn't see a nice guy like that suffer anymore," said one of the female hostages.

PART IV

[Doug's Mad]

Dress Ant Pug

Where to start – is that an exclamation or a question (then is that an exclamation or a question) … and so on. Draft proofing a house, or in this case a home (constituted quite literally by the pitter–patter cacophony of feet up and down the stairs before rising time), 'simple' furniture that would keep most African villages fed and clothed and bathed and vaccinated for a year, art – just contemporary enough to be trendy and sufficiently abstract so as to give off an all–too–familiar air of knowledge in the ever–widening sphere of social 'how big's ya canvass' and of course the one item completely out of place, tacky, obscure, personality statement to just take the edge off home maker contrived meets expensive – the one object which normally defines a man – in Doug's case, his old school case, with hedgehog picture slapped on the front and curling on all four edges and so ugly and out of place in the minimalist study. That it worked ain't no easy feat in an old Victorian home, which made Margot's excuse plausible if somewhat rare.

"All I'm saying is that when I'm bent over on all fours and you're going hammer and tongs the draft sometime catches me and you know I'm not good with the cold."

"What does hammer and tongs mean?"

"You know you don't feel the cold like I do, that's all I'm saying."

"You've never referred to it as hammer and tongs before."

"Oh for God's sake, shall I just blow you?"

"That would be such an honour. Don't bother. I'll call the draught proof guy in the morning."

A dual duelled rollover in perfect symmetry, each sliding legs and heads forward into the pillows to form a disjointed X; butts transitorily converging then inching adroitly away in equal and opposite paroxysms, the X, pulled apart like the manual amputation of a flying ant's wings, now greater than less than: > <.

This is a first – I AM SURE OF IT.

CHAPTER 15

Deal Low Segregation

The list raged on: firing air–rifles from a grassy (more like shingle) knoll at incognizant teenage vandals and graffitists every couple of days until there wasn't anyone to aim at anymore (job done); appearing outside the school en paedo–neighbour route between his house and bus stop so that he started taking the half–mile longer less scenic route in the opposite direction; failing to allow any seemingly minor misdemeanour like littering and swearing to go unconfronted. During all this heroic antisocial cleansing there was never any real male–bonding that took place between Reg and Doug. Well there was in the truest unsaid activity–based male camaraderie normally associated with fishing but Doug couldn't help but feel he was no closer to knowing who Reg really was. Of course he was more than happy to play Sam to Reg's Frodo as the burden of the societal degradation weighed heavily and any opportunity to make that difference and improve things appealed. Really appealed. It was in line with what Doug had always striven to stand for. The family interaction levels suffered though.

But it wasn't all work and no play: Reg managed to slip something into Doug's post anti–teen unhappy slapping routine celebration whisky so that Doug, now mere putty in Reg's grubby puppet master fingers, submitted without his usual (even if now ever–increasing) protestations. Actually, Doug was sure he'd dreamt it when he woke up the next day – yet he was more exhausted than usual which meant it had to be real.

Driven to an industrial building in the dead of night, somewhere south of the river, they'd made their way into an elaborate set designed in post–apocalyptic Terminator–take–off style and given laser guns. Harmless enough – playing laser quest tripping on something had to be, at minimum … different. Energetic even, like a good run. The clue might have been when they strapped on their laser vests without the luxury of another shred of clothing. When the lights dimmed and Doug could faintly hear Reg's demented screams descending in a faraway direction coupled with angry female screams and actual Terminator music, he vaguely remembered seeing a sign exclaiming 'Sex Quest'. Strangely nervous, creeping through the darkened tunnels and fake skull pebbled pathways, Doug shot at the first dark yellow blurs which beseeched his left to right vision like the swipe of an Impressionist's brush over the horizon. One he thought even shot at him because his vest vibrated, the large red light in the middle blinking thrice.

"How many have you snagged?" whispered Reg, appearing from a smooth panel above Doug's head and pulling him into crouch position. "They're better this year, although two more hits and I'm giving one to their lowest scorer. Look at the board! Someone called Veronika. Hell yeah. But if I'm hit again I'm into the cell. Win win! Otherwise we've got to get the cyborg and steal the hand so that we get a freebie at the end."

Immediately Doug's light went off again, Reg literally forward rolled to safety and fired in the direction of a naked black woman, her purple nipples illuminated in the false dusk–light appearing from the female version of the vest like two eyes, the red Rudolf nose buzzing below them. Doug shook his head yet she remained, her body bent over, glistening with sweat. Then she parted her legs and Reg made his way over, darting his head down like a man with little time to spare. Then the two of them were gone and a new electricity filled Doug as though he was racing someone. Now he wanted to win.

The next half hour saw Doug amass more points than anyone on the screen, but not before the siren went and Veronika's name flashed with the words 'room 4' next to it. He even thought he saw his Veronika in room 4, a girl of similar build, hair and muscle tone grinding her way through

Reg's torso.

It couldn't be her – she never likes it on top.

Then Doug's turn: despite his promising recovery, the slow start meant his 'comeback' was just too much to catch the leaders. He found himself chained up akimbo in the cell, one woman per limb chaining him into submission. He didn't bother to struggle, dipping in–and–out of consciousness and unable to comprehend time's gallop, jumping and slow–motioning all in one. He was now also sweating and each vest–clad enemy proceeded to whip him so flimsily that he had to request a bit more effort be put into it. Tiny red lines decorated his back and arse and the stimulation had him feeling as though he'd been brought the starter but was not able to eat it. So he got angry and hard, all four taking turns passing him from mouth to mouth until the siren went again and they unclamped his bonds and scuttled off, his testicles still muggy from the attention.

It became easier to hit the moving targets. Perhaps Doug's levels of fitness, perhaps the tiring assassins – either way marksman Doug slaughtered into the lead in the following round, breaking the hundred barrier with such ferocity he roared when he exploded across the gaping mouths presented in front of him like an all you can eat buffet. This was after a VIP invite into room 101 where a participant's black rose tattoo above her coccyx made vivid splashes in Doug's brain, appearing in front of his face, then below his navel, then distorted as he entered her backside, one of the petals fluttering as he went in and out just barely beneath the skin. Both remained armed, content to hold the weapons without stopping the powerful, persevering, purposeful pumping, the reverberations flaying their downward facing breasts.

And it didn't end there. Reg became lost to the world and Doug the owner, ruler, supremo of the underworld Laser Quest 'fuck your way to triumph' until he'd probably been through all sixteen opponents and some a few more times than once, twice, thrice. But dear gawd his aching body did not touch on the pain in his head the next morning.

"Where were you?" asked Margot, pulling on a running bra and rendering Doug a million miles away from survival sex. "Last night. I heard you come in late." The words jigsawed pieces of the evening back as Doug remembered going back to Reg's and completing the marathon on Deloris in the downstairs loo while Reg swam. Was that son–of–a–bitch reality biting now? The best of the fantasy–build Terminators hadn't been a touch on Deloris.

"I've got a problem," said Doug, "at work. I'm unable to solve it; creating allies in the worst places. It's never been like this."

Everything became laboured that day. Even reluctantly agreeing to let Veronika go down on him in the disabled toilet at work was a chore, his thoughts dispelling the immortal words Leo claimed you'd never find yourself saying: "Could you please stop sucking my cock?" And the long overdue meeting with the boss and showdown with Pinky never materialised into anything significant. Or perhaps significant now had a new bar height or had dropped a few rungs? What would be the perfect smug opposite of a midlife crisis –

having one? Was the irony such that not having one was the cliché versus embracing one full throttle, both sweaty, steaming Porsche key holding palms seizing the crisis (a funny green–blue–black long necked bird of a crisis) and clasping the air from the chamber then holding it close to one's breast so as to become united? At one with the crisis, so that it remained a crisis and not crises. How had his dad done? Either he'd been past it when Doug awoke out of proving his worth up the parental hierarchy or he'd just been cool enough to come out of it looking like a man in complete control of his destiny. What worried Doug the most is that his anger was becoming ambivalence.

Subconsciously he went backwards first: digging up some old friends who he'd outgrown but who he now felt were interesting. Leo, all fat, eco–friendly and long since unhappily divorced, resentful daily immersions into his past transgressions and wishing he'd grown up earlier. Pepe, institutionalised with long bursts of uncontrollable sobbing during chaperoned visits. He discovered Michelle had been killed by a stalker, a full wedding and consummation ceremony taking place in her apartment postmortem, ending up conciliatorily sleeping with her best friend while they Googled the perpetrator's earliest release date. He then leapfrogged from tolerance over compromise into the more standard couples genre: arguing. Not being argumentative but reciprocating what was clearly a change in tone from Margot; all comments, actions, gestures now had that extra bite – an expression of some dissatisfaction of what … being a mummy? Low sex output? Him in general.

This made turning to crime easier. Doug needed to get the stash sold and Sonny Boy's name erased from the equation. He was the new dawg in town and the only way was to infuse a higher quality product into the mix yet keep the price the same. Brand it and do some research about types of 'buzz' – the target: a happy buzz in these recessionary times.

And he started painting too. Initially with a keen eye and a bit too gifted for novice, he started rubbishing his increasingly impressive works so as to ensure the constant lacuna from the mantelpiece, the freedom afforded in shitting oil and acrylic not only shackle shattering but consistent with the satisfying new constant in his life. Reg had been right – this act wasn't him; doing things well all the time is tedious. To evolve you need to royally fuck up – and make a big fucking deal of it. So that people turn their noses up at you and forget your wondrous traits. This was not an overnight decline though but rather a systematic unravelling of thirty plus years of careful smug crocheting.

Perhaps I'll fuck the neighbour's daughter. She's legal now and wouldn't that wipe the knowing grin off her face. Something to take away the tedium of that same smell and grunt from Veronika. Not that it's bad but Kerist I'm running out of interesting ways to do it. I'd rather watch myself in the mirror than her – does that make me gay? Jeez, is my whole life about sex? What about a resolution to abstain for a while – to attain the higher level of actualisation. I'm better than just that.

Graham had hired someone new into the team who was

stealing most of Doug's thunder. This meant that Graham was more able to subtly berate Doug – a veiled 'fuck you' slithering across the entire firm; the ultimate acknowledgment that Doug had been the powerhouse behind the progression for years. And, almost like those reality shows where the audience love a loser coming good and shining at the end, Graham actually started blossoming. It made Doug wonder whether he'd played the relationship all wrong from the beginning when he saw Christie operating in consummate support mode, making the boss look good but ultimately Christie look good to the boss. He even liked the way she dressed. Steven, now acquiring a bigger slice of the management pie, became too busy really to bother at the lower echelons meaning his unwavering sponsorship of Doug dissipated. Doug's behaviour could only become more anarchical, like the only way to express displeasure at authority in a corporate existence was buck against it. Without any real understanding of what this would achieve he started 'Operation Undermine'. It just felt right; instinctual. And good. Warmth on the face after a day of dark rain.

One medium, slightly foamy, semi–skimmed, circumcised, urine–infused coffee coming up! Finished with a delicate garnish of exudate from the increasingly unrestrained brain–matter–smooth balls. A graphic memory never forgets.

Throughout these annoying disruptions Doug had neglected his parenting duties to the point where the kids' behaviour began to deteriorate to comments in their jotto workbooks well less than 'Outstanding' 'Exceptional' and 'Superb'. Although Doug did shift back into making more time for them (mainly because he just genuinely missed their honest company), he made more of an effort to let them fail – so that when the 'Needs to try harder' 'Missed key points' and 'B+' reality excreted across their homework pages, they'd understand earlier rather than later what it felt like to be less than perfect. Flawed. Not the best at everything. A lesson Doug sorely missed but was now making up for.

A good by–product of severe life change and general upheaval for Doug was weight loss. So much so that his stomach muscles began to stick out like piano keys and the indentations above his jaw line skateboard ramped up to his pronounced cheekbones, his eyes and saluting lashes now abnormally big for his face. It wasn't that he didn't feel like eating – there were just more interesting things to do than gorge your face full of tuna, Pringles and Pepperoni Passion.

CHAPTER 25

Den No More

When something changes, the first jaw–dropping, knee–jerking, sphincter–clenching moment is negative. On average. As all those lifestyle change managers will (or you'd image they would) tell you – we as a species are naturally averse to change; yet change is healthy, a necessity to continue evolving – to explore new avenues in our constant spiralling towards inevitable death. Once upon a time there was a man named Doug and a woman named Margot. They lived in a terraced house in North London. Their lives were simple; simple and ultimately boring: eat, sleep, work ... watch TV. Eat, sleep, work ... watch TV.

Eat. Sleep. Work. Watch TV.

Eat. Sleep. Work. Watch TV.

Eat. Sleep. Work. Watch TV.

Eat. Sleep. Work. Watch. TV.

Eat. Sleep. Work. Watch. TV.

Eat. Sleep. Work. Watch. TV.

Watch TV. Watch TV. Watch TV. Watch TV. Watch TV. Watch TV. TV. TV. TV. TV.

In this tale there could be no other option but change. Being reluctantly thrust to the top of the food chain would mean that all that regularity, all that monotony, all that reality had to change. And when that change rolled into town like a giant granite donut bulldozing every man, woman, child and channel in its path, Doug was probably left jaw shattered in pieces on the floor, knee snapped forward at a right angle and anus so tight a microscopic needle pushed by a hundred men wouldn't have found its way through.

"What's happened to Janine?" Doug asks, blinking as though he's just woken up.

"The couch now has a permanent dent in it from your slouching. You didn't come to bed ... again. What was it this time? Hostage drama?" says Margot, Dysoning under Doug's raised feet. "And who's Janine?"

"Is that how we're treating it now? Writing her off completely. Makes sense I suppose."

Margot grabs the remote peeping from beneath the side of Doug's buttocks, drawbridge raised erect in service, and flicks to the stored programmes on the Sky+ menu. "3%

space left – any chance someone else in the family could watch something recorded?" Margot laments.

"Most of it is education stuff for the kids. See: Discovery, National Geographic."

"That's not even funny. Plus there's loads of older shit on here – mostly viewed. Can't you get rid of them once you've seen them?" Margot flicks down the list. "X Factor ... Rugby ... a marathon ... some crappy low–budget ITV two–parter ... porn – urghhh ... Documentary on the Riots ... Queer Eye for the Straight Guy ... Come Dine with Me. My God, you watch a load of tosh, you know that?"

Doug's head hurts so much that he can't move. He's stuck inside his body looking out as a Lego pirate might stare out of his angular, colourful Lego castle. Expressionless yet expressing something. The smile painted on for eternity or until some violent child scratches away to just leave the eyes. His stomach is bulbous, pressing his shirt towards the ceiling, the shirt indented into his bellybutton like the animate tip of an exclamation mark. He can feel his breath is unsavoury from the way the sides of his tongue itch and his chest is tight – the double tap, gap, big tap irregular beat of his dormant heart seemingly slipping his ribcage apart.

"I need to know what's happened to Janine," says Doug, crying.

"Whatever. Just open the windows for some light at some point this year okay."

Doug looks up at Margot and he doesn't recognise her: who is this woman living in his house, cleaning, bitching ...

... raising the kids effortlessly; looking seamlessly brilliant all the time; going down on Janine all the time ...

"I'm going for a run."

"Yes and I'm swimming the Channel after East Enders."

"We need to talk."

"Talk to your favourite thing in the world, because it doesn't answer back. I'm cleaning."

"I need to know what's going on. I need to know what happened to Janine."

"Well then do that – you've only a week to wait. Perhaps you could get your hands on a pirate version – from the internet."

Doug feels his phone buzz in his pocket: it's a text message from Reg.

Blast from the past ... wah–hey.

Almost as if his spirit is flicked up into the air like a booger from a crusty kid's finger, Doug's now visibly chipperer. He fumbles with the device, accidentally deleting the text, picking it up and scanning for Reg amongst his contacts. But nothing.

His name isn't there.

Margot, with less chance of fitting into a pair of short denim shorts than toothpaste getting back into the tube, leaves the room carrying the broken–wheeled Dyson under her arm like a fireman's hose, her tracksuit bottoms halfway down her arse. Trudging past Doug, either numbed by recent catastrophic events or in denial. Will the hokum dull the pain or even eradicate it … pulling the arrow tip from the wound and forgetting to suck the poison out.

The screen flickers.

{ ↪ ↼ ↪ ↼ ↪ ↼ }

Moping down the street, Doug notices a billboard of Veronika. Wow, what has become of dear sweet sexy Veronika? He's not even played a thought in her direction since the retrospective Janine yarn and now there she perches, a yoghurt spoon angling into her mouth.

She's become a memory, one where each chapter has been chipped at, eroded – not the slow fading decline of a sunset. As though their time together was an oil canvas brutally defaced with a chisel and blade rather than a watercolour submerged in an industrial sink, the colours muddying into an insipid brown to hover above the coarse unbleached yarn as the only reminder. Instead Doug sees the remnants of the oil undercoat, jagged edges adorning the canvas like the tips of a child's mountain range drawing.

Did she even eat yoghurt?

Doug's mind, now needlessly clouded by confusion and reminiscence, has no other option but to resort to base associative euphemisms.

Was that my one and only weakness all along? One and only seems a bit flattering, non? When everything was perfect, was sex the only way to fill that void, that space, that gap? (That hole ... Oh Gawd, you are pathetic!) But Veronika was just there and I just sort of fell into it, didn't I? Did I make Janine into the Veronika prequel or was Veronika the main to Janine's nostalgic starter? This is all just too linear: do we have to have this bullshit progression from stability to meltdown to redemption to – what? Death? Insanity? Realisation? Accountability? Who wants anything to do with my existence other than those close to me? Any age–induced mantra must be to make every day an interesting adventure and avoid the big tragedies. But what is big?

Without completely acknowledging his directional incompetence, Doug wanders into one of the less salubrious parts of town. Approached by two hookers, he politely refuses then accidentally buys some smack off a well-dressed drug dealer thinking it was Wrigley's Extra Ice Peppermint. He portentously pops it into his jacket pocket, not spotted by four police cars speeding by breezing old brown leaves and mangled papers across his path.

Is this Tottenham? It looks too American. I was expecting more kebab and sari shops.

Suddenly all is quiet and Doug feels alone ... no ... lonely as he catches a news excerpt through the bars of a strip joint window offering free hand–jobs and swears the newsreader is Deloris. He's chewing the Wrigley's and there's a pressure above his bicep all the way around so that the earthworm vein now pulsates and shifts blood up and down the pipe, each undulation and camel hump slide of the ringed wormearth's body contortion.

"I've been looking for you," a voice lurches out; Sonny Boy's scratching the freshly welded burn of a tattooed serpent with a dusty blade. Doug's surprised because he's little and bald: a combination one often doesn't see; aren't gangsters meant to be big, shaven and bald like a cartoon version of a chicken's arse?

"Are you part of my dream? I'd hoped to dream you up to be more, well … glamorous."

"Where's my suitcase?"

"Wait, so this is where I argue with you and we fight and then I kill you and emerge as a hero who took down a local drug dealer much to the adulation of the wider lost–faith–in–the–police–system public. It's something a little spectacular but not too much so that we've been choreographed to within an inch of our lives – The Matrix is so two thousand and nought. And we'd have to avoid that I'm crouched in my own blood hunched over like a dog about to die with you hesitating to deliver the fatal blow before I symbolically reach for the suitcase lying on the ground next to me and swipe it across your face so that the lock you couldn't open rips open your throat. Or! Or! Wait! Redemption! Someone pitches up to save me, redeeming themselves in the process and proving they were local all along despite a minor diversion. Reg? Deloris? Janine?"

"That's emotional, but I left something which I know you

got. I don't want to ask for it back again. If I have to, I'll be returning with another souvenir, perhaps your wife's head."

"Do I have the power to magic the suitcase to this street? Guide me …"

And now there's a gun in Doug's mouth. No he can't taste the metal but the holder keeps disappearing from view: is he waking or is there some sort of bonus hallucinatory drug laced on the revolver's barrel?

I know this look. Gawd, you're not anybody this season if you don't have a weapon protruding from your mouth like a giant fishing human–hook. The dental work that this is about to destroy if–

Then total darkness, but not very very dark room darkness, rather space darkness: shiny dark; endless dark; floating dark.

{ ↪ ↩ ↪ ↩ ↪ ↩ }

When Doug awoke, he had a beard, was in a well–lived in hospital bed and there was a bullet hole out of the back of his neck. And unlike those home movie transitions he didn't slowly raise a floppy–paw eyelid with the room fading from previous mental image injected into the brain to the next, but rather drew–his–sword eyes open awake: spanked awake. The bright of the room invading him; entering him; raping him, the unwelcome visitor keeping the eyes transfixed open on the pulsating glow of the fluorescent light as though the possibility of closing them again might render him blind or comatose or dead for the rest of whatever remains. A waking coma. Wakeful yet unable to move, a direct taut chain keeping his head still as the light pours into his black–hole pupil drains, filling him to the brim with sensory content so that something had to give, something had to spill over, something had to explode.

With the scream the pipe in his throat not only dislodged but came ejaculating from his face with such ferocity it shattered on the opposite wall pulling adjoining cables and cords with it in slipstream unison, pilot fish being led to their demise. But instant relief, unshackling after months of oppression. And no team of white clad eggs rushing in to sedate, no alarm bell beeping, no flat line; just silence and painfree vision, the beaker full and moving harmlessly from overconsumption to welcome acceptance.

When Doug tried to speak it was at no one in particular and for no other reason other than it felt like the right thing to do. Like an itchy scratch that only inflames the rash. The sound emitted was more Ewok than the distorted deep Darth Vader you'd expect after having 200 hours of surgery to repair your tonsils. Janine hands Doug an iPad.

He types: "Are you my Guardian angel?"

"No I'm just a visitor." She points at the iPad then points the room's remote control towards the wall–mounted television but nothing happens.

Control Remote.

"I'm tempted to ask what happened to me." He hands it back to her, that familiar scent of her neck smearing into his nostrils, the olfactory sense's turn to be reacquainted to actual living life. He feels the distantly familiar weight of her buxom bosom on his clavicle which ignites that almost dormant sense reclining down his inner thigh. She doesn't notice him ejaculate into the bedsheets and the sensation is so laced with negative connotation (with Janine in the room … again) that his only give–away is a long–overdue blink. A blink so welcome his lubrication of the eyeball is more impressive than the orgasm.

"I don't know. I just arrived back in town and thought I'd visit. I heard you were here. It's been eight years. You have grey in your beard."

"Where's Margot? Is she here? Sleeping in the waiting room? Talking to the doctor?"

"Is she still alive?"

Veronika walks into the room carrying a cue card, holding it right up at Doug's face. It reads: "You're Alive … So Thankful for That", the time taken to write the letters in geometric perfection apparent.

"Do you two know each other?" thinks Doug. Neither raises an inkling of a plucked eyebrow in the other's direction, Veronika almost sitting on Janine's lap as she sidles past into the path of another chair. Doug can smell her; all of her: the hint of cinnamon encircling her collar bone like a sea rescue safety belt, the tiny discharged intimation of sour raspberry now outside her cunt, the cream–smelling odourless hand cream.

"I can talk," he says, raising his pelvis to stretch his lower back, an involuntary twitch of sorts, completely inappropriate given the number of similar metrical engagements posed to his visitors either behind, in between their legs, standing above their back–holding acrobatics or underneath like trying to hammer a nail from an awkward angle beneath a house.

Would it always come back to this? Is this my explicable, despicable, inescapable affliction – that it all comes back to Adam's failings in lusting after busty, apple–swilling Eve? Or multiple Eves?

Is that the single source of enjoyment I can hold, touch, feel, understand and relish? Do I seek this out or is my excuse of going with the flow, being the tag–along male victim in the Eves' conquests enough justification to realise that this, not the smugness, will tear all things important to me apart. Is that Janine taking off Veronika's top?

When Doug woke up, possibly having blacked out again after the months of pain medication, Janine and Veronika were still in the room – both killing time with (*post–coital?*) menial/handy tasks, Veronika reading a book and Janine knitting (*knitting?*) … Janine killing kittens. Deloris enters, flustered, burgundy cheeked, the two asymmetrical prints of Doug's hands decorating each line–separated oval like his kids' wall–displayed artwork at the old nursery.

My kids? The centre and light of my life – where have they disappeared to in all the mayhem? Is this me 'taking care of stuff' before devoting completely to their raising and perfection ahead or is the smug perfection something I just know they'll acquire on their own? Be the best without even trying. Be the best without even trying. Be the best without even trying. Be the best without even trying. Be the best without even trying. Be the best without even trying. Be the best without even trying. Be the best without even trying.

Deloris kisses Doug softly, leaving a dark purple smear of lipstick between the corner of his nostril and the greater than shape of his mouth. Or would this situation have to be less than in Doug's world? This … this … gathering of conquests; mini–loves; ego–creators; squealing pleasure seekers.

It's always the build–up; imagining what it'll be like. The anticipation burns like a hot fish baked on the shore, the scales pop–flaming in domino succession and rolling up into a ghost–rider–headed grenade. Lobbing it into the sea doesn't even extinguish. Is it the anticipation of what might occur which never has or a glamorised rehash of the reminiscent replay of past exploits? Those 'moments of inspiration' – intended to impress or genuine indulgent re–enactment of some sloppy porn site?

Doug recalls his round two with Veronika and paid–for–friend, yet this recollection is so real it's as though he's starting side by side with his trusting self, watching the curved indentation at the side of his buttocks tense and relax, tense and relax whilst all the time both girls point back to his actual self. He had them piled on top of each other like two smooth welcoming bags of fertilizer, their openings ever so slightly misaligned: two upside down exclamation marks in different sentences, the Word editor just short of aligning centre. He has to do this – it's part of his perfection – how can he double–tap at onepointthreesevendegrees to the upper left each alternating stroke, so, almost making the rectification unnecessarily difficult, shifts Veronika at the bottom, who'd conveniently turned her head to kiss the base of Christina's exposed neck. That neatening of the deck restores the longitudinal rhythm and the actual thought of repeating exit and entry, watching the full length of his manhood disappear between the four different shapes of labia, makes him want to finish in a hail of cream–coloured paintball bullets, creating a beautifully formed natural rock formation waterfall where the flow seeps through the fissures. But because he's there doing it the appeal dissipates, while his twin next door to him anticipates and imagines, at a lighting up of the national grid feverpitch, what it will look like; what it will feel like to see it happen. The Doug, hammering away, having got through the anticipatory magic of the genital Jenga stack, now wonders what all the fuss is about. This has to be the reason one exists: planting fodder into the memory bank for the future; ignoring the now because the now is never all that whilst hoping beyond hope this enriches the future. The Doug next door is the future and the anticipation makes him explode into the hospital sheets, the material quickly darkening as fast as, say, if the expulsion had been lighter, fluffier, less dense. Perhaps it's his urostomy bag overflowing but that exclusively male, chew your arm off with guilt post–come sensation put there by some cruel god seeps over him, making each and every time hardly worth the effort. If things were the other way around, wouldn't that be perfect. Perfect because this incessant pursuit would never happen: start off with unwavering guilt and shame followed by that pinnacle of ecstasy then into the act supported ably by the imagining of how that ecstasy might occur then topped off by the single greatest feeling above all else – anticipation.

When Doug came to, his sheets had been changed and he smelled faintly clean. The room felt like no one had been in there for a very long time, the window a crack ajar with no real breeze to mention and an intimate moribund feel to the air. Forgotten while the world resolved towards perfection. In what felt like a day a male nurse, whom Doug had never seen before, walked in mute and did some stuff which put Doug back into a haze, this one without the unsuppressed joy of sexual encounters. Doug remained convinced the nurse had mouthed, "You're ready to go home now."

CHAPTER 35

← →

Soap & Ace

This hospital room feels bigger. Such that the walls and ceiling are so far away Doug is unable to comprehend whether he's inside or outside. But he can feel from the air, the hint of stuffiness laced with sprinkles of house dust mites, that the room 'contains' him. He's struggling with his sight but he's not blind: everything haloed so that the inner rings blurs, the middle doughnut obscures and the outer periphery is abnormally crystal.

"I had to get you out of that hospital," says a voice

seemingly somewhere up in the rafters. "It was doing my head in, and more importantly doing your head in. I didn't know where else to bring you. Home didn't seem right somehow."

Doug tries to speak back but can't, immobilised into merely blinks, nods and shakes. His mind shouts, "I need answers!"

"I had to eradicate some of the evidence including that one person who was going to make it all wrong. I do still love you, despite all of 'it'."

She kisses him on his head, lingering long enough over him for him to roll his eyeballs up and recognise Janine's (or is it Margot's … or … Michelle's … or … wait … Beth's!?) cleavage scent.

"Everyone in that place was making all this crazy talk about how our quest had changed you; how it was bad for you so I removed you from the situation as quickly as I knew how and brought you here. Do you know who's buried under this warehouse?"

When London screams it wails. Always perpetuated by the boomerang audibility of a siren, squealing to the rescue, always too late. Or the groan of congested folk elbowing in the same solitary direction to be better, be perceived better and inch up (the ladder) or inch down (the gym). Here in this place there is none of that – no mothballed frustration outside the windows and flimsy walls waiting to burst in and rip Doug back to the race, just the quietest mouseless rustle of grass clumps. Surrounded by emptiness.

"God, I've always wanted to say this: no one can hear you scream out here. Look at me, the big horror film director. I need to cleanse you so we can be together without hindrance, so we can be the same." She fishes around a small black toiletry bag; Doug notices her hair falling forward and seemingly off. She takes off her clothes and steps into view but Doug's eyes still haven't conformed to the new visual stimuli, only making out the ghost–like cream–coloured form without any break in contour except for the hollow sea eyes below the rounded unhappy smiley dome. She's holding tweezers and quickly darts in like a viper to rip an eyebrow hair from Doug. Before he can continue his screaming, she places tape over his mouth and proceeds to remove each of his eyebrow hairs one at a time, a few seconds gap between each to allow the pain receptors just enough time to spark then recline into a false sense of refuge. The eyebrows take half the day with most follicles leaving a blood bead which she kisses each time leaving her mouth encrusted with shaded layers of dry erythrocytes.

"You must remember when you made me shave my pussy then I shaved your anus and your balls. It was so beautiful, that feeling of freedom, I decided to have all my hair permanently lasered off and now I'm giving you that gift so we can lie together without this grimy barrier between us. I do so love you and I know every woman wants to change her man in some way but I know how you need to be so we can prosper."

Doug then lost all his eyelashes and his head hair, passing out from the pain when she reached the crown. Sequentially and from north to south in the front first, the underarms followed then chest then stomach then pubic then legs then feet. Then on the third day she rested departing for extra food and sustenance supplies, leaving the tweezers a school plastic ruler length from his eye level on a table, the edges seemingly blunted and the shafts arched.

Is this some form of Stockholm syndrome: am I missing her now that she's gone or do I fear dying alone like this? This must be my punishment. I can feel each pore enflamed which makes it real. I'll have to try and draw strength from this somehow – embrace the pain or find a distraction. When I was nineteen, I had an affair with one of my lecturers, a married woman unable to shed the bulge above the line after three goes at childbirth. I remember making her so self–conscious as my nineteen year old hips jelly wobbled the bulge that she started exercising frantically and tore open the caesarean internal cut through the muscle which almost killed her. That's one hair's worth. Then we carried on and she eventually did get back into ridiculous shape so that a spirit level would sit flush between belly button and pubic bush (the line now more of a Nike tick than a full smiley) only for me to move on with someone more my own age, a fellow member of the Economics 202 called something or other. That's two more follicles.

When she returned, she removed the tape from Doug's mouth, kissing him on the cheek more casually than a soap star's tenth take when returning home from work. Removing a carton of milk from the bag, the pouring act into Doug's mouth causes violent convulsions.

"Sorry lovely but you must keep your strength up."

"I know why you are doing this and I support you all the

way. I deserve this. For everything."

"This is not a punishment; this is an affirmation of our love, our union."

"I've pretended all this time to care; to be seen as the one who cares – to spout continuous words telling how I'm the one who is selfless. But I'm not – I'm the one who has to finish first, be gratified, be fulfilled. So if you need to do this to reach some sort of enhanced place, then you do it. And keep doing it until you are fulfilled."

"No. No. No no no. This is not for me – this is for us. I'm going to prove it and make love to you right now. With the job not completely done you'll see how the decaying smell of anal and bum hair sweat makes our union sordid and impure. You showed me the way and brought me into your world now I want to make sure we enter that next world together."

She puts her hands between his legs pulling free the dried wax, wiping the flakes up his flank and across her face. Doug's non–responsiveness is no surprise so she rams the tweezers down the traditional exit route fish–mouth, eliciting a new tone of wince, scream and erection from Doug so that her spittle could run down it like a melting ice cream cone. Her breath is on top of him and he now completely notices that she does not possess a single hair on her body – he can feel there is no abrasion with her arched back thrusts, and above her eyes all the way to the rounded apex of her head is milky smooth.

"You look utterly ridiculous," he says, "which makes

fucking you now better than ever."

She lets out a banshee scream, double–punching his velvety chest until the red outer fist marks pock his naked body like a Leopard print.

"Go as long as you like. Until you're done." Doug notices the slight loosening of his right hand bind, her wild triage knocking the knot into a loop shape around a metal bed bolt. Doug realises to get this undone he needs her to unleash that fury again until he's actually free and the strength returns into his right fist enough so to knock her face into a chin to breast slump, whilst still inside her.

Without knowing it, Doug had started the process to make a baby inside her.

Is someone born a killer all the time or can they be made? If I put my forearm around her throat and stop her from ever breathing again will that be the justice she deserves or the justice I deserve, knowing I've finally graduated from smug dad to life–taker?

Never had food and drink tasted so sweet and been inside Doug's stomach so short – his wild palm–cupping arcs into his mouth with a swift chew–chew and chug often including packaging, straws and other accessorised objects only for his body to reject the intrusion in the most violent of fashions. On hands and knees crying, heaving and descending with the wires of bile to the floor. Doug lay on his back breathing deeply, his heart pinballing around his chest cavity in a seemingly fruitless act of escape.

Then came the urge to return to one of the constants – go

for run. Barefoot, he clothed himself in her clothes, tearing the pair of snug fitting jeans into some semblance of shorts and using her overcoat as the lone item on top. There was no weakness in his legs, each having shed the inner teardrop bulge above the knee and the meatloaf flare on the outer edge but that muscle twitch fibre desire remained. Stretch those legs. Explore the surroundings.

An hour in, Doug discovered he was nowhere familiar, in fact the excursion felt like it was a completely different country, not a soul about and no movement around him other than the odd cloud gathering then dissipating. Something had to bring him back. Did he have to go back and end her life to return to reality? Was it even her? Had he checked? Could it be a cult follower? Or was the surreal stalked the stalker?

He turned on his heels and stopped, the sweat from his hairless body mixing with the geographic blood patterns and other aged bodily functions mixed together in a Body Shop swirl. This was the extreme backwards, Doug now running through time and back into his childhood. Sitting in the dormitory at his boys–only boarding school, effortlessly acquiring groupie followers and quiet admirers as one might pick up bits of gravel in the grooves of a boot's sole. A blend of aloofness sprinkled with Midas–like achievements and a healthy rebellious displeasure for the more tyrannical of the teachers left him unable to do wrong, which meant all 'this' deception, pain and narcissism was the counterbalance; filling the void or just progressive drama akin to complaining about a seasonal salad dressing's acidity when African children starve every day?

How did the story go this way? This lack of structure, reason or empathy, Doug now hovering above his teen self, trying to understand it all. Fight through the embarrassment and find out what is real, what is not and what is forgivable. Of course 'that' isn't – it can never be but the rest just might be.

Doug retuned to the warehouse and strangled the inert body of Michelle until he could feel only his own pulse beating through his fingertips into her neck. At that moment he found his hands scalded in the hot water of a familiar sink, the water red and the lines perfectly along the veins of the hands next to him. Margot slumped in his arms, eyes rolled up and more real blood than he'd ever seen.

CHAPTER 45

←→

V Core Dead & Renewed

Reg tap–tap–taping his heel on the Victorian–tiled floor, sitting moments away from Doug.

"What took you so long to come back?"

"You did."

"I didn't miss you at all in the beginning but I think I need you now. I killed Michelle."

"That's fine. They're always there as window–dressing – more alluring extensions of me."

"What were you doing? Who was involved?"

"Alluring in that way you like of course. Not the enhancing you from middle class tedium type, but the 'I'll pretend to care about it before defacing it when it touches its toes' type. Deloris gave you the disease which you gave to me which I didn't ever give to Margot. That was all in your head and hers for that matter – given the post–Janine fallout. After you and Margot murdered her baby."

Doug's lip bled quickly and stopped, the bite protruding through the skin then back out again like a fast–extracted thorn.

"I hadn't thought of that for a while; hadn't let myself."

Reg stood up and approached the television.

"Where's Margot?"

"In the hospital. Where you've just come from. Who knows. It took too long for you to get to her – like you didn't want to; like you wanted her to take the blame for what happened."

"I don't think that's right."

Reg turned on the TV, hovering over it, God–like, leaning over to check the cables at the back before retreating to the same chair. Doug's attention shifting – his call to arms; the dog whistle now alerting all the history so he fell into the screen, transfixed, trying unsuccessfully to pull himself back to Reg.

"I need to show you something. You need to show you something. There are hostages in your head and we need to free them."

Reg now finding the list of recorded titles, the free space flashing 0% in lipstick red …

Tues 20:30 – RECORDED & VIEWED –
BBC / ITV Soap Series Link
How to Initiate a Cult – 3 episodes
Porn Idol – 2 episodes
Went Up a Hill – 1 episode
After Life – 4 episodes
Skeletal Artefacts – 1 episode
Gengineering – 3 episodes

"But first I want you to think; to remember. To dive back into those early and recent moments, experiences, guilty pleasures and tell all. No divine flashbacks just everything that you've ever encountered from when it all started going wrong." Reg lights a joint. "I'll be here as a soundboard only – I'm not helping – it's all down to you."

"The mayhem of when we moved into that property – pre–kids. And that moment which you only realise years later when the marital sex isn't enough. So you start … helping yourself out, as it were. And blaming your spouse – my dear beautiful patient faithful Margot, when specifically your appetite for variety and death–defying risqué acts become normal … stable … predictable … boring."

"And this 'helping yourself out' – is this the first act of selfish betrayal?"

"Years of pent up teen hormones and angst and an unwavering worship of the female form makes it all acceptable in some way. As a man you are allowed to not outgrow wanking, aren't you?"

"I've never stopped. In fact over the thought of your wife a few times, but I know that's not helping. It's difficult to change my spots. Carry on."

"Then Janine to incinerate the monotony and the industrialisation of how hard you portray the decent–doing–dude. Resistance should never be futile or that's at least how the 'moral high–ground' me used to think: if you resist once and do the right thing, you're fine, then you do it again and you're not so fine, and again then you can casually blame the initiator, in this case Janine, because at least you tried. And you're not fine prior to the act because you're weighing societal moral perfection against the missed opportunities that presents – what's the perfection payout?"

"But once you act the perfection wanes if not completely dissipates – so you've cashed in but you've lost what made you in the first place. Do you regain it through months of getting morality back on track?"

"You think you do and it's alright but then the next time is easier. It's like you've fallen off a horse and the pain of the fall becomes so distant that the next time you feel your foot slip out of the stirrup and your butt wobble off the saddle you almost lean into it. You know how to fall, how to avoid the hooves and roll to safety."

"What's unique about that period? Your friends any different from the norm? Janine?"

"All very follow–on. Incremental simplicity ticking the boxes as we go – buy flat, upgrade job, tire of university friends. So much more simple than the next period – bullet points rather than lengthy metaphor–laden, dramatic, gun–wielding prose."

"So is the simplicity real or is it the complexity?"

"I need to find when that break occurred. Was it when you and Deloris arrived? Even what … what happened before then was … simple compared to what followed. Like a soap opera but with less colourful accents."

Doug's unable to look at Reg any longer, boring a stare–hole in the wooden floorboard going under the house through the foundation and somewhere long forgotten.

"I don't think you can go back after something like this; something so normal for people watching BBC or Sky News that it wouldn't even make the headlines other than perhaps some markets statistics on the subject."

"You don't have to talk about it."

"But I want to; I have to now because something happened that day shortly before you arrived. We killed him … her … it. We did it together – it was mine and Janine's and it embodied how far everything had spiralled from the chosen path. Margot and I made her do it and we watched how the extraction also ripped the soul from her face. The what if? The hope? The it could work? What did we do just given the timing wasn't right and vessel a third party?"

Without blinking or moving, Doug's eyes were watering like a disconnected intravenous drip. Not programmed crying, just long overdue, pulling him to his knees to retch a few times and lie back on the floor.

"This is crying for someone other than you and the perceived impact of an act which might have dropped you from grace. This is real."

CHAPTER 55

Maybe Baking

Doug held onto nothing sacred any longer. Workdays merged with an almost complete eradication of any memory involving regular, menial activities: had he brushed his teeth that morning? He could smell deodorant but it might have been yesterday's smattering; or the day before's. The top orange rind of his eyelids hurt so much that the only respite was keeping them wide open – even blinking hurt – fellow office inhabitants thought he was perpetually deranged or just mocking them.

"Is that the same shirt you had on yesterday?" "Do you

remember our conversation?" "Isn't that your responsibility?" – all common place in Doug's day. One evening he woke up with a jolt in front of the television stinking of sex but couldn't remember how he got there. Was the scent that he could taste with the tip of his tongue lingering in a foreboding memory–cloud above his aching brain Veronika? Or was it Margot? Or was it the television?

The thing about thinking there's something wrong with you but being completely inert, completely unable to ask anyone for help with dealing with it (depression? mental illness? schizophrenia? disease? mind tricks?), is that you try to place yourself back in happier more mundane times. Simplicity or simple because they're no longer the here and now – worrying about getting out for a run or the kids' success in the classroom or the sports field as the primal distraction to avoid life's harsh realities? But what were life's harsh realities? Does choice spoil the human soul? Does getting genetically laden with superficial gifts result in amassing those societal rudiments you know mere mortals are unable to attain ... hot pussy, winner children, making everything look easy. If that was the yang, this was the motherfuckerslapinyourfacebatonupthearseispitinyourfacem oonyourightonthenose yin.

He was a fire breathing yin Dragon, deeply opening his hip and groin – or so his Chinese scriptures taught him.

When his beard grew it now portrayed Emma Bridgewater dispersed dots of grey. Doug failed to notice but, had he done so back in the day, it might have actually added to the persona – his imperfection making him more perfect; the inconsequential nature of the imperfection making his consequential perfections even more solid. But now it just made him look old and scruffy. An old horse on the farm waiting to be shot. He'd never craved people, even in his heyday, but they'd always craved him which is where the seismic shift in Doug's life had occurred: his indiscretions and misplaced adventures had expelled the hangers–on; the peripherals, his loose north magnet impelling the smaller lighter north magnets away, slipping off the science experiment table and into the recycling bin.

"Please may I speak to my mother?" he asked the operator at the care home.

"Is that you again, Mr Perfors?" She paused. "Um we've been through this – your mother is not with us anymore."

Doug took to watching excessive pornography. Without any desire to masturbate he began cataloguing nineties and noughties porn stars in a confutation of Reg's work. He researched each one and ranked according to number of appearances, quality of the scene, tasks performed and correlation to the next performance with high variety scoring the highest. His consumption of these scenes and images began to wash over him, eventually as though he was fucking the star but with the disillusioned dreariness of a business transaction. One day he found himself at a sexual health clinic even though he was relatively convinced he'd done nothing – wasn't that something all responsible performers in adult entertainment undertook?

On consecutive days Veronika and Margot visited the house. When Veronika arrived, Doug's immediate thought was to firmly place the heel of his hand into the groove between her shoulder blades, shove her over the desk littered with his scribbles of mind maps, peel her jeans over the top edge of her buttocks then offer a corny line which had bombarded his subconscious for God knows how long now. But that was suddenly crumb flicked from the table like a horse double hoof back kicking a novice rider out of shot, when he saw her eyes produce drops of water at the sight of him.

"I haven't stopped thinking about you," she said, staring in the hallway, too afraid to hold him but too drawn to him to avert her watery gaze.

"I've not been thinking about much," Doug replied. "Just letting all this think for me." He pointed to the explosion of papers, printouts, post–its and cut–outs strewn across the floor, stuck on walls, shoved behind radiators, propped up by crockery: a paper–eating elephant's diarrhoea.

"Have you been eating properly? Your cheeks look thin, underneath your beard."

"Why have you come? Here? Now?"

"I'm getting married. A man I met on the Internet. I wasn't initially drawn to him like say when we met, but he's stable; and reliable; and the world doesn't have to move to make a life with someone."

"So is this the final hurrah visit? Is this my send–off or yours?"

"It's not like that. I came to see how you were and to say goodbye. I'm not sure there's room for you in this situation."

"OK goodbye and all the best of luck." His voice void of any sense of irony or resentment.

"I also meant to say that I've got a baby inside me and I'm not certain it is his."

Doug looks quizzical like a dog hearing a high whistle, cocking his head robotically to one side whilst performing a quick backdating calculation. 'Dating' he chuckled to himself. But the problem was he'd lost unequivocal track of time, space and, most pressingly, sexual encounters. The tedium of their encounters had cascaded to the extent that he often forgot where he'd come from in the taxi home. The story he'd provided to Margot had felt true, so true now that he wondered whether he'd done anything wrong at all. Perhaps this was all just a schoolgirl crush and they were merely 'dating' – holding hands in the park, watching movies, drinking wine all the time resisting the primal urge to penetrate and orgasm. Or perhaps it was just a schoolboy crush.

"I'm not sure I'm in the best state to ask whose it is; I know it's not mine."

"It's yours."

"But the timings don't work; we haven't been together—"

"Since that last time and I felt it happen. I felt you impregnate me as I dug my nails into you and ripped scars in your arse. I felt each one of the little yous struggling up towards my impregnable egg and burrowing through to make this … this … boy inside me. It can only be yours. It would only be yours. You're the only one able to make a baby inside of me no matter when it happened. It's like they waited, somehow hidden inside me, hiding from reality until the right moment to expose themselves, the strongest and most agile leading the attack to be us three."

Smug Dad

Doug could feel something happening to him: was this the sensation Reg had talked about identifying? The frustrating clicks kept happening, incessant, familiar, menial clicks, directed elsewhere. He had to find a way to break this and ascertain what was real. Veronika was real: she was standing in from of him like some art gallery patron staring at a work she couldn't understand, couldn't fathom, the colours all merging in inexplicable messiness and confusion: Doug. He opened his mouth as if to confront her further then stopped – stopped by something. With the next click he was inside her, all the way so he could feel his groin muscles strain against hers, his the bow of a violin pressed deliberately on the f–hole and c–bout. Next click they were smoking and the next she was gone and Doug was alone again surrounded by his images, a bunch of twisted expressions and merged genitalia; a spectrum of tan, pink, pale, brown and golden. Bodies piled up in display – a genocide war dump without the dignity of burial, clothing or individuality. Doug felt like he now laid among the porn dead, his skin sweating oil down both his flanks and the line where his buttock cheeks collided, dripping uncontrollably – an aerobics class of calorie burning intrusions, extractions and focus. He could feel the heat of another then another, first piled on top of him, then encircling his, a revolver chamber of over–salivated sphincters beckoning him in. When he chose the most familiar he couldn't help but notice it had changed, it all felt different somehow – tainted, unloved, neglected. He could feel it was Margot who turned on him, pressing both heels into his pectorals and flipping her head back like a beer top slammed off on the side of a bar. Doug could taste the alcohol on her skin.

"God I'm so glad we did that," she said.

CHAPTER 65

High 7 Lea Milled Wren

When Doug awoke from the restless sleep he'd been forced to endure after a night of scratching all over his body like an octopus with fleas and the incessant hum of faulty electrical wiring somewhere in the house, the television was on but with the sound off. He'd not remembered moving the television to the bedroom and, upon discovering that the lounge television was also on with the red mute button adorning the top right hand corner – a beckoning symbol for respite from the humming – couldn't in fact remember buying the bedroom television. Both channels were the same

– infomercials.

Doug got up and shaved – a bloody affair given the length of the beard with the result somehow comforting mentally but also uncomfortable physically in that his skin felt like broken chocolate when he winced, smiled or gesticulated in any way. His body was weak so he went for a walk to a nearby cafe and ordered a dozen poached eggs with proportionate salmon portions, altogether costing £48. It filled his stomach like the flame–induced air into a hot air balloon and, after browsing at his local bookstore, he felt marginally nauseas only to quell the spasms by yet more food – a sausage and crispy bacon bap from a trendy street food vendor (whose name was Edgar). Edgar had three children and two grandchildren, all of whom he adored – much like Doug and his children, even if his behaviour hadn't much shown it of late. He knew he needed to see them – Magnus, Giorgia and little Kenz – with their adoring faces, innocent eyes and loving arms, but without Margot knowing. It would just complicate everything, and this for the first time provided real purpose for Doug.

Through some form of memory soundbite he'd remembered where Margot was staying pre rough monkey sex and post lots of Vodkas. There'd been some reference to him paying the bills so it had to be five stars and an instruction to stay away – it was too early and too raw. Why he hadn't enquired 'too early since what' and what exactly had irritated the surface to the extent that it was chafed, numb and blue fillet red was beyond him. But remembering the hotel was enough of an incentive to begin.

The hotel was tucked down a sloping alley away from the

bustle of a less than normally bustly part of the West End and, when Doug came upon the place (not quite revelatory Columbus but also not disassociated Rome conquering either – somewhere in between), he pinched his collar at the top end to make them more pointy like a German Shepherd's on-alert ears, and walked through the revolving door with purpose. Through the doors he made his way to the foyer, strutting as though this was his commonplace routine, and plonked down in a low set yellow–beige chair between an oversized woman drinking a latte dressed all in white and three burka–clad (women? men? beings?) standing aimlessly waiting, while a man stood furiously gesticulating some way off at reception like a gambler watching his horse finish second. No one seemed to notice him which was kinda the point – he had cleaned up sufficiently so that those who had spent the most recent times with him would have keeled over in impressed congratulatory back–slaps, but maintained a subtle disguise for those who knew the old Doug; the pre (what did they call it nowadays?) mental capitulation Doug. His shades were big bucks baby (or so the courier explained), his hunting attire sufficiently over–the–top–Kentish–shooting–toff–father to strike the scent from him – he even wore a tweed hunting cap.

He knew he needed some luck – it was about fucking time surely? But it didn't arrive for some time – that evening in fact. He had to come and go, hiding in the toilets and intermittently walking up and down the emergency stairs, in and out the lifts and along corridors so as not to loiter in the foyer too long and be seen to do anything other than what most people do in hotel foyers: wait. His luck emerged on the

fifth floor when passing room 502 an audible emanation of
'boom' came trickling through – the 'boom' of Magnus
getting one over on his sister and clearly having been cooped
up too long in a hotel room. Doug revisited the site a few
more times, loitering only as long so as not to arouse
suspicion. His opportunity emerged when he heard Margot
announce an imminent shower, followed by the jet stream
pitter–patter in all directions as the multi–angled shower
turned the open space into a WWI attack, enshrouded by
enemy fire from all inescapable trenches. He even thought he
heard the drop of Margot's clothes to the bathroom floor,
losing valuable seconds in being dragged back to a time when
that was commonplace, her bowl–shaped buttocks cheeks the
last imagined vista before entering the watery cross–fires.

Doug knocked with the most delicate angle of his knuckle.
Nothing. Again – same pressure, different tempo. Still
nothing. Change of tactic – tapping all fingers across the door
– an impenitent patient in a waiting room. Footsteps towards
the door.

"Who's there?" said Giorgia, tip–toeing to look through the
non–existent keyhole (replaced inconsiderately by the card
slot and lock).

"It's Daddy," whispered Doug.

Quickly another furry carpet flurry of footsteps, these
heavier and with more purpose.

"Dad!" said Magnus seeking verification with optimism but
circumspect enough not to fling the door open. Well-trained
… stranger danger.

"Shhh buddy, yes it's me. It's your dad."

"What's your mother's maiden name?"

Very well-trained – I must have been a good father, thought Doug.

"Stipps," said Doug. "Don't call your mother. Just latch the door and open slightly so I can show you my face."

A long silence – a bit too long for comfort still with the shower raining up, down and across Margot.

"Muuuuummmmm," shouted Giorgia.

"Yeeesssss," came the shower–depth voice.

"Nothing, Mum," said Magnus. "She just wanted to know how to change the channel – I've showed her." Magnus's hand was now over Giorgia's mouth.

"OK," came the shower response followed by the wet–fart sound of a plastic bottle emptying its final contents.

The door opened deliberately without the latch: the training failed!

Magnus's eyes danced with delight when he saw his father, his cupped hand falling from Giorgia's mouth, her eyes following suit. MacKenzie, sensing a gathering, now miraculously disentangled from LazyTown, Sportacus flips towards the door, arms aloft. Doug, overcome, fell to his knees crying uncontrollably, but not in that he could have maybe controlled it – instead that literally his brain, body and soul completely overrode all control, restraint and manly social indoctrination to syringe endless water from his dictating nictitating membranes. He hugged the children, kissing them quickly and repeatedly and forcefully on top of their heads like a bee with eternal life and a bottom not designed to be ripped in kamikaze glory from the body when confronted with fight–or–flight danger.

"Where have you been, Daddy?" said Magnus, quickly evolving from joyous reunion to curious circumspection.

"What did Mummy tell you?"

"She said you were sick and went away. And you weren't coming back."

"Look buddy the last while has been a bit of a blur and I don't know what to tell you except that I love you all more than anything in this world and I never have stopped. Everything should have been about you – and it always was until I lost my way. I don't quite know the damage I've caused through my actions but I know I can fix it; fix us. Don't tell Mummy I was here just yet but know we'll be together again soon. I'm going to make it all right again."

"What's been the matter?"

"I'm not quite certain but somewhere along the line you have kids, fall in love with them then when it all seems too easy start behaving selfishly – like it's all about you. Then you remember it never was about you – but about you guys and making sure you're okay and looked after and have all the opportunities. Never trying; being spoilt with you and Mummy all along was why I got it all wrong. Never having to try. But now the trying begins – you just look after each other and Mummy and I'll be back before you can say—"

The shower stopped suddenly, the silence interrupting Doug and almost jolting him back, an aftershock post–bomb pin–ball back down the hotel corridor.

CHAPTER 7⁵

'Tis Demin Ahead?

To get to a point of redemption (or at least some level of reality certainty) Doug had to find Janine and rekindle whatever it was that made him believe their time together was real. He knew there was a routine progressive banality about that pre–kids phase of his existence which couldn't be made up – couldn't be fabricated – could be who he was. It was like imagining walking into an ice–cream shop and ordering broccoli – his fucked up path since then more likely to be the full–frontal, high–fat, caffeine–loaded, naked ice cream masturbation session covered in M&Ms, sprinkles, nuts and

Oreos.

Redemption. In whose eyes if not the selfish seeking of guilt alleviation? But even if achieved or sought or touched, like the tip of your penis in a MaSye Tanzanite Excessive, it never eradicates the memory. As if by ... by ... magic! That can be the only redemption; the only true redemption. You don't fuck yourself out of a situation: possibly the hardest post–adolescent lesson Doug had ever learned. But it wasn't post adolescence, and it wasn't ego; and it wasn't horny. Was that his biggest shortcoming: boundary pushing? Was being smug a licence to be a victim in all exploits of a carnal nature? Janine had not so much awoken this thing as merely pissed pure brazen oil–and–paraffin onto his fire. The fire of his inadequacies – his misguided chivalry which was (ah well the way the papers and the experts and the rights activists and the forward thinkers put it ...) misogynistic sexism. Was it better to realise his shortcomings and soldier on like the water in a violent waterfall destinying to the bottom? Or change? Put big boy pants on and beg for redemption – in his own eyes first then others. As if by magic. The flick of a switch.

When Doug awoke ... only shitting you ... before Doug could exercise any sort of heroic restraint, he was cat–slapping–a–woollen–balled into the back seat of a car that smelled like the stale had been blinged and fucked out of it. The seats were an unnatural orange–like puke after drinking Fanta and Doug knew this because his cheek was grass–orange stained against the leather as his next door BFF (for now) kept the heel of his hand indented into the gap between Doug's jaw and his cheekbone. Hollow and involuntarily curved: the bit sucked in by a model being mocked by some fat Kentish bloke: the funny one that everyone feels sorry for. Of course Doug transposing this funniness in the writing is his attempt at comical redemption – like the funny fat guy everyone says is funny but not fat but who everyone thinks is 15% funny than if he was thin. That or the lead up to a funnier lighter sequel because your closest family and friends say they don't like your sick pornographic mind. And you tell them it's just a story; a momentary lapse from reality; a TV show sent to shock and be forgotten.

Doug chuckled beneath the palm. He was a funny guy – you have to be, being a bit older and not fat. But the situation wasn't funny – quite serious indeed and familiar. The car took a corner then another, halting, speeding then doing a full double 720 degrees before coming to rest. Gawd that felt good! The release of the palm more than the double doughnut, Doug making a mental note that if a banking colloquialism didn't already exist of a similar ilk he'd introduce it: the irony of infinity versus two zeros (read two recessions or whatever the rock bottom opposite of £££ was) side by side in uniform defiance and symmetry.

When Sonny Boy roused Doug by throwing cold water over him in a drug–funded mansion AND was wearing bright yellow trousers, Doug was wise and scarred enough to know that this was a programme. But maybe it was a cerebral double–bluff: so clichéd that it had to be real, Sonny Bill stroking his stubble moustache down each side, the forefinger and thumb divorcing each other momentarily then back together not by fate but by habitual physics. Sonny Boy took out a yellow hanky and blew his nose, dainty squeals radiating from one nostril then another – now that wasn't textbook; not late night crime drama. Without a second blink or blow or snort Doug has secured the lit smoke from his lips and plunged it into his own arm.

When Doug switched back on the burn had scabbed and Janine was lying next to him smoking a cigarette, her forehead smeared with moist and the sides of her nose propping up haphazard lines of coagulated cum. Her breasts still heaved up and down but with a warm down mandate, the duvet protecting her lower modesty, wound tight to hold her small hips and tucked at the sides under the curve of her lower back. Sex and redemption like sin and salvation.

{ ➥ ➦ ➥ ➦ ➥ ➦ }

Training through robotic lineups of empty, derelict warehouses, Reg bobbled from side to side, a skittle wobbling before toppling and being joined by the dragged down mob of further toppled skittles; the skittle graveyard. On his left Deloris, her hand on his cock, pulled from his fly protruding at attention like a person on another person's shoulders at a boring concert. Pink furry furious futile fluffy unicorns fucking on rainbows … pink fluffy unicorns fucking on rainbows. What am I trying say here? What is the narrative arc: Reg glancing across at Deloris and nodding, an acknowledgment that despite her most sensual tugs and moist gobby mouth and inviting pussy he would never come. A resolute soldier refusing to die in battle. The battlefield passing in a taupe blur of angular derelict warehouses (yes repeat but fuck you that's just the way it is). The train disappears then Reg – copying Craig in Casino Royale tied to a chair, abusive knotted rope wielding (this time bitch) flying around him – submissioning (not fundling downstairs with a Marvel fan) to Deloris in an act of accepting depravity; an apology of sorts.

A website this time. Can we get away from this? No because a ban on all screens for his kids should be the same: Doug staring at the barbed wire wound tightly around the man's neck, his hired fake captor orange and fake–titted, a microbikini of questionable bad liver yellowgold – with a strained feeble arm 'apparently' winding the wire to a painful skin penetrating act of 'people pay for this sort of shit'. But why Reg and why now? And why apocalyptically empty square warehouses? Or is that just the right cinematic theme to accompany this?

Doug enters the room, stepping through the screen beside hired Polish beauty Lemka who suddenly becomes Deloris, the lines of stomach muscle forming parenthesis around an eat your ice cream off dented belly, turning ever so slightly into a double spoon I'm a mumMy and I gym the fuck out of this aging body but my personal trainer tells me I'm in Victoria Beckham's league (does she deserve a star turn here for having the poster pin–up body for post–childbirth digital skulduggery?). Deloris has not got a muffin top but the spread above the arterial micro gold slits of bikini bulge in giveaway mumMy territory.

"Why are you here, Doug?" she says, tightening the barbed

wire around Reg's neck.

"For answers. For you," Doug replies touching himself to check if he's real: Wreck It Doug modern cartoon version flitting from one unreal world to another.

"Is this the moment we reveal all?" says Deloris. "Where everything ties up in a neat ribbon to explain your evil ways?"

"I hope so. Can you help me there?"

"I need a tighter strangle," Reg pipes up.

"But you're not submissive; never submissive," muses Doug, confused at his own interpretation. "If you're proper retro TV you need to at least pretend to be in charge."

Deloris is now strapped to the chair, Reg holding the weapon of destruction clad only in the latest Man Size Skeletal Range masculine thong for 'straight gal and gay bloke lovers of the perfectly formed male derrière everywhere'. Deloris not naked. Never naked. A woman's completely naked form never a true male fantasy. Partly clad.

"Why isn't Janine here?" Doug asks.

"She's so boring she's real. No one could ever romcom the life out of something like her. She loves you and Margot which makes her less binary than anyone from your fledgling low budget TV collection," mutters Deloris through the muffled restriction of a dirty rag cloth looped into her mouth.

"So you are real and this is not real or you've never been real?" Doug, perceiving progress yet apathetic to the answer, squinting his eyes in punch–drunk boxer recoil.

"Or is just one of us real?" says Reg whipping across Deloris's back so she arches and squeals in delightful agony, then pauses, then comes, then wishes she had hands free, and not the phone because this isn't a comedy – that's the sequel.

With the computer off, Doug realises he's made love to Janine again, despite his pain and hers they do it drunk on intimacy. The umpteenth time is a gram more functional than the rest – penetration through spit–laden labia failing to mask physics. Doug goes down on her, his smell now overpowering hers like the two have been wrestling all night long and his has won over, half–nelsoned that musk to a point of sperm–sweat–faecal dominance. When it is over (again) Doug can't help flipping from depraved sex cliché to contemplative about kids and the general well–being of the female after invasion. This must be his upbringing: the surge of testosterone leaving him void of anything further for half an hour and over stimulating his decency and nurturingness. Like it needs to compensate for having put his cock in her bum then her mouth then her bum then her mouth. "I'm a good dad and man," his inner message yells as he tries to squirm away from her adoring stare. But this is Janine after all, not Veronika so the stare is more like nothing.

Nothing. Nothing. Nothing.

{ ↪ ↩ ↪ ↩ ↪ ↩ }

Where does this end? Is there some magical point with all the pain, all the mayhem, all the ball–busting angst, all the suffering, all the loose ends, all the misunderstandings, all the channels, all the button pressing envelopes (the crumpling of a piece of paper perhaps) together wrapped in a neat mauve ribbon? Do we deserve that? Is that something we've paid good money for? Is that the life affirming moment we all crave, salivating at the teeth for that one moment that ensures humdrum is shuffled back into the life deck and ameliorated is dealt? It starts and ends with Smug Doug and his misunderstood wicked ways. His misunderstood wicked ways as induced by those alluring goddesses enticing his seed. Doug because of Eve. Smug Dad to continue the phylogenesis.

In a dark corner – wait, let's call it a room, Doug stands attention erect in the centre of a circle of chairs. His body – Mattel He–Man toy plastic–like, controverts his lazy expression: awaiting sentencing, a resigned low expectation brow as one might slap onto the counter of a new coffee 'chain' offering the 'best coffee in London'. A more expression awakening tag line perhaps – 'better than the obvious aromatic piss served every day in Costa'. Doug twitches.

How long since I thought through what was important to me? I have to save my children for me: shield them from my misdemeanours and raise them in a way that makes sure they dodge the pitfalls – the ones I broke both ankles in. Is Margot too far gone – can we come back from the trauma that bastes our life turkey until we've both burnt under the grill, cowering as Christmas mouths move in to chew? I feel my head inserting into a mouth and they methodically, ungreedily masticate my brains and skin and bones into mush. Then I'm back in the room unable to move in my Man–At–Arms plastic body prison. I'm not green but I'm bulked and ripped to a point of being unnaturally unable to brush my teeth: my bicep too big once my arm is bent.

In the gloom surrounding Doug – the perfect circle – empty chairs are littered facing outwards. Not chairs but seats jutting out of this air; bookshelves almost or more like TV stands but stable enough for bums. They're levitating but not in a sci–fi remake of a remake whoooooooooooo look hands under the seat TV magician sort of way, rather just there: bookmarks inserted into Doug's life. A library card shoved into jelly, cemented and awaiting landing.

Reg (Doug thinks by the saunter) steps up, his face obscured like a sinkhole, carrying a copy of a VHS porno. He's indubitably talking to Doug but the words are indecipherable. He nods and sits facing the other way inserting the VHS into an old silver player, grabbing a remote and slouching down as though readying for a wank.

There was once a mouse – true story, urban legend – with each foot caught in a mousetrap. Initially his mechanical logistics were unwieldy, pained, but eventually he learned to live with four tiny broken ankles and wooden slabs following him around wherever he went. Some argued he'd put his own feet into each trap, sequentially and methodically – a form of masochistic evolution, a Rhodentia Jesus suffering for our turpitudes. The pussycats who had placed the traps knew that one further trap, a fifth targeting the tail, would kill the little mouse, unbalance him such that they would have no choice but to remove the traps, smooth their whiskers and place the Dougmouse's broken little body on the altar to rise as the vermin Son of God.

Put his foot in it. Then again. And again. Then once more.
Now only my tail remains.

CHAPTER 85

Chew Numbs

How does one go about telling a story from here ... with your thumbs? It defies everything prior; everything past; everything in the lead up box ticked by thoughts being at least a million miles ahead of one's fingers. But not the thumbs.

Doug had to resolve. He had to summarise it (Twitter interruption mofo Alab Hassan) in a way that would facilitate navigation: that management consultant training kicking in like a morning americano. He had to make a list; not a beautiful, flowery, incessant, unnecessary, literary list but a business list; a funny bulleted list (fun this autocorrection –

how do you turn it off angry face red exclamation man's question mark); not a bulletin – a simple chronological shopping list giving each a plus and a minus; a Real and an Unreal (but not like the surfer dude 'Unreal' just 'might not have happened').

So it needs a title, Doug decides sitting in his dimly lit study, the lamp shade worn and wonky, the door creaking by design. He hears a fly or could hear a fly and this disrupts the flow: a trap door slamming across his stream so that the piss flies here and there and on the seat and floor and pyjama pants and hands. Eew.

"Where is that fly?" thinks Doug, imagining the fulfilling moment of blasting its insides through its brains with his worn slipper, now almost flat from wear (left thumb bias autocorrecting to water). An old porno pic hiding behind a newly hung family picture catches his eye and it is like someone's insides being blasted through her brains, the feigned organism (thumbs!) only countered by the cartoon like (phone buzzing WTF) invasion. Doug scrumples the picture, whipping it behind his back towards the bin. And missing. Of course. Like the cut–off stream. Extinguished. Failed.

The fly again. No not the worst ever episode of Breaking Bad, a serious green–blue country fly that lands on you and somehow makes you itch, like you've caught a disease instantly and start lepering away. A pus–like sore growing and exploding in the face: always back to porno – "Can we try snub this habit?" thinks Doug taking the cap off the T for the numptyith time.

"Come out come out, you little buzzing … Buzzing …

Buzzing …"

No words seem clever enough so Doug abandons the comparison like a post transfer window sportsperson. Almost at the stop.

Avoiding Twitter becomes like not taking a daily shit. It's there: the monster and, like some overblown form of expression, it wants to come out (a baby's head pushing pushing pushing until it is released) yet has to remain. You know it is there and you don't forget. What if someone unimportant says something important. Note to self: Tom Hanks is the worst tweeter in history. K – k

CHAPTER 95

Cooper Solid Cereal Miller

She's so hot yet she fucks people up. Regularly. Like seriously regularly and with consummate ease. Perhaps the first few weren't that easy – all average looking men falling over themselves and their dicks like a dominoes of puppies – colliding, cascading, cacophonying to get her attention.

How in Christ's name do they believe they have any real chance other than to provide dead expressions? "Is that what she loves the most?" she reflects. And the tease is so spectacular.

"I'm going to get it; I'm really going to get it! From her. Oh my Jezus! Until I'm not and there's an object dive boarding from my head, protruding in parallel with my hard–on."

She feels a bit sick thinking about the first. Likely more impulsive self–defence than maniacal pre–meditation, but still bucket loads (bloody literally!) of disposing and cover–up planning. Like did he text his mates on the impending conquest or did he make a scene at the club where people would remember him? The first definitely shaped her toddler steps – nice quiet loner in a crowded bar. Unobtrusive. Indistinct. No marked facial, racial or personality traits. Just a warm body to remove the life from – no real revenge at this stage either, just good old fashioned practice makes perfect. Oh so shittingly different to her first female victim.

❨ ↳ ↰ ↲ ↳ ↰ ❩

People judge people. Fat people, for instance – a significant target of commuter and restaurant disdain. As though their additional space is offensive somehow, depriving others of sacred space. And the additional afflictions: bad breath, body odour, snoring, drooling, inappropriate mastication technique, small cock, flabby tits, additional chins, Golden Arches rolls pushing out to say "Hello and I'm offensive."

And we do blame them, judge them for their lack of self-control; their lack of intent to out body perform the twenty-something gym instructor.

"There's one snoring right next to me," Doug thinks as he commutes to the airport. "Not her or him," he reflects, but "one" and not as in "one should always wash one's hands after wiping one's derrière" but rather "one of those in that cage over there; yes that ONE!"

As if to drag the universe back to equilibrium the aesthetic gods throw Doug the biggest bone – a cataclysmic specimen of such beauteous portions, even Doug betrays his usual non–gawking demeanour and philosophy of never making a woman feel uncomfortable by looking her (not one) up and down. He can't resist looking the fat one up and down when she coughs on him though (replenish the stock of antibacterial hand gel! Replenish the stock!).

She notices Doug's disdain at the fat one and shoots a look of approval his way. Well done for judging her fatness, her laziness, her lack of body charm. Doug smiles at her body charm; the living embodiment of David Niven, charm dripping, oozing, caressing from every perfect pore on her body. "She must have a flaw," thinks Doug. "A double uvula or a hairy belly or maybe a hairy butt hole: Gawd forbid."

"He might be a tad too hot to kill," she giggles to herself, resisting the urge to overtly squirm. "For the first time in … well, forever … this might not be a slam dunk. He has this look, like he might turn around and say, 'please take your mouth off my cock because I have a stunning wife, 23 perfect kids and a happiness unbeknown to most mere mortals.' He is confident but not swaggery confident, just that he knows how his shit works, how to get shit and how to control shit. Will he try to tame me? Show me who is boss in the sack or wait until I've come so hard I've dislocated my skin before pleasuring himself? Likely the latter."

Smug Dad

The train jolts, throwing the fat one into the vacant loo to be flushed out of the carriage and Miss Hotness Psycho Serial Killer and Mr Smug Delusional Unreality together, her the slap of cool ham onto him the soft acquiring buttered bread. They are forced to kiss. Not really, but their mouths do touch as the train tilts further, driving a fart from fat one dissevering Doug and Nell's glances in mutual concern. "Think I'll fuck him then kill him quickly," she thinks. "Think I'll check I've not made her up," he thinks.

CHAPTER 06

Boil & Topple

"Sometimes you get so excited about doing something, then you get to it and you wonder if it is all worth it."

"It is."

"Ladies, it is all worth it. From the keeping him believing he is mad to the constant sex: all serving a purpose."

"We are intelligent, resourceful and determined women, so this little 'display' is the symbolic cornerstone we should all go to cerebrally when things get tough."

"Like when he's inside you and you look so deeply into those lonely eyes that you think you can save him and hearts are literally pouring from his tear ducts."

"And you're the only one he has ever shared this with!"

"Right, that exactly when you think back to us throwing these items into this silly pot."

"It will drag each and every one of us back to this reality."

"This purpose."

"This foundation for the future."

"It will be painful."

"There is growth within each of us already."

"I can feel mine."

"Me too."

"They are his. We know that. But that is essential."

"Have we been too cruel?"

"What the fuck?"

"You know it is okay to feel both those extremes of emotions – sympathy and retribution."

"He serves a purpose."

"Now remove your clothing."

Each disrobed and stood around the dark ceramic pot, the night sky shrouding each in a different kind of warmth. The shroud was present but silent, holding each still. Enshrining the pot, far enough away from the flame, were items of animal, plant and human organ origin.

"The potion will symbolise the emergence, rise and fall of Douglas Perfors."

"We're not really going to drink it are we? They didn't in the book. Won't we get ill or something?"

"The potion also represents our evil, collectively and singularity. In doing this we acknowledge ourselves. The lonely intruder. The smitten accommodator. The pandering nymphomaniac. The mother superior. And the integrative whole of our creation – taking the good, expelling the bad and remembering that this would take evolutionary excellence to a higher level. Ensuring the continuation of the species and the elevation of the gender beyond any dad's comprehension."

"Is anyone actually wearing a butt–plug? I heard this was his latest thing."

"That would constitute clothing and render this little gathering null and void."

"Oh my god!"

"It's gone, I promise. Where were we?"

"This potion will not only push our Smug Dad towards destruction, it will foreshadow the evil and excitement in his soul."

"… to control and manipulate."

"… and elevate."

"First thing that has to go in is what we know as it represents the greed."

The liquid in the pot was now crazy hot, bubbling and splattering the night nakedness; firing at any of them. Foreboding. Daring. Entice. Each would retrieve an item from the floor, some still frozen from storage and cool to the touch, throwing it into the cauldron and citing a good and bad memory in sequence. A load, poured into the cupped hands, then draped up through birthing entry point up the breastbone and across the mouth, the shocking white lighting the scene. Lost into the pot forever.

"That's definitely going to upset my tummy," thought each of them.

A slice of severed penis – the swamp snake – not Doug's

evidently as this had a purpose to serve, but an unluckier, less fortunate male nevertheless. An eye. A large tongue. And a woman's fur.

"Not as neat as any of ours," thought each of them.

The neighbour's dog's tongue. The helmet of another penis – this one black with the hole widened and splayed like two petals; the black snake's forked tongue. A worm – the remainder. A lizard's leg. A bird's wing.

"Far off the distant hoot of an owl would be like so apt right now."

A worn out old fashioned scale, many an anxious moment spent hovering on one leg and spitting out the toothpaste to get the reading down – the dragon's scale. A tooth, likely wild animal, the root bloody and hastily removed (or bought from the lowly paid zookeeper).

Four kitchen knives produced, wrapped in a Cath Kidston tea towel. It was a sacrifice each knew they had to make, so they began cutting into their flesh, wild screams sonic booming into the sky and ecstatic stomping hops around the grizzling pot. Each would retrieve from a different region, some opting for perceived pain free points, others hunting out the masochistic pleasure. The flesh wasn't mummified in some cases, but this was the exact prophesy they were remedying. A toy shark's gullet and stomach. MacKenzie's. Or Giorgia's. No, 'Kenz's Jaws' scribbled on in pink Fine Point Sharpie, marvelling at her pinpoint maternal use of the possessive s even at an age too young to comprehend; subliminal educative advertising. Poison from the earth – Japanese knotweed, dug up under trying circumstances in the dark. A Christian's liver, this one real – an avid churchgoer drinking himself to death and dying praying in the pew. Liver cirrhosis. It was rotting inside and out in the open. He'd always refused to take communion so the liberally stretched inference was no baptism to speak of. A goat cheese and bile soufflé, the former gathered during the gastroenteritis episode, stored and doused on the Essential Waitrose English Goat's Cheese. Pine tree slips – the easiest of the twenty–three.

They laughed. Exhausted. Bleeding. Wild eyed. Climaxing. Each kissing the water then delicately hovering o'er and dunking, their legs straddling the pot burning into their limb flesh, the Tartar's womanly possession mingling into the potion. A baby's finger.

Her baby. It wasn't his but it was hers. And it had happened. Still born. Porn excursions were no different to prostitution they deemed. Modern times dictated upgrades and big huge supreme gestures of sacrifice. A bottle of Tiger beer – none of them supported the cruel Chinese custom of Tiger bones as aphrodisiacs so couldn't bring themselves to accept the Tiger's stomach, so elegantly offered by the zookeeper's assistant.

And finally the blood. So much of it. The easiest of all. Bottles and bottles. Stored up each month at the same time in the same way, their faces raw as they ingested the potion. Inside to outside to bottle to water to inside. The full circle complete.

"I am Janine."

"I am Deloris."

"I am Veronika."

"I am Margot."

"Hi Ladies, did I miss anything?" said Nell, emerging from the darkness. "I think he'll put one inside me too."

CHAPTER 16

Wavey Hall Wagner

"Tell the story; the one about when you pretended to be a big shot movie producer and those two wannabe actresses gave you a blow job … at the same time!"

Reg sat more in dazed disassociation than anything. The airport lounge was unusually quiet and his 'wish I never bumped into' cohorts ostensibly held onto some of his more embellished stories a bit too fondly.

"Who remembers this shit?" he said out loud by accident, a blurring Reg hitting the business class grade vodka back, the crack in his neck audible.

"Go on – the one when you ran that casting couch in that hired office block and those two babes applied to an ad you and your mate put out. It is a classic! It's well special!"

"You might have noticed that all this talk of coercion to enhance a woman's career is not particularly en vogue at the moment. That fat toad from Miramax, although taking that sort of abuse to a newly industrialised level, has opened up every single dumb dickhead pushing a little too fervently for a sexual favour. Now more than ever no does mean no. And besides that was a long time ago. And besides I was actually making a film until I realised I wasn't. So they just might have been in the film before the head, but really the quality from the one with the jagged teeth was of such a painful disposition it would have been an insult to the entire porn industry to cast her."

"Aw mate – you were making a porno! Legend!" And they start double high–fiving like chimps causing Reg to wonder if he was that much of a dick (check) or whether they were that much of a dick (check), so more like an AND rather than OR scenario.

The lounge continues to empty and flights are called, one woman sprinting towards the over–salted soup, gulping it down like cold morning I'm late for work tea, and heading out to boarding, the soup trailing down her mouth like an asymmetrical ginger dirty Sanchez moustache.

{ ↳ ↰ ↳ ↰ ↳ ↰ }

This was part of the training: part of the therapy. Imagining whoever you meet of aesthetic appeal in the throes of ecstasy and or excited pain at the end of your projected pointed penis could be addressed in three ways. One, look directly into the person's eyes and imagine all their hopes, dreams, shortcomings, aspirations, real desires and soul. Keep your eyes on their eyes. Do not avert to objectify territory including in your mind. "I imagine her having a fantastic rack" replaced by "I imagine her wanting to travel the world and make up with her father." Doug tried and succeeded on One. Despite Nell slapping back more of a coital stare than any cast member from Vikings.

Two, do not make porno boundaries your go–to place. Imagine love and lust as one rather than reverting to anal and girl–on–girl. Intertwine sexual desires with real feelings, not just make her come so hard the nails draw blood. Yes, be a selfless pleasure providing lover but this is not a school exam where the results are shared in the ladies' gym changing room. Doug normally had a problem here. His mind normally couldn't help contorting his subject onto all fours or looking up at him or showering in his finale. Yes, he was a selfless lover capable of putting himself a distant second but this was deemed too closely aligned to the 'path to porn' so he was instructed to steer clear.

Three, don't do it out of boredom. The classic irony amongst being too busy raising kids and holding down high stress big hours jobs and showing a genuine interest in (mainly kiddie) extracurricular activities and gym and running and socialising and and and, was that deep down the modern dad's purpose had become tedium. Like social media for teens, when bored stiff looking at porn. That is until the site you've become accustomed to and familiar with becomes too diversionary (to other shittier sites or big cock ads) or too young – a modern phenomenon Doug had become increasingly uncomfortable with. He'd discussed it with the group and the consensus rang true – not matter how perverted there was no desire to lower the age dial from woman. So he'd stuck to big tits and MILFs to make sure. He'd now get a book out and read or write a short story. Preferable to spicybigtits.com.

The three step porn cure had been working a treat for Doug until the encounter on the train. It was not that this woman imbued wholesomeness such that nothing even hinted Doug towards his obsession but rather that her demeanour was clearly willing him back in, like some straight white male Hollywood fantasy where the sap gets the girl. She was daring him and Doug, of sometimes stubborn disposition, was resisting her attempts to shove his head back down the 'everything is porno' vortex wormhole. And this pissed her off. She saw dirt; he had dirt, but like a flasher unwilling to flash he kept it concealed behind his unconventional suit. Did she say she'd kill him slowly as a result? Did it count if he didn't think it but DID it to her like the hair pulling, arse slapping, butthole fingering, ATMing, monstercocking cowboy that he really was? She'd fuck him at the airport she thought. In the business class private cubicle while all the old men clambered outside for a day–old newspaper.

Do what you love doing. A harmless starter after all.

{ ↦ ↤ ↦ ↤ ↦ ↤ }

That moment when everything changes; or everything should change. A full cream milk wholesale bargain re–evaluation of who you are and why you do the things you do and most importantly shouldn't do. A reembracing of one's core kindness values such that mistakes don't happen again. But is this really possible? Does the slate wiped clean like XC60 wipers (where the water actually squirts from the wipers directly in the new model) actually succeed in changing 40years of carefully honed nature–driven character? Doug hoped to fuck it would. Of course he'd been happy, even delighted, with his personality traits in the past – blessed upon him like a genetic lottery, ardently believing he was one of the good guys.

But he really wasn't. This dawning realisation of being flawed and wanting to alter not alternate his persona towards something less like the fully accomplished, perfected bodied, all achieving Smug Dad and more like a likeable, flawed, kind-hearted human being was not a step in the right direction but more like a forward roll followed by triple pike into handstand ending with back flip onto knees then head.

He couldn't amply squash the sex monster – this was one of his few genuine joys in life – but he could adapt this dark non–seatbelted passenger onto something more like the man his father wanted him to become when he popped out screaming, all limbs, goo, crumpled skin and eyelashes. He also couldn't help but notice how sex with Margot was way more exciting and fulfilling when he was kind to her rather than when the sides of his muscular butt cheeks quivered like sunlight across a troubled ocean in the full length mirror.

Of course to get to this magical potentially unattainable nirvana he would have to break some eggs; face some demons; uncover some harsh realities and stare his worst fears and nightmares in the face – his face too close up – a movie poster zoomed in too far.

He was a sex addict.
He was a porn addict.
He was a TV addict.
He was in denial about what was important to him.
He was an egomaniac.
He was a control freak.
He hated his own weaknesses.
He was an occasional drunk.
He was delusional.
He was Smug.
He was mad.

Was.

CHAPTER 26

Serene Delinquent

A square. Corridor. With doors on either side. So an inner set of chambers and an outer – belly buttons – innies and outies. A circle would have been a bit more woah, SciFi your ass, beam me around the rooms Scotty et–set–er–rah but deal with the square (and accept the obvious parallel to Doug who some would call a square but as Reg would undoubtedly testify "not those hanging off the other end!").

The square was the symposium where Doug would discover his reality. Bound with a razor blade pressing up under his scrotum, blunt enough not to insert the cool metal past the point of eunuch return yet sharp enough to keep his mind focussed. Plus they'd been emptied by her: she had to sample the goods before inadvertently helping him discover what was real before actually slicing him up into little bitty pieces of cheating, indecisive, ungrateful man flesh ... Doug's mad?

Was she an innie or an outie? A ninny or a shouty? Doug knew not the former as he was blindfolded and gagged throughout but the inner ear hairs and membrane had received so much abuse, he knew she was a shouty.

Before any doors were opened, Doug put her and Reg and Janine as outies: crouching behind each outer door ready to skewer his advance, prove his worth and establish his innocence. OK the first one counts but Doug could only hope in vain for the latter two – readers already siding with the long-suffering partner in direct response to his whoring. Was whoring worse than murdering, he wondered as she wet and attached the spaghetti electrodes and dropped Doug into the square corridor. An akimbo splat on the carpet. He could taste it; it had recently been cleaned. And the cleaning product had strawberry in it just like her lip balm. This he knew for certain. It felt nice on his cheek, not rubbing against a puppy nice, but nice as an annoying unreachable itch being scratched. Doug lay there. Not silent as his breathing was deafening to his own ear, but he lay there on his front flipped full circle from the position she'd tied him up in. But that was now another realm – something he couldn't recollect. Only the square corridor and the doors all closed. Numbered.

From the carpet, no not the red carpet (well maybe), Doug

almost arose, anxious to not discover what awaited behind each door. What if it was not to his satisfaction? What if it was merely a projection, further clouding reality and taking him to a sphere of subconscious only known to those in oblivion. Fuck off – this is not Inception!

Door number 1, up and to his left, the number 69 embalmed in Vaseline above the handle. The door was blood red, a type of blood rich in nutrients and iron, and vascular. Gold ♂ ♀ symbols flank the numbers, small globes of white trickled throughout the Vaseline and on the gold numbers. Then 96 at the top of the door written in brown – light orange rancid brown. Doug could smell it was shit. Maybe best to avoid door number 1 (or was it door number 96?).

Door number 2. Completely green – bottle green – a stick man looking at another stick man, the latter looking straight ahead. Door number 3 – yellow – not a golden yellow but a cool rose–coloured yellow, broken petals decorating the base of the door. That was Doug's chosen first standing. Come what may. Be what will.

Standing up from the warm embrace was harder than Doug imagined, Velcro tearing himself up and out towards the yellow door. Upon entering initially just darkness then the slam of the door behind him; he'd walked in without feeling like his legs were moving. Soft contemporary music playing in the background, the distinct smell of good red wine, a meal prepared and sobbing or moaning.

Veronika comes into focus, naked and exposed, her mouth and vagina sealed shut, smooth skin covering each. Yet she is able to speak.

"I never deserved what you had to give but I only wanted more. A Disney film. That's what all girls want."

Doug's kryptonite: sex. He's atop a giant naked woman, standing waist deep in her belly button, the skin surface soft and unsteady. A sweet smelling tan bouncy castle. He can see down between her legs, the sides of the vulva open and flowing, an inviting water slide at a child's water amusement park.

Raise your hands if you're having fun. Here we goooooooooooooooo.

Doug carefully climbs out of the belly button. He can hear the heartbeat, soothing and rhythmical; no movement of the breastbone but felt beneath his feet. He stands below the navel and there is not one hint of a garden path. The perfect woman? The hairs would be noticeable at this level and, although no path, the route towards the ankle high pubic forest undeniable. Doug swings around. A breast man his misogynist friends would say. A woman's man? A women's man? He can't resist looking, the mounds ahead of him, their sheer volume stirring his compartmentalised aesthetic kryptonite: just one look and the day is ruined with horniness. But never just random horniness for Doug; loving horniness with just the right smattering of smug ego to impress enough to shout to the back–archingly grateful recipient, balancing what should be a healthy relationship.

But they never have been. Not for Doug.

The breasts now change intermittently. Veronika's.

Margot's. Janine's. Margot's. Nell's. Deloris's. Margot's.

Doug's now on his back being dragged by his nostrils, an invisible force taking him to another door, flinging him up against it so his back slaps against the top half, collapsing back onto the soothing carpet. The door is labelled 4 and is a deeper shade of red, hundreds of ♂ symbols littered in black Sharpie ink, a prisoner's count of remaining days, except counting in men. Doug squints forward and notices a few ♀s scattered throughout; you tend to notice detail when you're after it. The smell on the door is new.

Inside, the door slams behind Doug into his behind causing an involuntary thrust. Dark of course but liquid dark – the room swimming, red rivers oozing in a million directions, an assortment of males screaming for help, gasping for air above the blood only to be sucked back into the torrent. And model Z–cards everywhere. Wanted supermodels for catalogue work. Nell, the supermodel serial killer, looking as alluring as intense holding a Cristal flute in one hand and a screwdriver in the other. The men begin flying from the bloody rivers piling onto her screwdriver, her arm muscle tensing to hold the weight, countless skewered men ready for the braai. Then the odd woman for good measure, Nell's twitch of expression one of ephemeral guilt. It's never the same as killing a man.

Then Doug being drawn by his anus towards the human piled screwdriver, fighting against the current, flailing in the opposite direction until his tuchus slams down onto another good looking man's ear, his face swollen for the protruding tool. And Doug forced to ride it, even enjoy it – a merry go around; Nell raising the sword in victory then lassoing them all off in one fell whip above her head: bloodied men with holes where there should and shouldn't be meeting the walls. Slap slap slap. Remaining there each of them, a moose head trophy freshly hunted; presented for exhibition, Doug the centrepiece; the newest relic; the mouse's tail.

Green door number 2. ⚢. I'll be ready. Whenever you need me. There's a monster – literally a bloody, drooling, scaly, multi–eyed monster in the room wearing a red swimming costume, pulled so high up, on the edge of surrenders inside. Actually two monsters fighting to the death. Over Doug. Big fuck off green monsters. Intrusive neighbourly monsters. Doug looks down at his hands as they start turning green; not Hulk warm–fuzzy–Marvel green, but green that if you really zoomed in on; looked intently at, you might get sick. A green so repulsive your repulsion would make you Exorcist sick. Doug gets Exorcist sick whilst continuing green.

Is there any bodily function that remains sacred?

When each of the monsters grabs an opposing pole of Doug they tear him clean in half. But he remains functional, the top half able to think and nose pick, the lower … well we know where this is going so flash ahead to the female monster lying in the sand smoking a cigarette, Doug's lower half being congratulated by the upper. Two beings; two monsters. Four in the room then just Doug's legs walking down the aisle with the Deloris monster, her belly taught and ripe. Forever and always. I'm always here.

Is there an intermission?

Doug on his side on the carpet once again but back as a whole person, his left side submerged into the carpet fabric. It itches that left side to form a bellowing red raw rash, boils and welts which he is unable to scratch fully because his left arm is contained in the foundation below the carpet. He seems to be dropping into another room, leaving his skin behind before he is cast through the keyhole of Door number 1.

Just his muscles, organs, sinews, gristle and bones remain and he wonders whether the bodily function conceived and heaved in the green room has contributed to his new projection behind this door. Because literally everything is projecting. Doug is orgasming every few seconds as though shedding tears, with each semen expulsion becoming more intense and painful. The room is shitting everywhere, all over him so that the faeces mingles with his exposed muscly sinews, infecting. There's lube everywhere; Vaseline as well so that nothing ever actually touches. Janine's room. And blood to round off the unholy concoction. Doug thinks he drowns in it, ingesting all the wrong stuff into all the wrong places until his breath stops.

Darkness in the corridor and the carpet has been cruelly removed. The four flanking rooms' doors banging in chaotic unison, playing a tune. Doug loses all his fingers and toes, stretched like one of those sticky man toys except the spheroid different coloured ends are guillotined off rather than erratically stuck to the wall in declining places. The outie rooms then fall silent, the doors cowering away to close about as silently as hoping not to wake a patient. The innie square takes over, lowering Doug into the gloom.

Has to be the big kahuna. Margot.

Inside the room there is no evident pain, despite Doug having no digits remaining at the end of any limb. The room is empty with four shady figures inhabiting each of the corners, way down below – a square grain silo. Doug watches as his bloody stumps turn into Apple product adaptors. He is still stretched and he can feel the strain of reaching towards the four corners but without pain. Duty yes and perhaps responsibility but not pain.

Magnus is the first to be plugged into, his eyes lighting up and his smile exploding in Doug's heart. Then Giorgia, the cheeky monkey curling into a ball, womb like position. MacKenzie the next to log in, leaving Doug with only one foot unplugged and Margot, the angel superior, approaching in a blinding light to complete Doug's circuit.

Epiphany of unadulterated joy.

And redemption?

CHAPTER 36

←→

Rear Hoe

Who could know how rock bottom feels? I mean, what is rock bottom? Some seascape, deep as an Attenborough narrated scene complete with wide–eyed fishes and plankton that suck on sand with the sole goal of evolving; no real horrible concept of bettering to be anything more than something on a chain? A shark. Jesus! The most evolved; and now is it a red wine extravaganza of boring ashtrays filled with the same burnt bumf that fills every boring discussion?

I absorb or pretend to absorb. I am an amoeba; a

professional one, continually adapting to prove I know what
it takes to cut it and make colleagues and contact and cash
and content and any Cs, mostly all ending in unt.

This is not how it was meant to be: not what the soil and wind
and cavewomen expected; no divine intervention to say man
shall lead a pretentious existence of false smiles, lots of nods
and constipation of real emotion.

Maybe there is this bright sunshine that exists in a dark
corner to magnify some small one in eight billion moment
that can make a human being feel better than a mere cog.
Nothing corny like an 'I love you' or a smile or dangerous
sex, but an unconventional moment of sheer bliss: a polite
call centre operator able to solve a problem, an on time train;
a wrongly forecast crappy weather day. Maybe someone who
doesn't spout bullshit; someone who looking at you can see
through the baldness, the unkindness, the marry–like malice
below to a kid who maybe didn't want to be an astronaut, a
cowboy or a doctor but rather a hero. An important person.
Someone able to make a difference where bees fear to make
honey and bus drivers are polite but not so polite that when a
teenager massacres a middle–aged father with 2 point 3 kids
he smiles and reports in to police 2 point 3 days later and gets
a 2 point 3 K Sun deal for how he saw the blade imbed in a
skull. A poor man's skull. A rich man's skull. A no longer
man's skull.

Someone who cares.

When I grow up I want to be a Hero.

Not a doctor or a scientist; or a lawyer or vet. I WANT TO BE A HERO.

Just an old-fashioned hero will do just fine; will do just dandy.

CHAPTER 46

Bestiality Writes

Doug awoke. Now awoke is an interesting choice of words. Not because he was asleep. But because he was not woken: he brought himself back to consciousness. Margot lying neatly beside him. Curled up. Quiet. Distant dreams invisibly melting across her forehead, her ribcage swelling up more suddenly than down but not sudden at all. No formation of wave or moon sucking tides to tsunamis in this sleep pattern, just a rhythmical sea of breathing. Normal. Back to normal. It felt like that anyway. For Doug. Captain of his own owness again.

Kenz, Giorgia and Magnus still sleeping; Doug slipping a non–intrusive glance in then out again, resisting the temptation to smooth the hair from their brows. Do not disturb. So he doesn't. The house fixed or outwardly functional. Again it seemed. Doug not floating but walking softly down the stairs, an explorer of sorts, rediscovering all he once held; all he once owned. It exists.

The lounge. Lived in. The remote controls, worn to the bone. Doug aches when he picks one up, so he puts it down, reticent to make the same mistake. But he must. Saturday morning rugby from Australasia the normal eye, ear, nose and throat fodder. It has to be a Saturday thinks Doug – the morning calm and spirited anticipation that can only be on a Saturday envelopes Doug, tickling his skin and stroking his bones and (ever so) gently blowing warm, chewing gum scented breath air on his neck. Saturday embraces Doug.

His backside magnets into his chair and his feet are atop the leather twice restored footrest. He's been here before, pointing the damn remote at the box. Saturday disappears, wisping out the window, Doug cold, exposed, raw, diseased. His sleeping beauties double, triple, quadruple the distance from him now. He's locked into position facing the box, there is no escape. His favourite place. His reality. Margot asking which to delete from the recorded list.

"Nothing!" he yells but not audibly. "This is who I am! This is all I have!"

Listed programmes, some viewed, some kept, some new. Zero percent space remaining.

"Home Invasion" – partly Viewed – Synopsis available.

Doug views from where he's left off as a naked man enters a suburban detached home and is grabbed by two terrorist–looking fellows. He's forced to the ground by one of the men, while the other steps back in semi–disgust at his own actions. Not quite method but solid acting school. A good looking woman and three children scream in the background.

Doug stops the programme, reverting back to this list. "Expiry Date" also partly Viewed. An 18 with Mature Themes, Scenes of a Sexual Nature, Violence, Sexual Violence and Strong Language. A grocery store – a big one, all the characters sweating, some holding guns, some crouched on the floor. A tense and visceral scene Mark Kermode might say.

Further down the list: "How to Initiate a Cult" only a small portion viewed, the blue line failing to stretch to the end in hopeless inactivity. Restricted R. The first word repeated on the line below yet this not viewed at all: virgin TV territory and seemingly a series. "How NOT to Murder a Boyband".

Doug glances down at the cup in his hand, the bitter, burnt taste of coffee beans in his mouth. Yet he's thirsty; thirsty nausea as his vicarious television existence points into his being. It was always the pouting pointing, the exaggerated 'this friggin remote doesn't work' shaking at the TV, Moses's stick to part the Red Sea.

CHAPTER 56

Loo Trove

"Does it have to end like this? All wrapped up in a neat sweet sweaty bow? All the characters satisfyingly cast as good or evil? Alive or dead? Resolved or redeemed? Can it not just be about love, sex and regrets? Not knowing what you have until it is plucked from your person: a thorn, painful and sometimes irritating yet holding all your blood in so that when you extract it you miss it, all the purple blood spraying from your body. I want to show her I still love her but I don't want to taint what we have by dredging up the misdemeanours on both sides, two fishing trawlers scraping the scabs from the bottom of the ocean heading towards one another, identical mobile icebergs. Shelving the memory so it no longer is a memory; like when you tell someone else's story so many times it becomes your own – your reality; your truth. Will the truth actually set you free or just alter an already tainted reality such that who you are after the drama becomes a pissed down version of your countless years of personality and integrity marketing? Your advert is seen and they buy you and the product is past the sell–by date. Expired."

"How did you end up this way?"

"Was it my past? A generational thing? I look at the kids nowadays – today's kids – and they're mainly like this and like fucking that but, apart from the obvious grammar and elocution shortcomings, they're nice. Nice. There is no edge, no hidden motive or agenda or message. When we interacted as teenagers I would say 95% of every human exchange was either bullying or mocking or public humiliation or practical joke or sex. The other 5% probably the same. So you were always guarded, always on the lookout for some other kid's edge or upper hand. Oh my god the poor gays kids – they were persecuted such that no matter how much they denied it they were tormented with the uncertainty of everyone else knowing. One chap's name was Sugar which tells its own story, but basically who you were was either drummed out of you in denial or you felt the shame. Now obviously I'm not gay but I'm clearly driven by everything sex and ducking and paranoia to the point I can't trust a soul and end up waiting for the angle. The sideswipe. I can't get through a day without wondering. I'm either made that way or the environment made me that way. Either way I'm sorry. I'm sorry, I am. That way."

CHAPTER 66

Chaste Lap Turn

"So how does it end?"

"Not well."

"So it ends?"

"Well not exactly. But there is an end, an ending. Of sorts. Wide open for the third in the trilogy." She giggles. "Sorry. Not fair, I know. This is your life after all."

"Is this the 'life was always great' realisation and now you hanker back to 'how it was' or has so much happened that the only route is to continue the destruction, keep digging, so that none of us end up in any neat little bow at the end of all this? Or somewhere in the middle?"

"Or something completely different; mesmeric in nature so that all are left crouching, ears in hands, complete in the altered state of storytelling and brain fucking. So that each and every episode has a reason; a point in the journey without end. But there must be an end."

"A violent end. Presumably?"

"Apt violence."

A person's eyes should tell you if they are real. The life deflating from each in utopian unison should at least tell you something. They might disappear like a genie: poof! they're gone or maybe a glassy stare: two insipid marbles fixated on a faraway nothing.

"I've got to do this. You first. Then Janine's Boyband. Then Sonny Boy. Then Reg. Then Magnus."

"Why Magnus?"

"Because he's not real. Like the rest of you. Programmes. Episodes like the cult, the afterlife, the reality porn, the dystopian future; not lasting long enough for a second series and scarcely memorable. But the big guns, ploughing through my life year after year, series after series, boxset after boxset. There has to be one who is hiding in the real normal light of day; one that escaped from their stories into mine. And if she's not then it's all unreal and I'll make myself the next casualty."

Rewind. Rewatch as the first time wasn't that clear, no screaming kids, whirring mower, low flying plane or flat screen non–soundbar issues to blame … he's standing over Magnus, his lifeless body crumpled together while Margot's legs twitch and her breathing slows down, inebriated from orgasm. He must be responsible. Couldn't be Magnus? Couldn't be one of the twins? Couldn't be a child? Couldn't be a child. Beyond his reckless sanity litmus tests there were lives at stake – actual juvenile lives – so this was one role of the dice where the shock factor of reality was not worth the diving head first into a shallow ice bath reality realisation. But Margot … now that was different. None of his blood coursing through her capillaries; none of his legacy snuffed out like spilling a drink; no innocence. Was he really blaming her for his unfortunate circumstances; his misdemeanours; his pig–headed fucking, weak ego and easily coerced libido – or was she really to blame?

Really.
To.
Blame.

❴↪↩↪↩↪↩❵

It had to end differently. The smut was not what defined Doug; it was his least endearing quality (or more like affliction) but he needed not to be the victim and take a smattering of responsibility, whilst imprimaturing his more endearing traits to be the mountain range and render the smut as shadow. He wanted to start again: shove the VHS cassette into the VHS Recorder and hit record on a blank screen, so the tape shows pitch dark black, the only trace perhaps the odd grey speckled flicker underlining the bottom of the screen like a stage. Better yet: erase all and every television recording. There! 100% free space. And don't forget the scheduled programmes and series links … all in the digital bin too now. A clean slate. Without the evidence.

Doug woke up next to Margot. She looked peaceful; not dead peaceful just peaceful enough for Doug to take a silent breath and enjoy looking into her rather than at her. It was all fine. Misdemeanours and misunderstandings and mistresses erased. He could hear the kids awake and traipse downstairs to watch something mildly educational. Then off to rugby? Normal order reinstated.

Margot stirs. Glances up in the void between awakening confusion and safe love. He's forgiven. She's forgiven. It's forgiven. She wiggles her nose ever so slightly: a hands free scratch of sorts. Funny she never used to do that. But that's okay isn't it? A few habitual idiosyncratic oddities to counter the emotional pain of deceit, diseases and unholy discord. Doug matches her uncharacteristic behaviour by reaching deep within his buttcheeks and giving a purposeful scratch. Not even followed by industrial strength hand sanitiser. New man.

So the sun rises, they hoof the duvet off in perfect unison, raise ridiculous successes, grow old together painting landscapes and imbibing expensive wine in France, one dies, the other bereaves, time passes until they're only iconic stories told to their grandchildren? Nope: there has to be some dark before the fork prongs of light scatter pickupsticks of hope across an otherwise unsuspecting audience. But maybe this is that story where the third act breaks tradition and ends with a resolution more shrouded in domestic and interpersonal nirvana than actual programmatic reality versus entertainment projection.

Doug wrapped his hands firmly around Margot's neck, only stopping to check if it was real, if she was real. If this was all a projection and he was stuck in his jammies in the middle of the night with four fingers pointing down his pants then killing her would only serve to get him further through the story. Inevitable. Her death. A scriptwriter's dark joke: more noughties than teens but still relevant, especially the 'this film didn't actually have an ending' motif.

'That's the next film.'

Until the audience realised the writers never actually had an ending in mind: the Lost heaven waiting room curse.

But Doug had an ending in mind. He would kill until his reality was real. Each death would equal momentary salvation: meeting the person again perhaps another reality but at least his, something amiss he had licence to kill. Not quite double oh seven but it suited his ego. He'd forage on with something derided; something that was real but shouldn't be; something hateful ... Boyband, perhaps.

How do you murder a Boyband?

He held his wrists as taught as he could imagine they would go: extreme ear holding for a 'wow you've grown' nephew. At first, she flinched then relaxed as though fate acceptance embodied the pillow like some sort of white cloud full of rain bringing dark storms and thunder to an arid grief stricken desert. When the rest of her body began to puppet in defiant disgust, her legs and arms bird flapping to fly away – escape – retreat – give–up, Doug momentarily (liberal use of the word as the wrists remained fisherman line tight) relented, believing it might be real. Would he be scuppered at the first hurdle proving it was all actually real, dinkum, actual?

She gave way after what seemed like an eternity so this meant Doug could actually now murder a Boyband.

The phone rang next to his ear, mid act, a jolt to the temple, almost a blow, shifting Doug sideways so that her slowly limping body regained a modicum of hope, emitting one last rodeo thrust to dislodge Doug from her person. The phone, still ringing, and Doug knowing full well it was a distraction technique to pull him from this reality into another unreality. Sonny Boy wanting more drugs. So Doug gave him his home address and, before Margot's body had even begun to decompose, Sonny Boy was sitting cross legged on Doug's dining room table, palms raised. Expectant. Or something. The Boyband would have to wait.

So Doug knew that real or not taking someone's life was not going to be simple smug easy like everything else in the past. To pull this off he had to make sure he was right flat bang there, hovering above Sonny Boy's face whilst the quivering eyes went from discharging to worn out, eighties, lifeless, chipped, scratched frisbee. Dull. But he was a drug dealer so one would assume that somewhere during his fetid past he had himself taken a life or hundred and would defend himself more forcefully than The Jungle Book's Shere Khan. And he had already shot Doug in the back of the mouth.

Doug looked around the room for something to strike with. No brooms but this was not real so there had to be something magical, surely? Something spiritual? Something relevant. Doug picked up a nearby suitcase, full to the brim with bowling balls, and swung it towards Sonny Boy, homerunning him off the dining room table and crumpling into the crockery cabinet. That loud a clatter would have normally woken Margot.

In half an hour, Doug had taped Sonny Boy's mouth shut with tape that really just won't quit. Like a fine ass just basically refusing to quit. He had taken a toothbrush to clean Sonny Boy's nostrils so as to ensure the pipes were clean and full suction could be achieved. Two hours later Sonny Boy's chest was white. Shining powder white: a gooey concoction of mucus, tears, decorations of blood and literally a suitcase of the least pure, rat poison infused, ephedrine spiked, cocaine. There was none left and Sonny Boy was moments away from either a heart attack, brain haemorrhage or both. Doug had forced him to snort his entire stash which meant the eyepopping faux death moment was coming. Doug was giddy with excitement. Then he pointed.

Doug awoke next to Margot, her breathing soothing and rhythmical. A song was playing in the background, from the depths of the house somewhere perhaps, one of the kids' rooms or a car stereo outside the front door. An unmistakable Boyband record creeping up, tentacles flailing into Doug's battered skull. Punishment? Well he knew Margot was real and Sonny Boy wasn't. That is unless he went downstairs and discovered his dining room had acquired a ghetto chic, complete with illegal substance and dead drug dealer. Perhaps even a dead hooker as we were dealing with the most obvious of television clichés. Doug pointed at Margot and nothing happened.

{ ↪ ↩ ↪ ↩ ↪ ↩ }

How to deal with a problem like Reg? Well start by finding him. Where would your overfriendly, subjugating neighbourhood rogue normally be hiding, other than inside the television? Trawling through sufficiently insalubrious establishments was illogical and Gollywood enough for Doug so he did it. Cue montage across all their regular bar and club haunts – a brief montage but many age nevertheless – then a few shaking bouncer heads like an ill–fitted road sign quivering in the wind, that extra public sector funding elsewhere. Then a few strippers, golden boobed, glittering in the red purple strobes, also shaking heads with a sprinkle of acknowledgment nods that they did indeed know him, eyelashes smiling back up at Doug, their erect arches desperate to penetrate him. Then the music fades as Doug enters a lower brow establishment, where naked women walk around with beer mugs filled with coins; no wait, no fade … the music screeches to a halt, decimating on impact. Doug's face filling the screen in genuine dismay and disbelief.

Veronika dancing on stage, toking on a double headed dildo as though it was something she'd performed before. Looking resplendent as ever even if a bit tired, the jewel standing out in the crappy crown. She doesn't see Doug. At first that is. Allowing Doug to circle the stage, avoid a few more clinking beer glasses and settle in a begrimed corner, the stool of choice less sturdy that a drunk dad dancing at a wedding. Had he actually come looking for her too? Was she real? Did he have to kill her too? He imagined strangling her with the dildo, watching the horror drain from her brow and colour erase from her eyes. He knew there was a part of him that loved her beyond her accommodating lust, but perhaps this departure from decent society meant she was tarnished? That or she'd learnt a whole bunch of new tricks that could literally blow Doug's mind. Well the baby quantity of tricks they'd not tried in the past anyway.

{ ↦ ↤ ↦ ↤ ↦ ↤ }

You find the end somehow. One finds the end somehow. No matter how dissatisfactory or loose ended or frustratingly unfair, a conclusion will Geronimo! towards cowardice at its most finite. So when that sense that the programme is at an end and the credits roll or one has started something that has been interrupted (doorbell, annoying WhatsApp, quirky Twitter post, imminent shit, exhaustion doze–off, nagging wife, nagging husband, nagging children, obligations early the next morning, mental health issues, blackouts, insanity) there is little left. Doug's life. 'Twas time to kill Reg.

Reg's embodiment of all that Doug didn't want to be, then all that Doug wanted to be in breaking the shackles of smug perfection, meant that Doug had to remove this part of his –

  a) Brain b) life c) neighbourly presence d) wife's infidelity e) own infidelity.

But why, you ask, does it suddenly become murder? Could

Doug not casually sit down with Reg, explain his seemingly psychotic dilemma, agree to disagree (maybe light wrestling, knowing Reg) then part ways ten times the wiser? Because resolutions this important have to end with death being taken; there is no gay (as in happy) middle ground – the hula hoop has to drop to the floor. Eventually.

So Doug would plan Reg's death according to the episode most prominent, most surreal in his psyche. And allow Reg some resurrection from his sins. Reg was in Mexico; of course Reg was in Mexico, where else could he be? Hiding out with drug lords in the Cotswolds? In fact he was being housed by a wealthy far right green millionaire parading him as a long lost cousin, which Reg would of course relish initially then categorically destroy the story until a midnight flee to Central America, holed up in a brothel filled with hearts of gold.

The setting was more dated saloon than patchy fluorescent brothel. This didn't surprise Doug. The bartender had a moustache bigger than any cat Doug had ever seen and, as we know, he had seen a fair menagerie of cats. The bar had only one type of drink but the screen flickered so the viewer had to assume it was merely 'strong liquor', Doug ubiquitously wincing from the forced shot.

It happened quickly. Reg slumped over the bar in obscure self-awareness flung his dark brown poncho open, firing a shotgun from beneath. The shots swayed past Doug, he rolled sideways shielding an innocent super unnecessarily beautiful prostitute, her scream his ultimate hero tonic. But this is when it got dark because Doug should have fired a miracle between two toppled tables shot into Reg's throat, then dragged him onto the dust patch outside to demand the truth or at least tease the last dying breath of morality from Reg in setting Doug free with the truth. But this didn't happen. It couldn't. And they weren't really in Mexico in a bar.

Doug dragged Reg from his bedroom by his eyes down the street, Deloris kicking and screaming next to him, alerting the street and likely the po–po. The neighbourhood would never really be the same. With Reg's eyeballs oozing all over Doug's thumbs, the little bird–like innards lubricating so that each slip meant the reinsertion needed to be more penetrative than the last. Doug had to shut that bitch of a wife up before the whole fucking neighbourhood was alert, awake and aware so he swung the back of his hand at her. Did the trick with a small volt of something showing Doug a premonition of walking down the aisle with Veronika. Was this the happy less than perfect ending? A wedding night of regret, anal and having to pretend to care? Or was this the real deal? The real deal only given the circumstances?

"They're going to get me, Doug. Part of their plan all along. Two then three with her past flame and four with your broken winged stray. Five might have even been the two plus above my league I was lucky enough to, but her eyes only wanted to end mine. They used me to grind down your reality and ultimately your sanity, inserting themselves outlandishly while you inserted yourself, making the dangerous melange of sex, viewing pleasure, middle class relationship obligation and procreation. It was you they chose – but they only wanted elements; Dad made Mad and Doug's Smug offspring.

"I was the only one on your side really."

A flicker and too many white clothed faces staring at Doug, a halo of artificial light dispelling their angel status and rendering Doug blinded. By the light. But the flickering a television light. They had him strapped to a chair in a hospital, an intersection of wires coming from his head and wrists. The channel was changing and Doug was malfunctionly mad. Reg was there shaking his head. So was Margot. Crying. Doug felt sure the watcher had become to watched.

The sex test would follow, too explicit for this exposé. Sorry. Send a request to the writer and he'll she'll they'll perhaps open up about this open sore in Doug's hypothalamus. Study or cure.

CHAPTER 76

Queue Your D

"You're cured," said Margot.

Doug's eyes were not awake: a familiar sensation. His legs were numb; he knew walking wasn't something imminent.

"Doctor says with enough rest you'll be back to normal. Like before. Before the TV." She put her hand on Doug's inner thigh. He felt nothing.

"We could get back to normal. Me, you and the kids. Take walks – do school runs – argue. Normal stuff. Now that the fucking TV is on the skip and you're fixed. Forever."

Doug tried to force himself back to the dining room with Sonny Boy's remains, back to giant labia water slide, back to

Veronika's threesome, back to Mexico, back to finding celebrity bones, back to DP Laser Quest, back to cults, back to Porn Idol, back to potbellied televisions on their sides, back to profitable dystopian YA fiction, back to pointing. But he couldn't. He didn't feel normal but he felt stable, like Atlas with the world removed, spinning uncontrollably towards the sun into explosive oblivion. In his mind he stood up, pushing his shoulders back and smile crying. He loved Margot and was sure he had hurt her but relished being the victim able to blame extraneous circumstances. Death metal played while he shook off his past.

Before long, he was back home, the kids jumping all over him once again, his body filling with the procreative satisfaction he'd forgotten for a while. Where the TV was stood an ornate sculpture of an elephant, the actual elephant in the room. He knew he'd have to talk to Margot about this eventually but was just relishing reacclimatising: putting on weight eating normal food, not having grotesque sexual thoughts every waking second and embracing the most simple joys in life. The cool feel of water on skin. A shoe fitting. Unflattering underpants. He was normalising just as Margot wanted him to.

Well into his recovery, Doug almost had a dream about Veronika and Janine and Deloris and Nell. He could feel their presence on the other side of a door and imagined them lunching together but without menace or nudity. They were there but they weren't there; on the other side of the door for a moment, then a swift justice of pre–planned cerebral extrication. Gone before any damage was consumed. And despite the dream Doug slept well. When he awoke there was no manifestation of any dream just the grateful feeling that this was in the past and he could get on with his life.

This would have been completely laid to waste had he heard the scream from the converted basement below. Five female screams; in joyful bloodlust. One male; in pain. The basement that had been renovated was no longer a fly zone for Doug. Perhaps in time or perhaps it was part of the methodical cure. Was this the feminist end we'd all been waiting for? Reg lured into believing he was helping Doug then caged, raped, murdered, eaten, poohed out – getting his just deserves after captaining his pathetic universe a little too misogynistically for the likes of the protagonist gals. So was Doug beyond retribution as this was another hop towards a master plan or was there enough to love about him that made all concerned genuinely concerned?

Saving Doug to save Doug.

But would the victors be able to share the spoils?

He was still Perfect Perfors, after all.

CHAPTER 86

←→

Snail Behave

"Men are toys," said Deloris, "to be played with, broken, discarded."

"Then a new one sought and bought," said Nell.

"Or perhaps just bought," added Janine.

Reg was still alive at this point. Just alive. Like a fly that's been swatted from every angle but lies twitching on the windowsill, legs intermittently curling, body unable to Superman off the ground. And Doug could have saved him if he'd have known, or been well enough to know. Or been able to walk.

"I don't believe Doug would lift a solitary finger to help

you," said Margot pointing at Reg's draped body.

"After everything you put him through," said Deloris.

"And you put him through!" giggled Janine.

"But he might want to do the right thing?" asked Veronika.

"Be the fucking hero," said Margot. "Again."

Reg moaned so Janine and Nell fought over placing a metal pipe in his windpipe, his head hanging flaccidly back, upside down, both jumping up across it – an active punt in Oxford – splitting his trachea without putting him out of his misery. Then both fascinated with the effect, the pipe metronoming between them – shoved and caught – anchored by Reg's Globus Hystericus trachea. Repeated. More mess of course; red mess everywhere but the girls so friggin organised; all over this, the plastic sheets engineered to gather pockets of blood so Reg could stare at his own reflection as he hung from his genitals.

"I love how this always has to be about sex," said Janine, "for these simple men folk."

"Reg always said we congregated late. Women. Clans," said Deloris. "That men gathered ritualistically in sports and conquests pre settling down to couple and procreate, but that woman realised this unity later. Our solidarity forms more solid once we've made our babies."

"And we figure out that the weaker sex has served its purpose," said Margot.

"But what if we haven't yet," said Veronika, stroking the bump.

"You're not still the weakest link, are you?" said Nell. "The purpose might or might not be extended – depending on

Doug."

"There's one of him in all of us," said Margot. "All boys – I just know it. We'll raise them all right, so that they don't treat breeding as a self–congratulatory pleasure; an indulgent whim."

"But we all did love fucking your husband," said Deloris. "Even if some of the conceptions were … orchestrated."

"We had to do what we had to do. Bubble Bubble!" said Janine. "But gawd he knew which bits to push and pull when."

"And we let him push and pull because of who he was inside rather than out," said Veronika.

"Then when he deteriorated, he became even more appealing," said Margot, "because of all of our maternal instincts. To save him from himself. But make sure he passed on the good bits."

"And come doing it," laughter abounding. "Repeatedly."

"Think I only liked him in the beginning because of you Margot," said Janine.

Reg hadn't moved in a while now so the girls took turns slapping him back to consciousness. It didn't work.

"We're good people, ladies," said Margot. "I do believe that. We had to make some tough decisions to get to where we wanted to be and live the life we all wanted to live. Either by a collective purpose or external sexist force forcing us towards the ultimate solidarity. The ultimate male in bed with all of us; in all of our lives; all of the time. So if we stay the course, it all works out. If it doesn't, we start again. With a new generation. And a much bigger message. How not to murder a

Glossary

CHAPTER 01 ← → Paradise Shattered

CHAPTER 02 ← → Perfect Day

CHAPTER 03 ← → Porn King

CHAPTER 04 ← → Sitcom

CHAPTER 05 ← → Gastroenteritis

CHAPTER 06 ← → Precarious Vicarious

CHAPTER 07 ← → Daydreaming Confidant

CHAPTER 08 ← → X Factor

CHAPTER 09 ← → Point of No Return

CHAPTER 10 ← → Gay Rape

CHAPTER 11 ← → Cracks Emerging

CHAPTER 12 ← → Perfection Angel

CHAPTER 13 ← → Dinner Party

CHAPTER 14 ← → Magnificent Child

CHAPTER 15 ← → Dead Wife

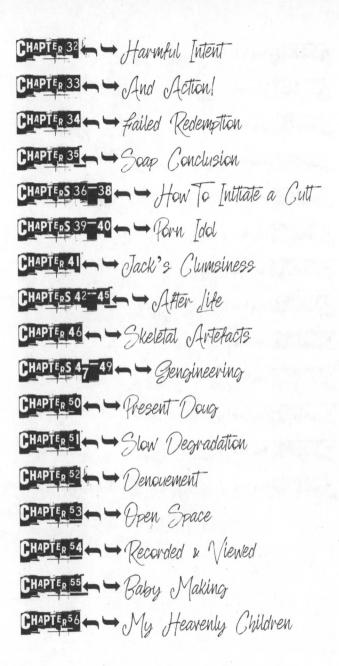

Coming Soon: the prequel to Smug Dad – How to Murder a Boyband.

Newspaper Article, 2001

Boyband slain in New York hotel room

US based boyband LoveBoyz tragically lost their lives in a midnight chainsaw romp in New York yesterday evening. The Los Angeles based God-loving band were on their summer tour when Jim Phillips, a twenty-four-year-old delivery boy, entered their hotel room at around 11:15 pm with a chain saw concealed beneath his overcoat. Sources say the band were indulging in illegal substances with a large number of minors which meant Phillips was easily able to gain access to the band's room under the false pretence of being a member of their church congregation. Hotel staff are not claiming responsibility stating that the band clearly issued authorisation from the room. Hotel residents claimed the noise from the slaughter was not dissimilar to a 'horror movie', the band's screams heard some three floors above. Detective Kirk Coolidge of the New York Police Department was put on record saying that there was no connection between Phillips and the murder of British based boyband ...

CHAPTER 1
BIG FaT ARSe

So there's this big fat arse in front of me, blocking the path and turning an already depressing morning into one that makes you want to turn around, flip your umbrella the correct way and go home. But you don't. And there the arse looms, dominating the width of the concrete walkway, the seam on the worn denim moments away from a symphonic tear. With each stride it takes on another impossible dimension, percolating beneath the faded material, the unsymmetrical ovals buckling into an angry felled eight. There should be a law against this sort of thing; a code or something which prevents people like this ruining other people's mornings. And not because they're fat (oh no, that would be too easy to categorise and scorn them with that) but because they're taking up the whole pavement, maliciously blocking it so that hard-working, decent people like me are prevented from passing; so that our pursuant arses are all bunched together behind the one that momentarily holds the power.

I need to get past as the 'alarm didn't go off' excuse is getting way too stale and my umbrella's impotence means I'll look a complete state after another unforgiving downpour.

And it's Monday, what a bonus. A WeightWatchers advert catches my eye and I momentarily forget that I'm late. Obscured by a lamppost and damaged by the relentless rain and glue from old posters, a distorted picture of a happy fat person with what looks like a tape measure lassoed around her waist seems to grimace back at me. Her thumb is raised towards me.

I force myself to relax and slow down a little, letting the rain pelt my forehead, trying not to wince from the stinging sensation. Someone impolitely coughs behind me and I'm not sure whether they're hinting for me to move or the Arse. More fruitless coughs follow and everyone's now jamming into my back like discarded trolleys in a supermarket loading bay.

The pressure behind me becomes too much so I make a desperate break for it, spotting a gap above his left love handle as he raises his hand towards his mouth, but it's like I'm a pebble on a bouncy castle as I get shunted backwards, relegated to the back of the 'arse-passing' queue, a swathe of burbled discontent scolding my feeble attempt. I'm at the back of the queue when my replacement at the front attempts another Kamikaze surge, this time making it through, turning towards the man with the arse and shaking her head as she speeds forward into the throng ahead.

The man finally comprehends that the sole reason for the jam is him and tries to press himself to one side against a chipped rail as the professional mob gush through the opening. His embarrassment is clear and the crimson appearing in his already rosy cheeks makes me stop, offer some sort of indecisive benevolent gesture and proceed through the diagonal shower. He smiles as I leave.

Acknowledgements

Dedicating this to my Mom and Dad (neither of whom are Smug by the way) just felt right as, although the narrative is more concomitant with my life as a parent rather than a child, stellar parents deserve a significant doff of the gratitude cap for shaping the formative years, including from a literary perspective. Always encouraging, daring me to dream and unshackling the creative powers that might or might not be, my Mom and Dad have not only been instrumental in all my writing exploits but that pesky little adventure called life too. So, thanks Mom and Dad, this novel is dedicated to you both. And perhaps that's the beauty of expression through telling a story ... getting lost in your own overactive imagination often takes your narrative down some dark paths which I suppose you'd often rather your family and friends didn't know anything about. But heck, they love you for who you are even if your writing now provides tangible evidence that there is something seriously wrong with you. Besides, reflections and ramblings of an all-round decent fellow might not be the 'couldn't put it down' mantra all us authors are striving for. My publisher asked me to describe Smug Dad for the cover in 3 words ... I provided 5 ... Disturbing; Surreal; Redemptory; Ribald; Nihilistic. Mom and Dad, after this trilogy is complete ... life-affirming feel-good sports drama, I promise. Likely Rugby or Cricket ...

Smug Dad began life on a muggy summer's day 2009 in Muswell Hill, North London with the final edit a mere 12 years later, a surfeit of life, keyboard tapping, missing train stops lost in the telling, blocks, hiatuses, self-doubt, children, provision, reality and good times in between. The memory of wandering upstairs to start this idea I was immensely excited about, a slight calm in the parenting battlefield apparent, is as vivid as if it were yesterday, the blank page daring me to take the plunge. As a Dad myself there was reference to the familiar paternal base of Smug Dad but with the more vicarious and outlandish elements it was fun to exercise the more fanatically phantastic and uncompromising places of one's imagination. Smug Dad forms part of what I've called The Boyband Sandwich Trilogy with noughties prequel How to Murder a Boyband to be published directly after Smug Dad and contemporary How NOT to Murder a Boyband almost complete serving as the sequel, so the two Boyband novels as the sandwich with Smug Dad the meat in the middle!

I'd like to acknowledge the editorial wizardry of Kirsty Jackson and the team at Cranthorpe Millner – collaborative tough love and support but with the ultimate goal of making the novel as good as it possibly can be, covering all elements of the publishing process, the likes of which have been enthralling and regimented in equal measure. Each step, working with Kirsty and Cranthorpe Millner, is like unwrapping a gift making all the blood, sweat and (mostly) tears worth it, bringing characters to life, tightening narratives, removing the self-congratulatory literary moments, mopping up the grammar and inspiring to the point where you realise why you write and tell stories. There is so much to take into my future writing so I thank you for that and cannot wait for the next chapter, promising to use ellipses more sparingly …

Writing has long been my tumultuous bedfellow, a trail of experimental English essays leaving a factioned faculty of (sometimes) smiling, head-scratching, admonishing and adulating in equal measure English teachers but perhaps signifying tangible belief and recognition at age 16 when, posed with only 30 minutes to write a school essay, I wrote a satire on Biblical beginnings and, without a second read (timeframes missed in those days were deadly), it went on to win a national award – The Alan Paton Creative Writing Competition and was published including in a national newspaper, leading me astray towards the completely false belief that the first draft achieves anything real! Mrs Lewis … Standard 9 whom I wrote The Garden for remains one of my favourites, as does Mr Willis … Standard 7, never afraid to reward outlandishness! In my spare time I'm prone to other forms of writing, specifically film and television screenplays and daring to dream even further having embarked upon a soupçon of independent filmmaking, the foundation of which I'm hoping book trailers, montages and family anthologies edited in DaVinci Resolve will serve as the equivalent of Fincher's music video introductory path.

As I said, daring to dream.

With so many people to thank for this journey and the culmination of Smug Dad being published, perhaps I'll save for the 45 seconds at the Oscars. Being a writer comes with incredible highs, made higher by the perceived lows but I have been extraordinarily fortunate to have an unrivalled family support base and readers willing to give me the honest feedback.

Please do stay in touch at jasonroche.co.uk

BV - #0094 - 061022 - C0 - 197/132/29 - PB - 9781912964796 - Matt Lamination